SCU[illegible]

'You have had it all [illegible] do what is asked of [illegible]es. You are in now [illegible]ace of time you wil[illegible] guerilla, partisan [illegible] one. The training [illegible] will be times when yo[illegible]ill be no let up. When the [illegible] with you, you will be able to ta[illegible]erman army as if you were Errol Flyn[illegible]od have mercy on your souls.'

Also by Michael Hughes

THE GIRONDE INCIDENT
THE INFILTRATOR
SPECTRE OF MARALINGA

SCUMBAGS

Michael Hughes

A STAR BOOK
published by
the Paperback Division of
W. H. Allen & Co. PLC

A Star Book
Published in 1987
by The Paperback Division of
W. H. Allen & Co. Plc
44 Hill Street, London W1X 8LB

First published in Great Britain by
W. H. Allen & Co. Plc 1986

Printed and bound in Great Britain by
Anchor Brendon Ltd, Tiptree, Essex

ISBN 0 352 31844 9

Chapter One

Britain, the small island isolated and fighting alone against the might of Nazi Germany was dependent on ships. Ships were her lifeblood.

In Liverpool, the most important seaport, literally hundreds of men and women were labouring, following the course of thousands of ships ferrying cargoes to the war-torn nation: plotting on giant maps where ships had last been seen before being sunk by German U-boats. The cargoes were being prayed for: willed on by those whose very existence depended on their safe passage.

The Royal Liver Building, although blacked-out according to regulations and appearing deserted in the dark night, was still an impressive sight. Behind the walls of the large building men and women had earlier shaken hands when a convoy arrived from the other side of the Atlantic. Some of the ships had docked. Others waited in line along the river for a spare berth while the tail-enders sat at anchor in the estuary until their time came to move upriver. And still more ships were on their way.

Up to one hundred ships could arrive at one time to be unloaded, and such was the demand for their cargoes that they did not have to wait long. Unloaded, refuelled and turned around in record time they went back across the Atlantic to the United States and Canada, or south and east to Africa and Australasia never certain, although under escort, that their destination would ever be reached.

From the ships came men: brave men, men without

whom Britain would have starved. They came ashore quietly without fuss or acclaim, either walking or accepting a company agent's offer of a lift to the Royal Liver Building. Most walked. Most wished to savour the safety of dry land away from the constant fear of U-boat attack, the sleepless nights, the terror as the ship lifted when a torpedo struck home. All they wanted was their own company for an hour or two while they picked up their pay and enjoyed a quiet drink in a pub before going home to their families.

At all hours of the day and night tired, dejected men, sometimes still in shock, pushed through the doors of the Royal Liver Building. Inside, they waited calmly in line before presenting their seaman's book and signing for their hard-earned pay, all too aware that they might only have two or three days' grace before rejoining their ship for the next perilous journey, never having time to forget the moments of terror of the previous trip.

Four men, none under fifty, emerged from the building. Outside they stood in a huddle. The little moonlight there was showed money pass between them. George Read, a fifty-seven-year-old grandfather and bos'un aboard the *SS FARNE* collected money he had loaned the others over a two-month period. Together the others handed him £17 which, when added to his own pay, totalled £90. A tidy sum, but worthless in a way for Britain's shops were virtually empty.

Still, Read thought, his wife would be pleased: and she would be even more pleased with the leg of bacon in his giant duffel bag sewn into a canvas shroud. The *FARNE* had just returned from the United States where there was no shortage of food. He had felt guilty while there, dining in restaurants and eating the finest meals while back home his family was existing on the basic minimum. The leg of bacon, and several cans of preserved fruit, helped to salve his conscience. The cans of fruit would delight his grandchildren.

Hiding in the shadows of the Liverpool blackout were three desperate men. From their hiding place they watched the four seamen exchange money. They also knew what went on behind the black windows of the Royal Liver Building. They knew that within the walls were immense reserves of ready cash, and that each seaman who left took a proportion of it with him.

Read said his farewells quietly, muttering that he would see the others in a few days' time. He watched them slip into the night then just stood and looked up at the silent sky. He thought back. He had given up the sea-going life but hadn't completely severed his links. The company had found him a comfortable position as a watchman on the wharves and he had looked forward to an easier life watching his grandchildren grow up. The war had put an end to his dreams. So many experienced men had been lost in the Atlantic that the old timers had been asked to go back, to volunteer to make the hazardous trip across the North Atlantic. Pride and patriotism had sent him back, but he was tired: too old for the stress and strain that now went along with the job.

He began a slow, tired walk through the dark streets to the tenement building less than a mile away where his wife would be waiting. She wouldn't know he was back. She never knew. For security reasons families were never told when a ship would arrive, only when they went down.

Only his familiar knock on the front door would tell her that his ship was safe, that he had survived another trip. She would know instantly from his face that it had been bad: not a wink of sleep for ten nights. Every other hour there had been an alarm and every night a tragedy. Off Cape Cod the convoy had comprised ninety-one vessels: fifty-two reached Liverpool.

She'd still be happy, though. And his grandchildren: they would be delighted. In his bag was a toy for each of them: clockwork, the likes of which hadn't been seen in Britain for nearly two years.

His mind went back to the sea again. Thinking that one day he might not come back, he did not hear the three men creep up behind him. There was a sharp stab of pain at the bottom of his spine and he went down, temporarily paralysed. Hands roamed over his body and through his pockets. He yelled with anger and frustration. He wanted to get up and defend himself but his legs refused to obey his command. He yelled louder, swinging his heavy duffel bag with all his strength and felt it connect with a body: and as suddenly as the attack had started, it stopped. His own voice echoed for an instant then the night became still once more. Whoever had attacked him had gone. He raised himself to a sitting position and listened. Somewhere within earshot there was the sound of animal-like softness sliding into the darkness.

The pain subsided and he managed to stand on shaky legs. His money had gone, which made him want to weep. The company sent his wife an allotment to keep her going while he was away, but she depended on his leave pay to make up shortcomings. And it was gone, stolen by young hoodlums who would probably faint at the very sight of a gun.

More tired than ever, George Read, tears running down his face, trudged heavily on his homeward journey.

Chapter Two

The same evening, 400 miles south of Liverpool, an incident occurred which at the time bore no relation to the robbery of George Read. In time the incidents would relate but for the moment Lt Oliver Woolcott's thoughts were a world away from Liverpool.

Off the coast of Brittany Woolcott knew that his first trip as commander of a submarine was having a charmed life. The boat had surfaced nearly three hours before and the law of averages stated that they should have been blown out of the water several times. But, incredibly, luck was on their side. So far they hadn't as much as spotted a piece of driftwood.

With him on the conning tower were two lookouts who scanned every inch of the horizon through night-glasses. Both were experienced sailors. Neither of them spoke and their movements were slow and purposeful. Woolcott did not disturb them. They would immediately report anything that might put them in danger.

His own eyes were glued to the shoreline, still hanging on for a recognition signal that was two and a half hours late. His orders had been to surface at exactly 2030 hours, signal and receive a prearranged reply, then wait no more than thirty minutes for three Allied agents to row out. At 2100 hours, regardless of the agents' position, he was to depart. The orders had been precise and Woolcott had exceeded them but it was a clandestine trip and instinct told him that his passengers had been delayed. By his own volition he decided to wait.

With stern to shore, the screws turning slowly to fight the tide and the currents, Woolcott began to have his first doubts when the three-hour mark passed. He recognised that in enemy-occupied France it would not always be possible to meet contacts on time, and for that reason he had waited. But he also recognised that the longer he waited the more he put the life of his crew at risk. Sooner or later a sharp-eyed German somewhere along the coast would spot them and the luck that had so far stayed with them would be no more.

At 2345 hours he decided he had done his best. Valuable information would be lost, but he would have to get into safer surroundings.

'Stand by, number one,' he spoke into the voice tube. He heard Second Lt Huntingdon repeat the order below. Before the order had been finished the crew would be at their stations, the stress they had been under increasing as they knew they could be caught at the last minute.

'A signal, sir!' one of the lookouts said sharply.

Woolcott pushed his glasses to his eyes and swept

the coastline. There was nothing for a few seconds then a lamp began to blink.

'What does it say?' he asked the lookout who stood beside him. The other was still watching the sea.

'CUE, MISS-CUE, sir.'

Woolcott nodded. He had read the same but two people had to read the signal and agree on its contents. Ashore their contact had flashed DASH-DASH-DOT-DASH for the letter Q, then DASH-DASH-DASH-DOT, mis-spelling the letter.

'Prepare to receive shore party,' Woolcott spoke into the voice tube again.

The crew would feel even more stress now, Woolcott knew. Having sat idle for more than three hours was bad enough but now, with their goal in sight, their chances of discovery were greater than ever. The shore party could have been followed and by making for the coast would alert the Germans to the fact that a submarine would be off-shore. If this were true any number of ships and planes could be heading towards them.

The signal came again.

'Return the signal!' Woolcott said quickly.

The lookout flashed the same signal once and immediately afterwards the lamp on shore blinked.

'ARE, sir,' the lookout reported.

Woolcott grunted his agreement. He had signalled CUE-MISS-CUE in reply, which to those on shore meant they had to miss the letter Q and go on to R.

'Flash ARE.'

'Yes, sir.'

Woolcott sensed relief. He had, he thought, done something worthwhile. So far the boat hadn't fired a shot in anger. It had come straight from Barrow-in-Furness following trials to take part in the clandestine operation: and although he was the boat's captain he was the greenest man aboard. Previously he had been on a corvette and had taken part in plenty of action, then along had come a notice asking for volunteers for the submarine branch of the service. Even now he couldn't explain why he had volunteered. He had just done it and they had snapped him up. There followed two months' intensive theoretical training, then a week aboard boats in the Irish Sea and off the west coast of Scotland in practical exercises, then Barrow-in-Furness.

Second Lt Huntingdon already had three trips under his belt and before long would get his own command. It seemed a mystery why the present command wasn't the other way around but the Sea Lords must have had their reasons. Of the crew, one man had done one trip and the others were seasoned campaigners.

He was glad now that he had volunteered. Aboard a surface vessel war seemed to progress mechanically. With the corvette it was like getting on a bus in the morning for a specific destination, then returning in the evening to sit before a warm fire.

The submarine was completely different. They had a destination but there were many unknown perils they could encounter on the way. There was a sense of intrigue in not knowing what would happen, which complemented a streak of romanticism within his character.

The sea was coming up, he noticed. On arrival it had been smooth. Even in the dark it had seemed blue but now it was changed. The surface was choppy. He could feel the boat rock slightly, a rocking that would increase until they bobbed like a cork.

But that was the power of the sea. One minute it was blue and calm and the next angry and green, as if some unseen force below the surface stirred the depths, bringing it to the boil as heat would a kettle.

'Party arriving, sir.'

Woolcott raised his glasses again. A tiny rowing boat was within fifty yards of them. Two bulky figures, their backs to him, were rowing furiously. He lowered his head to the voice tube.

'Reception party on deck!'

The after-hatch opened almost immediately and four dark-clad figures scrambled through.

More anxious minutes passed until the tiny craft

stopped abruptly when it collided with the boat. The two men powering it were exhausted and reached up for assistance, being pulled aboard and unceremoniously bundled down the hatch. Their oars were also taken aboard. Left behind they would tell a tale: and the final act was to sink the smaller boat with a steel bar smashed through its bottom.

'Increase revs to half,' Woolcott delivered the instruction to leave the Britanny coast.

The boat shuddered as the screw bit into the sea. The rocking stopped, being replaced with bucking as the bow pushed into the waves now mounting with the gathering storm.

With the French coast left behind Woolcott sighed heavily. Thank God, he thought, then realised that his hands were shaking.

'Full revs!' he shouted into the tube with a slight tremor in his voice.

The noise of the diesels reached the conning tower: a reassuring noise that told him the danger was over. Now he could relax and meet his passengers.

'Number one, up-top!'

Second Lt Huntingdon appeared and took over, Woolcott waiting ten minutes until his subordinate's eyes became accustomed to the dark before going below.

He had expected young, tall, tough, fighting Bretons and was surprised to meet two heavily-sweating middle-aged men dressed for a business trip. They wore polished shoes, suits, leather coats and homburg hats, and each clutched a briefcase to his stomach.

'Our thanks for waiting, mon capitaine,' one of them said in heavily-accented English.

'There were supposed to be three of you,' Woolcott replied in fluent French.

The speaker smiled, relieved that they could communicate. But the smile was brief.

'We had our problems, capitaine. We were betrayed and ambushed on the way. Our friend was killed.

However, we did manage to get the information he carried.'

'My commiserations,' said Woolcott. It was the first time he had met an agent of any kind and he wasn't quite sure how he should react to the news that they had lost one of their number.

'We hope his death will not be in vain, capitaine.'

'Will his family suffer?'

'Perhaps. We all sent our families away, capitaine. When a man goes missing the Gestapo presume he has joined the Resistance, and so take his family in for interrogation, which is not very pleasant. We took the precaution of sending our families away, but now that the Gestapo is certain of our whereabouts there is no guarantee they will be safe. If they *are* caught they will be tortured and murdered.'

'If you could only have brought them with you . . .' Woolcott made a gesture with his hands, leaving the sentence unfinished.

'Women and children cannot run like men, capitaine. We can only pray that they are safe.'

Woolcott suddenly felt inadequate. Reports of the Gestapo torturing and murdering their helpless prisoners were so numerous that they had become commonplace. But now, hearing it from the lips of someone with first-hand knowledge, the horrors of what the French people were suffering made a fresh impact on him. The two Frenchmen had embarked on a journey knowing full well that it could mean the lives of their families. Yet they had done it, in order to fight the tyranny that had murdered thousands of others. That took courage, a courage he doubted he possessed.

'Would you like some coffee?' he asked.

'We would welcome coffee, capitaine,' the second man spoke up. 'It was very cold out there.'

Coffee laced with brandy was brought. The two Frenchmen sipped slowly from their cups and shivered and Woolcott noticed that they still clutched the brief-cases to their stomachs. They had offered no names and Woolcott decided not to ask for any. Watching them holding information they had risked their lives to take to England, he felt proud in their company.

The boat dived before dawn. The two Frenchmen were asleep in the wardroom, sprawled over the table with the briefcases under them, ready to jump at the slightest hint of danger. They still had their hats and coats on.

Daybreak was long past when they surfaced again. A radio signal went out informing the Admiralty listening station that they were approaching Falmouth, and at 1100 hours they entered the harbour.

'I shall be going ashore, number one,' Woolcott told Second Lt Huntingdon. 'Have the crew inspect the boat and do any necessary repairs before they rest.'

'Very good, sir.'

Woolcott carried a small case containing the boat's log. After each trip the log was sent to the Admiralty to be studied. It would be in London within hours.

Two cars pulled up alongside when the boat berthed. Someone Woolcott had never seen before emerged from one and asked for the Frenchmen, who were already on deck waiting for a gangway to be lifted into place.

'Morton: John Morton,' the stanger introduced himself. 'Captain Woolcott?'

'I am.'

'Many thanks for your trouble, captain. We heard there was some kind of hold-up. Can't tell you how relieved I am that they are safe.'

'It was my pleasure, Mr Morton,' Woolcott replied, at the same time wondering how the other man could have heard anything. He wasn't Navy.

He was probably attached to some Secret Service department, Woolcott thought, but like the Frenchmen he did not portray the image Woolcott had of spies and agents. Morton looked more like a harassed schoolmaster or worried businessman. The jacket of his suit was too small and allowed only one button to fasten, pulling the jacket across his middle like a rope. His detachable collar was dirty and the front stud seemed to have come loose, and down his lapels was the ash, now ingrained, from hundreds of cigarettes.

'I'm afraid I can't wait long, captain. Must get these chaps to London at once. Thanks again.'

The Frenchmen were being ushered into the car. They waved to Woolcott in gratitude, then the car sped off and Woolcott never set eyes on them again.

The second car was for him. It would take him to Falmouth Naval HQ where he would make his report, after which he would enjoy a rest. The trip, short as it had been for his first foray into enemy territory, had also been an eye-opener. He looked forward to more of them.

Chapter Three

Victor Brack paused in his work and watched with curiosity as a submarine was towed into the Boston Navy Yard. At first it did not register, then in a flash the memory came back. As an apprentice he had watched the very same boat slide down the slipway, twenty-three years ago in September 1917: right there in Boston at the Electric Boat Company's Victory Yard.

'Well, I'll be . . .' Brack said to the boy alongside him, an apprentice, just as he had been all those years ago.

'You seen it before, Vic?' the boy asked.

'I helped build that old girl, son. I was a kid like you, then,' Brack drawled in his acquired American accent. 'This is the first time she's been back.'

Brack and the boy were atop the stocks alongside a cruiser being constructed in the dockyard, having a bird's-eye view of the old submarine's arrival.

'How can you tell?' asked the boy.

'The way a baby can tell its own mother, kid. You just know.'

The rest of the dockyard had stopped work to watch the boat being towed in. They had heard previously that it had been involved in some kind of accident or collision at the Portsmouth Naval Base down in Virginia, and was coming home for repairs. She was one of the old T–Class, distinctive by her small conning tower, built too late to take part in the First World War and now completely out of date. Possibly she was the only one of her class still afloat.

'What's she come back for, Vic?'

'Repairs, they say, kid, but there don't seem to be any structural damage. Must be internal. Hitting the bottom too hard or slamming into a sand-bar can take an engine off its mountings, y'know.'

'Jeez!' the boy blew through his teeth.

Brack thought no more of the old submarine once it had been towed into the covered dock area but turned his mind to the evening to come. A convoy was due to leave Boston two days hence for Britain and, leading his unit, he intended to sabotage as much of the convoy's cargo as possible.

Brack had been born in Germany in 1901 and brought to the United States by his parents at the age of twelve. He couldn't speak a word of English then and found life hard in his new country. The Americans seemed to resent his presence – even though a great many could not speak English themselves – and said so. He was a foreigner to them. Although they still spoke in their mother tongue they had come to America ten and twenty years before and considered themselves American.

The resentment spurred Brack on to speak English like an American. He mixed with true American boys his own age, picking up words he did not understand, repeating them until he had the right accent and, with continual usage, began to understand. In two years he mastered the language, speaking with an accent that shocked his parents but made him acceptable in America's streets.

War was raging in Europe when Brack began his apprenticeship, and each evening when he returned home from work his parents would be sitting at the kitchen table discussing its progress. A German victory seemed assured and Brack senior impressed on his son never to forget that he was German first and American second. He should always be proud of his origins and never say or do anything that might harm Germany.

Brack listened but did not take much notice. He wondered at the time what they were doing in America if they were so proud of Germany. Why weren't they in Germany, his father in the army and he working in a munitions factory?

It wasn't until America's entry into the war that he began to take notice of his father's words. Germans in America suddenly became outcasts. Shops owned by Germans were broken into and looted. His mother was spat on and his father physically abused in the street.

At work Brack took verbal abuse, but there lurked in him a cunning which he put to good use. Vehemently he cursed Germany and the Kaiser, claiming he was American and proud of the fact. His accent corroborated this and thereafter his workmates left him alone.

But not his parents. His mother became afraid to leave the house and eventually his father lost his job. Brack was angry but he contained his anger in order to keep his own job. He maintained two faces, one for work and one for home. He became the family breadwinner, fanatically German and avidly reading the newspaper reports on the war, vowing that in the future he would do everything in his power to aid Germany.

At work he kept up his American appearance and soon found that he was not alone with his thoughts. There were many apprentices and young tradesmen with a German background who wanted to do something but were afraid. They only needed a leader to spur them on: Brack. Thus was formed a secret brotherhood and a campaign of sabotage began.

It was too late to do anything about the T–Class submarine. She had gone on her sea-trials. But there were other vessels being hurriedly constructed and each of the brotherhood did what they could to delay the launchings and fitting-out.

The campaign was all too short, however. The entry of America into the war brought it to a speedy conclusion. Germany surrendered and reparations in Europe began. Germans in America became respectable again, but it had all been too much for Brack's parents. First his mother died, then his father: both broken-hearted. Brack was on his own. He blamed America for their deaths and vowed revenge.

The brotherhood was never disbanded. With the war over there was no point in further sabotage, but they could help each other and their fellow-countrymen in bankrupt Germany. Funds were raised. The brotherhood bought into property and used the property to house new emigrants from Germany. German engineering expertise was used to form companies in which only Germans were employed, and by the time Adolf Hitler came to power in 1933 the German community on the eastern seaboard was both impressive and influential. It also blended with the background of American society.

It was with almost manic relief that Brack received the outbreak of the Second World War. Again America was not involved but hundreds, then thousands of ships began transporting cargoes to beleaguered Britain. The brotherhood, much stronger and more efficient than it had been in the previous conflict, emerged in secret from behind its pillars of respectability to begin another campaign of sabotage. The brotherhood had gained control of some waterfront unions: indeed, in some cases, entire ports. Cargoes were delayed or mysteriously set on fire; ships were blown up or sabotaged so that their departure was indefinitely postponed. Contact was made with Berlin through German consulates and a chain of communications established. Brack became an important part of the chain.

The evening went well. A diversion was created. A large fire broke out in a warehouse containing crates of packet-food due for shipment to Britain. While teams of men fought the fire and all eyes were shifted in that direction, two freighters loaded with small arms, also destined for Britain, had holes blown in them below the water-line, causing them to sink at their moorings. Trucks waiting to be loaded had sand put in their sumps and others set on fire, all of which created chaos which echoed round the Boston wharves, and gave the brotherhood time to get clear and return to their homes. And, before the evening was over, news of the episode was transmitted by wireless to Berlin.

The next day Brack's apprentice asked if it would be possible to have a look at the old submarine.

'Why not, kid. I'd like to see the old girl again myself.'

The appropriate permission was sought and before long they were walking across the yard.

'Jeez!' the boy whistled with wonderment when they entered the covered dock area. The submarine was sitting on keel-blocks in a dry-dock. Sections of her hull had been cut away to reveal the inside and workmen were swarming all over her.

'What's happening?' Brack asked a workman, one of the brotherhood.

'Being broken up,' replied the other. 'Been working non-stop since she arrived, I'm told. They've already taken one engine out.'

'Damaged, was it?'

'Not really: nothing a few turns with a spanner wouldn't put right. She's just being scrapped, that's all.'

'A pity.'

'She's too old, Vic. Compared to some of the boats the European countries have, it's like the Pony Express trying to compete with the railroad.'

Brack nodded, a touch of sadness on his face, then said, 'Can the kid have a wander around?'

Chapter Four

John Morton was sadly disappointed. He had three men and a woman primed, ready to be ferried to France, and the Royal Navy had turned down his request for transport. He could have approached the RAF but there were no decent dropping zones in the Le Havre area and he wanted the agents in quickly. Using the RAF – assuming they would have given him the use of a plane – his agents would have to be dropped fifty miles south of Le Havre and find their own way north, in an area seething with German troops. The only way in was by sea.

'They don't seem to understand that this is a different kind of war,' he told James Witherspoole.

Witherspoole nodded. He knew what Morton meant. One arm of the services believed wars should be fought according to rules binding on either side. An air-marshall he knew of was dead against bombing raids over Germany on a Sunday, claiming that it would anger God. And the same air-marshall also believed that if the BBC broadcast cricket scores Goering's Luftwaffe would not bomb London while the MCC played at Lords.

Which was absurd. The Battle of Britain was at its height and Goering did not seem to know that cricket was played at Lords.

The air-marshall's view was not supported by all the services, although all agreed on one thing: that wars should be fought honourably. Secret agents were an underhanded method of fighting and anything underhanded was not in keeping with the traditions of the fighting services – a view that would alter as the war went on.

Morton had just returned from the Admiralty and reported his conversations there to Witherspoole.

'They did us a favour on the Brittany trip, they said, but no more. They have more important things to do than ferry boy scouts on camping trips. Most frustrating, it was.'

Again Witherspoole nodded, equally sad. There were countless jobs to be done on the European Continent and not being able to count on the navy's support would only serve to prolong the war.

'I've had a similar talking to by the Air Ministry while you were out, John. They've been extremely helpful so far but every request I made today was turned down. Said they would inform us when a plane was available and if we have an agent ready, then well and good: if not . . .' Witherspoole paused and became angry. 'Dammit, John, they're shortsighted, boneheaded, moronic idiots!'

Both had had the priorities of the RN and RAF explained to them in no uncertain terms. The first priority was to damage or destroy enemy ships and installations. One way of achieving this was to be in the right place at the right time, not skulking along the coast of France waiting for an opportunity to put someone ashore.

Whilst the RAF had been fairly obliging and the RN less obliging in the past, both services maintained that it was a waste of fuel, time and energy, and a misuse of manpower to continually take part in what they termed as 'unethical and unprincipled warfare'. Why use great quantities of fuel, put hundreds of sailors or airmen at risk just to land perhaps one man in France who might be caught as soon as he landed anyway, when the same resources could be utilised to sink a destroyer or flatten a munitions factory?

Witherspoole acknowledged that the RN and RAF were hard-pressed to ensure the safety of the country. The Battle of Britain was still raging and although Britain was winning, the death list of pilots was appalling. If the losses could not be made good Britain would be in more trouble than she was now. Similarly at sea, scores of naval craft were being sued to protect convoys from U-boats, leaving the home defences stretched to the limit.

Whilst recognising that the human and material resources of both services were severely strained, Witherspoole was annoyed because neither service seemed to realise that trained agents dropped into France were the very people who could immobilise a dozen enemy planes in one night, or flood a dock while a U-boat was being repaired, thus easing the demand on the major services.

'Do you know,' Morton said, his thoughts elsewhere, 'it would be ideal if we had our own transport.'

Witherspoole agreed. Theirs was not the only small group continually requesting the use of a plane or submarine. There were dozens of groups all trying to get people in and out of Europe. Each occupied country had at least two factions in London, one sponsored by the pre-war government of the country in exile, and the other sponsored by London. Some nations had groups of different political persuasions, each claiming to be the main participants in resisting the Nazis in their homelands, and all with their own Intelligence services demanding or requesting transport. Often the factions were at loggerheads with each other, and on occasions violence erupted between them. As their demands and requests for transport were turned down, animosity between them and the London goverment was created.

'Yes,' Witherspoole said slowly, 'that *would* be ideal. Maybe I should make one or two enquiries.'

'Good. By the time the RN and RAF understand what we are doing is vital to the war effort, it might be too late.'

Morton and Witherspoole wore no uniforms. Both were civilians, university graduates who prior to the war had commanded responsible positions in industry and commerce. Witherspoole had been employed by the Ford Motor Company as an industrial engineer at the Dagenham Manufacturing and Assembly Plant, while Morton had been an insurance adjustor.

After Dunkirk the Secret Intelligence Service realised that with the fall of France information on what was happening inside the Nazi fortress of Europe was vital if Hitler was to be defeated. The SIS also realised that by utilising opponents of Hitler, and the general population of the occupied countries, the fortress could be eroded from the inside. With this in mind an instruction came from the highest level in Whitehall to 'set Europe ablaze'. Men and women with first-hand knowledge of Europe were sought out. Street maps, clothing, newspapers and even picture postcards were collected: anything that might provide information to help agents dropped into an occupied country.

While the SIS struggled to carry the fight back to Europe using professional and trained agents and saboteurs, an even more secret organisation was formed by amateurs: Special Operations Executive.

Formed in July 1940 in an office at 64 Baker Street, its existence known only to a select few, the SOE began recruiting ordinary people: people with special skills, and among those approached were Witherspoole and Morton.

As an industrial engineer Witherspoole possessed a planner's mind. Mass production depends to a great extent on exact timing. Parts must be manufactured and assembled to a pre-timed process, on occasions involving sequences measured in seconds. Within the time sequence each part must fit into the next and so on, until the finished article comes off the end of the production line. The finished article must conform to the details within the procedure. The quality of workmanship must be nothing short of 100 per cent. The material must be of a standard that will do the job for which it is intended, and all must be performed by men with the correct attitude towards the task.

It had been part of Witherspoole's job to ensure that the men with the right temperament were employed: that the men with the appropriate skills were employed: that they had the proper tools with which to carry out the work: that the materials they worked with were neither too hard nor too soft; and that they had sufficient time in which to complete each task.

SOE badly needed people with Witherspoole's ability to plan and organise, and one evening while leaving the Dagenham works two men stopped him in the street. Would he care to help the country in important war work? Witherspoole had said that he would. The men gave him an address in London and advised him to be there at 11 o'clock the following morning.

Witherspoole followed the advice and was taken to St Ermin's hotel in Caxton Street where a minor headquarters had been set up. There he was informed that his employer would be contacted and told to forget about him until the end of the war. He was now, he was told, part of the most secret organisation ever established.

John Morton had had a similar experience but with a slightly different approach. As an insurance adjustor he had for many years investigated claims made on his company, and was considered to be at the top of his profession. Morton was young but exhibited a brilliance that was the envy of men with many more years' experience. His mind could determine quickly if a claim on the company was false: if the claimant had deliberately sabotaged his own property to obtain payment; and this ability was sufficient for the fledgling SOE to approach him. If Morton knew the methods people used to cheat insurance companies, it was reasoned, then he would know the weak points in buildings and machinery, and know exactly how to place an explosive where it would cause most damage. In short, Morton was a textbook for sabotage.

He had been asked to investigate a claim in Central London. A stamp collection valued at £5,000 had been stolen from the apartment of a businessman, formerly wealthy and now down on his luck. He had gone into Central London visualising weeks of investigating the claim, at the time convinced that it was a false one. Money was scarce and those who had money were buying gold for investment. Crooks also knew how investors operated and a knowledgeable one would not go for stamps. There was no market for stamps with the country in so much strife and the maximum a crook could expect to receive for his efforts would be 10 per cent of the catalogue value. Even to get that he would be lucky: more likely to realise 5 per cent, which would not be worth his while when gold would bring upwards of 75 per cent of its current value.

Morton was somewhat surprised to find the address he had been given was an office in a Salvation Army hostel, and even more surprised to be met by a middle-aged woman who apologised for inconveniencing him. There was no stamp collection the woman said, then told him that she represented an important organisation involved in war work, and there was the matter of a steam locomotive somewhere in Europe she wanted put out of action. Could Morton describe to her how to use the minimum amount of explosives yet cause the locomotive a maximum amount of damage?

Morton immediately responded to the request, going into great detail; the woman then thanked him and left the office for some time, returning to ask would he care to offer his services to the country for the duration of the war. Morton readily agreed.

Although they worked as a team it was evident that Witherspoole was in charge. Instructions from Witherspoole were phrased to sound like suggestions, and a certain look in his eye told Morton the indirect instruction should be carried out without delay. Morton did not really mind. He was only twenty-eight and Witherspoole in his fifties. Witherspoole looked after the office side of things – something Morton was loath to do – while he travelled a lot. The job was more demanding than dealing with insurance claims: a bigger challenge. If they needed a suitcase manufactured in Poland, for example, it meant visiting people not only in London but throughout the country: and Morton liked to travel. The trips also built up long lists of useful contacts where skills or items of necessity could be obtained, all of which Morton and Witherspoole put to excellent use.

Quietly and efficiently SOE became a formidable organisation and, because there was never any regularity in its movements – they could be dormant for a week then suddenly have everyone working non-stop for thirty-six hours – the nickname 'Baker Street Irregulars' emerged. And the organisation became huge. Morton soon learned that they were only a tiny group within it, and that during every hour of the day and night men and women were being recruited in one capacity or another. But no one seemed to know who was at its head. Morton would never know. He would never know that the organisation was controlled from a skyscraper in New York, and that even as they discussed the merits and demerits of the RN and RAF, recruits were undergoing intensive training in different parts of the world prior to being dropped into Europe.

He would also never know that the only person in the British government who knew the man who gave birth to SOE was a personal friend of James Witherspoole: Winston Churchill.

Lt Oliver Woolcott was still at Falmouth. His boat was ready to leave at a moment's notice but so far no orders had come through. The waiting frustrated Woolcott. His first mission had been highly successful and he had hoped another, similar, mission would have been given to him.

Then a signal arrived. A messenger came by motorcycle bearing a naval telegram.

'This is it,' Woolcott smiled at Second Lt Huntingdon.

Huntingdon looked over Woolcott's shoulder as the small buff envelope was eagerly torn open, and sighed with disappointment. The telegram instructed Woolcott to proceed to London with his personal belongings on the first available train.

'Another command, sir,' Huntingdon suggested.

'I hope not, number one. Not now that I've become used to this boat and know the crew.'

It was late evening when Woolcott arrived in London. A car collected him at the station and drove him to the Admiralty where he was immediately ushered into a room filled with enough gold braid to paper a wall. Five senior officers were in the room. He counted an admiral, a rear-admiral, two captains and his own Captain SM.

His immediate superior, Captain, Submarines: in Charge of Flotilla, approached him.

'Lt Woolcott, allow me to introduce Admiral Sir Adrian Usher . . .' his superior went on to introduce the others and invited Woolcott to be seated.

The admiral and his entourage seated themselves behind a long desk facing Woolcott, all eyes on him, examining him, yet their expressions betrayed nothing.

'We have your log here, Lt Woolcott, from your trip to Brittany,' his superior said, pushing documents across the desk. 'Would you please read it through and confirm it is a true and accurate record of events.'

'It is, sir,' Woolcott replied.

'I should like you to read it through nonetheless, Lt Woolcott, so that there can be no misinterpretation of facts.'

'Very good, sir.'

The older men behind the desk remained silent while he read. Once or twice he looked up and saw the same thing: each sat impassive, like a statue, waiting for him to finish.

'The log is accurate, sir,' Woolcott said after a time.

'There can be no doubt about that, Lt Woolcott?'

'None at all, sir.'

'That being so, I now wish you to read this document . . .' another was passed across. 'It is the original copy of the instructions given into your care prior to undertaking the mission. Your signature is appended there. Please read through the document and verify that you accepted, read and understood the instructions, and signed them to that effect.'

Woolcott read through his original instructions again and agreed that he had followed standard procedure.

'Would you say, Lt Woolcott, that the mission – your first – was successful?'

'Very much so, sir.'

'Why would you say that?'

'Vital information about the enemy was brought out, sir.'

'That is so, Lt Woolcott. Some cloak and dagger people were extremely grateful for your efforts.'

'That is pleasing to know, sir.'

'Undoubtedly. However, having the gratitude of the cloak and dagger people does not necessarily mean that you have the gratitude of this panel. Your orders were specific, Lt Woolcott, and you disobeyed them, did you not?'

Woolcott was taken completely by surprise and could not reply. He had honestly believed he was going to receive a commendation. When he did find his voice it stumbled, his throat partly closed, dry and tense.

'I. . . I. . . used my own judgment.'

'I shall remind you to think back on the document you just read, Lt Woolcott: your original instructions, then tell the panel if you did or did not disobey those instructions.'

Again Woolcott was struck dumb. Yes, he pondered quickly, he had, but the mission had been highly successful. . . This was below the belt.

'We await your reply, Lt Woolcott.'

'Well,' Woolcott drew a deep breath, his lower jaw trembling. 'In a sense I suppose I did, but . . .'

'You suppose?' he was interrupted. 'Let me remind you Lt Woolcott, that I recommended you for this command because you convinced me that you could bear the responsibilities necessary to assume a command. I shall also remind you that when one assumes the responsibilities of a command, one obeys instructions except in the case of an emergency. Your mission was not an emergency: therefore by disregarding your instructions you risked the lives of seamen indispensable to the war effort: not to mention a submarine which is irreplaceable. Would you not agree, Lt Woolcott?'

Woolcott wanted to protest but decided against doing so. In the eyes of the panel he had disobeyed his instructions and that was that.

'It was with great reluctance, Lt Woolcott, that the submarine was loaned to these cloak-and-dagger people: and had it not been for pressure from a higher authority the mission would not have taken place at all!' the Captain SM leaned forward to utter the last few words in an angry tone.

Admiral Sir Adrian Usher assumed the position as spokesman now, his face beginning to turn pink with anger.

'The Royal Navy has no place for any man, seaman or officer, who disobeys an instruction, thereby risking the lives of others, Lt Woolcott. Therefore, it is the decision of this panel – a decision taken, I might add, not with reluctance but with vehemence – that on cessation of hostilites you will appear before a court-martial and be charged with this most serious offence. Until then you are relieved of your command and will not be appointed to any other. Instead, you will assume duties in the clerical section of the Admiralty, thus releasing for active service an officer more suited to the command you have relinquished. Do you understand, Lt Woolcott?' the admiral's voice was booming now.

'Yes, sir,' Woolcott replied quietly, his own voice barely heard.

'Then you may go. Ask the sentry outside to direct you to the clerical section.'

Woolcott stood and saluted, then turned and marched from the room. Outside he stopped, stunned, and leaned against the wall to recover. His body trembled.

'Are you all right, sir?' the sentry asked him.

Woolcott could hear nothing. He was shattered, for the moment mentally destroyed. At the age of twenty-six his career as a naval officer was over.

The sentry gripped his arm and spoke to him again, this time Woolcott responded in a hushed tone.

'Just got some bad news, that's all,' he said hoping

the sentry would not sense the cause of his shame. 'Can you direct me to the clerical section?'

'Certainly, sir. Take the elevator to the next floor down. On leaving the elevator the clerical office is through the second door to your right.'

'Thank you,' Woolcott mumbled and swayed off in a daze. Behind him the sentry smirked. He had seen others come out that way. This one wouldn't be the last.

In the elevator the words *If I had only* echoed through Woolcott's mind over and over again.

Chapter Five

'They should be arriving soon, sir!' a brawny sergeant snapped to attention as he replied to the officer's question. 'I gave them fifteen hours to complete the course, sir, and told them less than politely that I would be very cross if they took more than twelve.'

The officer lowered his head to grimace. To put it mildly the sergeant was a bastard when it came to training recruits for the new commando units, but he made sure that those who passed the multiple courses were at the peak of perfection. The sergeant had been a training instructor for several months now while he, previously behind a desk in London, was a newcomer. He hadn't got used to the sergeant yet and found some of his behaviour quite distasteful.

'Do you expect any failures, sergeant?'

'There are always one or two, sir.'

They were in a commando training camp twenty miles from Fort William in Scotland, where scores of recruits, all volunteers, were undergoing the most gruelling exercises. And there was no such thing as ninety-nine out of a hundred. Every volunteer had to attain perfect marks, otherwise they were 'returned to unit'. No one was given a second chance. Only those who could withstand the harsh discipline and demanding runs across the Scottish mountains carrying a hundred pounds of equipment were accepted. There were other tests, tests so demanding they took a man's stamina and mental aptitude beyond their limits, and on completion each graduate became a human death machine.

It was nearly noon. Mist had only just begun to lift from the bleak Scottish moors. Twelve hours before, on the stroke of midnight, a group of twenty-two recruits had set off on a test: all young men aged between nineteen and twenty-four, each one seeking some kind of adventure apart from that offered by the regular army. Carrying their hundred pounds of equipment they were to run – not walk – fifteen miles across dark and mist-shrouded mountains to a checkpoint. At the checkpoint there would be no period to rest. Immediately they arrived they would be steered in another direction, another fifteen miles to a second checkpoint, and again there would be no rest. From the second checkpoint it was a further fifteen miles back to base, mid-way along which was the castle of a Scottish earl. They were to enter the castle unobserved, still carrying their equipment, remove some small trinket and leave a receipt – the only evidence that they had entered the castle – retreat and complete the run.

The first man appeared, exhausted, his battledress soaked with mud and sweat, practically collapsing at the officer's feet.

'On your feet, boy!' the sergeant bellowed. 'You have your uniform and equipment to clean yet. Get up, boy!'

The young soldier was nearly in tears. He had expected some kind of pat on the back for being the first to return. He struggled to regain his feet and staggered, his eyes appealing to the officer to keep the bullying sergeant away. The officer had his head turned away, his ears screwed shut to blot out the raucous voice of the NCO.

'Get up, boy! Get into that hut!' the sergeant screamed at the top of his voice. 'If you give up now,

Christ, I'll have your balls off and use them as pepper-pots!'

Within minutes others began to arrive, like the first worn out and ready to drop. Again the sergeant began his abuse.

'You miserable bleeders! You're like a lot of girl-guides who've just experienced their first period. Move yourselves! Get in there and clean your gear . . . and I want it bloody spotless!'

Several backsides were kicked as the sergeant followed his charges into a hut at a rapid pace. From the outside the officer could hear bawling and shouting.

'You snotty-nosed wankers . . .'

The officer shook his head. Commandos were an innovation to him. What was the war coming to when it turned men into animals?

The remainder arrived, being bulldozed into the hut in a similar manner to the earlier arrivals, and after thirty minutes the entire group streamed naked into the open with their equipment. All were spotlessly clean. The equipment was laid out on groundsheets where the sergeant, seeming to enjoy himself, examined every item in detail.

The recruits were cold. Some of the nearby mountains already had snow on them and each day the snow line crept lower and lower. The sergeant wasn't bothered.

'Where's Wilson?' he suddenly shouted, making everyone, including the officer, jump.

'Are we one short?' the officer asked timidly. He was beginning to feel sorry for the recruits.

'Wilson, James, sir. Short-arsed Londoner. Thinks he's a comedian, sir. Sharp as a shithouse rat!'

The officer wished the sergeant wouldn't bawl so much.

'Oh, yes,' he remembered.

'I'll have him, sir, don't you worry. I'll stick his cock up his arse and drag him all over the bloody Grampians, sir!'

'You have something against him, sergeant?'

'Never liked him, sir. Too cocky for my liking, sir.

Little bastard, wasting my time like that! Christ, he won't know if his arse-hole is punched or bored by the time I'm finished with him, sir!'

The officer winced. The howling and bawling was bad enough, but the language . . .

'He is still within the time limit, sergeant.'

'Someone's coming,' the sergeant pointed along a narrow, winding road snaking across the moors. An old car was bumping towards them.

'Where the bloody hell did that come from?' the sergeant asked incredulously to no one in particular.

Slowly the old car approached them, then stopped. From it emerged a very irate Scottish earl, his gillie and Private James Wilson. The two Scottish gentlemen had double-barrel shotguns pointed at Wilson.

'What the hell's going on?' the sergeant strode forward, resuming his bawling.

'Slight mishap, sergeant!' Wilson snapped to attention.

'Mishap, indeed,' the Scottish earl echoed. 'I found this man robbing my home and when challenged he attacked my staff. One man has a broken jaw, another a broken leg; and heaven knows what it has done to my wife's nerves!'

'You failed, Wilson!' the sergeant screamed in a voice the officer imagined must have been heard right across the Scottish Highlands.

'And what about this?' the earl demanded, holding out twenty-two hand-written receipts. 'I shall take these to my MP and create the biggest stink since war was declared.'

'Wilson!' the sergeant seemed to be on the verge of apoplexy. Someone had to be blamed.

'Worn't my fault, sergeant,' retorted Wilson. 'Me equipment was faulty.'

'Faulty, my arse!'

'No, sergeant,' the officer put in, 'let him explain.'

'Go on then, you slimy little toad!'

'Well, sir,' Wilson seemed unsteady on his feet. 'I 'ad gone into a bedroom an' there was this little cracker still akip. I takes a pair of 'er knickers, pats 'er bum an' slides out . . .'

'My daughter . . !' the earl screeched, his face purple and his Adam's apple bobbing in rage.

Wilson went on. 'I 'ad a look in one or two uvver places an' went downstairs, an' 'alfway down me pack breaks – 'onest, sergeant. The bleedin' fing fell down the stairs making a God-awful racket an' suddenly these two great 'airy jock-straps attacks me. Well, you says we wasn't to be captured; we was to treat the test as being under battle conditions. So, I defends meself. I'd of got away if it worn't for the shotgun, sergeant. I mean, you'd of 'ad a go at me if I'd shot 'im.'

'Let me see your pack,' the sergeant moved beside Wilson. He looked into the soldier's eyes, turned and gave the officer a peculiar glance.

'I don't know what it is yet, sir, but something's not right here.'

'The pack, sergeant. Check the pack.'

Wilson held out the pack which both the sergeant and the officer examined, and much to the sergeant's disgust it was faulty.

'I'll put a chitty in for new equipment, sergeant,' said the officer, somewhat relieved. 'This lot has seen too much service.'

The sergeant nodded and glared at Wilson. The soldier looked straight ahead and the officer wondered why such a weedy looking person could have been considered for special duties. Given the task of forming a commando unit himself the officer would have gone for the taller, stronger type. Wilson was barely 5 feet 4 inches, on the thin side with a prominent, broken, curved nose. He reminded the officer of a London wide-boy: a keenly alert mind always on the lookout for something illegal. In short: a crook.

The sergeant was still glaring at Wilson, then he pushed his head forward until their noses nearly touched. An instant later he yelled, turned sharply and bawled in his aggravating way.

'He's pissed as a fart, sir!'

'Quite,' the Scottish earl came forward, this time brandishing an empty bottle. 'When my staff apprehended him he had already consumed half a bottle of my best malt, and then having landed two of my staff in hospital calmly consumed the other half. I shall expect the army to make full restitution.'

The officer was full of apologies, placating the earl in gushing terms, promising that the finest care would be given to his staff and that a case of the aforementioned whisky would be delivered to his home in the shortest possible time.

'What do we do with this soldier, sergeant?' the officer asked when the earl had taken his leave. 'If it hadn't been for the faulty equipment he would have passed the test.'

'What, sir! With a bottle of electric soup inside him? He'd never have got back. He'd have flaked out somewhere on the moors and half the bloody unit would've spent the rest of the day looking for him.'

'We don't know that, sergeant.'

'He failed, sir. Begging your pardon, sir, he's not worth a wank in a brothel.'

'Then I shall leave his future to your recommendation, sergeant,' the officer said, rather than argue the point. He just wanted the matter over and done with.

'Thank you, sir!' the sergeant bawled and whirled round. 'Right, you hook-nosed piss-hole! You and I are going on a run. Alongside me! Move! Knees up! Faster!'

The officer shivered momentarily. He recalled his own drilling instructor from years before. Like all recruits he'd hated the man, but he'd been an angel compared to this one.

The sergeant was more than a hundred yards away now, the soldier by his side, his voice bawling orders and abuse as he pushed the unfortunate miscreant through another punishing course.

'All right, men,' the officer dismissed the other shivering recruits, 'you can have your meal and turn in. But remember there is another course tonight.'

The sergeant was disappearing over a rise, his voice still audible, still swearing and abusive.

He was wasted up here, thought the officer. There were people in London who were looking for men like him. Perhaps he would pass word along.

Driving away in the old car the Scottish earl had similar thoughts. Mentioning the fact to his gillie he said: 'Had some remarkable attributes, that chap, wouldn't you say?'

'I would indeed, sir,' replied the gillie.

Chapter Six

'We've done it, John!' James Witherspoole said jubilantly as he entered the small office they used in St Martin's Lane. 'We have our own transport.'

'Sir, you mean . . .' Morton rose from his chair, a smile on his face.

'No, not a plane, John: a submarine.'

'A subma. . . but, sir, how did you talk the navy into . . .'

Morton had taken to calling Witherspoole 'Sir'. He didn't really know why. It just seemed the right thing to do.

Witherspoole held up a restraining hand. 'I didn't. I asked one or two questions in the right places and the upshot of it is that we are to be given a submarine for our own independent use. All *Most Secret*, of course, but just what we need.'

'But how could the navy be persuaded to part with it?'

'I believe it came from the United States actually.'

Witherspoole hadn't asked too many questions, nor would he be given any answers were he to ask. He would be in his grave before the name of William Stevenson would be made public. Stevenson, a wealthy Canadian industrialist, was in fact the man responsible for setting up the organisation of which they were part, and only three people in the world knew his identity. They were Winston Churchill, Franklin Roosevelt and William Donovan of US Intelligence.

SOE was but a small part of the much larger British Security Coordination, to be nicknamed BSC or British Sugar Corporation, an organisation controlled from New York, the last place, it was hoped, that German agents would expect its headquarters to be.

Stevenson was a genius. As a teenager he had improved on Samuel Morse's system of telegraphy and foresaw the use of wireless communication as a weapon of war. Using his engineering abilities he very quickly became wealthy and when war broke out put his entire business empire at the disposal of the British government, during the war spending much of his personal fortune to defeat Hitler's Germany.

Britain had asked the United States for ships, submarines and planes, and the Lend-Lease Bill was being furiously debated in Congress.

Obstacles were constantly put in the way by pro-German sympathisers who predicted Britain's early defeat, and who wanted to share the rewards of the new German Europe. Months of debate and negotiations lay ahead but Stevenson had become impatient. Through Churchill, Stevenson approached Roosevelt and Donovan and a series of secret deals were made, deals the American public knew nothing about and the proceeds of which would never appear on any balance sheet.

Churchill himself had negotiated the purchase of Flying Fortress bombers. These had been stripped down on small remote airfields in the United States, crated with false labels and shipped north across the border into Canada, and then on to England where they were reassembled and put to immediate use. So, when the request came through for a submarine no eyebrows were raised.

'Where is it, sir?' Morton asked.

'Over in Boston, I believe. She was to be scrapped, I'm told, and the request saved her from being cut up.'

'How will she be brought over?'

'I'm not sure. I was just told that she would arrive in the next few weeks. Has to be carried out with strictest secrecy, John. If German sympathisers over there get wind of it there'll be trouble. Officially the United States is not supplying us with any major equipment. And we're jolly lucky in more ways than one.'

'Why's that, sir?'

'Well, by the London Naval Treaty of 1930, apparently, this type of submarine was to be sent to scrap, but somehow or another the Americans managed to hold onto it as a training vessel.'

'She's old, then?'

'Apparently so, but we can't look a gift horse in the mouth.'

'Absolutely not, sir.'

In Boston, Victor Brack was stopped during his lunch-break by a member of the brotherhood.

'Something fishy going on, Vic. All work on scrapping the old boat has stopped. Two of the main engines have been taken out and lots of pipework removed. We've been told to replace the pipework and box her up for a trip.'

'With only two engines?'

'That's right. She's to leave as soon as possible for a place called Jonesboro up in Maine. We've looked it up and it's nothing more than a fishing village and,' the other man paused for effect, 'it's only forty miles from the Canadian border.'

Brack grimaced. Months before Berlin has asked German agents in the United States to keep a close watch on the Canadian border, as it was strongly suspected that war materials were being spirited into Canada for shipment to Britain. But the border was long and it was impossible to watch every inch. Nothing suspicious turned up at the normal, busier crossing points, but there were thousands of smaller, more remote points where the two governments could conduct their business. To date, the brotherhood had found no evidence that the traffic was taking place, and now it seemed that their patience was being rewarded.

'I'll get someone up there and find out what's going on,' Brack said.

Lt Commander Roger Sherman couldn't understand why he had been ordered to move at once for Boston. For weeks he had done little else but act as a filing clerk, then out of the blue came orders. And the orders were explicit. He was to inform no one where he was going, not even his parents, his estranged wife or father-in-law. He would be flown to New York and there catch a train for Boston, then make himself known to a Mr Josiah Bartlett whose address he'd had to memorise.

Sherman was tired when he reached Boston and introduced himself to Bartlett.

'You must be curious about all this, commander,' Bartlett commented.

'Some,' Sherman replied.

'Unfortunately I cannot explain anything just yet, but in time you will know all there is to know. For the time being suffice it to say that you will be taking over your old command.'

'That old tub?' Sherman showed surprise. 'I thought she was to be scrapped.'

'She still is. Anyway, let's get cracking. She's just about ready to go and all she needs is her captain.'

Within thirty minutes Sherman was in the dock area where the old submarine had been floated out of the flooded dry-dock. Once aboard he was shocked.

'This isn't fit to sail on a duck pond.'

'It's only a short trip, commander. And between you and me, don't take everything at face value.'

The crew was already aboard, less than the required number for normal operations, Sherman noted: nothing more than a skeleton crew. All the civilian workmen had been taken off and the crew were under orders not to speak to anyone other than their fellow-submariners and officers.

'You leave at once, commander,' Bartlett handed Sherman a bulky envelope. 'These are your sailing orders. They must not be opened until you are free of the three-mile limit. They must be destroyed after reading and the contents must not – repeat, not, be conveyed to the crew. Good luck to you, commander.'

That was that. Bartlett was taken off by launch, leaving Sherman on the conning tower bewildered by the speed of it all.

Victor Brack watched the old boat leave, his suspicions aroused more than ever. The crew had arrived in a bus with blacked-out windows and they had waited on board the bus until the boat was cleared of civilians, and while making their way up the gangplank they had kept their faces covered. Then the captain arrived, just as quickly, and no sooner was he aboard than the boat was underway.

He asked himself why. The boat was out of date, too old for service, yet an importance had been placed on its boxing-up as though it had been the most modern boat in the fleet. No one in Boston seemed to know why, but the man heading for Jonesboro soon might.

Jonesboro in Maine was a 250–mile journey by sea which, with 50 per cent of the boat's propulsion removed took forty-two hours to complete. The maximum speed attained was eight knots and was seldom reached because of rough seas.

Following his orders Sherman stopped his engines five miles off Jonesboro and waited, drifting in the currents, and told the crew to stand-by for disembarking. Hours seemed to pass before a large launch came speeding out from the shore and tied up alongside him. The crew made no comment as they climbed down into the launch but each of them, sworn to secrecy, wished they knew what was going on. Then without a word having passed between Sherman and the captain of the other vessel they parted, the launch speeding back the way she had come.

Sherman was alone. Within minutes of the launch's departure he experienced an eerie sensation. Under him was 1,000 tons of submarine drifting in the open sea, helpless against nature with no one to help him were an emergency to arise. It made him feel like the Ancient Mariner.

He went below and dragged a partly finished bottle of bourbon from his bag. The boat hummed. He looked around to where men had sat calling out ranges and bearings. The wireless had been left switched on and was still tuned to a Boston radio station. The atmosphere was weird. He took a swig from the bottle and went back up-top, taking it with him.

He had done a lot of drinking lately, ever since the . . .

'Christ!' he swore aloud. He hated to remember.

His eyes swept the ocean, looking for other shipping, knowing there would be none. The Navy and Maritime Services had ordered all shipping out of the area for a specific number of hours. He was all alone.

An hour went by and the bottle was finished. He threw it far from the boat and continued his waiting vigil, watching far to the north-east from where a launch should come.

When it came he was half-drunk. Darkness was nearly complete and he was thankful that those in the launch could not see his haggard face. It roared alongside and boathooks pulled them together. Silently, wearing dark clothing, men jumped aboard and disappeared down the hatches. The launch disengaged itself and took off and Sherman called down the voice-tube.

'Engines full ahead.'

In a North London pub George Taylor sipped from his pint of beer. No one took any notice of him. He was just another soldier in uniform enjoying a drink.

Taylor finished his pint, lit a cigarette and walked out into the cold night. He paused outside and drew in the fresher air. Because of blackout regulations all doors and windows in the pub had been sealed, making the atmosphere inside abominable. He closed his eyes for a moment and stiffened, sensing other bodies close to him. Suddenly the cigarette went flying from his fingers and strong hands forced him against the pub wall.

'Don't give us any trouble, Taylor,' a voice said in his ear, 'or we'll use you to sweep the street.'

Taylor nodded and relaxed. He couldn't be bothered fighting. The hands gripped tighter as an army truck came speeding round a corner, squealing to a halt by the kerb.

'Get aboard,' the voice said, 'and no tricks.'

The Military Policemen were itching for Taylor to start something. He had given them the runaround for weeks and at last they'd caught up with him. In their books a deserter deserved shooting.

Taylor climbed into the truck, helped by kicks and punches, and sat on a bench seat along one side.

'On the floor, Taylor!'

He obliged, took out another cigarette and began to light it.

'No smoking!' a boot kicked his hand.

Taylor sighed. It was all part of the dehumanising process: all part of the army's way of bending a person's will to its way of thinking. He had seen it all before.

Fifteen minutes later he was half-dragged and half-thrown into an office where the colonel in charge of his regiment sat waiting for him, his face a mask of stone. Flanking the colonel were his senior officers, each of them staring at Taylor and seeming to promise the worst.

'You have led us a merry dance, Corporal Taylor,' the colonel said, trying to keep his temper. 'What do you have to say for yourself?'

'What would you like me to say?' Taylor replied in a tone which, although not insolent, was lacking in respect.

'What would you like me to say, *SIR!*' a voice roared behind him.

'Well?' the colonel lifted his eyes. 'My officers and I would dearly like to learn the reason for your persistence in being absent without official leave.'

'I don't much care for the army, I suppose,' Taylor said with a shrug of his shoulders.

'I don't much care for the army, I suppose, *SIR!*' the voice roared again.

Taylor turned his head to look at the face behind the voice and said: 'Keep your voice down, old son. None of us are deaf.'

'Where did you find him?' the colonel asked the sergeant in command of the escort party.

'Where we suspected he might be, sir.'

'Did he give any trouble?'

'He was no trouble, sir,' the sergeant smiled boastfully. 'We are capable of taking care of any trouble his kind can come up with, sir.'

'That's something anyway,' remarked the colonel, remembering the last time they had Taylor cornered. With a lump of timber he'd crowned the escort and made his escape.

The colonel could not understand Taylor's attitude. He was twenty-nine, with eleven years' service behind him and could have been an officer had he cared to apply. In the early thirties when Japan invaded China Taylor had been stationed in Shanghai, and immediately following the Japanese invasion volunteered to go to the northern areas of the country to teach the inadequately-trained Chinese armies how to fight as soldiers. He had spent five years with the Chinese, not only training soldiers but fighting alongside them in the remote mountainous ranges that spanned the country from north to south. The Chinese had decorated him several times and had been saddened when he was recalled with his regiment to England.

Since then he had been a thorn in their side. He had gone to pieces, doing as he pleased with complete disregard for army discipline, and had it not been for his record he would have been court-martialled long before; a step the colonel was reluctant to take since it would have damaged the reputation of the regiment. Yet he would have to use the threat of the ultimate.

'You do realise, Corporal Taylor, that your conduct calls for the maximum penalty at a court-martial?'

Taylor shrugged and looked around. There was a chair handy. He drew it towards him and sat, still facing the colonel.

'The prisoner will stand!' the now familiar voice roared and a boot kicked the chair from under him. Taylor landed in a heap on the floor. The colonel, taken aback, lifted himself from his chair, just slightly, then resumed his statuesque position. He would talk to the guard later.

Taylor rose slowly. He was beginning to lose his patience. On regaining his feet he turned to the escort, his eyes icy and demanded: 'Who did that?'

'You will stand to attention and face the colonel!'

'Was it you?' Taylor asked from deep in his throat.

The escort was made up of four tough soldiers who sensed a fight about to begin: just as they had been hoping all along. Their fingers touched the batons at their hips and they spread their legs, balancing on the balls of their feet in anticipation.

'Was it you?' Taylor asked again.

The escort sergeant smirked, his face telling Taylor what he wanted to know and then all hell broke loose. Taylor's right foot suddenly appeared from nowhere and caught the sergeant under the chin, felling him like a pole-axed bear. The rest of the escort party were meanwhile on the move, but not as fast as they should have been. Taylor was on them like a hungry animal seizing its prey. His hands and feet moved so fast they became a blur. The colonel and his officers sat frozen in a tableau. They had never seen anything like it. Grown men were being thrown into the air as if they were pieces of paper. The snap of bones breaking was sickening and the scream of men in agonising pain tore at their nerve-ends.

Very soon it was all over. The escort lay stretched out on the floor and Taylor faced the colonel again. He could have told the colonel that the Chinese had taught him certain methods of fighting that the army had not, but decided against it.

'You were saying, colonel?' he used a form of address for the first time.

Behind him the sergeant was stirring. Hatred was in his eyes. He got to one knee, grasped his baton with both hands and launched himself up.

Taylor heard the swish of quick movement too late. His body reacted as the Chinese had taught him, but a millisecond delay was all the sergeant needed. Taylor blacked out as the baton crashed down on his skull.

Victor Brack brayed with triumph when a messenger brought a long report back from the north. An earlier report told him that the crew of the old boat had been seen in Jonesboro, but not the boat. They had come ashore in a launch and been taken away very quickly in a bus similar to the one that had brought them to the dock in Boston. The long report in his hands now was more revealing. Members of the brotherhood along the east coast of the United States and Canada had been told to be on the lookout for the boat, and it had been traced. She was in Canada, at Halifax, Nova Scotia, having supplies taken aboard, and crewed by Canadian sailors. A few discreet questions had revealed that she was to sail for England very shortly.

It was important that Berlin knew exactly how many ships and submarines Britain had in her fleet. Each was documented in Berlin and as each new vessel left the slipways in docks throughout the world, they, too, were added to the detailed files.

A submarine was serious. Nothing this large that Brack, or Berlin, knew of had been sent across. A submarine could do more damage to Germany than a hundred tanks, and it would cause that damage if it crossed the Atlantic.

Brack smiled. He could have the pro-German lobby in Congress accuse the government of breaking her neutrality. That would really set the cat among the pigeons. But it would do Germany no real favours. By the time the news hit the press the submarine would be well on its way and denials would be made.

No, it would be more appropriate to sink the submarine shortly after she left Halifax. The move was supposed to be secret – otherwise why would they have gone to the trouble of trying to disguise the fact – so, why not let London know that Germany's Intelligence was so expert that nothing could escape her notice, thus making it futile to attempt the same thing again?

That night a coded signal was flashed to Berlin where, from records, German Naval Intelligence very quickly produced every detail of the boat. Orders were sent out to several U-boats in the Atlantic to stand by off Nova-Scotia and await the departure of the newly-acquired British boat and sink her at the first opportunity. That she was reputed to be deprived of half her propulsion should make the task easy.

Completely unaware of anyone called Victor Brack, Lt Commander Roger Sherman supervised the preparations being made aboard his boat. It had come as something of a shock when he'd read his orders. Not only was he to take over the boat at Boston, but he also had to sail to Jonesboro where the crew would be taken off and replaced with Canadians. From there he would sail to Halifax and prepare to sail to England. *He* would sail to England: not an English captain, and on reaching England would await further orders.

Sufficient supplies were aboard, although no torpedoes or worthwhile arms: nothing with which they might defend themselves should they meet a crisis.

The sailing orders were precise. The boat was to submerge immediately on leaving Halifax and remain so for as long as possible, surfacing for the first time during darkness to recharge the batteries, and from there on be submerged by day and surfaced at night.

Sherman predicted that only a miracle would take them to England. The Canadian sailors who had come aboard off Jonesboro had been so shocked at what they found that Sherman couldn't have blamed them if they'd wanted to get back off. Most of them hadn't been born when the boat was launched and to them it had come out of the ark. They had got the remaining two engines running – simple enough – but they'd had to be instructed in carrying out other operations. To their credit they had picked it up quickly but they had been on the surface at the time and in safe waters.

Going across the Atlantic would be different. They would be a target then, not only for German U-boats but also for British U-boat hunters, for all identification markings had been removed.

Chapter Seven

James Witherspoole and John Morton were appalled when they saw the submarine they could call their own.

'It's disappointing,' Witherspoole complained. 'I confess I expected something more reliable. I knew it was old but . . .'

Morton expressed the same sentiments. The boat was empty of its crew and lay in the shelter of a tiny cove at Polperro in Cornwall. Polperro, in peace time a popular tourist resort, was deserted except for a few locals who were used to ships and submarines lying with them for a few days. Tied to buoys, the boat was rusted, and looked a derelict wreck. It had suffered engine trouble on the way over and only just scraped through.

With propulsion depleted, the boat had managed to keep to its eight knots on the surface and six knots submerged, and with a zig-zag course had taken just over thirty-one days to complete the crossing. In that time there had been 122 alarms but they had come through safely, although not without damage. Immediately on leaving Halifax the boat came under attack and only swift evasive action by Sherman prevented disaster. In turn the boat had been attacked by American warships protecting American shipping, by British and German ships and submarines over and over again, and even by a French destroyer. Many of the outer plates were buckled as a result but she had made it.

'Not very nice looking,' Morton said. 'What happens now?'

'She'll be towed somewhere for repairs and fitting-out, then we have to find ourselves a permanent base.'

'Where?'

'I shall have to see what is available, John.'

'Well,' Morton sighed, 'we have a boat. All we need now is a crew.'

'That's a point,' said Witherspoole. 'Let's ask around, shall we? There's bound to be someone with people to spare.'

'What about the crew who brought it over?'

'Nothing doing there. I'm told they were loaned to us without the knowledge of the Admiralty, and as soon as the boat arrived they were whisked away rather sharpish before the Sea Lords could learn they were here.'

'That was a pity.'

Witherspoole and Morton returned to London where they began putting out feelers. Visits were made to departments of the Admiralty, pleading for able-bodied men, but the Sea Lords shook their heads. The navy wanted nothing to do with subterfuge.

'Then if we can't have a ready-made crew,' said Witherspoole after an unrewarding day, 'we shall have to beg, borrow or steal one. Perhaps we should start contacting people who have helped us before,' he added with a smile.

Morton smiled in return, his eyes twinkling. 'That's the ticket, sir.'

Berlin, disappointed that the underpowered boat had reached Britain, and anxious to learn of her whereabouts, radioed agents in Britain with instructions to establish her port of arrival, her eventual base and the number allocated to her by the Admiralty. The boat should be easily recognisable by its stubby conning tower, Berlin said.

Corporal George Taylor awoke with a massive headache. He tried to move and discovered he had been tied in some way. After a while his head, although still painful, began to clear and he looked at his surroundings. He was in a prison cell. A single light bulb burned above him. The walls had no windows and the door had the usual peep-hole in it. He struggled to free himself and only made himself more uncomfortable. A strait-jacket restrained him, holding him in its lunatic grasp and refusing him freedom of movement.

In a room not far away his colonel debated what to do with him. Recommending the most decorated man in the regiment (albeit Chinese decorations) for a court-martial wasn't the done thing.

Since his capture every day had been the same. Taylor had originally been housed in a cell with bars, with meals being pushed to him through a grille, and at each meal as the food was being passed through he tried to grab hold of the soldier on duty. Sometimes he caught them and so far two broken arms had resulted. The last straw came when a psychiatrist tried to talk to him. Taylor went for the psychiatrist like a man possessed and it took ten bulky guards to subdue him. Later the psychiatrist was treated for a nervous condition.

Taylor had had to be restrained. The guards had beaten him unconscious and although none of his bones had been broken he would be sore for several days. Still unconscious he had been put into the strait-jacket and thrown into a cell without bars. He was still there and the colonel was at a loss about his future.

'I believe it is psychological,' remarked a junior officer.

'Psychological!' the colonel snorted. 'Did you see what he did to the chap who visited him?'

'I did,' the officer replied, 'but I still hold that belief. I mean, if you look at it, he practically gave himself up: yet he could have taken off had he wanted.'

'He was arrested. He did not give himself up.'

'Think back, sir, to the time when they brought him in and the way he handled himself. The guards never knew what hit them. And he was so calm about it afterwards. Remembering that, imagine what he could have done to the guards when they were in the street? In my opinion, sir, he let them take him.'

The colonel became quiet for a few moments as he pondered the thought, then said: 'By God, you're right! So, how do we get through to him?'

'We need a miracle, sir.'

'I wonder if the bugger's mad,' the colonel said to no one in particular.

The miracle came later in the day in the shape of James Witherspoole. The colonel took a telephone call that informed him of the imminent arrival of a civilian who would offer no name, but would produce a warrant card bearing a legend the colonel would recognise as very high in the ratings of security. The warrant card would act as an instruction and should the civilian make any suggestion regarding Taylor's future, the colonel should act on the suggestion immediately.

'How can a civilian know about Taylor?' the colonel looked to his officers with an air of puzzlement. 'And what on earth could he suggest for him other than a court-martial? Damned bureaucrats!'

No one could reply to these questions and as the evening neared every officer on duty at the barracks waited at windows with their necks craned to see the mysterious creature: and were more than surprised when they caught sight of an overweight elderly man entering the gates.

'Good lord!' the colonel ejaculated. 'My information says he is an important person with clout. One would expect him to have a car and driver, but this chap looks as though he's just come off a number eleven bus!'

Escorted, Witherspoole entered the colonel's office where, after producing his warrant card and making one-sided introductions, he came straight to the point.

'I may be able to take this chap Taylor off your hands.'

'You'll take him?' the colonel blurted. 'How? I mean to say, there are procedures . . .'

Witherspoole held up a hand. 'If I could just talk to the chap, colonel, I can decide quickly, and if he is what I want . . .' he let his words trail off.

'Well, yes . . . of course . . . by all . . .' the colonel became flustered. 'Major,' he spoke to one of his officers, 'escort Mr . . . er, this gentleman to the cell block.'

As Witherspoole left the office the colonel poured himself a drink. He didn't know how the civilian could get away with simply taking Taylor into his charge, but if he could it would solve the problem of a court-martial.

At the cell door the major assigned as his escort brandished a revolver.

'That won't be necessary, major,' Witherspoole remarked. 'All I need is a chair and some time alone with him.'

'But, I can't let you . . .'

Witherspoole waved a finger. 'If he's tied up he can't harm me.'

'You don't know this character, sir. He's a nutcase, but if it is your wish . . .' the major signalled for the cell door to be opened by the duty guard.

'Lock it behind me, would you?' said Witherspoole.

Taylor looked up from his prone position on the concrete slab serving as a bed when the stranger entered, dragging a chair with him. He struggled again, trying to get to his feet and inflict hurt even while wrapped in a cocoon.

'Please,' Witherspoole smiled, 'there is no need to struggle,' his tone was friendly. 'I have only come to talk to you.'

He wasn't a soldier, Taylor thought. Possibly another trick-cyclist trying another tack. Well, he would get short shrift.

'That's better,' said Witherspoole, pulling his chair close. 'Can't stand for any great length of time, you know.'

Taylor studied his visitor. He saw a fat and partly balding man: a red face that said he enjoyed a good drink and that if he wasn't careful he'd have a heart attack. When he spoke several layers of fat below his chin wobbled.

'I understand you've been giving your superiors a bad time?' Witherspoole said with a chuckle.

'Who are you?' Taylor asked.

'My name is unimportant. I am here to offer you a job: purely and simply that.'

'A job?' Taylor became still. 'I'm in the bloody army.'

'I can get you out, old chap.'

'To do what?'

'Oh, little tasks here and there.'

'Here and where, and who do you work for?'

'I can't tell you that, but I have nothing to do with the army or any other of the services. Just be assured that I need reliable men. I thought perhaps you would be ideal.'

Taylor gave a short laugh. 'My colonel doesn't think I'm the ideal soldier.'

'I'm not looking for soldiers, corporal, I'm looking for reliable men. There is a difference.'

'To do what?'

'I can't tell you that just yet,' Witherspoole repeated, then suddenly: 'I say, would you like to be free of that thing?'

'Wouldn't I just!'

'Then allow me to undo it. Dreadful way to treat a chap.'

With the strait-jacket off Taylor stood and moved stiff muscles. 'If I ever get my hands on those bastards who done me over,' he said angrily, 'I'll crucify them.'

'All in good time, old chap. Please sit down and listen to me. Would you like a smoke?'

Taylor nodded and accepted a cigarette.

'Will you work for me?'

Taylor nodded, 'But I'd like to know more about it.'

'There's time for all that. First of all, tell me why you've upset so many people?'

Taylor sat on the concrete slab and let his shoulders droop.

'I don't know how to explain it,' he began. 'When I first joined up it wasn't so bad, you know, the drilling and what-not. You expect that. But I spent some time in China and we didn't have time for blancoing and bullshit. I was involved in fighting the Japanese and it was a different kind of fighting. We didn't line up in front of each other and invite the other to fire first. There were no trenches. There were no masses of infantry going forward with tanks to back them up. It was totally different. More hit and run. We attacked in small groups and caused some havoc then shot out of it. We didn't need officers. We didn't do things just because an officer said so, even though the order had no meaning. Your mind adapts to that kind of fighting and you see the futility in what we know as recognised war-making. Anyway, I was brought back and I just couldn't stand all that marching up and down, the yelling and bawling and snotty-nosed officers with no experience belittling me just because they had pips. I didn't know what to do about it so I done a bunk. I was hoping they'd chuck me out for being a bad boy but they wouldn't have any of that. I had to be punished. Once I tried to explain and they thought I was being insolent. But I wasn't. I had respect for the colonel and his off-siders, but they just didn't want to see things my way. Every time I went before him I had to snap to attention and do all that bit . . .' Taylor shook his head with frustration. 'Does that make sense to you?'

'I do believe I understand what you mean, old chap.'

'I don't fit in any more.'

'Exactly! But you will fit in for what I have in mind. As I say, I am not the army, but with me you would be working with a small team.'

'Okay, I've nothing to lose by giving it a go.'

'There will be discipline, old chap, harsh discipline if necessary, and lots of training. You may be required to undertake a considerable amount of sea travel and take orders from a superior and . . .' Witherspoole took a deep breath, 'I can have you out of this cell in five minutes. Once out, however, you become my property, and there will be no second thoughts.'

'You mean I come back here if I don't go along with whatever you are offering?'

'No, I don't mean that, old chap. If you leave this cell and be discharged, and you do anything which might upset my plans, I'll have you shot. How does that sound?'

Taylor looked up. A silent chuckle was on the older man's face. A twinkle was in his eye, and a signal warning that he wasn't joking. A thin smile broke across Taylor's face. He understood now.

'That sounds more like the war I could get my teeth into. You're on!' he stuck out his hand.

Witherspoole chuckled loudly, shook hands with Taylor then called for the cell door to be opened.

The colonel was quite taken aback to see Taylor and before he could ask the obvious question Witherspoole gave him another surprise.

'All I need is your signature, colonel, and Corporal Taylor will be officially discharged – out of your hair.'

'But, I just can't . . . there are forms to be filled . . . complicated procedure.'

Witherspoole delved into a tattered briefcase and produced several documents.

'Everything is here, colonel, rubber-stamped and signed by the appropriate people. All they need is your signature.'

The colonel shook his head with amazement and signed. The fat man *was* important, he decided, if he could get someone out of the army that quick.

'Thank you, colonel, and now I shall bid you a very good evening, Mr Taylor and I have things to discuss.'

Witherspoole returned the documents to his briefcase and to Taylor said: 'You're not in the army now, old chap. How does it feel?'

Taylor looked around him. The guards who had taken

him in and beaten him with their batons were to one side. He went close to each one, staring into their faces, then stepped back.

'I'll remember you,' he said in a tone that was a promise more than a threat. 'We'll meet again, and when we do I'm going to make each of you suffer. Right, sir,' he smiled at Witherspoole, 'when do we start?'

A few minutes later the colonel and his officers watched Taylor walk away with his new-found friend. He was thinking that he would have given his right arm to learn how someone like Witherspoole could transform a barbarian into a civilised being.

Chapter Eight

A radio signal arrived at Hicomintel HQ in Berlin – German High Command Intelligence Service – which decoded read: NIB BROKEN, REPLACEMENTS IN TRANSIT.

Intelligence officers shook hands at the news. They smiled, and yelled out with triumph and generally behaved as if Germany had just won the war. The news went higher up the ladder of responsibility and within the hour telegrams and telephone calls of congratulation flooded in. Promotions were certain to follow.

While the congratulations were being passed round Hicomintel HQ six RAF officers were being driven across the Iberian Peninsula. Cooped up aboard a battered Mercedes truck sitting on bench seats facing each other, three either side, the officers were in a pitiful condition. Each was restrained, one ankle manacled to the floor and hands cuffed behind their backs. They also showed signs of having been severely beaten.

The truck bumped over unpaved roads out of sight of the general population and prying British agents, stopping only to refuel and to change the armed guards who kept the prisoners company in the truck's rear, ensuring they did not attempt to escape their bonds.

Their fate seemed in no doubt. Since being abducted they had not eaten. They were weak, not only from hunger but also from the beatings they had received before the journey began. Since then they had heard no one speak, not even at refuelling stops, hearing only the knock of metal on metal when a spout was pushed into a fuel tank. Except when the two guards in the rear changed, the doors were always locked. Bodily functions were carried out where they sat, making the atmosphere inside unbearably nauseating for the guards – who had the privilege of relieving themselves in the open – as well as themselves. So far as they could ascertain there were five guards, three in the driving cabin and two in the rear, the two always armed with Schmeisser MP38 sub-machine guns: deadly at close range.

The guards were in civilian dress and in a continual state of agitation. Were the truck to crash or need repairs, anti-fascist Spaniards might possibly catch sight of its cargo, and if that were to happen the operation could transform itself from a triumph to a disaster. British agents and anti-fascist sympathisers – and many people in Northern Spain had not forgotten the atrocities meted out by the fascists during and after the civil war – could quickly organise their forces and rescue the prisoners. As these prisoners were manacled and obviously ill-treated Berlin would be put in an embarrassing position, having contravened the Geneva Convention, and it would perhaps spawn retaliation on German prisoners in Britain.

Nor would Spain escape. On paper Spain was neutral, but allowing German agents to take British fliers out of the country, in chains, bound for Germany, could result in that neutrality being lost and therefore making the country liable to attack by Britain. Spanish shipping would become targets for submarines and the country would suffer hardship, a hardship she could ill afford since she had not yet recovered from the catastrophic civil war.

For three days and nights the truck rolled and bumped across the dusty roads, and it was with relief that the guards sighted the frontier post where arrangements had been made for an uninterrupted crossing. This rarely-used frontier post nestled several miles north-east of Albana in the province of Gerona where, bribed with gold, both Spanish and Vichy French officials sat behind shuttered doors and windows in their respective stations waiting for the truck to pass through.

The barriers were upright, the immediate vicinity deserted. No lights showed from the single-storey, stone-built frontier posts. Midnight had passed an hour before and even in nearby Albana few people stirred. The driver of the truck dipped his headlights and murmured to his companions, who nodded in reply.

The first post went by and they were on the strip of no man's land. Seconds later the truck went through the second imaginary line separating the two countries.

'Thank God,' one of them said.

'We're not finished yet,' said another.

After the frontier there was only fifty miles to a private hangar at Perpignan airfield where an unmarked plane waited, and although the German abductors were more at home in France than in Spain, they could not relax their vigilance. Vichy France was alive with British agents and sympathisers and the same conditions applied as in Spain. The only compensation was that across the frontier Spain would not be embarrassed.

At three o'clock in the morning the truck finally came to a halt. In silence the rear doors were opened and the prisoners motioned to be quiet. The stench reaching the open air was overwhelming. Keys jangled lightly as their manacles were undone then rough hands pushed them onto the cold tarmac, from where the snouts of sub-machine guns ordered them towards the waiting hangar.

Ten minutes later it was all over. The plane took off

on its way to Berlin and the five guards, all German Intelligence agents, climbed back into their truck and drove to a farm on the outskirts of Perpignan. There they would rest before driving back into Spain the next night for more pickings.

Private James Wilson was enjoying a spot of leave in his native London. He still wore his army uniform but did not know what the future held. Except for the incident at the home of the Scottish earl he had passed the commando training course, but the incident was still being dealt with. They hadn't given him RTU, nor had they told him he was in. He had just been told to go on leave and await a decision. It was a bit annoying not knowing.

Not that he minded the leave. Already he had filched some army stores and sold them on the black-market, the proceeds of which were now safely tucked away in a bank account ready for the day when the war was over. When that day came he would go into business for himself: strictly legal, of course.

The girl with him had had enough to drink. Her eyes were glassy and she'd been giggly for a good half-hour. It was time, he thought, to get her back to his mother's house at Bow and give her one.

''Ere, let's 'ave you, luv,' he took her arm. 'Let's go 'ome.'

'Home where?'

'Me mum's place. It's cosy there.'

The girl giggled some more and Wilson knew he was in for a good time. His mother had gone to stay with a relative and the house would be empty.

Outside the saloon bar the girl staggered against him. 'Ooh, it's cold!'

'Not for long, luv.'

The girl was still giggling when two civilians approached them.

'Private James Wilson?' One of them asked.

Wilson said nothing. His eyes quickly swept over both men. Nothing said they were in the army.

"Ooo's asking?' he let the muscles in his body ripple as he'd been taught.

'We are.'

"Ooh are you?'

One of them came close and spoke in low tones. 'It is to your credit that you are cautious, Private Wilson, but there can be a limit. You are to come with us. Your leave is cancelled.'

'Leave it out, chum. I've got four days left.'

One of them shook his head. 'Your leave is cancelled, Private Wilson, from this instant. You will accompany us and do it quietly. If you do not you will be charged with a variety of offences, including, for example, disobeying an order; insulting an officer; disgracing the King's uniform; drunk on duty; and rape. Now, just come along and forget the young lady. We shall see she gets home safely.'

Wilson shook his head. It was the first chance he'd had in weeks to get his end away and he wasn't giving it up just like that. Remembering his training he switched his weight onto one foot.

'And you can cut that out, Private Wilson. Either of us could wipe the floor with you. We teach the oriental arts. Now, do you come or do we have you arrested?'

Wilson nodded. What was the point of getting into a ruck? They'd only stick him away and he'd never get into the commandos.

'Sorry, luv,' he said sadly to the girl.

Chapter Nine

Two half-drunk seamen with yet another horrific Atlantic trip behind them, lurched along one of Liverpool's darkened streets. In the pub they had just left they had been fortunate not to spend a penny on drink. Hearing that they had survived a torpedo attack after which their ship went down, other customers stood them all they could swallow. It was the only way the ordinary Britons could show their gratitude.

Further along the street on the opposite side, three men prepared to go in for the attack. The three were experts at relieving others of their cash and valuables and during their stay in Liverpool had lived well.

The two drunken seamen followed a zig-zag course along the sidewalk. They were trying to sing a popular tune which, to the trained ear, sounded more like a band of Apaches on the warpath. That they could be assaulted and robbed in their home city was far from their mind.

Across the road the three robbers prepared themselves. They would allow the pair to go by, then dash across quickly, fell and rob them then retreat in the same manner.

They rose on the balls of their feet, waiting for their dark-featured leader to give the signal, when, seemingly out of nowhere, a group of men suddenly surrounded them.

'Don't move a muscle, gentlemen,' an upper-class English accent warned. 'There are two of us to each of you, and we have firearms pointed at your heads.'

The three froze, wondering what to do. The drunks had passed and were on their way, singing their heads off.

'I strongly suggest that you relax,' the accent went on, 'then turn and put your hands against the wall. You will be searched and God forgive you if we find any offensive weapons.'

The would-be robbers hesitated. 'Move!' the accent hissed.

Jolted out of their hesitancy the three turned quickly and pushed their hands against the wall that previously had been their shelter, where a brisk patting-down produced no weapons of any sort.

'That,' said the accent with emphasis, 'was extremely wise. Now, I further suggest that you remain as you are until transport arrives.'

Three black cars, their headlamps taped over to leave

only pinpoints of light, rolled to a stop alongside the group. Without another word being spoken the three men were split up, one to each car, flanked on both sides by a determined armed member of BSC. Inside the car hoods were pulled over their heads and, in line, the cars pulled away from the kerb heading for the Mersey Tunnel.

Much later the cars, still closely in line, pulled into the rear of the seventeenth-century Providence House in the centre of Chester. In total darkness the three robbers were taken inside, guided along a corridor and into a large room where they were helped into deep armchairs, then hands removed the hoods.

They blinked, fear coming into their eyes. Where they might be they had no idea, and the men now facing them appeared grim. No guns were visible but their absence did not make them feel safe.

The dark-featured member of the group looked around. The room was palatial, furnished in a way he had only seen in Hollywood films depicting English stately homes. His companions also began to look around them. One of them gasped, causing the other two to follow his eyes. Piled on the floor in one corner were all their belongings, everything they owned between them which they believed was safely hidden at their lodgings.

'Ah,' said the accent from earlier, 'I see you recognise certain articles.'

The speaker was no older than thirty, tall and distinguished, dressed as if ready to spend the night at a club. He wore a long black overcoat with a white scarf showing from behind the lapels, white collar and black and red tie.

'Now then,' the accent smiled, 'Let's see who we have here . . .' he began to sort through identification papers taken from the robbers in the car. 'You, my friend,' he nodded at the dark-featured individual, 'You appear to be the leader of this industrious little trio . . . Jesus Reyes Heroles, born on February 17, 1917 at Ciudad Juarez in Mexico's Chihuahua Province. Taken to El Paso in Texas – illegally, one hastens to add – at the age of three by parents Luis and Sophia. First brush with the law at the age of seven and sent to a reformatory for six months . . .'

Heroles' mouth fell open. No one, but no one, knew of his early life.

'Graduated to the ranks of the hardened criminal classes as years passed and spent four years between the ages of nine and fifteen in various houses of correction. On release following a two-year sentence, two weeks before your fifteenth birthday, absconded to New York where, after an initial successful period of criminal activities, joined the merchant marine to escape justice. Left a trail of unsolved crimes ranging from petty theft to robbery with violence around the world. At present, on your return to the United States, there awaits a five to ten year term in Sing-Sing Penitentiary.

'And your gallant comrades . . . You, my young friend . . .' the object of his attention was a nineteen-year-old, less experienced than Heroles in dealing with authority and visibly terrified.

'Lyman Halls, born on July 8, 1921 to Joshua and Ernestine Halls in their rented house at Wheeling, West Virginia. Joined merchant marine in December of last year while on bail for robbing an all-night drug store. The drug store being your first step into crime it is believed that you panicked and ran when given bail, fearful of a possible term in one house of correction or another. Jumped ship with Jesus Reyes Heroles and have been his partner in crime since.

'And last but not least, William Hooper, born March 27, 1911 to Thomas and Sarah Hooper at Ann Arbor, Michigan. Sailed on Great Lake steamers from the age of fourteen for five years then moved on to ocean-going vessels. Free of crime until a visit to Rio in 1934. There, you became involved in a fight with sailors of the German Navy, resulting in three sailors being treated for knife wounds and you being gaoled for two years at the request of the German Ambassador who apparently had some financial arrangement with the constabulary in the country. On your return to the United States you managed to get yourself into some undesirable company and before long found yourself before a judge for the second time, on this occasion receiving six months for assault, intent with a deadly weapon and demanding money with menaces – or whatever phraseology is used in that part of the world for the aforementioned crimes. Knowing that the sea can hide many crimes you departed those fair shores again, in time meeting up with Jesus Reyes Heroles and jumping ship here in Liverpool.

'There is much more, gentlemen,' the accent smiled, 'although for the time being it is of no consequence. I just read that to you to indicate that we know much more about you than you realise.

'And now, what should we do with you, I wonder? You have robbed a goodly number of British seamen in the past few months. What would you say that deserves – five years? Ten years?'

'Hey!' Heroles spoke up. 'We ain't robbed nobody.'

'Haven't you, by jove?' the accent mocked Heroles. 'Then my informants must have made a ghastly mistake. You see, I have a long list of crimes here purportedly committed by you three . . . You do know what purportedly means, by the way? Of course you do.'

Heroles realised his captor was making fun of him and made to rise.

'I shouldn't, old chap. Our revolvers are tricky things when they go off, and I shouldn't want to make a mess of the carpet.' Accent took a chair, sat on it the wrong way round, leaning on the back and dropped the smile and facetious manner.

'Gentlemen, this country is at war. Our enemy is all around us and we have our backs to the wall. Now, we are very alert to enemy agents possibly entering the country, and to ensure that they do not we scrutinise every stranger who comes near our shores – and I mean everybody: no exceptions. So, do you honestly believe that you could jump ship and run loose without our knowing? We have had you under observation from the time you left your ship. Yes, we could have picked you up at any time of our choosing, but we decided to see how you would fare in an austere environment. And you have had a long enough holiday, I think. It's time now to go back to work. A chap I know in London can make use of you. The job will be dangerous but having observed you at work I believe you will rise to the occasion admirably. Danger seems to suit you, don't you think?'

There was a pause while he waited for some kind of response, and it came, as he expected, from Heroles.

'Nothing doing, buddy. You can lock us away if you like, but you won't be able to do that without first informing the US Ambassador.'

'Can't I?' their captor raised his eyebrows. 'Now I thought differently. I thought that since the US Ambassador has no idea that you are in this country, and that since all reference to you in the register of the American Merchant Marine Service has been removed, no one at all would know you are in this country. What's more, when you stand trial for murder I would think the Ambassador would disclaim all knowledge of you. . . Wouldn't you?' the smile returned.

'What do you mean, murder?'

'A chap by the name of George Read. I don't suppose you saw his face. He died as a result of the injuries you inflicted upon him.'

There was a silence while the security men waited for a reaction, which came this time from Lyman Halls, the youngest of the trio.

'We didn't mean to murder anyone. We was only after money.'

'But you did, my son, and murderers are hanged in this country. Of course, if one of you were to tell me who actually committed the foul deed he would almost certainly be let away with a light sentence.'

Again there was a silence, and the Englishman smiled as the silence became prolonged.

'I'm pleased,' he said.

There was nothing wrong with George Read, but the Americans didn't know that, and they were staying loyal to each other even with the threat of the rope hanging over them. Exactly what the Englishman wanted. If they were prepared to be loyal to each other in the face of the hangman then they would have the same loyalty in a skirmish.

'Do any of you wish to hang?'

Heads shook.

'Thought not. As I mentioned earlier, there is a chap in London who can use your talents. If you agree to work for him you will not be charged with murder. In fact, you won't even appear before a court. Does that not sound fair?'

Lyman nodded as expected, then Hooper, and Heroles last.

'Then let me welcome you to Britain, gentlemen. There will be no need for you to return to your lodgings. Your landlady has already been informed of your departure. In about . . .' the Englishman looked at his watch, 'twenty minutes a truck will arrive to take you to London. When you arrive in London you will be supplied with more information. I shall leave you now, and I can safely assume that you will not attempt to do another bunk can't I? I wouldn't want to interview you again. Goodnight, gentlemen.'

The Englishman hadn't volunteered a name, nor would he at his next port of call – Strangeways Prison in Manchester. For identification he used a card exactly the same as James Witherspoole's.

The governor of Strangeways stayed on to meet him: an order direct from the Home Office, which was not to the governor's liking. Normally he was home by 6.30 in the evening, and waiting at his desk doing no more than twiddle his thumbs until the early hours of the morning was much against the grain. His visitor was important, he had been told, and was to be afforded every assistance.

Not being given a name was irritating, and when the

visitor strolled into his office wearing a patronising smile the irritation became anger.

'What's all this about, Mr . . . ?'

The visitor still smiled and gave over his card. 'Nothing spectacular, old chap. I only wish to interview one of your inmates.'

'Interview a prisoner? What the devil for?'

The visitor tapped his card and smiled that irritating smile.

'Which prisoner?' the governor was tired and wanted to go home.

'Chap by the name of John Harte.'

The governor rose from behind his desk and opened a filing cabinet, pulling from it a manila folder.

'Harte, John, sentenced at Salford Crown Court to twelve years for robbery. With good remission could be out in eight years and has completed eighteen months. You sure you wish to interview him? I mean, the police were satisfied there was nothing more he could tell them – not that he said much at his trial, mark you.'

'I do indeed, old chap, and I should like to interview him as soon as possible, and alone.'

The governor nodded. 'I'll have him sent for.'

'Quietly, if you would. I shouldn't want any of his colleagues to know that he was interviewed at this time of night.'

'Colleagues – ?'

'Or whatever they call each other.'

John Harte arrived in the governor's office after afew minutes. He smelled of stale sweat, urine and prison. Prisons seemed to have a smell peculiar only to themselves, thought the visitor.

'Please take a seat, Mr Harte. I should like a little chat.'

Harte looked at the governor, who nodded. He was dressed only in singlet and shorts and did not look at all like the man London was looking for.

'What do you want?' he asked sleepily.

The governor was closing the door behind him,

leaving the pair alone. The visitor smiled again and asked how prison life suited Harte.

'It doesn't.'

'Didn't think it would. Just my way of starting a conversation. Would you like to get out?'

'Are you nuts? Every man-jack in here would give his right arm to be on the outside.'

'You haven't answered my question.'

'Of course I bloody would!'

'You can get out. In return you would be expected to carry out certain tasks for which there might not be any reward.'

'What sort of tasks?'

'Nothing extraordinary. You would be expected to use the talents that got you in here.'

'Where?'

'I can't say.'

'You mean,' Harte suddenly came awake, 'you're offering me the chance of getting out of here if I commit a crime for you? You're off your trolley, mate. As soon as I done it the law would be round my place beating on the door.'

'The police would not be involved.'

'Oh?' Harte sat up.

'Everything you would be asked to do would be strictly legal in the eyes of the government. It would be dangerous, though.'

'And I wouldn't have the law after me?'

'Correct. And not only that, I could have your sentence quashed.'

'Just like that?'

'Just like that.'

'Then I'm not going to pass up a chance in a million. You're on.'

'Good,' the visitor rose and called the governor.

The governor had heard whispers about it but had never actually met anyone who could speak from experience. The visitor placed several documents on his desk and said quietly: 'All duly noted and signed by those who matter. Your signature will release Mr Harte into the custody of His Majesty's Government, myself being the official representative.'

The governor signed, but not without giving both his visitor and Harte a look which said *I wish I knew what you're up to.*

Harte was given clothing and taken immediately to a car waiting outside the large gates at the entrance to the prison, where the visitor left him.

'Goodbye, Mr Harte. I doubt if we will meet again. In a few hours you will be in London where no doubt you will be given much better accommodation. Now I must fly to Glasgow.'

The very mention of Barlinnie Prison is generally sufficient for Glaswegians to let their heads sink into their shoulders and shudder. Synonymous with dread, Barlinnie sat alone among fields, stark, its interior cramped, inmates crowded together in conditions where fear ruled and nerves were so taut they snapped at every hour of the clock.

The visitor felt the atmosphere the second he stepped through the small gate set aside for those who were other than evil. The atmosphere seemed to cling to him, telling him that he should not be here, that if he did not leave immediately he would become one of them.

Even the wardens on duty seemed tainted. His pass and identification card were taken quickly from his hand and passed back just as quickly, the movements sharp and jerky. The governor was the same. When they shook hands the governor stood away, turned slightly to one side lest his visitor swing a boot.

'Who do you want this time?' asked the governor.

'Beg pardon?'

'I've had people like you here before. Who do you want?'

'I want to know something about a chap by the name of Christopher Edward Livingston.'

'Livingston?' the governor's head went back. 'A bliddy nutter!'

'I understand he knows no fear?'

'Right!'

Barlinnie's governor was a bag of nerves himself. Every word he uttered came out as if he were a sergeant-major barking out an order.

'A psychiatric report states he has a genius IQ, but just does not know how to use it.'

'He's a nutter! I couldn't care a monkey's what the trick-cyclists say!'

'Has he been violent since coming here?'

'Christ, it was violence that brought him here! He only knows violence!'

'Has he been violent since coming here?'

'Of course he bliddy has! He's a nutter!'

The visitor made a mental note to speak to the Home Office on his return to London. If the governor wasn't replaced he would end up in a hospital.

'I should like to speak to him, if I may.'

'Livingston! He'll go off his nut if he's disturbed.'

'Will you fetch him or shall I go to him?'

'I'll send someone for him . . .' the governor went to the door muttering that the bliddy Home Office should leave them alone. What the hell did London know about running a Jock prison? Then they send up poofs wanting to talk to them at five o'clock in the morning!

Screaming and bawling heralded the arrival of Christopher Edward Livingston. Foul language reverberated along the stone-walled corridors. Furniture crashed as six prison officers fought to drag him through the outer office used in daytime by a secretary, into the governor's private office. Two officers were already bleeding from the mouth and Livingston was just about to smash his forehead into a third when the visitor shouted.

'Stop or I shall shoot!'

Livingston froze in a split second. From the corner of his eye he saw a revolver pointed at his head. He allowed his body to relax then turned, ignoring the prison officers.

'Who are you, Jimmy?' he said.

The visitor smiled. It seemed that everyone in Glasgow was called Jimmy.

'As soon as we are alone I shall explain, old chap.'
'You can't be left alone with this lunatic!' the governor barked.
'I don't think Chris will harm me. Will you, Chris?' The revolver went out of sight.
'Depends what you want, Jimmy.'
'Give us a few minutes, gentlemen,' the visitor appealed to the governor and his officers.
'Smoke, Chris?' the visitor asked when they were alone. 'Please sit down and take the weight off your feet.'

Chapter Ten

At the entrance to a small hotel in the Wimbledon area of London, Thomas Nelson, a thirty-two-year-old American from California checked the name against the slip of paper he carried then went inside. Behind the reception desk John Morton looked up when the door opened and immediately liked what he saw. The six foot one American, broad across the shoulders, walked with an easy but purposeful and confident step.
'Good evening,' Morton smiled.
Nelson handed over his slip of paper. 'I was given this in the city and told to come here.'
'You are?' Morton lifted his eyebrows.
'Thomas Nelson.'
'Nelson . . .' Morton looked down a list. 'Yes, Thomas Nelson. Thank you for coming Mr Nelson. You have no luggage, I take it?'
'I was told I wouldn't need any.'
'Good. Through there . . .' Morton pointed, 'is the reception lounge. There is a fire burning in the grate, food on the table and plenty of drink. Please help yourself. Others will be here soon and then you won't be so alone.'
'You mean I'm the only person here?'

'I'm afraid so.'

Nelson shrugged. 'So what. Okay, I could do with a meal.'

Morton smiled again and watched the American walk off.

The hotel hadn't seen a guest in six months since the government had closed the premises, intending to hand it over to the army for the duration, but SOE had managed to pull strings and it was now to be a staging post for agents either going out on or returning from missions.

Morton hoped the others would be as likeable as Nelson, although he couldn't imagine how they had managed to find an American. America wasn't involved in the war. But there were some American airmen with the RAF, men who had been flying for British companies and who volunteered their services on the outbreak of war. Perhaps he was one of them?

He lifted the telephone and dialled a number in Central London to speak to James Witherspoole.

'The first of them has arrived, sir.'

'Which one?'

'A Thomas Nelson.'

'Yes, decent sort of chap that. Volunteered, actually.'

'Did he, sir? How did he know about us? I thought no one knew.'

'He didn't. Nelson was working in France when the Nazis invaded. He was a contract engineer responsible for constructing a dam near Pontarlier close to the Swiss border. He didn't like what he saw when the Nazis arrived so he moved out, and not a moment too soon, apparently. The Nazis wanted the plans for the dam and Nelson took them with him. He became a wanted man then and barely made it. Walked across France into Spain and then across to Portugal. Bought a passage to London and walked into Scotland Yard, the only place he could think of, and asked if the plans would be of any use to us. Strewth! Certain people went potty over the plans. It was a windfall. Now we know the strengths and weaknesses of the dam and its surrounds.

'Nelson said that after what he had seen, he would be quite willing to go back there and blow the place up. That was filtered along the line and he was offered to us. An approach was made and he threw in with us.'

'Very noble of him, sir.'

'It was indeed. Some of the others weren't so willing, though.'

'Yes, sir, I know.'

'Anyway, John, I shall be along later. Just have some things to clear up here and I'll be on my way.'

'Very good, sir.'

Witherspoole put down the receiver and returned his attention to his visitor. 'You have been most helpful, Desmond,' he said. 'I just hope everything turns out the way we hope after all this.'

'I'm sure it will, old chap,' Desmond Fairhurst replied. 'You know where to find me if you need replacements.'

'Not too many, I hope.'

'Well, I shan't keep you, old chap,' Fairhurst rose and offered his hand. 'Good luck.'

Fairhurst, the tall Englishman with the upper-class accent who had utilised the services of BSC and MI5 to find a crew for the old submarine, tidied the white scarf around his neck and went out into the night.

An hour later Witherspoole was in the hotel at Wimbledon. With Morton he stood in the manager's office and watched through a one-way mirror at the men assembled in the reception room where only a few months before music had played at weddings and birthday parties. The company that ran the hotel took no chances. Party guests could become unruly and from his office the manager could spot the troublemakers early.

It was also ideal for SOE purposes. The reaction of men and women coming and going could be studied without their knowledge; a must when there was so much at stake.

'How do they look, John?'

'A right motley crew, sir, to quote a well-known saying. No two the same, really.'

Through the window they watched thirty-three men, some drunk, some sober. Several sat alone, others were in small groups, in pairs, some talking and some listening, the conversations exactly the same: thoughts exactly the same. Each wondered what it was they would be asked to do.

'Which one is the Pole?' Witherspoole asked. Morton pointed to a smallish figure sitting alone in a corner.

Kazimerz Barcikowski stared into his glass of beer as if the contents had some hypnotic appeal. A round face, topped by shiny black hair, sitting on a thick body devoid of fat, looked lonely.

'A sad case there . . .' said Witherspoole, recalling the information supplied by Fairhurst and MI5.

Barcikowski, thirty-seven years old, had been a very happy man until a year before. Then came the Nazi invasion. A captain in the 2nd Warsaw Cavalry Regiment, he had led his troops in a charge against a German Panzer division. Formerly a romantic, he discovered to his agony that horses and lances did not even have nuisance value against the invaders. The regiment, decimated, retreated to Warsaw to regroup and found their beautiful city practically destroyed by enemy bombing. The regrouping never happened. Such was the speed with which the Nazis were advancing that all fighting men, regardless of their previous designation were thrown together in battalions and taken west to meet the enemy advance. Again the Polish ranks were decimated and this time there was no retreat. It was every man for himself. Barcikowski took four weeks to get back to his home city, fighting along the way and hiding to avoid being shot out of hand, and on arrival found that the Nazis had begun a programme of annihilation. He found his parents, wife and three children dead, horribly mutilated beforehand. Barcikowski then went north and escaped to Sweden, then London.

In London Barcikowski made it known that he

wanted to do something to defeat the Nazis and MI6 took him in to train as an agent, but again disaster overtook him. While in London on a break from training Barcikowski overheard two men in an alley speaking German in low tones. He snapped, went after them and strangled them both with his bare hands then told the police he had executed two spies.

The dead men turned out to be German Jews employed by the BBC to broadcast propaganda to Germany, and the police were far from impressed with Barcikowski's explanation. MI6, in keeping with its policy, denied all knowledge of him, and Barcikowski found himself before a judge who sentenced him to death, but commuted the sentence to life imprisonment in consideration of his sad loss at home. Fairhurst had kept track of him and interviewed him at Wormwood Scrubbs.

'Poor bugger,' said Morton.

'MI6 wouldn't take him back again. Thought he couldn't be trusted on his own.'

'But were prepared to let him hang.'

'We are at war, John, and in war there are various types of casualties.'

A tall man, drunk, waving a bottle of beer in one hand and singing at the top of his voice, stumbled into Barcikowski. The Pole did not even see him. He continued to stare at his beer.

'Which one is that?'

'Livingston: Christopher Edward.'

'Yes, our Scottish friend. A strong chap. Bit of a strange one, and at the same time unfortunate. He is twenty-three, not very well educated but given the opportunity could be a brilliant student. Apparently he has a genius IQ. I haven't heard him speak yet but I'm told that he doesn't have the harsh, broad Glasgow accent. Been in and out of prison for violence and is considered to be the most dangerous man in Scotland, but I am told this is due to frustration, from having a first-class mind but not being able to use it. He doesn't realise how intelligent he is, but he knows there is something different about him. This tends to confuse him and the confusion becomes frustration, which results in violence. He was once attacked by eight thugs, took them all on and gave as good as he got. On one occasion he was shot but it didn't stop him going after his assailant and half-killing him. Had the police not come along he would have. To protect himself he took to carrying an open razor which, I am reliably informed, he can use with great effect. Like most Glaswegians he calls everyone Jimmy, and is himself known as Razor Eddie.'

'How did we manage to get him out of prison?'

'By using the Special Powers Act. The Act gives the government the right to do just about anything it wishes. And Livingston is not the only criminal. Which one is Hopkins?'

Morton pointed.

'He's another. Only nineteen and destined to spend the better part of his life behind bars. He was at Dunkirk and reports say he gave a good account of himself. Unfortunately Stephen Hopkins is a thief. When he returned from Dunkirk he managed to carry with him seventeen Lugers looted from dead German officers, which he sold to the London underworld. He was arrested and escaped soon after, wounding an MP in the process. Recaptured, he escaped a second time, on this occasion setting fire to a truck as a diversion – got the type of mind we can use. They caught him again and sentenced him to five years' hard labour in an army prison in Wales where they hack away at a mountain for rock to form the bases of gun emplacements. He is a hard and determined man. In Wales he took everything they could throw at him. Generally they break a man's will in a matter of days but Hopkins had them outfoxed. It seems he did everything expected of him just to spite the army, to show that he could not be reduced to a whimpering idiot. Still, he was glad to get out. He jumped at the chance of working with a select group.'

'Should be useful to have around, sir.'

'And Rush Stockton?'

'Over by the window, sir, by himself. Hasn't said much at all.'

Rush Stockton did not seem to have any outstanding features. In a group of four people he would have been the one to be ignored. He was of average height, pale complexioned, and his head hung forward, as if he were hiding his face in embarrassment.

'Haven't fathomed this one yet, John. All we know about him is that he is American, twenty-five years old with no fixed address or occupation other than that of thief. Recently he was apprehended while robbing the home of one of the Sea Lords, whose address isn't generally known. Since his arrest until yesterday he never uttered a word: not even during his trial, nor when the judge gave him eighteen months. Which prompted MI5 to investigate him. The identity of everyone who enters the country is checked yet there is no record of a Rush Stockton having come in. This was the name on a driving licence he carried. MI5 tend to think he may be working for American intelligence.'

'One to be watched, eh?'

'Very much so.'

'I should think they will be ready for bed soon, sir. Most of them have had too much to drink.'

'Good idea. I shall speak to them in the morning.'

Chapter Eleven

There were a number of sore heads in the reception room the next morning, and much less talk than there had been the previous evening.

'Good morning, gentlemen!' Witherspoole greeted them warmly. Hot tea and toast were brought and the group invited to help themselves. Witherspoole poured himself a cup, took several slices of toast and sat at a table on a raised platform where a three-piece band once played to happy crowds.

'My name is James Witherspoole,' he said between mouthfuls, 'and my colleague is John Morton. We both work for a new organisation involved in the war effort. I won't claim that we work for the government, because the government doesn't know about us. In fact, we are very secret.

'You chaps have been brought together because you have something to offer. Some of you I have had the pleasure of speaking to, not really telling you much but enough to let you know that the work you shall become involved in will be extremely dangerous. Some of you have had the same conversation with John, here, and the remainder with some gentlemen of another organisation. You all have something in common. You are misfits: an embarrassment of some kind to someone or another. You don't fit in to the world desired so much by your lords and peers. Now, I don't say that to be insulting. It is said to have you appreciate that none of you is any better or any worse than your neighbour, as I am sure you will discover as time goes on.'

'How awfully observant,' a cultured voice in the room drawled.

Heads turned to see the speaker. He was sitting to one side, one knee crossed over the other, and smoking a cigarette held between two fingers in an effeminate manner. He waved the fingers in a kind of salute to those looking at him.

'Yes, it was, wasn't it?' Witherspoole retorted jovially, then said: 'Gentlemen, allow me to introduce to you Charles Edward Andrew Harewood, a son of one of the country's notable figures and second cousin to a very important personage whose name and title shall not be used here.'

Harewood stood and gave a light bow.

'Here!' former private, James Wilson put in. 'You ain't related to . . .' he winked, *'you know who?'*

'He most certainly is, gentlemen, and the black sheep of the family, I'm afraid.'

'What did you do, mate? Or do we call you *Duke* or something?'

'I'm sure our tubby friend up there will be only too glad to supply you with my family history,' Harewood drawled.

'Well, since you suggest it, I will . . . Gentlemen, Mr Harewood – or *Duke,* was a captain in the Household Cavalry. Unfortunately he has a weakness for the female species, which eventually brought about his fall from grace. Duke kept a string of mistresses and his family turned a blind eye, believing it normal for a young man to sow his wild oats whenever the occasion arose. However, what his family drew the line at was the seduction of first cousins. Duke not only satisfied their curiosity into the appeal he had for women, but also made two of them pregnant. Both ladies being part of the retinue of . . .' he coughed twice, *'you know who's better half.*

'The family was shocked to the core, the young ladies in question quickly whisked away to parts unknown for a period, and for punishment the Duke's funds were cut off. Which did not deter our noble friend . . .'

Witherspoole was cut off by Harewood standing and speaking out.

'What our rotund friend there is about to say is that to keep myself in the manner to which I was rightly accustomed, I filched the regimental silver and sold it to a well-known London fence. After that I was disowned and I am now at the mercy of some boy scout movement intent on making me work for a living.'

Harewood gave a sweeping bow and retook his seat to some applause and cheers.

Witherspoole nudged Morton and smiled. It was the sort of thing he wanted. The group had to get rid of any inhibitions they might have and trust each other.

'Good on yer, Duke, mate!' Wilson shouted across. 'I wish I'd been with you. I'd of given your cousins a right going over, an' I'd of took you to a fence what gives the best value in London.'

Harewood stood again, briefly this time and said:

'Many thanks, my friend. I shall remember that next time. And what is your claim to fame?'

'Ain't got none. I was 'aving a sup with a bird an' a couple of blokes tells me my leave's finished. They takes me off somewhere for a while: God knows where it was, then they brings me here.'

'And who are you, sir, if I may be so bold as to make the request?'

'I was Private James Wilson, but I don't know what I am now.'

Witherspoole took over. 'Private James Wilson is no more. He is plain Jimmy Wilson, one of my lads. And Jimmy's claim to fame is that he owes someone a bottle of malt whisky.'

'You what?' Wilson looked puzzled, then remembered. He laughed.

'Won't you let us all in on *your* secret, old chap?' Harewood called out. Wilson looked to Witherspoole who nodded, so he told the others about his commando training, going into great detail, using his cockney accent to good effect, gesticulating with his arms and generally entertaining his audience. By the time he was finished the room was in fits of laughter.

'A man after my own heart,' Harewood laughed with everyone else. 'And you, sir?' He looked in Barcikowski's direction. 'What dreadful deed have you committed to have been relegated to this rapacious rabble? What horrible secret lurks behind that morbid fizzog?'

'Eh?' Barcikowski shook his head. 'I understand not.'

'Polish?'

'Polski, yes.'

'Captain Kazimerz Barcikowski, late of the 2nd Warsaw Cavalry Regiment . . .' Witherspoole said.

'An aristocratic Pole!' Harewood smiled and went to shake Barcikowski's hand. 'How nice it is to meet someone of one's own class. How do you do, dear chap.'

'Kazimerz murdered two German Jews in London

and was sentenced to death at his trial,' Witherspoole added.

'How awfully balking for you, old chap!'

Barcikowski shrugged and turned his eyes to stare at the floor.

'Well, now that the ice is broken, I am sure you will soon confide in each other. Therefore let us go on. The reason you are here is because you are going to become the crew of a submarine . . .' he stopped to let the words sink in. No one spoke.

'You have all had it spelled out to you. You either do what is asked of you or you suffer the consequences. Even the volunteers. You are in now and in you stay. You shall stay here for the remainder of the day and then tonight, after dark, a bus will arrive to transport you to where the submarine is based. Once there the hard work will begin. In a very short space of time you will be expected to learn everything there is to know about the boat, and at the same time learn how to be a guerilla, partisan and underground fighter all in one. The training courses will be punishing. There will be times when you will cry with pain, but there will be no let-up. When the instructors have finished with you, you will be able to take on the entire German Army as if you were Errol Flynn.'

'And may God have mercy on our miserable souls,' Harewood chanted.

'And may God have mercy on your miserable souls.'

'Here, chief,' Wilson spoke up. 'Where is we going on this submarine?'

'That is still to be decided.'

'How do you mean?'

'Jimmy, basically we are odd-job people: garbage collectors. We shall be doing things other organisations will be loath to touch or do not have the facilities to do. When you are suitably trained something will come along.'

'I don't know if I fancy it now.'

'Too bad, Jimmy, old chap. It's either that or RTU.'

'I'll stay where I am!' Wilson retorted in mock horror.

The group was left to its own devices for the remainder of the day. Newspapers, magazines and a wireless were provided and with everyone beginning to get to know each other Morton and Witherspoole returned to Central London, to the Lyons Corner House in Tottenham Court Road where Witherspoole had booked a table for midday.

'No tea just yet,' he told the waitress when they took their seats. 'We are waiting for a third party.'

The third person arrived shortly after midday and Witherspoole rose to meet him.

'Lieutenant Woolcott? Witherspoole, and my colleague John Morton.'

Woolcott removed his cap and sat down.

'Pleased to meet you, gentlemen, and what is wrong with my father?'

'Nothing, old chap. That was just a ruse. How else could I have taken you away during office hours?'

'You must have some good connections to get a signal past the clerical officer.'

'The best.'

'Well, Mr Witherspoole, since there is nothing wrong with my father, what is so urgent that you had to use official channels to see me?'

'I shall come to that. First, let me apologise for having caused you concern. It is a rather shabby trick to play and I can imagine the distress you felt when your father was mentioned. But, as I said, it was the only way I could get you away from the office. If I had gone through the normal channels I would never had got within a mile of you. The navy and I don't see eye to eye at times. For instance, your trip to Brittany was for my benefit. I arranged that.'

Woolcott looked at Morton with sudden recognition. 'Now I know where I remember you from. That little excursion cost me my command, and a future.'

'Yes,' Witherspoole nodded sympathetically, 'I've read the transcript of the enquiry.'

'You've re . . .' Woolcott leaned forward with surprise. 'But how could you . . .'

'How I know is of no consequence. What is of greater consequence is that I can offer you a position as second-in-command.'

'On a boat?'

'Exactly that.'

'But where? How? The Admiralty controls the emplacement of personnel.'

'Not on this boat.'

'I don't quite understand you.'

'Of course you don't. Just let's say that the navy is not the only organisation with a submarine. John and I have one and we have gathered a crew together. All we need now is a commander and his number one. I am asking you to be the number one.'

Woolcott closed his eyes and grimaced. 'How I would love to be back again, but,' he opened his eyes, 'I would never be given permission?'

'It would have nothing to do with the Admiralty.'

'The Sea Lords wouldn't allow it.'

'The Blessed Sea Lords don't have to know anything about it, old chap.'

'They would have to give their stamp of approval.'

'Not if you came with us now and didn't go back to the office.'

'You're not suggesting . . .'

'I am.'

'That's desertion, and with my track record I could be before a firing squad.'

'Yes, you could, couldn't you?'

'Yet you are still asking me to?'

'Very much so.'

'Dear God!'

'I can't force you to, old chap, but if you did decide to come with us I would take all steps to protect you should Naval Intelligence attempt to arrest you.'

'Who do you work for, for goodness sake?'

'I can't tell you that.'

'Then what kind of protection could you give me?'

'Right at this moment I have no idea, but I'm sure we'd think of something. Wouldn't we, John?'

'I should say so, sir.'
'The very idea frightens me.'
'Undoubtedly. What I can promise you, though, is that if you come with us now, the navy would not see hide nor hair of you for several weeks. In fact, it is possible the navy might never clap eyes on you again.'
'That sounds better. But, God, you're really asking me to do the impossible.'
Witherspoole did not reply. He just smiled, his eyes twinkling, and waited for Woolcott to make the next move.
'You want me just to get up from here and go with you,' Woolcott repeated the request, 'and to hang with the Admiralty. Just like that?'
'Just like that.'
Woolcott's bottom lip began to tremble, then his hands. He screwed his eyes shut then shook his head vigorously from side to side. 'Jesus God!'
'I need a reply, old chap. Very soon we have to meet the boat's commander.'
Woolcott took a deep breath. His hands were shaking so much they made the table vibrate.
'I'll do it!' he said quickly, his words hissing. 'I'll do it, but God help me!'
'Well done,' Witherspoole said, visibly relieved.
'Then let's go,' Woolcott wanted to be away from the place quickly.
'Not until we've had our tea, old chap.'

Later in the afternoon a car braked to a halt outside a small lodging-house in West Harrow. Morton was driving, with Witherspoole and Woolcott in the rear.
'We are expected,' said Witherspoole as they alighted.
A woman opened the front door as they approached and nodded to Witherspoole.
'How is he, Mrs Clark?'
'Upstairs in bed, sir, same as usual.'
'Ah, well, all good things must come to an end.'
In a room upstairs they found the man who was to become the commander of the submarine, although he

didn't look as if he could command a wheelbarrow. He was unconscious on top of the bed. The bedroom stank of vomit, patches of which stained the unconscious man's shirt and trousers.

'Lt Commander Roger Sherman,' said Witherspoole, 'United States Navy, now appointed as commander of our boat.'

'Good God!' even Morton was appalled.

'Appearances are deceiving, John. The commander brought the boat across the Atlantic. He knows her inside out.'

'How did we manage to get him?'

'He is another embarrassment. There is a story attached to him which I won't bore you with, but when I heard it he seemed the type who would fit into our little scheme. I made one or two enquiries and the equivalent of the Sea Lords in the United States seemed only too pleased to give him to us on loan. Of course, they believe he is on loan to the navy.'

'Is the story the cause of this?' Morton pointed down at Sherman.

'I would imagine so. Anyway, Captain Woolcott, the reason I wish Commander Sherman as captain is because he has commanded the boat on more than one occasion. It is not because you are not capable.'

'I understand, sir.'

'The boat is old, you see, and he has the feel of her.'

'We shall have to get him sober.'

'There is a doctor on his way.'

Chapter Twelve

Lt Commander Sherman was sober by nine o'clock in the evening. He had been shaved, bathed and given clean clothes, and on arriving at the hotel in Wimbledon looked respectable. When Witherspoole introduced him to the crew there were smiles from the Americans.

'I'm glad they've got the sense to put an American in charge,' one of his countrymen, Richard Henry Lee, said jovially.

'And yet another from the colonies,' Harewood chipped in in his cultured voice, although inoffensively.

'And his second officer, Lt Woolcott.'

Woolcott's English voice brought a cheer.

'Now we are complete,' Witherspoole said with satisfaction.

'Not quite, sir,' Sherman said pointedly. 'I count thirty-five men including myself and Lt Woolcott. The old T-boats had a total complement of fifty-four.'

'Unfortunately we cannot run to that number.'

'Our chances of survival are practically nil then, sir.'

'We'll see. You may even find that you have more than enough.'

'I doubt it, sir.'

'Time will tell. But now let us get down to some hard facts, gentlemen. You are now part of an organisation that has no connection with the army, navy or air force. You are responsible to myself and my colleague John Morton, and we are responsible to others. Do not be offended if you think information is being withheld from you. This will be deliberate. You will appreciate that security is paramount and the less you know the better. You will be told sufficient to carry out a mission and no more. The boat you will be joining is now at a place called Bucklers Hard, which from now on will be your base. Very soon a bus will arrive and take you there.'

'Where's Bucklers Hard, sir?' someone asked.

'It is on the Beaulieu River in Hampshire. The river and Bucklers Hard are deep in the New Forest on the estates of Lord Montague, out of bounds to civilians except for those who live and work there, making it an ideal place to operate from. I shall warn you now that the moment you get there you will begin training. You will be taught how to fight and kill dirty, how to use explosives and every conceivable type of weapon, and possibly even have a trip to Scotland or Wales for some mountain-climbing and cliff-scaling. And in a matter of days, rather than weeks as is the case with the navy, you will be expected to know your boat inside out.

'From now on Captain Sherman will have the power of life and death over you. You will notice that I do not use the title Lt Commander. Captain Sherman is no longer with the US Navy therefore that title is superfluous. However, since he will command the boat he is still your captain. You will treat him with the respect his position entitles him to and I am sure that given this respect, he, too, will have the same respect for you. I shall expect you to be loyal to him and to each other. Anyone who betrays that loyalty is likely to be shot, as is anyone who deliberately puts another in danger.

'If you are caught by the enemy you can expect no mercy. You will no doubt be tortured in a most bestial manner and then when drained of information shot in the back of the head. It is important then, that if any member of the group is captured and he cannot be rescued, all reasonable attempts should be made to prevent him talking. And don't have any misgivings about the capabilities of the Nazis when it comes to making people talk. Sources tell me they can make a horse talk if they want to. Now, that has probably frightened some of you, and it was meant to. I want to make sure you know what to expect.'

'The bus is outside, sir,' Morton reported.

'This is it, gentlemen. Off we go.'

Berlin was frustrated. Reports filtering back from agents in Britain were blank where the old T-Class submarine was concerned. Even the Admiralty had no knowledge of it. Of the numbers recently allocated to submarines all were spoken for. The old boat seemed to have disappeared.

The New Forest looked gloomy in the early hours of the morning. Mist slowed the bus to a crawl, and at times it was forced to stop sharply when trucks and Land-Rovers suddenly appeared from nowhere.

Explosions could be heard, some loud and some muffled. Rifles cracked and whistles blew.

'Sounds as if the bleedin' Nazis have invaded,' a cockney voice said quietly.

When the bus eventually reached its destination the night was still. Mist still covered the New Forest. The group shivered when they alighted. Buildings showed up, dark outlines against the grey-white mist. They could smell the sea but had no idea of its direction.

'Bloody hell!' someone whispered. 'Look!'

The dark silhouettes of figures running towards them became evident. They moved back. The figures stopped, turned and ran back the way they had come.

'Who the bleedin' hell were they?'

'People like yourselves,' said Witherspoole.

'It's bloody spooky.'

'I am going to have a word with some people,' Witherspoole said. 'In the meantime John will guide you to the first training exercise. Look after them, John, would you?'

'Will do, sir. Follow me, gentlemen.'

Morton led them in single file several hundred yards into the forest then stopped. Before them was a timber-walled corridor, the walls ten feet in height and the corridor eight feet wide.

'Are you ready for the first exercise, gentlemen?' Morton asked.

'If we ain't now we never will be,' an American voice replied.

'That's the spirit. Okay, this corridor we have here is fifty yards long. Along it are trenches, holes and rocks. Sticking out from the walls in some places are branches from bramble bushes thick with thorns. You have to negotiate this corridor.'

'Seems simple enough,' a voice Morton did not yet recognise weighed up their situation.

'Not that simple, old chap. Somewhere along the corridor are twenty of the toughest instructors these courses have. They are waiting for you. To get to the end you must get past them, and they will try to stop you. They may have weapons and they may not; I don't know. Whatever, to stop you they will knock seven kinds of shit out of you. To get past them you must do the same.'

'You what – ?'

'When you have reached the end of the corridor you can then find your way back to the bus. I shall be there waiting for you. Then you can have a cup of tea and get to bed. Off you go now.'

'But . . .' someone made to protest but Morton slipped into the mist out of their sight.

'We're committed,' Woolcott pointed out. 'We'd better get on with it.'

'I'm scared!' Seventeen-year-old Tommy Stone whimpered.

Stone looked exactly what he was: a boy. He was small for his age, still had puppy-fat on his face and should have been at school. Wrapped in the adventurous tales he had heard from others who had served in France with the BEF he had joined the army in the place of his brother. Immediately he volunteered to train for special duties and spent two months in Scotland before his real identity became known. The commando training school rather swiftly returned him to his unit, creating a dilemma for his commanding officer. Stone was too young to be in the army and the commando training course had taught him too much to be allowed loose on the public. A solution had to be found. The CO considered keeping him locked up until his eighteenth birthday, which would have been illegal and Stone would have been entitled to some leave during that time. No one knew what to do: until Witherspoole got to hear of him.

'It's okay, son,' George Wythe gripped his shoulder. 'You stay with me. I'll look after you.'

Stone moved close to Wythe, his hand holding the older man's sleeve. He was terrified. Even up in Scotland they hadn't done anything like this.

Had Stone been told of the reason why Wythe had been brought into the group he would have run a mile.

Wythe was the oldest, forty-one years old and a native of Birmingham. At Dunkirk Wythe had been part of the rearguard checking the German advance. He had gone without sleep for a week and led his men time and again against the enemy. Then the war caught up with him. He charged what he imagined to be a Panzer division, shouting orders to his men and yelling battle cries. The French villagers who found him and returned him to a medical unit told of what they had seen. Wythe's unit had in fact been wiped out by bombing. For an entire day he had charged an imaginary enemy. For an entire day he had shouted orders at a unit that no longer existed. Even when the French who found him guided him to the medical unit he still shouted orders, and continued doing so until a needle was pushed into his arm.

Brought back to England Wythe was taken to a mental hospital where he spent a month under sedation. At first it was believed he had gone completely insane. He hardly spoke, kept to himself and at times suddenly shouted for his men to fix their bayonets. The army didn't want him after Dunkirk. He was a casualty, useless for military purposes.

After three months doctors reasoned differently. Wythe was back to normal, but being rejected by the army could cause a relapse. If he could be given a position where he could keep in contact with the war he could be completely cured. Wythe, the doctors said, was a brave man and should not be kicked out like a worn shoe. The army shook its head, then his name was passed on to Witherspoole.

Woolcott led the way. Gingerly he stepped into the corridor, keeping to the centre and feeling with his feet for obstacles. The others followed.

'Christ Al-mucking-Fighty!' someone swore.

After ten yards the first obstacle appeared. A Canadian, John Hancock, stepped into a pool of mud and a thorny branch suddenly whipped across his face.

'Jesus!' he jumped back holding his hands to his face.

Someone fell into a pit six feet deep and had to be

hauled out. A yard further on a similar pit filled with slime claimed two victims, then out of the blue came an unearthly scream.

Tommy Stone cried out with fear, clung to George Wythe for support and waited for the worst. Nothing happened. No fierce men came at them from the darkness.

'Hey, you guys!' one of the Americans, Joseph Hewes, pulled everyone up. 'They've just blocked the entrance.'

En masse they looked round. It was true. The entrance to the corridor was blocked by another timber wall. No one had heard a thing.

'Bastard!' Jesus Reyes Heroles shouted.

Heads spun. Heroles was being kicked and punched by several hooded men. Others were storming in from behind them.

'It's them!'

George Taylor wasted no time. He threw himself over the top of those in front and waded into the assailants. Others followed suit. Young Stone held back; violence was not part of his make-up. Then a calloused fist him him in the mouth and he went down screaming with terror. He looked for Wythe, saw nothing but arms and legs and began to cry.

Men were cursing, grunting as they fought to move forward. The reason for the end being blocked off became apparent. Forced into a corner the recruits would either have to fight their way out or concede and receive a hiding. The walls of the corridor shook as bodies crashed against them. Someone flew into the air and landed on top of the heap and was immediately pulled down into the mêlée.

Tommy Stone stopped crying. Adrenalin began to flow through his veins. He rose, his teeth bared in youthful anger, boiling inside, then threw himself into the fight. He never knew who he hit. He just kicked and punched, tore at faces and heads until the tempestuous storm within him blew itself out. Then came confidence. He went in with a purpose, looking for shapes he did not recognise, hitting hard and grunting with satisfaction when a blow landed.

The bunch was scattered now, stretching for twenty yards and more. A helpful arm pulled young Tommy Stone along.

'Come on, son,' George Wythe shouted. 'Let's get at them together. We can't leave yet.'

Men were on the ground, some unconscious and some moaning. Three ran for the other end.

'We've beaten them!'

No one knew who yelled but it put more heart into the recruits. Strength came from somewhere. Noses cracked. Yells and shouts spurred them on and from the darkness a whistle blew. From the mêlée men began running, pushing the recruits to one side as they headed for the open end of the corridor, and once again the night became quiet.

'Quick!' Sherman panted, 'Look for our own and carry them!'

Eleven of their number were laid out, seven attackers with them. The stronger members lifted the eleven unconscious ones, swung them across their shoulders and continued along the corridor. In front were Taylor and Woolcott. Each carried a rock in their hands.

'Lift something,' Taylor whispered back, 'anything. Don't be afraid to cripple them.'

The course was more difficult now. The pits and trenches were still there and carrying unconscious men only added to the strain. Taylor announced that he could see the end of the corridor and told everyone to be on guard, then from above came another attack. The dark hooded figures dropped from the walls and another battle began. This time the recruits were ready for them.

A sickly *thunk* announced the meeting of a head and a lump of rock. Teeth were smashed. It was no holds barred. Where previously some of the group would have thought twice before hurting another human being, minutes of fighting had taught them to defend themselves with any weapon at their disposal.

Before long the whistle blew again and the official

attackers withdrew. This time the recruits went after them, pulling them down and administering their own version of the Last Rites.

All of a sudden it was over. The attackers who were still standing disappeared and the recruits moved out of the corridor carrying their wounded, each experiencing a feeling of exhilaration.

'Stay together,' Sherman advised. 'Bunch up. Keep the wounded in the middle and the fittest stay on the outside, and if you find anything worth using as a weapon pick it up. This is a madhouse and we'd better be prepared for anything.' No one disagreed. Keeping the outside wall of the corridor on one side they trotted back to where the bus had stopped and found Morton waiting for them.

'Right, gentlemen, just keep behind me and we'll have a brew.'

A few minutes took them to a Nissen hut where an urn of tea boiled.

'Gordon Bennett!' Jimmy Wilson swore when he looked at his companions in the light.

None had escaped injury. Large bruises had already come up on some. Others were heavily gashed with blood soaking into their clothing.

'You'll be sore in the morning,' Morton remarked, 'but it was for a purpose. You will no doubt find yourself in a situation where the only way out is to trample your opponent into the ground, and to do it quickly and efficiently with complete disregard for his health. Now, how about a cup of tea?'

Although bruised and bloodied the group smiled. Each believed he had achieved something worthwhile. They felt proud.

Medical orderlies appeared to clean and cover wounds, stitching where necessary, and handed round aspirin tablets.

Food in the form of sandwiches arrived, then a civilian stormed into the hut in a fit of anger. Behind him were four men wearing army battledress without insignia, and carrying primed Sten guns.

'Right, you bastards!' he roared. 'Who used the knives?'

The hut went quiet. No one spoke. They just looked at the civilian with blank expressions.

'Is there something wrong?' Morton asked.

'Wrong? Your men were told to fight their way along the corridor: not told to stab my people to death on the way!' the civilian screamed at the top of his voice. He looked as if he wanted to put his hands around someone's neck and squeeze hard. 'Some of these bastards carried knives, and among my squad there are twenty-three stab wounds. One bloke alone has seven!'

'Are any of you carrying knives?' Morton queried, his tone serious.

Again no one spoke.

'Come on, lads,' Morton urged, 'that's not playing the game.'

Still no one replied.

'Right, so you want to play it funny?' the civilian was beside himself with rage. 'Okay, I'll do the same. You will come out here one at a time to be stripped and searched, and pity help those I find knives on. And don't be under any illusions about my level of authority here. I run this centre. Since you are all wankers and rub-outs of some kind I can do anything I like with you, and there will be no come-back on me. Get that into your heads right now. So, you. . . !' he stabbed a finger at young Tommy Stone. 'Come out here!'

Stone shrank back. George Wythe put a protective arm across the youngster's chest and his eyes met the civilian's, defying him to come and get Stone.

'Leave the kid alone,' Jesus Reyes Heroles said slowly and got to his feet. A knife still stained with blood appeared in his hands. 'He wouldn't know how to use a knife. I've got one, and if you want it you're gonna have to come and take it off me.'

'That goes double,' Casar Rooney, another American, rose to his feet brandishing a knife.

Razor Eddie also rose although he carried no weapons. He casually strolled from the group and took up a position behind one of the newcomers holding a Sten gun and said into his ear: 'How's it going, Jimmy?'

Yet another American, William Paca, waved a knife, and the whole hut seemed to be on the move. The armed guard found itself surrounded and Heroles moved to confront the civilian, daring the other man to take his knife away.

'Actually,' Harewood's cultured voice broke the tension, 'I would venture to suggest you have met a Mexican stand-off.'

Someone laughed.

'So you think you're clever?' the civilian began to back towards the door. 'We'll see about that. I'll still have the last say.' He nodded to the armed guards and stormed out.

Jimmy Wilson exhaled heavily. 'Gordon Bennett! I thought we was in for it there.'

'I think it's time we all turned in!' Morton shouted above the din of thirty-odd voices suddenly trying to talk at the same time.

Outside the Nissen hut the civilian's mood changed completely. Smiling, he shook Witherspoole's hand.

'Congratulations, James. That's one of the best teams I've had the pleasure of being involved with. They haven't even been together twenty-four hours and they're sticking by each other.'

'Yes, I am rather pleased. But are your chaps okay?'

'They'll survive. I must say the knives were unexpected, though.'

'None of them serious, I hope.'

'One or two deep wounds but nothing that can't be put right. They'll have a few weeks' holiday in hospital and one or two extra perks.'

'I'd better go in and tell them how displeased I am.'

'Okay, James. Goodnight.'

An argument was raging when Witherspoole entered the hut.

'You don't stab someone to death when you're doing bayonet practice,' Morton was saying. 'You use a dummy.'

'Leave it out,' James Adams, another Londoner, said. 'For all we knew they could have been carrying knives – or anything for that matter.'

'But they weren't.'

'We didn't know that. And anyway, you didn't say we weren't to use weapons.'

'That's not the point,' Morton, in on the deception, continued to argue.

'It is,' Casar Rooney put in. 'What happens if we meet the same kind of situation wherever you send us? If you've never been in that situation before you've got to stop for a second to think about what to do. But the other guy doesn't stop to think. He's in, and by the time you've decided to kill him he's got a blade tucked up around your heart. I know.'

'You speak from experience, I presume?' Harewood asked.

'Sure do. I had a spell in Spain during the civil war and we didn't hold back to decide if he was friend or foe. You got in there and killed him before he killed you.'

'That'll do,' Witherspoole pushed his way into the throng. 'There's no need to dwell on the subject any further. The damage is done.'

'So what happens now?'

'You continue training.'

'And what about that guy who came in?'

'I shall try to pacify him.'

'He comes near me I'll drop his guts on the floor,' Heroles promised.

'I don't think we need go that far.'

'So did we do wrong, sir?' Razor Eddie asked.

'Very much so. You've got to take into consideration that the men who fought you in the corridor all volunteered to do the job. They didn't have to. I mean, would any of you volunteer to get punched and kicked about from morning to night? They do it because there is a need to produce men and women tough enough to face similar situations in Europe. Now, if we start stabbing them there will be no more volunteers.'

'You mean women go through that as well, sir?'

'Of course. Everyone who goes through here does the corridor. And you do it more than once. During your training you will be woken up at all hours and given ten or fifteen minutes to get from your bed, through the corridor and back again.'

'You're joking?'

'Far from it: and I have a feeling that after tonight you will meet a far more determined foe. I shouldn't be surprised if weapons of some sort are used.'

'Then we'll also be prepared.'

'I want no more complaints.'

''ang about, guv,' Jimmy Wilson became angry. 'You'll make your bleedin' mind up! First you tell us that them blokes in the corridor is goin' to kick seven kinds of shit out of us, an' we've to do the same, 'cept we ain't allowed to defend ourselves in a way we see fit. Well, I for one don't go for that old cobblers. If someone's going to kick seven kinds of shit out of me, I don't care a bleedin' toss if he *is* a volunteer: if I've got a broken bottle in me hand he gets it in the moosh. If he's doin' over one of me mates an' he's got 'is back to me, he gets me knife, or anyfink I've got, up the bleedin' khyber!'

'Hey,' Hooper, one of the Americans pulled Harewood to one side. 'What's he mean by *cobblers* and *khyber?*'

'It's cockney rhyming slang, old chap. Cobblers is short for *Cobblers Awls,* meaning balls, and khyber is short for *Khyber Pass*, meaning arse.'

'Oh, yeah? Do they all speak like that?'

'Lots of them do – but not all the time.'

Witherspoole ignored Wilson's outburst and called for silence.

'Let's get a night's sleep,' he said, 'for tomorrow will be a long day. But before you go let me say that, even though you've upset everyone on your first day,' he leaned forward and adopted a conspiratorial air, 'I am proud of you. But I will deny ever having said that.'

There were smiles all round.

'It's them others you've got to worry about, chief, not us,' Wilson said, his anger gone.

'Quite,' Witherspoole winked. 'There's a chap outside the door now waiting for you. He'll show you where you sleep. Goodnight gentlemen, and good luck on the rest of the course.'

When they were gone Witherspoole sighed. 'I do believe we have them hooked, John.'

'They're good men, sir, all of them. I just hope they last long enough to achieve something.'

'As I do, John, but don't let's get sentimental. I've told you before: if and when they get their first assignment and they succeed, we will have achieved a victory in some small way. If, on the other hand, they fail, we will have lost thirty-five men society doesn't want and who can be replaced, and a boat the country didn't even have to buy. Nothing, John: we will have lost nothing. All of them, even the boat, are immediately expendable.'

'I appreciate that, sir. I was just thinking that if they can last long enough we could have an élite sort of group.'

'My word, John! Can't fault that argument. My sentiments exactly. But we must always work on the basis that they are immediately expendable. Anything else is a bonus. What have we got – fifteen Englishmen, fourteen Americans, a Jock, a Paddy and a Pole, two French and a Canadian: none of whom the world wants to know anything about. Take that bloody fool Harewood. He believes he is here to atone for his sins: thinks the family and the regiment might forgive him if he does something worthwhile. Actually the family requested on the QT that he be put in situation where he might be killed, and the regiment went along with that. Officially there should be a court-martial over stealing the regimental silver, with Harewood being drummed out of the service, and at his level of society what he did to his cousins has made him an outcast – although it wouldn't be the first time it's happened. Certain levels of society keep to themselves in more ways than one. It's just that in his case he didn't keep his mouth shut.

'Being what it is, the Household Cavalry could not afford the scandal of a court-martial and public drumming-out. Its image would be destroyed and anyone connected with it would be avoided like the plague. But with Harewood dead there would be a way out for everyone. There would be no court-martial and the Household Cavalry could invent some tale to cover the missing silver. Without a felon the crime could not be proved. And in the case of the family, there would be a complete denial of incest. The ladies in question would have their babies adopted and as far as society is concerned everything would be perfectly respectable again. And if that isn't enough, Harewood would become a hero.'

Morton raised his eyebrows for Witherspoole to elaborate. 'With Harewood dead all his sins are absolved, and because of who he is and the regiment he belonged to, he dies a war hero. History will then show that his nibs rates along with Nelson, and the fact that he was a thief and an incestuous womaniser will never be mentioned again.'

'All very convenient, sir.'

'Oh, John, you don't know the half of it,' Witherspoole chuckled.

'You've forgotten something, sir. You did tell our chaps about Harewood's sexual indiscretions. What's to prevent them from selling the truth to the press?'

'The fact that they probably won't be alive to tell anyone and, allowing for the possibility that they might – to use Jimmy Wilson's words – I couldn't give a toss.'

Chapter Thirteen

Buckler's Hard, the crew discovered, was straight out of history. In daylight they stood in awe looking at the spot where men-o'-war had been built as far back as

1745. From bank to bank the river was wide but with islands and sand-bars scattered between, and on all sides were trees: masses of trees so thick that one could see no daylight through them.

'I never knew this place existed,' Oliver Woolcott muttered.

'Few people do,' said Witherspoole, 'which is why it is still unspoiled by time. The first ship to be built on the river was laid down in 1696 further up-river at Bailey's Hard, and launched in 1698. In 1724 the Second Duke of Montague began building a town on this very spot and enticed workmen to move here from elsewhere with cheap rents and free building materials. Ships were built here until 1847 when the change-over to iron construction sent it into oblivion. It was an ideal location as you can see. There was no shortage of timber and the forest made it extremely difficult for spies to keep track of how many ships the fleet was building. Some of the town has obviously gone but not all. As a matter of fact you are standing in the main street.'

Two rows of cottages faced each other, a wide gap between them.

'A very wide main street you will notice. It is exactly eighty feet in width, which allowed horse-drawn carts to pull in the long timbers necessary for building the old tubs. Down there on the river front you can still see the stocks where the ships were constructed. When shipbuilding finished here most of the people moved on, leaving everything as it was, although many stayed on to do a bit of farming, fishing and salting. People still live here and are employed for the duration by the same people who employ you and me.'

'What about that lot?' someone pointed to a number of camouflaged launches tied up along the river bank.

'Being prepared for an operation of some sort, I would imagine. Lots of people are trained here, and not all work for our organisation. Different organisations send people along for training. They don't say why or where that person is bound for. They just ask and the training is given, and it would be pointless you asking anyone why they are here.

'Along there,' Witherspoole pointed to a long camouflaged shed further along the bank, 'is your boat. It is under cover being overhauled. Let's get along there. The sooner you learn about it the better.'

As they walked towards the covered shed Witherspoole continued to tell them about Buckler's Hard in its new role.

'All boating movements take place at night and blackout regulations are strictly enforced. Perhaps you will recall that whenever you entered a building last night you actually went through three entrance doors, each covered with black drapes. This is to ensure that not even the light from a match can be seen from the sky. German reconnaisance aircraft are coming over the south coast all the time taking photographs, and they must always see this place as a quiet riverside village. All work by day is carried out under cover and even when a boat is moved by night something else is put in its place lest those who evaluate the photographs in Berlin have their suspicions aroused.'

They were approaching the long shed and could hear the noise of workmen and machinery.

'She's an old boat, I'm afraid, although Captain Sherman knows a fair amount about her. She's 1,106 tons surfaced and her operating depth is only 150 feet. Overall length 268 feet and maximum breadth 22 feet: five watertight compartments and a small conning-tower: four forward torpedo tubes each taking standard British Torpedoes and no after tubes. Originally she had four main engines developing 4,000 shaft horse power. These were Nelseco engines, from the New London Ship and Engine Company. They were six-cylinder jobs and gave a maximum cruising speed of twenty knots on the surface over a range of three thousand miles.

'Two of them were removed before we got her and the other two are being removed now. In their place will be four V–16 MAN, engines, German: the Maschinenfabrik Augsburg Nürnberg type. If you are wondering why we are using German engines, it is simply because they were all we could get hold of, and personally I don't mind them because from what I'm told they're bloody reliable. The extra machinery will make the interior more cramped than it already is, but the V-engines should give you a top surface speed in excess of thirty knots, faster than most of the surface craft afloat . . .' he stopped speaking to allow gasps and sighs to subside. They were impressed.

'Originally, she also had two banks of sixty-cell storage batteries for submerged propulsion. These will also be taken out and a much larger two bank 126–cell system fitted, and where before the top submerged speed was 11.5 knots the more modern battery system should give you up to eighteen knots, again faster than many surface craft. And, since the pressure hull plating is only a half-inch thick and these speeds would shake the boat to bits, the plating will be strengthened. This will also allow you to operate at greater depths. Propulsion will be laid out in the diesel electric direct mode: two engines, two generators and a motor to each screw. I was told the horse power output of the motors but it has slipped my memory. Anyway, you will have no shortage of power. The motors, by the way, are American, made by Electro-Dynamic. All this, Captain Sherman, is the main reason the number of crew is curtailed. There just isn't the room. Does that make sense to any of you?'

Several heads nodded.

'Good, because it doesn't mean a thing to me. I'm only repeating what I've already been told.'

'What about fuel, sir?' Tommy Stone asked.

'You won't run out if that's your worry. I'm told that if you wish to carry lots of fuel you simply add more tanks. There is one drawback, though . . .' Witherspoole turned his attention to the whole group again. 'With the boat being so old many modern features are not included. The main ballast tanks are flooded by hand-operated valves linked mechanically by levers to the control room. Vent valves are likewise and so are the main drains. Also, the rudder and diving-planes have mechanical linkages coming from fore and aft to the control room. The linkages tend to wear, which results in having a certain amount of 'play' in them which, as time goes on, allowances must be made for. Would that be correct, Captain Sherman?'

'Sure is,' Sherman nodded, 'and I'd like to say here and now that this is the biggest load of junk that ever came down a slipway. When the US Navy sold you British this they must have seen you coming. Three of this type were built and all three were a disaster.'

'Everyone should try everything once,' the raw Brooklyn accent of Rob Morris said, 'except cab-driving and dealing in scrap.'

There were laughs and Jimmy Wilson said: 'That's our luck, mate. I'll tell you what: if it was raining bleedin' palaces we'd get hit with the handles off the shithouse doors.'

The laughter which followed this remark considerably reduced the alarm Witherspoole's latest revelation caused. Witherspoole was grateful for it and he went straight on to something else before anyone could query the reliability of the boat any further.

'Since you will be a kind of élite group I shall attempt to ensure that you have the best of food – much better than is supplied to the Royal Navy – and if and when you take part in a mission and you come across something you like the look of, I won't know that you have it.'

'Good on yer, guv!' Wilson chirped.

'Yes, I thought that might appeal to you, Jimmy,' Witherspoole smiled slyly. 'I understand you have contacts in the under-the-counter trade.'

'I can do a line on most things, guv.'

'Well, I don't mind you collecting a few knick-knacks, but obviously not if it puts your colleagues at risk.'

'A nod's as good as a wink, guv.'

Witherspoole continued to explain the features of the boat – keeping his narration positive – but Wilson was only half listening. Rob Morris had come alongside him.

'You sound like a guy after my own heart,' Morris whispered.

'You what?' Wilson whispered in return.

'I used to do a bit of business myself. That's why I'm here.'

'Yeah? Go on, mate.'

Morris was no taller than Wilson, much the same build, and his eye kept track of everything going on around him. A scar went down his forehead above his right eye and continued down his cheek to end at the side of his mouth: a relic from a gang-fight in Brooklyn some years before. The scar gave him an evil appearance and made him look older than his twenty years.

'I'd been into a good business,' he said, 'knocking over trucks and selling the loads through a little network I'd built up. There never was a shortage of customers. Everybody, didn't matter who it was, wanted something at half-price. But then I found that some of the trucks I was knocking over belonged to the mob. I'd taken them for a hundred grand and they put a contract out on me. No kiddin'. The word went out that there was five grand in it for anyone who put me down. Not only that, the cops got my name from some stoolie. I had to get out quick and the best way seemed to join the God-damned navy. I thought if I was out of sight for a while they'd forget me.

'My ship came to Britain on a courtesy visit just before Dunkirk,' he went on, 'and I was doin' a bit of business up in Glasgow – y'know, smokes, scotch, nylons and that sort of thing. I'd got into a good thing, then found I was in someone's territory up there. I got a visit from a few guys who warned me off and tried to take all my stock and cash away from me. The two guys with me were big – that's why I chose them – and I thought we would see this lot off. But, Christ, they're evil sons of bitches up there. We'd a pitch battle right in the middle of the main drag and one of my guys was thrown through a shop window. Christ, they couldn't even fight fair. Back home we settle differences with guns, but these guys had no guns. It was boots, broken bottles, knives and bayonets. We wasn't prepared for that and got the worst of it. Next thing, the law's there and we're in shore-side dress so they run us in. We clammed up about being sailors and next morning we get six months.

'So, I'm quietly doin' my time wondering what the navy'll do when I get out, when along comes some posh guy who visits me in the middle of the night. I'm officially classed as a deserter, he says. The navy hasn't been informed that I'm in gaol. With remission I'm due to get out and as soon as I do, the guy says, he'll hand me over to the navy. That would mean another stretch for desertion and after that I'd be kicked out, all trussed-up for the New York mob who still want me. There is an alternative, he says. I can work for some guy in London, who turns out to be Dinnerspoon, or whatever his name is, and it will keep the navy guys off my back. So here I am, and still looking for a line of business.'

'You're from New York? Never been there.'

'Brooklyn, New York,' Morris corrected. 'There's a difference.'

'You got any cash?'

'Not a cent. I lost the lot up in Glasgow. What the heavies up there didn't take the cops did.'

'Thieving bastards! Bent coppers make it hard for an honest tea-leaf.'

'Tea-leaf?'

'Thief.'

'Oh, yeah.'

'Okay, Brookie, maybe we can make a team. Once we have a good look round this place we might find something useful, and when we get a bit of leave I'll introduce you to a few people up the smoke.'

'Up the. . . ?'

'London.'

'Good on yer, mate!' Morris tried to imitate Wilson's accent and stuck out his hand.

Wilson laughed and shook hands, then said: 'I would count your fingers now.'

Morris looked at his fingers before the penny dropped then gave a laugh himself.

'So what about you, Jimmy? What did you do to get in with this lot?'

'Nothing much . . .' Wilson recounted his exploits in Scotland a second time. 'And from what the old geezer says I passed the course but made a boo-boo. They didn't nick me for touchin' the girl's bum nor for knocking the earl's servants about, but for taking the bottle of scotch without leavin' a receipt. They failed me on that, for God's sake. Then they says the earl was goin' to press charges an' I would get thirty days. I could get out of that, says the old geezer, if I agreed to work for him. It would be a bit like commando work but maybe more dangerous, an' since I weren't too keen on the army I agrees. Christ, now I'm lumbered with all these nutters trying to kill me. I tell you what, mate: if I'd of known what it was goin' to be like, I'd of took me thirty bleedin' days.'

The interlude of freedom did not last long. Witherspoole passed them on to an instructor who immediately set them off on a ten-mile run through the New Forest, during which stragglers were abused and kicked.

'I'm an SS trooper!' the instructor yelled while booting Harewood unceremoniously up the rear. 'I've come for your balls! If I catch you I'll wire them up and give you the shock of your life!'

The run was punishing and no one was allowed to stop for breath. If they did, men would jump from the shelter of trees and bushes to push them on, screaming that the first time they stopped while in enemy territory they were dead.

Nor was there any let-up when the run was finished. They were ordered to plunge into the river fully clothed, swim to the opposite side and return. Several were unable to swim, which made the effort more difficult since others had to help them, and even after that the punishment went on. Physical training exercises followed until dark and when the instructor left, the group lay exhausted on the cold ground.

'Thank Christ!' a very tired voice said. 'I don't think I could have taken any more of that.'

'It must be dinner-time,' another voice complained. 'I'm bloody starving!'

Dinner was delayed. Within a minute of the physical training instructor taking his leave another instructor arrived and ordered them to the corridor.

'You're joking!'

'The Nazis don't joke, squire,' the new instructor did not shout or scream. He just looked down at the tired, pathetic creatures who imagined they were being hard done by and spoke quietly.

'So you've run ten-miles and swam across a river, and done a few physical jerks. So what? You might be in France next month having to run fifty miles and swim across ten rivers. Every time you outrun a patrol another will be waiting further on. In desperation you might outrun that one, but if you're not fit you won't outrun the one after that. And what happens if you've got to stand and slog it out? Will you ask them if they're joking, just because you've run a few miles? If you can't slog it out, squire, you're dead. Now get up and get into that corridor. There are some very unhappy men waiting for you there. Apparently they owe you something.'

The corridor turned out to be a massacre. The group was in no condition to fight its way out of a wet paper bag. More were carried back to their sleeping quarters than could walk and medical orderlies spent two hours patching them up. No one felt like eating and they collapsed into their bunks where they immediately fell into an exhausted sleep, which was rudely interrupted in the early hours of the morning.

A group of instructors crept into the hut and placed dummy grenades alongside each bunk, then stood back. The grenades went off in a series of very loud bangs, interspersed with blank ammunition being fired from Sten guns and Webley revolvers.

Their nerves already strained, the group leapt from their bunks in terror and ran around in circles for several moments before gathering their wits, then anger set in. Razor Eddie, realising what had happened, threw himself at the nearest intruder and tried to throttle him. Others followed his example and a general free-for-all began, which went the way of the instructors until a light came on and stopped the one-way fracas.

'If the Nazis had disturbed you then, you would all be dead.'

The speaker let his eyes sweep round the hut to meet those of the group, each in their turn, then without saying another word turned and left, followed by the earlier intruders.

'He's right, you know,' Woolcott said when the excitement died down. 'We could find ourselves in any situation we've experienced in training so far.'

'And we've only been here a day,' added John Hancock, the Canadian.

'Bleedin' sadists, that's what they are, guv. Christ, look at us. A good advert for the casualty department.'

'He's still right in what he says, Jimmy, and we don't have any choice, remember. We're the dregs of humanity at the moment.'

'So what did you do chief?' Wilson asked Woolcott. 'I mean to say, you're a bit posh, an' that. Why ain't you on the bridge of some big destroyer givin' it plenty of verbals?'

Woolcott shrugged. There was no point in keeping his misdemeanour a secret.

'It stems from a trip I made to Brittany . . .' he told his tale.

'Rotten bleeders! You mean you got them blokes back safely, info an' all, an' the navy gives you the elbow?'

'I disobeyed orders, whichever way you look at it.'

'Yeah, but I mean, you probably did the country a favour.'

'Most probably, but the Sea Lords don't see things that way. They don't go much on cloak-and-dagger operations. That's not the done thing in their eyes. And now I'm a deserter.'

'How come?'

Woolcott explained about his meeting with Witherspoole.

'Gordon Bennett! The navy must be goin' potty lookin' for you.'

'Yes, I would imagine so. I just hope they don't find me'

Bill Hooper sat beside Harewood and nodded at Wilson. 'Who's this guy Gordon Bennett?'

'There's no such person, old boy. It's a term of exclamation, like "Good God", "Hell's Teeth", or "Bloody Norah".'

'Bloody Norah?' Hooper shook his head.

'I agree with Oliver,' Sherman said, ignoring this exchange of information. 'There's nothing we can do about the position we're in and we'll just have to put up with it. The only thing I can suggest is that we get stuck into it and show them we can do everything expected of us. Make them all eat their words.'

'I'd like to make them eat more than their God-damned words,' Heroles said angrily.

'Maybe we'll get the chance before we're finished.'

'I bleedin' hope so, guv,' said Wilson.

There were no more interruptions that night.

Chapter Fourteen

The next day began like the one before. Most of the morning was spent on the old boat learning the lay-out and being instructed on how the equipment operated, then after a break a bus ferried them to another part of the forest where they were to learn the arts of Oriental weaponless fighting.

'What you will see this morning, gentlemen,' said Morton, 'is something out of this world. I've no doubt you've all heard of Ju-Jitsu, the stuff they teach commandos and agents in other departments. Well, we are going to teach you another Oriental art – Karate, it's called. There are various styles of Karate, depending on which country you come from: countries, that is, like Japan, Korea and China. Karate has been hidden for centuries and very few westerners know of it, but somehow someone brought it to England and taught the art to a handful of privileged army personnel. A chap is going to teach you some of the less difficult moves. I don't know much about it but I'm told that it takes many years of training and practice to master the art and become a top exponent. However, I am also told that fit persons can be taught a certain amount in a few weeks, enough to cripple or kill an opponent who hasn't seen it before . . . Ah, here he comes now.'

A powerful man appeared, running through the forest wearing what appeared to be a pair of white pyjamas, and what the group would shortly learn was a *Gi*. 'Bloody hell!' Jimmy Wilson swore. 'Not that bastard!'

'You know him, Jimmy?' Morris asked.

'Know him, Brookie? That was the bastard what had me runnin' all over bleedin' mountains. Christ, he's evil.'

'My name is Williams, Sergeant Williams . . .'

He wasn't even out of breath. He stood, legs apart and hands on hips before thick mats already laid out on the forest floor, and glared at his trainees.

'You blokes are going somewhere, they tell me, and you've to learn how to fight dirty. Okay, I'm the one who is going to show you. Now, I don't know if any of you hold rank, and I don't bloody well care. I am in charge here and you will always call me Sergeant Williams. Have you got that?'

No one spoke until Williams barked out the question again, after which everyone replied in unison.

'Right. The first thing you'll do is strip off to your underpants and start running on the spot. Move!'

For an hour the group went through the most gruelling exercises in which their muscles and joints were stretched and twisted to breaking point.

'Now I will show you how to stand.'

Williams went among them punching and kicking those who didn't follow his instructions fast enough. Basic arm movements followed, then how to punch at the face and body, and how to block.

'Split up into pairs! One of you punch and the other block. Move!'

For a solid hour Williams had them do nothing else but punch and block then allowed a two-minute break which without exception each spent lying on his back.

'Okay, up you get. Now I shall show you chops and kicks, and for that I need a volunteer.'

No one was game.

'No problem,' said Williams, 'I see an old friend of mine who'll fit the bill nicely. Won't you, Private Wilson?'

'What, me, sergeant?'

'Yes, you, you little swine. Come out here!'

When Wilson got within three feet of Williams, the sergeant's right foot moved suddenly and a fraction of a second later Wilson was on his knees nursing a sore stomach.

'We call that a thrust-kick, a *Kekomi-Geri*. Delivered properly it can cave in a man's chest or stomach . . . Get up, Private Wilson, you haven't even started yet!'

Wilson rose, immediately to go down again with a howl.

'We call that the side-kick, a *Yoko-Geri*. And again, Private Wilson.'

This time Wilson took a kick on the shoulder, throwing him backwards into the arms of his comrades.

'And we call that the jump-side-kick, the *Tobi-Yoko-Geri*. Now you can practise the *Kekomi-Geri*.'

When the session was ended Jimmy Wilson was in a sorry state. His body was badly bruised and one eye was completely shut. His lips were so swollen he could hardly eat, but even in the circumstances he was able to joke which helped to keep up the spirits of the others.

'I'll tell you what, mate: if he was an undertaker people would stop dying.'

The day finished with a run and the corridor, again the group taking a beating and collapsing into their bunks afterwards. No one noticed that they had passed along the corridor in the fastest time so far, even though some had to be carried back

There was an interruption during the night and being drained of energy the group's reactions were much slower than on the previous night. The same instructor made an appearance and looked at them with scorn, commenting in a sneering manner: 'You'll never learn, will you?'

The next day began at five am for the group, with a ten-mile run followed by a swim across the river, then breakfast. Following this they spent several hours on the boat, and afterwards until dark with Sergeant Williams on the mats: and for the second day running Wilson became his tool of instruction. On this occasion Razor Eddie, Jesus Reyes Heroles, Casar Rooney and Joseph Hewes were missing. Sergeant Williams did not seem to notice.

'We shall practise yesterday's movements and go on to something else.'

'How awfully tedious,' Harewood remarked.

Williams glowered at Harewood then strode across. 'So the posh one thinks it's awfully tedious?' he made an attempt at mimicking Harewood's accent. 'And what would the fine gentleman rather have us do, eh? Or does he think the Nazis don't kill gentlemen?'

'Oh, I am sure they do, sergeant, old chap, but at least when I die it will be as a gentleman.'

'And some of us are not gentlemen, I take it?' Williams was rising to the bait admirably.

'As the famous man said, sergeant, old chap: to be born a gentleman is an achievement, to die one is a privilege.'

A second later Harewood was a tumbled heap on the ground.

'That,' said Williams, 'was a back-kick, the *Ushiro-Geri:* ideal for dealing with "gentlemen".'

Wilson was the object of Williams' attention from then on and the session became a repeat of the day before. He was kicked, punched and generally knocked about, and although none of the blows were too severe they were sufficient to aggravate Wilson's already sore body and re-inflame bruises and swellings.

The day's epilogue, the corridor, was just as fierce and again, without noticing, and with their numbers reduced, they traversed it quickly.

The nightly interruption came as usual. Around two o'clock in the morning men crept into the hut with their dummy grenades ready. The hut was as they normally found it: each man sprawled out on his back, too tired to have removed his clothes, snoring like a bull. The first man smiled. It was all so easy.

The smile was wiped off his face quickly. Unseen in the dark Razor Eddie slid from under the bunk closest to the door where he had been alseep during the latter part of the day. The length of timber in his hand swung in an arc catching the first man's shins. In an instant he was on his feet and joined by Heroles, Rooney and Hewes and threw himself at the intruders with a venom he hadn't experienced since someone had shot him in Glasgow.

The noise brought the others from their bunks and within seconds the intruders were overpowered, but not without being badly beaten first. The first three were unconscious and the others on the verge of it when the scornful instructor made his entrance. He looked down at his own men first then at the group, and without smiling said: 'You're learning.'

Medical orderlies arrived to take away the injured and when the hut was back to normal each congratulated the other. They felt proud. As a group they had achieved something together. Even the boy, Tommy Stone, had gone in like a machine.

'And let's give them a surprise tomorrow,' said George Taylor. 'Jimmy,' he motioned for Wilson, 'you'll most likely be the whipping-post again. I'll show you something: something he doesn't realise I know. Now, see if you can follow this . . .'

The saying that practice makes perfect was true where the group was concerned. The time for the early morning run next day was reduced by one-third, and those who only two days before could not swim somehow got themselves across the river without assistance. After the session aboard the boat they ran to the mats where Sergeant Williams waited, instead of using the bus provided.

'Any remarks to make today?' Williams asked Harewood.

'Time wounds all heels, sergeant, old chap,' Harewood smiled, 'as the man once said.'

'Good,' Williams took up a preparatory stance then his eyes narrowed, peering at Harewood with some puzzlement. Something about the remark did not seem right, but he decided to ignore it.

'Wilson! You don't mind volunteering, do you? Let's see what you've learned so far.'

Once again Wilson went down.

'We call that the hammer-fist strike, a *Kentsui-Ucni*. Up you get, lad, we've the jump-side-kick to try yet.'

Williams suddenly flew into the air with his right leg stretched out in front of him like a ram. Wilson saw it coming and took two steps back as Taylor had shown him, and as Williams' impetus decelerated he made a fist at his waist, stepped forward and thrust hard, his fist connecting with the arch of Williams' foot.

A look of surprise crossed the sergeant's face. Wilson's left hand reached out to cup his heel, lifting him completely off-balance, following which Wilson's right foot swung between the sergeant's legs. Williams collapsed like a sack of potatoes and groaned with agony. Wilson grinned, turned to his audience and announced: 'We call that a kick in the goolies, the *Knacker-Cracker*.'

The others cheered. They knew that from now on

the sergeant would have a little more respect for his charges.

Chapter Fifteen

Three British airmen lay in a ditch in freezing rain and watched a German patrol search for them. There were eight Germans, a corporal and seven privates, all protected by waterproof capes but all wishing they were back in the warmth of their billet. The darkness seemed more intense in the driving rain which seemed to break up the beam of their torches, showing up nothing but leafless bushes and sodden earth among which not even a hare could have hidden.

Two and a half hours earlier the three airmen had sat together enjoying mugs of strong tea at an airfield in England, prior to taking off on a bombing run. But the night hadn't gone well. They'd flown over the channel safely, but immediately they crossed into Belgium a violent blast alongside the right wing disabled their plane sending it into a downward spiral and destruction.

In the mess they had listened to a variety show on the wireless and had felt as if they had been part of a live audience, laughing, nodding to each other as near-the-knuckle jokes flowed. They had been part of a nation then, the majority of whom would go to bed that night still amused and looking forward to the next evening when yet another show would for a short while divert their attention away from the war.

They had also looked forward to the next evening and now it would never happen. The millions of other listeners would sit by their sets never realising that a handful who had laughed with them twenty-four hours before, would be cold, afraid and alone in a field in Belgium, liable to be shot by anxious Germans who no more wanted them there than they wanted it themselves.

The German torches retreated and in the murky skies overhead planes droned on their return trip, silhouetted when the beam of powerful searchlights picked them out. Scattered along the horizon were a series of red glows where planes had come down and their unloaded bombs exploded. Ack-ack was heavy. The sky seemed to be filled with fireworks. Planes lurched this way and that. One with two engines on fire left long streaks of yellow behind it.

'Poor bugger,' Flying Officer Douglas Payne whispered, 'he'll come down in the channel.'

Beside Payne, Navigating Officer Denis Lister and Flight Engineer Harvey Deane nodded. At least they had a chance of survival. The doomed plane could go down anywhere and in darkness the rescue ships, particularly in this weather, would possibly never find the crew.

'But what do we do now?' said Deane. 'God knows where we are.'

'We were over Gembloux when we copped it,' Lister replied, 'about twenty miles south of Brussels, so we can't be far from there.'

'Right, so what do we do?'

'I say we wait until daylight,' said Payne. 'We can see bugger-all in this weather but in daylight we can see what's around us, then take stock.'

The suggestion seemed sensible.

The hours passed. Now and again a German patrol searching for them passed by, but the Germans were only half-heartedly carrying out their task. For all they knew the distressed fliers could be a dozen or more miles away.

'I wonder what happened to the others,' Payne said in the early hours to keep himself awake. So far as he knew everyone got out safely, but more than two minutes had gone by from the time the first of the crew left, to the last, which could mean a difference of up to ten miles.

'I hope they're doing better than us wherever they are,' said Lister.

The rain seemed to be taking revenge for their raid over Germany. Since they'd bailed out it hadn't stopped. Water from the field ran into the ditch and it was gradually filling, up to the top of their flying boots now which made their position all the more uncomfortable.

'What I could do with is a cup of Naafi tea,' remarked Payne. 'I'd kiss the woman who made it even if she was the ugliest thing alive.'

A movement close-by made them freeze. Someone, or something was near. Payne looked around for a weapon of some sort and found nothing. Minutes went by and they wondered if they'd imagined the sound. Then it came again, and again they froze. Someone *was* out there, yet there were no torches. Lister made to move but Payne waved a finger. Moving would only make a noise.

'Englishmen!' a voice hissed.

Once more they became still. The voice was accented but the accent was unrecognisable.

'Englishmen,' the hiss came again, 'do not be afraid. I am a friend.'

The movement increased and a figure slid into the ditch. Payne saw a pair of bare legs and a skirt. It was a woman although they could not make out her face. She was drenched to the skin and covered in mud, her hair hanging loose like a witch.

'You will come with me please. I will take you to a safe place. Come!'

Without another word the woman sped along the ditch with remarkable speed since the ditch had more than a foot of water in it.

The airmen had no option. They had to trust someone. With their hearts beating rapidly they followed.

The woman kept to ditches, head ducked low, zig-zagging around fields and culverts for twenty minutes before stopping. She held up a hand.

'We have to cross a roadway here,' she said, panting. 'We go one at a time and I go first. If traffic comes get back into the ditch and stay there until it is clear to cross. If any of you are seen I shall leave you. That you must understand.'

'Okay,' Payne nodded, although he couldn't say if the woman saw it.

The woman crawled to the lip of the ditch and looked both ways. Payne noticed her feet were bare. In a flash she was away from them, out of sight into a ditch on the other side of the road. A half-track truck came by within seconds. It showed no lights and as it passed spray and mud spewed to the side of the road covering the trio from head to foot.

Payne went first, then Deane and Lister. The woman waited and waved them on. More ditches were negotiated and another fifteen minutes was spent in trying conditions before the woman rose to her feet and relaxed.

'We are here now,' she said.

They were in a farmyard, and had it not been for the squeal of a pig in a barn somewhere the farm could have been taken as abandoned and derelict.

The woman's feet slapped across cobbles to the door of the farm cottage where she gave what the Englishmen assumed to be a prearranged knock. The door opened but no light showed.

'Inside, quickly!'

They filed in and noticed the woman run away into the rain and darkness. Warmth hit them like a brick wall and lights came on.

'Welcome to Belgium,' their host smiled.

He introduced himself as Louis Carre and invited his guests to come closer to the fire.

'When you are warm you can bathe,' Carre said, 'then my wife will give you something to eat.'

'And if the Germans come?' Payne said.

Carre shrugged. 'We will know. There are people watching for them now.'

'How did you know where we were?'

'We didn't,' Carre replied in excellent English. 'We had search parties out looking for you. We saw your plane hit and knew roughly where you would come down.'

'Were there any others?'

'We do not know yet. By morning we should learn something.'

'You have taken a great risk, sir.'

'We have done it before.'

'I don't know how we can thank you.'

Carre's face became hard. 'By defeating the Boche, monsieur.'

Carre's wife appeared, a large, motherly woman. Her English was not so good but she made herself understood.

'I have the warm water, please. You will the undress each of you and come.'

Madame Carre would stand no nonsense. She clucked like a hen as she stripped off their muddy clothing, plunged each of them in turn into a large tin bath and scrubbed them clean.

Later, before the fire, wrapped in a blanket, Payne asked the question that had been on his lips since their arrival.

'Will we be able to get away?'

At that there was a knock at the front door.

'Sshhh . . .' Carre put a finger to his lips. His wife switched off the lights while he went into the hallway. Seconds later he was back and the lights were switched on. Carre had his arm around the shoulder of the woman who had brought them to the farm. Only it wasn't a woman, but a girl no older than fourteen.

'Our daughter, Annette,' Carre said proudly.

Warm and clean the Englishmen felt sorry for Annette. She looked as though she had just been dragged through every field in Belgium, but she was smiling.

Payne got to his feet. 'If there was some way I could express my gratitude . . .' he was at a loss for words.

Annette just giggled, pointing to Payne's middle

where the blanket had come adrift. His pubic hairs were showing. Embarrassed he pulled the blanket around himself and blushed.

'What is happening, child?' her mother asked in rapid French.

Annette replied in English. 'The rain has prevented a detailed search but all roads are blocked and house to house searches have begun. They are miles away at the moment and we have watchers out, so we should be safe for a few hours.'

'And then?'

'We get you away, my friends, but first you must have food. Anneliese!' Carre playfully scolded his wife. 'Food for our guests.'

During the meal Carre explained what would happen at daybreak.

'There is a curfew from dusk to dawn and tomorrow many people will be on the roads. Namur is twelve miles from here and an important football match is to be played there. Namur will be playing a team from the Boche Garrison . . .'

It was not lost on Payne and his companions that Carre referred to the Germans as Europe had in the previous conflict.

'. . . and the Boche commander wishes as many Belgians as possible to see their team being beaten. We will use his ego to get you into the town. You will be provided with papers which will pass any checkpoint on the way. Do any of you speak French?'

'We all do.'

'Excellent! The Boche do not know the difference between a good French accent and a bad one. You should have no problem. Can you ride bicycles?'

'Of course.'

'Good. Someone will ride with you to Namur, and once there you will be handed over to a friend. After that you will embark on a long and tiring journey.'

'Are we permitted to know where?'

'Of course, monsieur. You shall be taken into France,

then to Spain and into Portugal. We are part of an escape chain.'

'We've heard of the escape lines,' Payne nodded. 'They make life difficult for the Nazis.'

'And the Nazis also make life difficult for us, monsieur. If we are caught our whole family is shot. So, you must understand that if there is a danger of you being caught, whoever is with you will pretend they do not know you. They will disappear into a crowd if there is one at hand. You will then have to take your chances on being taken as a prisoner of war. Our people cannot afford to be caught, monsieur. It only needs one person to talk and hundreds of people will die: and the methods the Boche use to make people talk are most unpleasant, monsieur.'

'We understand, Monsieur Carre.'

Their host did not say that Carre was not his real name. If any escaping airman was caught the Gestapo generally applied some torture to extract information about the escape lines, and not all English airmen could withstand torture. They would give a name they knew and when the Nazis came looking for a farmer called Carre they would be disappointed.

'And now I must leave and make some arrangements,' said Carre. 'We shall not meet again but do not worry. At dawn your bicycles and papers will be here for you, and different clothing.' He held out his hand. 'I wish you good fortune.'

Seven hundred and fifty miles away as the crow flies, in the small village of Tomino in north-west Spain, two miles from the Portugese border, life went on undisturbed by the war ravaging the major part of the continent. Tomino knew something about war, however. During the Spanish Civil War the few hundred residents of Tomino were for the Republican cause, and being only two miles from the frontier had been an important centre for ferrying guns to the republican armies. At the end of the war Tomino had also been the last stage in an escape route for those sentenced to death by Franco's new secret police. Many of its citizens were taken away and never seen again, their properties confiscated and given to supporters of Franco who now commanded considerable influence in the village. The republican mayor had been executed and a fascist installed in his place. The local police force – all of four men – was disbanded and replaced with a fascist militia who made life difficult for the republicans who stayed on.

Life was good for some, particularly for people like Doctor Guillermo Acevedo Soberon. Acevedo, prior to the civil war, had been a struggling back-street doctor in the city of Vigo twenty miles to the north of Tomino. His practice had been in one of the poorer districts of the city: not because he had devoted himself to helping the disadvantaged, but because his reputation as a doctor was suspect. Although he displayed a diploma in his waiting room and could recite the names of his fellow students at medical school in Madrid, no one remembered him. His name did not appear on the roll of honour for the year in which he claimed to have graduated, yet the diploma was genuine. Vigo's medical council would not accept him as a regular general practitioner, which relegated Acevedo to the back streets of the city where his patients asked no questions and paid heavily for his services.

The civil war altered everything about his life. He became a spy for Franco's Intelligence Service, reporting myths about those who regarded him as a charlatan. Lengthy documents were compiled on his enemies and when Franco's forces conquered the country retribution came swiftly. Acevedo formed a secret police force, assumed command and took revenge. Hundreds of men and women in the Pontevedra province died on the stroke of his pen. Factories, shops and farms were signed over to him, making him within a matter of days a very wealthy and powerful man.

Never satisfied, Acevedo spread his wings. Using his new powers he confiscated other properties scattered about the province, one of which was the Casa Solariega de las Flores in Tomino. The Casa's previous owner, a wealthy industrialist who chose the wrong side in the war, had been Tomino's benefactor. The industrialist had spent huge sums of his own money to pave Tomino's streets, to install running water and proper sanitation. Those homes that did not have electricity were converted and under his sponsorship the village flourished.

Now Acevedo owned the Casa Solariega de las Flores, the largest and most impressive building in Tomino. Built on a hillside the Casa had a commanding view of the River Minho that formed the frontier between Spain and Portugal, and all the land between the casa and the river was part of his estate.

Surrounding the Casa was a high white-painted wall over which it was impossible to see. Only the second floor of the building was visible, and even this was partly obscured by tall trees. The grounds behind the wall were extensive and reputed to be among the finest in all Spain. Acevedo apparently spared no expense in catering for his whims, and although the money he spent remained in Tomino, it went to Franco supporters who had previously been rewarded with confiscated properties.

Acevedo spent most of his time in Tomino, being driven to Vigo once each week to listen to reports from his staff and sign warrants for the arrest and execution of Franco's enemies. On his return he was usually accompanied by a beautiful woman, generally the wife of a prominent citizen who wanted a favour of some sort, a practice the original inhabitants of Tomino regarded with disgust. Although they often witnessed the arrival and departure of these women, they never became used to the traffic. Tomino had prided itself on maintaining a strict moral code and felt now that the powerful interloper had degraded them. Whenever a vehicle of any sort, no matter who it carried, entered or left the Casa, they looked on with a burning hatred and at night prayed before a statue of the Virgin Mary for a saint to come and drive the serpents out of their life.

Seven miles away on the Atlantic Coast in the even smaller village of Oya, Horacio Aguilar Garcia, the twelve-year-old son of Horacio senior, sat alongside his bicycle and scanned the sea with binoculars. Horacio's wish for the future was to be a sailor. Each day following his school lessons, taken at home from a private tutor, Horacio hurried to a high point in the village and scanned the ocean for signs of shipping – warships in particular. The sight of a destroyer steaming past, even if it was barely within the range of his vision, excited him. On the walls of his bedroom were large pictures of warships and submarines, all German, for his father had instructed him from an early age on the might of Hitler's Germany and how that might would soon rule the world. On his bookshelves Horacio had volume after volume on ships. Even in the roughest weather when visibility was greatly reduced he could 'read' the lines of a ship and put a name to it. One day, he thought as his glasses swept the ocean, he would stand on the bridge of the biggest warship in the world as her master.

Farther inland in the riverside town of Tuy, five miles upriver from Tomino, Arsenio Farell was concerned. All day he had been on edge. Something, some inner alarm, told him all was not well. But what could he do? The question had crossed his mind a hundred times that morning. A whole month had gone by and no word. It hadn't happened before.

By midday Farell had made up his mind. He would break security. It would be risky, but it was a chance he would have to take. He had to satisfy himself.

Taking his time he walked to the post office and waited his turn for a call box. He dialled, listened for the number to ring once, then replaced the receiver, lifted it and dialled again. This time he let it ring. His heart thumped. It was common knowledge that telephone conversations were listened to by the secret police.

The number at Cousa, a town ten miles to the north-west, answered.

'Hello!'

'I would like to speak to Doctor Ochoa, please,' Farell said rather quickly.

'Your name, please?'

'Valdes.'

'Christian name?'

Farell put the receiver down. Something *was* wrong. Asking for a Christian name was not part of the code. Trying not to appear flustered he casually left the booth, keeping his head low, and went back to the end of the queue of people still waiting. He did not have long to wait. Within minutes the doors of the post office burst open and plain-clothes policemen rushed in. They dragged a woman from the booth he had just used and asked questions of others.

Yes, the general reply was, a man had been in the booth but he had finished his call and left. Descriptions of the man varied, which told the investigators nothing. They rushed out again and began a search of the immediate area.

Farell remained in the queue. He was grateful for the stupidity of people. They had not seen him leave. In fact, as soon as he emerged from the booth they forgot that he existed. They were only interested in getting closer to the few telephone booths the town had, and naturally assumed that when anyone finished a call they left.

When his turn came round again Farell rang the number of the local dental surgery which he knew would be closed at that time of the day. He let the number ring for half a minute then left the booth, looking angry, and muttering for others to overhear that the waiting had been a complete waste of time. Those in the queue sniggered. Farell was in his early fifties, gnarled and weathered by the sun, and the waiting people took him to be a grumpy old man.

He went straight home, changed his clothes and left again, heading for the river. A ferry was preparing to cross to Portugal. His papers were in order and being a bona-fide businessman exporting textiles to Portugal his face was known by the frontier guards on duty at the ferry terminal. They waved him through and minutes later the ferry was on its way.

On the Portugese side of the river Farell took precautions. Portugal was a hot-bed of spies, and agents of both Germany and England kept a constant vigil at crossing points to see who entered from Spain. Half a mile from the terminal he entered a two-storey building containing a number of shops, and without stopping left by the rear into a narrow, unpaved street. Houses backed on to the street and three houses along he turned up the path, entered without knocking and went to the window. No one had followed him: not that they ever had, but he had to be very, very careful.

Part of the house was actually an ironmonger's shop and through the wall he could hear customers arguing about prices. Farell went to the telephone in the room, pressed a button below the dial and waited. A key in the door leading to the shop turned. He swivelled round, keeping one eye on the window and dialled a number in Oporto, far to the south. When the number replied he spoke slowly and quietly. 'Ochoa here, I have had no mail or deliveries for a month. I telephoned the good doctor and he could not satisfy my query. I believe his NIB is broken. If this is so then I should have had an adverse delivery by now, and I haven't, which must mean that deliveries are continuing but are being intercepted and transported elsewhere.'

'Understood, Ochoa, thank you. Will investigate other end. Arrange another depot your end if you can and close down.'

Farell put the receiver back on its hook. His British controller in Oporto wanted him to take no more part in the escape line. He should try to arrange for someone else to take over his position, which would be extremely difficult, for not everyone had free access to the ferry.

And what about the others back along the line? What had become of them? This worried him.

Chapter Sixteen

The course was nearly at an end. The group had been to both Scotland and Wales to learn the rudiments of mountain-climbing and cliff-scaling. In other parts of the country they had learned how to use explosives, how to make booby traps, and under Morton's tutorage exactly where to place these explosives and booby-traps to ensure maximum effect.

To a man they were taught how to drive a variety of vehicles, always at break-neck speed and without lights up and down the Welsh mountains, using farm tracks as roads. In this, one of the Frenchmen, Michel Rocard, excelled. Rocard, it transpired, twenty-seven-years old, had been a test driver for the Renault Automobile Company prior to the war, and could handle anything on four wheels. Rocard was a handsome man, just above average height with a slightly tanned appearance. He was also athletic and drew admiring glances from some of the women agents who were training in the New Forest at the same time. A strictly enforced rule was that groups were not allowed to communicate with each other, a rule which everyone adhered to, but which did not prevent the women from looking Rocard's way.

Rocard had been in north-west France in the Vendée area at the time of the invasion, test-driving a new four-wheel drive truck that could negotiate a sixty-degree incline. German Intelligence knew of the truck and agents had already been assigned to its capture. Word reached Rocard an hour in front of the German agents that he was a marked man, that he would be taken to Germany with the truck and forced to help in the completion of its development.

Communications with the company had become non-existent. The country was in chaos with so many fleeing the invaders, and with no one to turn to Rocard hid the truck in what he believed was a safe place, then with his fellow-drivers and engineers commandeered a boat and sailed for England.

He was fiercely anti-de Gaulle. De Gaulle in Rocard's eyes was an upstart. Practically unknown before the war the general had come to England and assumed leadership of the Free French forces. Thousands rallied to his side but as many did not. France had capitulated and in the eyes of those who had wanted to fight on, one French general was no different from another. They looked to Churchill, the bulldog who refused to bow to the Nazi threat, and offered their services. Animosity built up between the two factions and in the streets of London, even at the height of the Battle of Britain, gunfights erupted and Frenchman killed Frenchman.

Rocard had been approached by Gaullist agents to provide all the information he knew about the Renault organisation. He refused, throwing his lot in with the London-controlled French. Attempts were made on his life and in self-defence during one such attempt he inadvertently killed one of the would-be assassins. Gaullist agents demanded he be arrested and charged with murder and, in an effort to keep peace between the factions, the Home Office agreed. But Rocard was too useful a man to languish in a prison. Word was passed along that if any organisation – not French – could use a resourceful Frenchman, they could have him. Witherspoole jumped at the opportunity and shortly after the Free French received a report from the police that he had escaped from prison, possibly at the behest of his supporters. In his absence the Free French sentenced him to death.

Rocard's fellow-countryman, Charles Henru, was also anti-de Gaulle. His views on French politicians were similar to those of Rocard. Following Dunkirk, although the British public were not aware of the fact, it had been touch and go whether the French government threw in its lot with the Germans. Both the government and armed forces had been split and it had been difficult to decide who really wanted to fight on and who did not. Henru also knew that many of the French politicians and senior uniformed officers who fled to England were pro-German, potential spies and saboteurs: information he had passed on to British Intelligence on his own arrival.

Henru was thirty-seven, and knew more about what was going on in France than many members of government and the armed forces realised. Before his hasty departure from France he had been employed as an announcer and programme presenter at Radio Normandie, the commercial radio station based at Fécamp beaming music programmes to southern England. All kinds of news items came his way and by studying them he and the other staff could determine whose sympathies lay where. Following the declaration of war Radio Normandie turned from popular programming to entertaining the British Expeditionary Forces by day, and to beaming propaganda to Germany at night. This made Henru a wanted man, and when the German forces invaded, a detachment of motorised troops was detailed to capture the transmitting station and its entire staff intact.

Henru had prior warning of their coming and waited until the last minute before leaving for England. He was aware of the influence of radio, and the station had files listing the names and addresses of listeners in England. It would not do, he had thought at the time, for the Germans to take over and use the files for propaganda, perhaps reading out the thousands of personal letters listeners had sent in over the years, making it appear they had been sent in only days before. So, with virtually the last boat available in Fécamp crammed full with documents, and equipment in the station smashed where possible, Henru and the staff of Radio Normandie made a narrow escape to England.

The BBC was already broadcasting programmes to France when Henru arrived in England, mostly using

Gaullists as announcers and presenters. The Gaullists approached him since his voice was well-known to the French, to broadcast freedom programmes and speeches on behalf of de Gaulle, but he refused. The main reason was that he had no time for de Gaulle or anything he stood for, but also because his family was still in France and as soon as his voice went over the air they would be arrested by the Gestapo.

Henru did not know where his wife and children were. When the Germans broke through Belgium he had been advised to get his family away from the channel coast. They went south hoping to reach L'Aiguillon-sur-Mer on the Atlantic coast, then everything happened at once. He had no way of knowing if they reached their destination or, in fact, if they were still alive.

The Free French were far from happy with Henru's decision not to become a broadcaster. Among those he met were men and women whom he knew would have collaborated with the Germans had they remained in France. The thought of working with them was repellent. They promised to trace his family for him, and when he still refused, threatened him: threatened his family. Henru asked for a day or two to think it over and went straight to the men who had interviewed him on his arrival. He confided what he knew about the pro-Germans within the Free French and how they'd threatened him, and asked if there was an organisation he could join that would allow him to do something useful against Germany. If necessary he was prepared to go back to France and work underground. Very quietly he was passed along to James Witherspoole.

Any fat the group had had on them before the training course began had gone. They were slimmer, muscular, their reactions razor-sharp and ready for anything. The ten-mile daily runs had been increased to twenty, and instead of swimming across the river they now swam down the deep boating channel to Lower Exbury Point and back again.

Training times also altered. Sometimes they slept by day and trained at night, and there was no let-up. The hard physical side always included a run, a swim and the corridor. Guards were posted while they slept and the interruptions continued, but ever since the third night they had never been taken by surprise. The only bug was the corridor. The number of attackers varied: on one particular occasion during the night when the corridor was enveloped in smoke, sixty attackers fell on them and they took the rough end of the stick, which resulted in Barcikowski losing the tip of the little finger on his left hand and Hopkins, the Dunkirk veteran, breaking one of his.

The boat was nearing completion and the sessions aboard were now simulations of movements. Test panels were installed and as orders were given each man attended to his station as if they were at sea, watching the instruments on the panels, stencilling in their minds the pressures that would save or take their lives. Then came the first sea trial.

Immediately after dark on a dirty Friday evening a blacked-out tug towed the boat downriver into the English Channel off Warren Flats. During the short river journey the group carried out a detailed inspection. One engine was idling and most pumps were in use. Joints and flanges along high-pressure water mains were visually examined for leaks, and glycerine applied to high-pressure air main flanges and joints. Hydrometers were applied to the massive banks of batteries to measure the SG reading. Two of the Americans, Carter Braxton and Thomas Nelson, elected engineers, made last minute adjustments to clearances and tolerances, set cooling water pressures, oil temperatures and pressures, nipped up leaking glands and generally made the propulsion equipment as ready as it would ever be.

In relatively deep water the tug cast off and stood by. Sherman ordered all engines on half-ahead. The boat shuddered a second later when it pushed into the might of the sea and a wave of apprehension swept through the interior. It was in everyone's mind that this was the real thing, not a mock-up on the Beaulieu River.

'Check for leaks!' Sherman's voice came over the tannoy.

There were no leaks. So far the boat was sound.

'All engines full ahead.'

The diesels roared as Braxton and Nelson increased the revolutions to a maximum, the roar becoming a deep *thrumm* as they took the 1,000 ton plus load, pushing the boat harder, fighting against a much heavier force, bucking as waves lifted the bows far out of the water.

Sherman did a tour. He studied faces and hands and saw the tell-tale signs of tension. For all the crew were probably the toughest men in the war, even tougher than commandos, they still had to experience the baptism of a first dive. Most wore a weak grin to let it appear they were not afraid. Some just nodded as he approached and turned their eyes away while others openly looked to him for words of encouragement. But in all cases white knuckles showed through tightly stretched skin.

He went to each man in turn and gripped their shoulders reassuringly, nodding and smiling, then returned to the control room. Woolcott was on the conning tower with Harewood and Bill Ellery, another of the Americans.

'Give me a bearing on the tug,' he said as he entered.

The reply came back immediately.

'Range?'

'Four thousand yards, sir.'

So far so good, Sherman thought, then climbed the tower and whispered to Woolcott.

The boat was still bucking and the instrumentation showed they were doing 27.5 knots. Now was the time to test their mettle.

'Dive!' Sherman shouted into the tannoy and sounded the alarm.

Within seconds Harewood, Ellery and Woolcott tumbled down the hatch, Woolcott bringing up the rear and fastening the stirrups on both the upper and lower lids. Even before the first man dropped from the ladder the engines stopped and an eerie silence roared through the hull. A sudden lurch telegraphed the boat going under and around him Sherman could see muscles stiffen.

'Group up!'

Power from the batteries flowed into the motors. Sherman noticed Wilson, on the range-finder, smile.

Then the boat's movement came to a sudden halt and everyone was thrown off-balance.

'Power off! Damage report!' Sherman shouted and ran forward, with Woolcott going aft. They had hit the bottom of the channel with an almighty thump.

A torpedo hatch leaked slightly but otherwise the boat was intact and, Sherman was pleased to note, no one had panicked. They had stayed at their posts. He didn't mention that the move had been deliberate.

'All motors slow astern,' he spoke into the tannoy, quietly this time, and listened for the reply.

'All motors slow astern, sir.'

Nothing happened. The nose was firmly stuck in mud.

'Stop all motors.'

'All motors stopped, sir.'

'Blow all tanks and all motors full astern together.'

They could hear compressed air rumble into the ballast tanks and water rush at pressure from the main drains. Levers and linkage rattled as the drains opened and both Sherman and Woolcott shook their heads. Witherspoole should have done something about the old-fashioned mechanical devices. Depending on the situation the devices could tie men up who could be utilised to better advantage elsewhere.

'Tanks blown, sir.'

'All motors full astern, sir.'

The boat groaned as it tried to free itself. Motors whined in protest at the job they were being asked to do and as the tanks emptied of water the stern rose at an odd angle with the bow still stuck. Spare equipment, crockery and men went tumbling to the floor and yells of concern echoed through the hull.

'Open all vents!'

'All vents open, sir'

The tanks filled with water causing the boat to sink to the bottom once more, but at the same time helping to loosen the mud's grip.

'Blow all tanks!'

Again air rushed into the tanks. The stern rose quickly, then with a sudden bump they were free. The boat went back like an arrow.

'Trim to fifty feet! Group down!'

Woolcott was prepared. He flooded certain of the tanks and the boat adopted an even keel. The revolutions dropped rapidly and very quickly everything became still.

Sherman sighed with relief. It was too easy to shoot to the surface after being stuck on the bottom in relatively shallow waters, and when that happened you were a sitting target. You had to use all your power to get free and level out immediately after.

'Well done, you guys,' he called over the tannoy. 'I can tell you now that was an exercise. Hopefully we will never get ourselves into that kind of position in enemy waters, but if we do I know that I can rely on you to take the correct action. I am proud of you. Blow all tanks. Group down and surface.'

Woolcott was smiling. 'It went well, sir, better than I hoped.'

'How long?'

'Thirty-two seconds, and the navy norm is thirty seconds maximum. But for our first time I would say thirty-two seconds was exceptional.'

Sherman nodded. 'We can improve on that, Oliver. And I'm rather surprised myself. When I had this old tub back home we thought we'd done well to get it down in under fifty seconds.'

They had already discussed the differences between the US and British navies. In the United States, before a submarine dived the commander waited until the report *the board is green* – meaning all external hatches and vents were closed – had been issued before giving the actual command. This used up valuable time which could mean the difference between life and death.

There was no such report in the Royal Navy. As soon as the alarm was given the engines were cut off, the ballast tanks filled and conning tower cleared. Reliance was placed on the sailors themselves to ensure that the boat was sealed. If it was not then a disaster occurred. Anyone on deck who did not get to a hatch in time was doomed. Nor did rank matter. The same ruling applied to a commander as to an engine-room artificer. Hatches were closed and that was that.

The general timing was no more than thirty seconds for a boat to submerge, and Woolcott had heard tell of one commander who had gone from fourteen knots on the surface to fully-submerged in nineteen seconds: a feat never repeated by any other commander.

Another difference were the hatches leading down from the conning tower. Both British and American boats had two hatches – familiarly referred to as *lids* in the RN – one from the conning tower platform into the conning tower itself, and a second through the pressure hull into the control room.

All British boats secured the hatches with stirrups, while some American boats used a dog and cam arrangement where a handwheel locked the hatches in place and could be operated from both inside and outside. Modern American boats had been changed to the stirrup method but some of the older types still relied on the handwheel, and this was one of them. The dog and cam arrangement hadn't been removed. It was still usable, but to be on the safe side stirrups had been installed and would become the means of securing the hatches.

Smiles were evident now that the excitement was over and Jimmy Wilson exhaled heavily. 'Blimey, chief, if that was an exercise I wouldn't want it to happen for real. Nearly pooped meself, I did.'

'I'm glad you didn't, Jimmy,' Sherman laughed. 'I might have been forced to open the hatch to escape.'

'Everyone should try everything once,' said Rob Morris from the hydroplane station, 'except typewriting and deep-sea diving.'

The trials continued all night. Every two hours half the crew were told to sleep and somewhere in the two hours an alarm was given, and when the first alarm sounded the diving time increased to forty seconds, gradually decreasing as they became used to the short periods of sleep until the time came below thirty seconds, the final dive of the night being achieved in a magnificent twenty-six seconds.

'Fantastic!' was all Sherman could say, considering much of the equipment was manual instead of hydraulic.

Two hours before dawn the trials ended and the boat was towed, astern first, back up the Beaulieu River to its covered, camouflaged shed at Buckler's Hard. Shore parties quickly tied her up, the tug disappeared further upriver and by daylight the New Forest was once again a quiet peaceful stretch of the English countryside.

Witherspoole and Morton were on hand, both with worried faces lest the trials had been a failure, and on hearing Sherman's report the worry became delight.

'Splendid!' Witherspoole was all smiles.

Over breakfast the crew discussed the previous night. To a man they admitted they had been afraid but they laughed now, feeling that it was somewhat childish for grown men to be afraid.

Sherman and Woolcott laughed with them but made no comment. A sea-trial off the south coast of England would be nothing compared to a depth-charge attack by a German destroyer. That still had to come. Would the crew panic then, they wondered?

The rest of the morning was spent on continued weapons training, followed by sleep, and in the evening a session in the corridor before boarding the boat again for another trial run.

The corridor they took in their step now. It was still violent and stitches were still inserted afterwards, but they went through fast without wasting time, felling their adversaries and running on, carrying their injured in front with a rear-guard for protection.

Periods of sleep were still interrupted but the intruders never got further than the door of the hut. Leaping from their bunks in a split second and arming themselves, they'd got it down to a fine art.

For a week the routine stayed the same and on the final two nights the time for diving was down to twenty-three seconds. Returning to base after the seventh night, they were presented with a surprise.

'Your training is finished,' Witherspoole said at breakfast.

'Bloody hell!' Jimmy Wilson gulped down a piece of bacon, 'you mean we're ready for the off?'

'When something comes along, yes.'

'You mean you ain't got a job for us?'

'Not yet.'

'Well,' Harewood drawled in his upper-class accent, 'I for one can say that I've never enjoyed myself so much in my life.'

'It don't look like it, Duke,' Morris laughed.

Nor did Harewood look as though he had enjoyed himself. When he'd first joined the group they'd seen him as a tall, good-looking, well-spoken aristocrat who tended to look down on those below his station. He was still well-spoken but a few other things had changed.

Although tall he had filled out, which seemed to make him look shorter. His good looks were marred by scars, cuts and bruises, and no longer did he talk down to the others. The fine head of shiny black hair he'd sported was gone: cropped down to the skull like the others to give him the appearance of a desperate criminal from a bygone era.

'Mayhaps not, old thing, but something inside me whispers that I thoroughly enjoyed myself. And, further, I do think we should have a bash at the corridor tonight for the last time . . .' Harewood's eyes twinkled as he looked round the canteen and the other caught on. The nodded, laughing at the prospect.

'Can you arrange that, exalted one?'

Witherspoole also caught on. He smiled. 'I will arrange it.'

'Jolly good. As the man once said: "Never depart Mine Host without first offering to return his hospitality".'

'Afterwards,' said Witherspoole, 'you can have a party. I've arranged for a consignment of beer to be brought in.'

A cheer went up.

'You can all get blind drunk if you wish.'

At 2245 hours the group approached the corridor. There was no artificial smoke. There didn't have to be: mist lay thick among the trees creating the eerie atmosphere of a graveyard at night.

Barcikowski led the way, his short but muscular frame bent over, taking lumbering, ape-like steps: a frightful sight for anyone to meet coming out of the mist.

Fifteen yards into the corridor it began. The entrance was closed off and men vaulted over the top of the walls screaming like banshees. Others leapt up from holes in the ground and seemed to fly through the air like darkened spectres. For an instant the group was taken by surprise. There had been no screaming on the previous occasions. They wondered if perhaps Witherspoole had sold them out this time.

The surprise was but momentary and an agreed plan went into action. The group did not attempt to fight their way through, but stood and fought where they were. No one carried weapons. Relying only on their training they became the attackers.

Young Tommy Stone jumped on someone's back and applied a neck-lock and as his opponent struggled to pull away the arm choking him, George Wythe kicked him in the groin. Stone let go then and the man doubled up moaning, whereupon Wythe delivered another kick, this time to the man's face. He fell to the ground like a sandbag.

Razor Eddie was in his element. He was back in the environment of his native city administering his forehead to mouths and noses in classical Glaswegian style: his tongue lapsing into Lallans, the language of the city, screaming words no one could understand.

Sherman, knowing that it was no time to behave like an officer or a gentleman, had someone by the hair, bouncing his face off the timber walls of the corridor.

Morris and Wilson had teamed up. Using a mixture of karate and street-fighting they very quickly bundled their opponents to the ground and executed their own form of the *coup-de-grâce:* a chop across the bridge of the nose and the famed kick in the goolies.

Whistles blew but there was no cessation of hostilities. When the original attackers attempted to withdraw they were pulled back and pounded. The whistles became impatient, their shrill tone sounding rapidly when the attacking force failed to appear. Someone looked over the top of the wall to see what was going on and called out for the mêlée to stop. Which was his undoing. Carter Braxton hoisted William Paca on his shoulders and Paca, with an almighty tug, pulled the unfortunate observer over the top and down into the bloody battle, where he disappeared among a forest of boots and legs.

When at last there was not one of the attackers capable of fighting on, the group stepped back. Most of the others were unconscious. A few were rolling in agony and one tried to sit up, but a well-aimed punch from the Pole's massive fist sent him back down again.

'Okay, you guys,' Sherman said, 'we go back the way we came.'

The partition at the entrance to the corridor was broken down by sheer force of numbers then torn from its hinges.

They had agreed earlier they would leave their mark on the New Forest. They would have one last go at the corridor and they would leave it the way they went in, proving they were tougher than all the instructors the course had to offer.

From the corridor they ran to the hut where they knew another group would be sleeping. These were the men who had interrupted their sleep ever since their arrival. The hut was locked – expectedly – but was soon opened by John Harte whose trade was burglary.

Using hand signals, Sherman directed everyone to their posts. Around the side of the hut Hancock and Halls stood by a blacked-out window facing each other, their hands cupped together, both of them braced. On the other side Jefferson and Stockton took up similar stances.

When everyone was ready Sherman whistled lightly. William Whipple, famed for robbing post offices, began to run towards Hancock and Halls, while Morris ran towards Jefferson and Stockton. The others began filing through the door of the hut.

Catapulted by those outside Whipple and Morris crashed through the windows into the hut taking glass and black-out curtains with them. The sleeping forms inside were awakened by the sound of breaking glass but, as the group expected, their reactions were not quick enough for the occasion. Bodies fell on them: fists and boots met their faces and groins and before long they were bruised and bloodied, trussed up with their own blankets and sheets.

A light came on and the instructor who some time before had sneered at their capabilities, entered. Sherman and Woolcott were ready for him. He walked between them, his face purple with rage, and a fist from each side crashed into his jaw, breaking it and making him incapable of speech for many weeks to come.

'I think,' Harewood broke the silence that followed, 'we have proved a jolly good point.'

Witherspoole was dragged from his bed in nearby Lymington in the early hours of the morning to be told what his men had done. This time there were no congratulations. This time it was serious. So many staff were out of action that the centre would not be able to operate normally for several weeks, which would have a telling effect on other agents being prepared for a drop. He would go back to the centre that instant and read the riot act or he would be no longer welcome there.

Witherspoole found his men drunk and lifted his shoulders in despair. What could he say or do? He'd set out to turn them into animals and had achieved exactly that. What did the centre expect?

He went into the hut to speak to them alone but said nothing. Instead he got drunk with them and was oblivious to the world by dawn.

Chapter Seventeen

Witherspoole hadn't drunk so much in his life. He awoke the afternoon following his binge with a roaring headache and raging thirst. His whole world was upside down and it was several hours before he could say anything intelligible. Noises made him jump, the thought of food made him want to throw up and wild horses wouldn't have got him within a hundred yards of a pub. Nor was he impressed by Harewood who, on waking from his own stupor, poured himself a drink and commented: 'As the man once said, old chap, the only cure for a hangover is to stay drunk.'

A day later, when Witherspoole felt well enough to continue normally, a job was offered to him. Excited, he called for Morton who was attending to affairs in London, to join him in the New Forest.

'I've just been approached by MI9, John. They would like us to look into the matter of a broken escape line. It seems that German Intelligence has penetrated the line and is actually running it.'

'What would they like us to do, sir?'

MI9 was the escape organisation, responsible for setting up the escape lines that criss-crossed Europe.

MI9 arranged safe houses and routes, provided money and mountains of false papers to the brave men and women who took stranded British servicemen under their wing and safely piloted them to neutral Spain, from where they could be taken to Gibraltar or Lisbon and back to England.

The escape lines took enormous risks. Security was paramount and a minor error could become a disaster. A wrong word at a checkpoint or a misplaced comma on an identity card, could mean arrest and an entire line destroyed. Families suffered also. If an escape line was uncovered the families of all those concerned were executed. Yet, as one line broke up, another was formed.

Witherspoole explained what MI9 wanted.

'That's a tall order, sir.'

'We shall have to oblige them, John. After all, it's this sort of thing we set out to do.'

'That's true,' Morton conceded.

'Get the lads together, John, and we'll give them a briefing.'

The briefing took place in the dormitory hut. Witherspoole arranged for a blackboard to be brought in and when everyone was seated he sketched a map in chalk.

'Spain,' he began, 'officially neutral, but as neutral to Germany as the United States is to Britain.'

He made no mention of MI9 but explained about the escape lines.

'Escape lines lead into Spain. Hundreds of men, women and children are involved and each of them risks their lives every hour of the day and night. Northern France, Belgium, Holland and Luxembourg are where the lines are in greatest danger, but that does not mean to say that anyone is safe in Vichy France. German Intelligence has people all over Vichy France constantly trying to penetrate the lines, and if the Vichy police or militia uncover a safe house along the way they arrest the agents and hand them over to the Gestapo in the north who, be in no doubt about their capabilities, very quickly extract enough information from the arrested agents to sweep up the entire line.

'The escape lines deal mainly with aircrew, although many hundreds of soldiers stranded after Dunkirk have been successfully brought back. And there is a very great importance placed on aircrew. Heaven knows how many bomber and fighter pilots there are at this moment somewhere in France and the Low Countries, all in hiding and waiting to go along one of the lines. It takes months to train these chaps, not to mention the enormous cost. To train just one fighter pilot costs £15,000, and to train the seven-man crew of a Lancaster, £25,000. This is a cost the country can ill-afford, and, I must emphasise, for each fighter pilot and bomber pilot stranded in enemy territory, there is one less fighter and one less bomber in the air. The Germans know this of course which is why they attach the same importance to capturing them as we do to getting them back.

'If the chap does manage to get into Spain it is not necessarily all plain sailing from then on. Spain, you must remember, is fascist, and is politically allied to Germany. As I said, she is officially neutral, but sources tell me that a Spanish division is at this moment serving with the German Army. And Germany, don't forget, learned about Blitzkrieg in Spain. If any of you do not already know, Hitler sent thousands of his troops, fighter and bomber pilots, to help Franco during the civil war. They gained invaluable experience there which they have since put to excellent use.

'So, having got into Spain what are our chaps up against? They are up against roving German agents who will attempt to kill them. They are up against ordinary Spaniards who will turn them over to German agents for personal gain. They are up against fascist militia and the Spanish secret police, and the highly organised German Intelligence networks. The fascist militia hand our people over to the secret police who try to emulate their German counterparts in methods of extracting information, and if they do gain information they come down hard on any Spaniards who are on our side.

Following interrogation our people end up in concentration camps – Miranda being the most infamous – and it is very rare that the diplomatic corps can gain their release. The Spaniards come under great pressure from the German Ambassador to keep them there for the duration.

'A number of escape lines cross Spain, one of which is code named NIB. German agents have penetrated NIB and now virtually control it all the way from Belgium. Unfortunately the people engaged in running the line do not know this. You see, whoever is at the start of the line knows the next person along, but not the one after. The second knows the third but not the fourth, and so on. They just pass our people from safe house to safe house hoping they will get to the other end safely. My sources don't know how the line was penetrated but have made fair assumptions on where. They believe German agents penetrated the line in a particular area of Spain, forced someone to talk and backtracked. All they would need is the name of the agent at the previous stage. They would watch that person's house and scrutinise every arrival, and sooner or later someone would turn up from a town or village farther back along the line accompanied by strangers. That person would then be followed and watched until he, too, had a visitor from another town or village, and so on. It would take many weeks of surveillance but eventually the entire line would be identified.

'The Germans don't always go in immediately and make arrests. Sometimes they stand back and watch, probably laughing up their sleeves at the efforts of those who still believe they are working in strictest secrecy. They follow the progress of stranded airmen being taken along the line, perhaps giving a helping hand here and there, and when the line reaches the stage where it has been broken, they pounce.

'Of course, this can't go on for ever. Somewhere in Spain there is a British agent, a Spaniard who is part of the line, perhaps the last link before the line crosses into Portugal. He doesn't realise that the line has been broken. He just thinks that there is no traffic for him. One stage back however, some unfortunate being is either languishing in a nasty Spanish gaol, or in his grave, having told his captors every detail of the part he played. German Intelligence, using the information, contacts the person further back using the correct codes, advising that there is a problem at his end, and any traffic hereafter should be moved to another location where they will be met by someone who will identify himself by some name or another. The chap has no reason to question the advice and appropriately guides his charges to the new location, hands them over and returns home. And that's the last anyone sees of them.

'But as time goes on the last link in the chain becomes worried. No word has reached him that people are on their way. This is unusual. He suspects something is wrong and breaks security, and using an emergency code contacts the second last link in the chain. The reply he gets is not that previously agreed, which confirms his suspicions. He then contacts his British controller in Portugal and passes on the bad news. That news then reaches London and London must do something about it. That is where you come in.

'The information we have is that the last three stages of the line were here . . . here and here . . .' Witherspoole marked the map on the blackboard. 'I have arranged for one or two maps to come so that you can look at the area in greater detail. Condomar, Cousa and last of all Tuy. Cousa was where the line was penetrated and taken over. Tuy knows this but Gondomar doesn't. When Gondomar receives his package he will in all innocence pass it on, straight into the arms of German agents. What you have to do is get to Cousa, contact a man by the name of Miguel Angel Ortega Gomez. A bit long-winded, I know, but it is important to have the correct name. I'm told that asking for someone called Ortega without giving his other names would be like asking someone in London if they knew a chap called Smith.

'The agent in Cousa who was a member of the escape

line is, or was, called Carlos Salinas de Gortari. Ortega will know something about Gortari. A signal has been sent to him to investigate and by the time you get there he should be able to supply information on what happens to our people. Working on that information you will trace the headquarters used by German Intelligence, determine if the head man is there and kill him – and anyone else who might be there for that matter,' Witherspoole paused for a second then asked: 'Any questions so far?'

'Yes, sir,' said Hancock, the Canadian. 'If we have so many agents over that way, why haven't they taken care of these Nazis?'

'A good question, John, and easily answered. On the Iberian Peninsula known agents of both sides follow each other about like lap-dogs. If they made a move the enemy would realise that we know, and we don't want them to know just yet. We want to get into their headquarters first, kill them and collect what information we can. Hidden agents run the same risk. If a British "businessman" suddenly appeared in the area German agents would at once smell a rat and clear out. No, the whole scene must remain unchanged. Germany must be made to think we don't know. The attack must come from the outside, from men who can cross a stretch of land quickly and fight their way in and out of a tight corner.

'So, what is required is that you will take your boat to a point on the Atlantic coast of Spain, exactly forty-two degrees north, where Captain Sherman will decide who actually goes ashore. You will be two miles south of the tiny village of Oya but will be hidden from inquisitive eyes. The location chosen is an area where large sharp rocks rise from the sea bed, some of them one hundred feet tall, reaching three hundred yards out to sea and half a mile along the coastline. Get as close to these rocks as you can then those going ashore can do so unseen. There is a small lighthouse on the rocks but it will give you no trouble as it is unmanned. Once ashore you find steep cliffs. These will have to be scaled, and in darkness to boot. There is a coastal road there, the C550. Keep clear of this road. Spanish patrols use it regularly watching for ships entering their waters and possible agents being put ashore. Skirting Oya make for Cousa. Cousa is eight miles north-east and a rather small village. Everyone knows each other: some are for Franco and some are not, therefore there is a lot of distrust. I can't advise you what to do there. You will have to decide when you get there which is the best method of finding and talking to Ortega.'

'Seems clear enough,' Heroles said. 'When do we leave?'

'In a day or two when the corking is complete . . . And there are drawbacks,' Witherspoole went on, his face becoming firm. 'If you are caught you will be disowned. You must understand that now. London will deny all knowledge of you, which will leave the Spanish authorities with absolute freedom to do with you as they see fit. There is good reason for this, you see. As I said earlier, Spain is officially neutral, but assists Germany in many ways, even so far as bolstering her army. Hitler would give his right arm for Franco to come into the war on his side, and that would be disastrous for Britain. Such an event could easily lose us the war.

'You being caught, armed to the teeth, could be taken as an invasion of Spain, a violation of her sovereign rights. Such an event would give those in the Spanish government who want to join the war the excuse to force Franco's hand. If that happened Gibraltar would be overrun and our access to the Mediterranean cut off. Every ship, submarine, plane and serviceman in that area would be doomed. Egypt would fall and our African colonies would topple over one by one . . .' Witherspoole shuddered. 'The consequences are too horrible to contemplate: therefore, you must not be caught.'

'Now,' Witherspoole consulted documents he took from a briefcase. 'I understand some of you speak Spanish. Joseph, Richard and Casar: you seem to be the best qualified to take part in the shore assignment. You have all had vast experience in guerilla fighting and speak the language like natives.'

'All three languages, sir,' said Richard Lee.

'Beg pardon?'

'There are three main languages in Spain, sir: Castilian, Catalan and Basque. I speak all of them. So does Casar.'

Joseph Hewes, Richard Henry Lee and Casar Rooney were American soldiers of fortune and adventurers who'd fought with the Abraham Lincoln Division against Franco in the Spanish Civil War. They had also fought in other wars about the world, particularly in Central and South America, and on one occasion had actually taken part in a raid against a British possession in the Caribbean.

Following the defeat of the Spanish Republicans they had gone over the Pyrenees into France, debating on whether to join the French Foreign Legion. Then war was declared. The trio went north to Paris to offer their expertise but the French army declined their offer, declaring that France had more than enough soldiers with fighting experience. For several months they remained in France, taking odd jobs and watching the situation along the Maginot Line. German troops were sparse along the other side of the line which, to men with experience of German tactics, meant Germany had no intention of attacking it.

They decided France was not safe and moved on to England where they found casual employment, until a stranger paid them a visit and informed them that they were in the country illegally: a prison offence, and with Britain at war they could well be charged with espionage. There was a way out of that, of course . . .

As well as being fluent in the three main languages of Spain, Lee also spoke German, Italian, French and Arabic. Hewes and Rooney could match him except for Arabic.

Nelson spoke French and some German; Jefferson: French, German and Dutch; Braxton: French and Italian;

Paca: Spanish and fairly good English; Barcikowski: Russian, Hungarian, German and French, with patchy English; Rocard: English and Italian; Henru: English, Dutch and German; Heroles: Spanish; Hancock: French; Harewood: French, Italian, German, Danish, Afrikaans and Latin; Rutledge: French, Dutch, German and Latin; and Sherman Spanish and some French; Rush Stockton brought a few mutters of surprise when he professed to speak not only French, Dutch, Italian and German, but also Serbo-Croat and Macedonian.

'How the devil did you manage to pick them up?' Witherspoole was surprised himself.

'I worked in the Balkans for a while,' was all Stockton said as a reply. 'I also speak passable Greek.'

Witherspoole shook his head. His own nationals were the most lacking. Few of them spoke foreign languages while the others could handle three or four. Then he shrugged. It was a throwback from the glorious days of the old Empire. In those days it was below an Englishman's dignity and station to learn foreign languages. With Britain supreme in the world everyone else was expected to learn English.

Changed days. While others were learning foreign languages the average Briton was going cap in hand hoping someone could speak English. Ah, well, he thought, if they get back I'll arrange intensive language training.

'There is something else,' Witherspoole said, his mouth tightening.

No one spoke. They could see from his face that what was to come would not be nice.

'When Berlin learns of what has happened – presuming of course you kill whoever broke the line – orders will immediately be given to arrest everyone concerned with the line. No doubt they will be tortured and shot so if any of you have reservations about the job say so now.'

Still no one spoke.

'Thank God for that. It is unfortunate but it is a part of the war we must accept. We could warn the line to get out now and go into hiding, but we are certain they are being watched and if they all suddenly decided to disappear Berlin would suspect something. The line therefore must continue to operate until you get into Spain. We will have some losses, but they will be offset by a more secure line being established. And now, some information on how to get inside locked buildings. John . . .?'

Morton came in front of the group and began making sketches on the blackboard. 'A locked door,' he said, 'and you want to get through. What would the average person do – anyone?'

'Smash the door down,' said Whipple.

'Pick the lock,' from Harte.

'That's about right, but let's examine each method. Smashing the door down makes a hell of a lot of noise, and if you have to get through locked doors in Spain the last thing you want is noise. And, yes, picking the lock is a good idea, but what if the door is bolted on the inside? I'll tell you what: just go and have a look at the doors in this building and see if there is anything that stands out.'

The group looked at each other.

'Go on. I'm not pulling your leg.'

They rose, began opening and closing doors, but did not really know what they were looking for.

'Okay,' Morton called them back, 'they are just ordinary doors: something we all take for granted. But let us take a closer look at one.'

All eyes followed Morton as he made his way to a door.

'Doors generally open inwards,' he pushed a door open slightly, 'and to stop it being opened people fit locks, and often internal bolts. They feel secure then. But are they? Our burglar friend here, John Harte, attacks the locks – is that not right, John?'

'I'll pick any lock there is,' Harte replied with pride.

'Any why do you pick the lock?'

'It's the easiest way of getting in without forcing an entry.'

'Exactly!' Morton smiled. 'Those were the words I wanted – forcing an entry. And if the door is too well secured, do you force an entry?'

'Nope, I go somewhere else.'

'Spot on! Just like the people who fit fancy locks to make the door more secure, you also miss the weakest part of the door.'

'You what?'

'Yes, John. One side of the door can have all the locks and bolts it wants, but the other side of the door never changes – the side where the hinges are. That's where the weak point is. Look at this door. It swings on two small hinges, each held to the framework by three small screws. At the most there might be four screws. So, as the door swings inwards what do we see? Just these two hinges. And what is between us and the hinges? Nothing but a timber frame held together with panel pins. All the frame does is hide the hinges from the eye and stops rainwater from getting inside. Allow me to demonstrate something . . .'

Morton took a small jemmy from a pocket and said: 'I shall go outside for a moment or two, and I should like you to lock the door behind me and bolt it.'

With the door locked the group sat on their bunks and waited. A few minutes passed and the door began to move, but from the wrong side. The hinged side moved slightly inwards then slid to one side off the bolt and lock, and then swung round as Morton lifted it out of the doorway.

'Bloody hell!' someone swore.

'If you'll gather round I'll explain further.'

Eagerly the group crowded round Morton and the first thing that caught their eye was the framework on the hinged side of the door. It had gone.

'I prised it out with the jemmy,' said Morton. 'Have a closer look and notice just how weak the frame is . . .'

'The frame is rarely made in one solid piece. That comes expensive therefore people generally go for a frame made up of sections. Now I shall do the same again but with all of you watching.'

They left the hut and walked to the opposite end to another door where Morton continued.

'I push the jemmy in here,' he said, finding the narrowest of gaps between the timber framework and the wall, 'and bear in mind that this hut is timber. In reality the frame is generally nailed to a wall, which is much easier to work with. I begin moving the framework . . .' Morton worked fast. The narrow gap became wider and he moved the jemmy down the length of the door, gradually prising the frame away from the wall.

'You will notice that I do not jerk the jemmy, but rather apply a steady pressure. Jerking it can result in splitting the timber, which creates noise, but applying a steady pressure in the right places will bring the whole length of frame away, nails and all. Actually it is much more difficult for one person than it is for two. Two people working together, working away from each other, can have the frame off in a matter of seconds . . .'

The length of framework was off and Morton laid it on the ground. There had only been the slightest of sounds and the group was highly impressed.

'Now you can just see the ends of the hinges, and again I use the jemmy, this time forcing it in behind the hinge-plate on the wall side . . . see, it's coming loose already. For economy reasons these hinges only have three screws and they will not be over-long. They tend to want to keep their grip and the timber around it splits: this you can't avoid, but by continually working the jemmy you will create enough slack for the door to start to move inwards . . . see.'

Both Woolcott and Sherman were amazed, some of the others less so. It had never occurred to them that one day they would be taught how to become a house-breaker and burglar. Nor had it occurred to them just how easy it was to break into a building.

Morton was working on the top hinge and already it was hanging from loose screws, leaning into the hut. He moved down to the lower hinge and repeated the process until he could see into the hut through the gap created.

'Now we turn the jemmy round and insert it between the frame and hinge, with the fulcrum against the hinge thus . . .' Morton levered and the hinge came away from the frame, then holding the door with one hand, bent down to do the same on the lower hinge. The door came free.

'We take hold of the handle with our left hand,' he said pushing the jemmy into his pocket, 'and the edge of the door where the hinges are with our right and slide it into the room at an acute angle. An inch or two is all that is required, and, voilà . . . !' he lifted the door and walked into the hut. The group applauded.

'You'd of made a good tea-leaf,' Wilson remarked. 'Where'd you learn that, guv?'

'Ah,' Morton smiled, 'that's something I shall keep private.'

'I wouldn't mind a go at that,' said James Adams, a thirty-three-year-old Londoner with a history of thieving.

'You will: tonight. I shall supply you with the necessary tools and you can pair off. There's a lot of doors in this training centre.'

'You mean . . .' Adams began, then laughed conspiratorially.

'I do. Oh, the boss and I will get our balls chewed off but we're getting used to that now.'

'We'll make a mess, chief,' said Wilson.

'Nothing that can't be put right, Jimmy.'

'Then roll on tonight.'

'And now,' Witherspoole put in, 'a late addition to your weapons training. Let's all go down to the range.'

Chapter Eighteen

In five minutes they were at one of the many firing ranges where targets were already set up and several funny-looking guns lay on the ground. Next to them were some odd items and a pile of newspapers, and as they arrived the anonymous face of an instructor emerged from the forest and without offering a name, went straight into his lecture.

'This,' he held up one of the guns, 'is a silenced Sten gun. It has all of the characteristics of the Stens you used in earlier training, but with some modifications. The barrel is shorter and perforated to release the gases quicker. This reduces the bullet's velocity but obviously not enough to lessen the damage it can cause. Reducing the velocity only means that it is subsonic and not supersonic. Supersonic causes the bang when the bullet goes through the sound barrier, while being subsonic there is no bang. Notice that the barrel is entirely surrounded by a casing. This casing contains a series of baffles which shuffle the gases back and forth until they lose their velocity, and then release them at normal atmospheric pressure and without noise. It is preferable to use the gun in single shots. The reason for this is that the bullets release gases quicker than the baffles can release them, and firing a whole magazine of thirty-two bullets can build up too much pressure inside the casing. However, in an emergency you can release the whole magazine at once, but it means that you must allow two or three minutes for the gases to disperse before you fire another, and that could be dangerous, depending on your situation. So, having said that, let's have a trial run.'

'Are these an innovation?' Sherman asked.

'Not new,' Witherspoole shook his head, 'just damned difficult to get hold of. They are made primarily for commandos and are on the secret list. We are unofficial and looked on as a bunch of boy scouts, so to get anything at all we have to beg, borrow or steal it. Getting hold of these took a lot of begging.'

The modified Stens made little more than a *pop* when fired. They were easy to hold and ripped the targets to shreds.

'They must never fall into the hands of the enemy,'

the instructor emphasised. 'I'd sooner you left a wounded man behind than one of these.'

Dozens of magazines were expended while they got the feel of the gun and the instructor was satisfied they were proficient, then they went on to another, although it looked more like a piece of plumbing than a gun.

'This is even more secret than the silenced Sten,' the instructor said, holding it up.

About fifteen inches long and two inches in diameter, only the stock, practically at right angles to the barrel, gave it any resemblance to a weapon. Two or three inches projected behind the stock, into which was a large knurled screw.

'. . . and is even more silent than the Sten. It is called the Welrod, an assassin's weapon, and fires either a 7.65 or nine-millimetre Short cartridge. Being silent it is obviously subsonic and the silencer is similar to the Sten with its baffles. The stock is the magazine and must be removed before reloading. This operation is simple. To unlock turn back the knurled screw and pull. To load just push in and lock. It is a single-shot weapon with two or three seconds' delay between each shot so make sure the first shot is effective. Okay, who wants first go?'

The Welrod was an SOE invention. Unhappy with being treated with disdain by the regular security organisations SOE had approached several gunsmiths in London, who before the war were renowned for manufacturing shotguns for the rich and famous, and asked them to come up with some weird inventions. The gunsmiths agreed and were whisked away with their tools to a secret workshop at Welwyn Garden City, where they met with a great disappointment. The workshop was there but no machinery. Nor could the gunsmiths' own machinery be used. Theirs was designed only to make shotguns and the weapons SOE was asking for called for a completely different design.

SOE was unperturbed. Armed with a list of requirements, agents located the required machinery in different parts of the country, owned by private concerns, and simply stole them with the intention of returning them at the end of the war. From then on the workshop turned out an endless supply of inventions that would help its agents in the field.

The Welrod was easy to use. Each of the group fired a score of shots and after the first four were surprisingly accurate.

Other weapons to appear were a spring-loaded metal cosh, a spike and knuckleduster combined, a flick-knife and commando hunting knife.

'Most people carry a weapon of some sort without realising it,' the instructor told them. 'A newspaper, for example: how many people realise that a newspaper can break a man's jaw or his ribs?'

Most heads shook, except Razor Eddie's. 'I've used it before,' he said.

'Ah, a Glaswegian. That's where it came from as it happens. Perhaps you would care to demonstrate?'

Razor Eddie nodded and came to the front, chose a *Daily Express*, folded it in half then rolled it into a tight cylindrical shape.

'Got to be rolled tight,' he said, holding it up like a truncheon. 'John,' he walked to Hancock, 'I won't hurt you. I'll just show you.'

The others looked on with an almost child-like curiosity as Razor Eddie tapped Hancock on the jaw with the end of the rolled-up newspaper. Hancock jerked his head back and touched his jaw.

'Hell!'

'And our friend only tapped him,' the instructor smiled. 'Imagine the result had it been applied with great force. A very clever invention that. It comes from the days of the large gangs that once terrorised Glasgow. They used razors for a while but the courts handed out ten and fifteen-year sentences for using razors and that died a death. Well, the gangs wanted something to defend themselves with and someone devised the rolled-up newspaper, and after that the police were powerless to arrest anyone carrying an offensive weapon. How could they arrest a group of people standing innocently at a street corner carrying a copy of the daily newspaper? Now the ribs, old son.'

Again Razor Eddie approached Hancock. He held the newspaper in front of him like a ram and pushed slightly. Hancock made a face when it prodded his ribcage. 'Used with force it can cave in a ribcage,' the instructor said, taking the newspaper from Razor Eddie. 'Okay, each of you take a newspaper and roll it up, then practise on each other. Watch your opponent's face. His face will tell you if it hurt. Go to it.'

For the following ten minutes the group went at each other hammer and tongs. There were thuds and grunts and one or two got carried away, tempers rising, trying to hurt each other, until the instructor called a halt.

'A pencil,' he said, 'an ordinary pencil is also a lethal weapon. Hold it between your fingers like a cigarette and let the end without the point fall into your palm . . .' he held up his hand to demonstrate. 'There is no need to grip the pencil tightly between your fingers: just use them to hold it steady, then punch as if you were delivering a blow. I won't ask you to practice on each other, though, for obvious reasons. A pencil does some horrible damage.

'Another weapon is the ordinary, everyday household key. Every key has a sharp edge or sharp corner of some kind. Held correctly and swiped across a person's face it will slice a deep cut. It's just as effective as the open razor, and to get that effect hold it between two fingers and clench your fist . . . like so.

'Now if and when you become involved in hand-to-hand combat and your opponent knows a few tricks, regular methods may not be applicable to the occasion so we resort to dirty tricks. Some of these you may or may not already know, and for those who don't it might come as a surprise. I've no doubt that the karate lessons surprised you all. You probably were amazed at how the human body could be used to inflict so much pain and injury: well, the dirty tricks department can be just as amazing.

'Imagine you are grappling with someone and he is

getting the better of you. He is much bigger and stronger and has you in a corner. You are unable to deliver a karate blow. Your back is to a wall and his bulk prevents you moving. What do you do? You're kicking and punching with no effect and sooner or later his strength will come out on top. Well, for all he is bigger and stronger he has the same weak spot as everyone else. Do you know what it is?'

'His cobblers,' Wilson called out.

'He has his leg covering that area.'

'His nose,' said Razor Eddie.

'Right! No matter how strong or powerful a man might be, his nose is no different to another. You go for his nose. Using the heel of your hand as a ram, push it up under his nose as hard as you can. If brought up from the waist the results are very messy indeed. As well as drawing a lot of blood, his nose will be completely smashed, he will be blinded for several minutes and he will feel as if someone has driven a spike through his head. You can practise this, but only gently. Just a tap will be enough to convince you of the effects . . .'

Never was a truer word spoken. Some tapped a little harder than others and one or two nursed a painful spot for a few moments.

'You can also push your fingers up his nose and pull hard: and there is nothing more frightening for a man than to look down and see his nostrils in shreds. Don't worry about the snot on your fingers,' the instructor added with a wry smile, 'you can always eat that afterwards if you're hungry.

'The eyes. Two well-aimed fingers stabbed in the eyes will not only blind him, it will also put the fear of Christ up him. His eyes will swell and be extremely painful, which will last for a few days before returning to normal. But he doesn't know that. When it happens he will imagine that he is blinded for life and the war won't mean a thing. His only thought will be for his eyes.

'And the throat: another vital area. Although a chop on the throat is most effective, the fingertips are more so. The chop, whilst delivering a painful blow, actually spreads the blow over a wide area which means that the force behind the blow is not concentrated in one spot. The fingertips concentrate the force. Don't jab. Hold your arm in front of you with your hand perfectly straight and flat, fingers close together and flick your hand as you would a whip so that the fingertips hit the throat in an arc, like so . . .

'And if someone has you from behind there are two main methods of forcing him to release you. Anyone care to volunteer?'

Steve Hopkins came forward and the instructor invited him to come at him from behind, putting a lock on his neck.

'One method is the unexpected. Just let yourself fall . . .' the instructor did just that. Hopkins bent forward to keep his grip, lost his balance and an instant later found himself on the ground with the instructor on top of him.

'It is a natural reaction to try to get out of a neck-lock by pulling on the arm or using your elbows on his rib-cage, and generally your opponent will expect this. But he will rarely expect you to fall. If you let your body become a dead weight he will either have to go down with it and by doing so will become off-balance, or release you. Either way he has lost the advantage and you're in there like a dose of Epsoms giving him some hockey.

'Another method is to run your heel down his shin: that is, if you're wearing heavy shoes or boots. Don't kick behind you. Although it hurts, your opponent can hang on, and within a few moments choke the life out of you. But – if I can demonstrate with our friend here – you do this,' he dragged his heel down Hopkins' shin, causing the recruit to yell out, 'you will make him experience the most excruciating pain and the body's natural reaction will be for the hands to go down to protect the injured part. At that point you make him sprout wings.

'Now, I want you to imagine you are creeping up on

a sentry, or someone who is between you and your objective. You have no weapons. You might even be wounded. You must kill this bloke and you can't become involved in hand-to-hand, nor must there be any struggle. Any ideas?'

Everyone looked at everyone else, lifting their shoulders in defeat.

'What about you, old son?' the instructor asked Razor Eddie. 'You've possibly used it.'

'The ears?' Razor Eddie suggested.

'Spot on! It's another street-fighter's ploy. You creep up behind him like so . . .' he demonstrated on Hopkins once more, but gently, 'and smack the palms of your hands over his ears, both at the same time. You don't need a great lot of force, and anyway it is difficult to swing both arms at the same time with any great measure of force. But it will do the trick. It will deafen him for a while and can possibly burst his ear-drums. It will also completely disorientate him. He won't know where he is or what's happening. Deprived of his hearing he will stagger and lose his balance, falling like a drunk man and as helpless as a new-born babe. Then you strangle him. You can try that if you wish, but very, very gently, just to appreciate what it feels like. And of course there is always the good old kick in the cobblers, although I don't think any of you need training in that art.'

The training session finished and the instructor left as anonymously as he had arrived, and Morton took over.

'One or two more points before we call it a day, lads. It is quite possible that you will be pursued. You will be on foot and your pursuers most likely in vehicles of some sort; therefore, immobilise every vehicle you think might be used to chase after you. I'm not going to ask if anyone has any ideas. I'm going to tell you how to do it. Don't do what they do in Hollywood films, lifting the hood and pulling out a few wires. That's balderdash and only for effect. In films we see the stranded baddies cursing while they watch their prey speeding over the horizon, their own transport at a standstill. That doesn't happen in war. In war spares are kept in the cabin and items like distributor caps and plug leads can be replaced in a matter of seconds.

'What you do is go for the parts that actually propel the vehicle. You go for the engine, the gearbox and wheels. If you are limited for time, slash all the tyres on the vehicles. A car carries one spare, a truck perhaps two, which can be changed fairly quickly by experienced mechanics, but all four will mean having replacements brought in from somewhere else. That can take hours.

'You can put sugar or sand in the sump and ruin the bearings. You can drain the sump and gearbox which will cause the moving parts to seize after a mile or two. You can snap off or bend the steering column or, if you have a heavy hammer handy, smash the cylinder head. Cast metal is very brittle and breaks easily.'

On their return to the boat a sharp smell of paint drifted up the hatch. The corking was complete and a gang of workmen were adding the final touch: painting the inside white.

'Bloody hell!' Wilson swore. 'What's all this for?'

'To maintain good light, Jimmy,' said Woolcott. 'If we get attacked and thrown about lights break at an alarming rate. If that happens the white paint will reflect whatever light we have.'

'With them fumes we'll all end up pissed.'

Woolcott laughed and turned to listen to Morris who was talking to Sherman.

'Don't submarines have names, chief?'

Sherman nodded. 'They're no different from any other craft. When they're launched they're given a name.'

'What was this one called?'

'The *Burgot*.'

'The whatgot?'

'The *Burgot*. All American boats are named after fish.'

'But we ain't an American boat no more, and we should have a name.'

Sherman thought for a moment and agreed. 'You're right. Hey, Oliver, how are British boats named?'

'Depends on the class,' Woolcott replied. 'My last boat was one of the 'U' class. The 'U' class had names prefixed with that letter, like *Unbroken, Undaunted, Unbending, Unrivalled*, and so on.'

'Yeah,' Morris pursed his lips, 'then with the way we're being treated we ought to be called the *Unwanted*.'

Sherman and Woolcott stared at Morris for a second then turned to face each other. Both were smiling.

'I like it,' said Sherman.

'Spot on!' said Woolcott.

'Hey, you guys!' Sherman spoke to those closest to the control room. 'See what the others think . . .'

In no time replies came back and the boat was thereby christened the *Unwanted*.

Chapter Nineteen

Snow was falling when the time came to leave. Everything was ready. The boat was fuelled, the fresh water tanks filled and sufficient food put aboard to last three months. Small items previously overlooked were brought by Witherspoole and Morton who spent the afternoon running back and forth, and who by now looked more like a couple of barrow-boys from a market rather than controllers of a group of saboteurs and assassins. Their clothes were soiled and rumpled, their faces red and puffed from constant exertion and their general demeanour that of not having sold anything from the barrow all day.

'No tug this time, captain, I'm afraid,' Witherspoole said apologetically. 'You have to get used to narrow channels.'

'Understood, sir.'

'Well,' the older man was hesitant, 'it's time to go. I'll just wish everyone a safe trip.'

Together, Witherspoole and Morton went round the boat and shook each man by the hand, using a two-handed grip and holding tight. There was both sadness and anxiety in their eyes. They made their way back to the control room and faced Sherman.

'What can I say, captain,' Witherspoole fought back tears. His personal feelings were that they had less than a fifty-fifty chance of succeeding. 'Except good luck and good hunting.'

'We'll need all the luck going, sir. A couple of torpedoes would have helped.'

Witherspoole shook his head, his face apologetic. 'I couldn't even get you a deck gun, captain. Good God, I had to steal the engines.'

'You did what, sir?'

'It's true. A small diesel power station on the east coast was damaged in an air raid and the electricity people decided not to use it any more. I heard about it and sent some of my staff along to see what they could find, and back they came with trucks loaded with your engines, motors and generators. The electricity people aren't very happy, I'm told. I couldn't get anything else. I'm sorry.'

'We'll do our best, sir.'

'Yes, you can't do any more.'

'Well, goodbye, sir.'

'What's that?' Morton pointed above the hatchway leading forward.

Sherman laughed. Above the hatchway in large letters written in blue chalk was *UNWANTED*. Where the blue chalk had come from mystified Sherman.

'Our new name, sir.'

'Appropriate,' Witherspoole nodded. 'Appropriate.'

'One final piece of advice,' said Morton, 'is to follow certain basic rules. One: if you follow someone, don't be seen yourself. Two: if you are captured and interrogated, keep your mouth shut. Three: if you ever have to change your identity, be bloody good at it. And four:

the best way to escape is to be bloody quick about it. Other rules you make up as you go along.'

A diesel roared. Witherspoole and Morton took the cue and moved to the conning tower ladder. They took a last look round, then climbed up out of sight.

'Prepare to cast off!' Sherman called over the tannoy.

Men leapt from the fore and aft deck hatches and slipped the mooring ropes.

'Slow ahead. Steer five degrees.'

Very slowly the boat moved out of the covered shed and into the Beaulieu River. The deck had a light covering of snow and in the forest around them the scene could have come straight from a Christmas card.

Both Sherman and Woolcott climbed to the conning tower to superintend their departure, and apart from passing instructions down the voice-tube they were silent for some time.

'How do you feel, Oliver?' Sherman asked as the stern of the boat eased out of the shed.

'Apprehensive: afraid, maybe. When I had a command I stood here just like this and felt excited, wishing I could get on with it. I had full naval backing then which I think gave me confidence, but this is different. We only have the backing of two worried civilians who work on a shoestring budget and who can't call on assistance if they need it. The last time I went out, there was a parade of brass on the quay to see me off, all smiling and sure of everything they were doing. But there's nothing sure about this job. I mean, look at our brass . . .'

The boat was in mid-river following the course of the dredged channel. Snow was still falling and both sides of the river were deserted except for two lonely, anxious men standing together watching them depart. Their arms were tucked inside their jackets, hands under their armpits, feet stamping on the ground to keep warm, their faces mere black blobs against a white background.

'I've got the same feeling, Oliver, and I think I know how they feel. They're thinking that we won't come back. Everything's against us.'

Woolcott nodded in the dark but Sherman was looking downriver.

'But dammit to hell, Oliver,' Sherman suddenly snapped, 'we'll see to it that we will come back!'

'That's the ticket, sir.'

'Hey, Oliver,' Sherman turned, 'we don't need the *Sir*. I'm not an officer in any navy now.'

'I don't think that that would be the right thing to do, sir. One must have respect for rank.'

Sherman stayed silent for what seemed to be an age before replying. 'Let's do a deal, Oliver. When we're together I'm Roger. When we're with the crew I can be the captain: okay?'

'A deal,' Woolcott smiled.

They were approaching a sharp bend in the river at Gilbery's Hard and conversation stopped while Sherman manoeuvred them slowly round. A fairly straight section along Fiddlers Reach followed then another bend at Lower Exbury Point, and the final stretch which took them into the Solent and at last the English Channel.

'Half ahead!'

The boat picked up speed in an instant and burst through the first wave.

'Engine revolutions to twenty-two knots.'

Again the boat surged forward.

'At least this is a feeling I like,' Woolcott commented.

Sherman drew a deep breath. 'I know exactly how you feel.'

First on lookout duty were Paca and Jefferson. Wrapped in thick duffle coats with scarves around the lower half of their faces they were anonymous. Their hands appeared gigantic, covered in gloves three times normal thickness, which made the glasses held to their eyes seem tiny.

'Surface craft ahead, sir,' Jefferson reported.

Both Sherman and Woolcott lifted their own glasses and peered into the gloom. Perhaps a mile in front were three submarines abreast of each other heading for the Atlantic.

'What are they, Oliver?'

'The regular U-Class, sir. Probably on their way to the Med.'

'Shall we give them a demonstration?'

'Why not?'

'Okay,' Sherman lowered his face to the voice-tube. 'All engines full ahead, maximum speed!'

'Jesus!' Paca swore from his position. The boat surged forward as if it had been pushed from behind, nearly throwing him off-balance.

'Hell's bells!' Woolcott could not help exclaiming.

A high wake shot up at the stern as the screws thrashed the water and the bow seemed to lift itself clear of the surface, coming down with a thud that shook the boat from one end to the other.

'I was afraid of this,' said Sherman.

'What's that?' asked Woolcott.

'These boats were badly designed. They don't have the shark-nosed bow, but are perpendicular and tend to hit waves like a brick wall at high speeds.'

Woolcott understood and said: 'Perhaps we shouldn't push it then.'

Sherman shook his head. 'We might be in a situation where we have to high-tail it out of somewhere, so we might as well get used to it now.'

They were catching up on the boats ahead.

'Speed?' Sherman called down the tube.

'Twenty-eight knots, sir!'

'This will make them sit up and take notice,' Sherman chuckled, then told the others below what he was doing.

Woolcott estimated the U-Class boats to be doing around fourteen knots and he could see the lookouts turning round to watch the larger, faster boat rapidly approaching.

'They don't know what to make of us,' he said, beginning to feel excited.

Officers were appearing on the towers of the three boats, all wondering where the devil the boat had come from.

The *Unwanted* bounced. From the towers of the three boats its pace resembled a speed-boat flicking over the top of waves. As it dropped a heavy wash was thrown out from both sides, seeming to pull the boat under the surface. One moment the decks were completely awash and the next the long cigar shape was nearly in mid-air, threatening to take off like a rocket.

Below, the crew held on tight. The pitching of the boat had already thrown equipment about. Thunderous noises echoed from one end to the other as waves crashed against the boat. Tommy Stone gripped a beam so hard the whites of his knuckles showed through, his eyes screwed shut with tear droplets forcing their way from the corners. George Wythe held on with one hand, the other reassuringly around the boy's shoulders, shouting above the noise that it was just the equivalent of road noise. The boy never heard him. Nor was the boy alone in his fear. They weren't on trials any more. This was the real thing and if it was an example of what was to come the future was nothing to look forward to.

Sherman steered them between the two boats farthest from the shore, the wash lifting the other boats high in the water, causing them to list to one side, then falling back suddenly to rock onto an even keel.

A lamp aboard one of the boats blinked in code.

'Any idea what it says, Oliver?'

'Wouldn't have a clue, sir, but I should imagine it isn't complimentary.'

Rush Stockton on wireless operating duty, head-phones hugging his ears, announced that one of the boats was transmitting a signal.

'What's it say?' Wilson shouted across to him.

Stockton just shook his head. 'Gobbledygook,' he replied.

The commander in charge of the small flotilla was in the process of contacting Portsmouth, demanding to know what fool had done the equivalent of push him off the road. He added that its speed was phenomenal.

Portsmouth did not know. Staff at the wireless station had a list of traffic covering the eight-hour period from

1200 hours to 2000 hours, and to their knowledge the three boats should have been the only vessels of any kind in that vicinity.

London was contacted by telephone, the Admiralty disclaiming all knowledge of a boat capable of twice the speed of the conventional U-Class and asked for a description. A description was provided, and as it still meant nothing the Admiralty gave instructions for the boat to be sunk.

By the time the instructions reached the commander of the flotilla the *Unwanted* was out of sight, miles away hidden in a snowstorm, its speed reduced to twenty-two knots to conserve fuel but still eight knots faster than those chasing her.

'That'll give them something to think about,' Sherman smiled in the dark.

Woolcott agreed, but added: 'They've probably reported us and there might be a dozen ships looking for us by now with orders to sink us on sight.'

'They've got to catch us first,' Sherman said with a touch of confidence, then leaning over the tube said: 'HE report!'

The reply came back almost immediately.

'Nothing, sir. Weather too rough.'

'Good.'

That was something anyway. Asdic was used to detect other vessels in the area, although generally referred to by the original Hydrophone Effect. It was only effective in calm or moderate weather as in rough weather the bouncing signals could not tell the difference between a ship or submarine and a wave.

'How do we split the watches, sir?' Woolcott asked all of a sudden. It was something that had been bugging him.

'What's that?'

'We only have two officers, sir. We need five or at least four watchkeeping officers.'

Sherman thought about it. 'Who would you suggest?'

Woolcott told him.

'Fair enough,' once again Sherman leaned down to the tube.

'Mr Kean and Mr Rutledge up-top please.'

'Rutledge,' Sherman said when they were on the tower, 'you have been appointed the equivalent of sub-lieutenant, third in order of rank behind myself and Mr Woolcott. Kean, you will also assume the equivalent rank of sub-lieutenant, fourth in order of rank. From now on both of you will take charge of a watch – two hours on and four hours off. While you are up-top either myself or Mr Woolcott will be below. You got that?'

'Yes, sir,' the newly appointed officers replied in unison.

Thomas Kean was taken by surprise. At twenty-five he had already seen six years' service as an AB with the navy, deserting twice because the life had not lived up to his expectations. Kean had been born on a farm in Yorkshire and being used to an outdoor life found being confined to an overcrowded mess not to his liking. On being recaptured following his first desertion he had spent three months locked in solitary confinement, nearly going mad in the process. On his release the navy, being what it was, imagined he had learned a lesson, and gave him a posting to Rosyth in Scotland, with a railway travel warrant and instructed him to report to the commander there within three days.

Kean never reached Rosyth. He went to Leeds, sold the travel warrant and joined the criminal fraternity of the city, where John Morton found him and struck a one-sided deal.

He looked every inch country-bred, being muscular and ruddy-faced with large calloused hands and red hair. Before the *Unwanted* the nearest Kean had been to a submarine was when they passed his ship, and then they were generally some way off, and here he was, he thought, in charge of one for several hours in every twenty-four.

Rutledge gave the matter no more thought. If they

put him in charge they put him in charge. He didn't care. One job was no different from another.

To date Rutledge hadn't said too much about himself. All he had said so far was that he'd been at Dunkirk: nothing more. Some of the others thought he was a bit odd – although he hadn't hung back in the corridor or any other part of the training. He was educated, they knew that from his speech, but hadn't yet discovered why he was an embarrassment to society.

'Mr Woolcott and I are going below,' Sherman said. 'You keep first watch, Mr Rutledge.'

'Yes, sir.'

In the control room Sherman unfolded several charts and with Woolcott began plotting their course.

'You know these waters better than I do, Oliver. What do you reckon?'

Woolcott knew nothing about the waters other than what he'd learned while training, but suggested a practical course: 150 miles off-shore around Cape Finisterre, well out of sight of boats patrolling the French coast.

For the present they steered into the middle of the Channel. At least there they would have some privacy. German shipping hugged the coast on the French side of the Channel and British shipping on the opposite side, leaving the middle comparatively free.

Five hours went by and the further they went towards the Atlantic the rougher the sea. At twenty-two knots the boat crashed and buffeted the way it had earlier at twenty-eight knots, forcing Sherman to reduce to a more manageable seventeen knots, allowing the tired and seasick to sleep.

At midnight Woolcott, relieved by Sherman, climbed down into the warmth of the boat, realising then just how cold it was up-top. The stench of vomit hit him. It was vile and he choked to keep his stomach from turning over. But it was to be expected. No matter how good a sailor a man might be, he might never conquer seasickness. There was nothing anyone could do about it other than hope the nervous system would become used to it. The smell of vomit, however, was something one never became used to.

He began a tour of the boat and found a good many asleep. Some were still, enjoying a trouble-free slumber, while others, tormented by something in their past, tossed and turned and moaned aloud.

Before long they would all be tossing and turning. The narrow bunks were fresh for the time being but as the days went by, particularly when below the surface, they would begin to stink. The bedding on the bunks comprised only a mattress designed to fit the narrow confines, a tiny pillow and a blanket. As a man left the bunk to take his watch another climbed in to take his place, lying in his predecessor's sweat, and sometimes his body waste, and having very reluctantly to accept that hygiene was not possible.

Man, Woolcott decided, was an extremely adaptable animal. At home he would sprawl all over his bed to find the most comfortable sleeping position, be out of touch with the world for up to nine hours, yet in the morning complain that he had a restless night. There was no sprawling aboard a submarine. The bunks were often no more than eighteen inches wide and rarely long enough for a man to lie at full stretch. Worse, the pressure hull curved over some bunks, making it impossible for a man to turn. He was forced to lie on his side facing inboard, knees slightly bent and his upper shoulder touching the curve of the pressure hull. Before the introduction of cork as a lining men often developed rheumatism as a result of their shoulder being constantly wedged against the nearly freezing hull.

If that was not enough there was the pipework. Woolcott hadn't bothered to enquire how much there was, but he imagined there must have been miles of pipework of varying bores aboard the average boat. For ease of design the pipework generally followed the most direct route from a delivery point to destination. Bunks, the item given the least thought, were installed wherever there was enough room, and if there was twelve inches of space between two banks of pipework a bunk was installed there. A man slid between the pipes, found the most comfortable position and closed his eyes, sometimes using the pipes above him to wedge himself when the boat rocked.

And men slept. The conditions would become abominable, unacceptable at first, but as time went on and relief followed terror they would climb into the bunks as if they were giant four-posters and sleep undisturbed. Others could be a few feet away singing and swearing: they would walk past, bumping into them, yet they would sleep.

Yes, Woolcott thought, man was a most adaptable creature.

The engineers were asleep alongside their charges, seemingly oblivious to the thundering roar they gave off. All engineers were like that, though. After a few hours they didn't hear the noise, but eventually it would leave them deaf as a post.

They already looked the part of experienced engineers. They wore a singlet, shorts and plimsolls. Oil mixed with sweat glistened on their skin, staining their bedding and clothing. Their mouths were wide open drawing in diesel-tainted air, yet there was still something peaceful about the way they lay.

Woolcott went forward, nodding to anyone who had an eye open, then returned to the control room, asking quietly: 'What's our position?'

'Approaching the end of the Channel, sir. The Ile d'Ouessant should be over that way . . .' a thumb jerked in the direction of the tiny galley.

Woolcott nodded and headed for his own bunk. The Ile d'Ouessant wasn't far from where he'd picked up the two Frenchmen and lost his command. Attempting to forget that night he climbed into his bunk and lay for some time before sleep came.

Chapter Twenty

An alarm came at 0250 hours. Woolcott, his mind primed for submarine warfare, hurtled himself from his bunk and into the control room. Before his feet had touched the floorplates the engines had stopped, and by the time he paced the few steps to the control room the lookouts and Kean were already down, Kean fastening the stirrups on the lower lid.

'Lids secure, sir.'

'Periscope depth,' Sherman said, his eyes slightly tired. Like Woolcott he'd come as he was: singlet and underpants and without shoes or socks.

'Periscope depth, sir.'

'Twenty seconds, sir,' a voice said.

Sherman made no comment on the diving time. His eyes were already glued to the periscope sights and sweeping the ocean above.

'U-boats,' he said, 'dozens of them, for God's sake.'

'There's a U-boat base at Brest,' Woolcott told him.

'Have a look, Oliver.'

Woolcott took over and gasped with awe. There must have been thirty of them, probably all heading for the North Atlantic. He watched them for ten or fifteen seconds and was about to order the periscope lowered when something else caught his eye. A small destroyer, previously hidden among the flotilla, had fallen back and was turning towards them. A large white wash at its bows told him that the destroyer's commander had ordered full speed.

'Enemy craft approaching!' he yelled out. 'Range!'

'Five thousand yards, sir.'

'Estimated speed?'

'Twenty-one knots, sir.'

'You wish to look, sir?' Woolcott lifted his eyes to Sherman.

Sherman shook his head. He had no experience of a war. Woolcott had and he wasn't about to question his judgment.

'Take her down to 250 feet,' he said, then quietly: 'Now we'll see if she can go below her designed working depth.'

Faces turned towards him. They recalled Witherspoole telling them that the boat had been designed to operate at a maximum of 150 feet. The boat had been strengthened but the parts of the English Channel where they'd carried out sea-trials hadn't been 250 feet deep.

'Group up,' he gave the order to increase speed. 'Maximum revs.'

The giant motors whined as power from the batteries surged into their windings. The boat shuddered as if someone was using it as a whip. The hull creaked as the pressure on the outside, increasing with every foot they dropped, caused the boat to shrink in size. Woolcott issued orders to correct their trim as they went down. Earlier he had tried to explain to some of the crew the intricacies of the submarine. They found it difficult to understand that as they went deep ballast had to be pumped from tanks at times to counteract shrinkage. And it had taken time to have them accept that boats did become smaller underwater.

As Number One it was his job to look after the boat's trim. Explosions could be taking place around them and he had to shut his ears off to them, concentrating on depths, pressures and ballast movements.

A muffled *kroomp* heralded the first depth-charge. It was some way off but the shock waves reached the boat and rocked it slightly, giving them a taste of what was to come.

The explosions came closer, each rocking the boat more than the last, until they were like a puppet on the end of a string. One explosion, very close, pushed the boat over on a sixty-degree angle. The crew were thrown against pipework and the edges and corners of equipment, screaming out with fear unashamedly, clutching onto anything that might give them support. The boat quickly found an even keel as the blast went by, throwing them back to their original positions, and again hurtling them painfully against solid objects.

The attack was over quickly. Above, the attacker was making the statutory circular sweep. Sherman imagined the commander on his bridge estimating how far the boat could travel in a given time at top speed, and he would base his estimation on eight knots maximum.

'Speed?'

'16.7 knots, sir.'

Sherman nodded and smiled. It was double what the enemy commander would be working on.

Explosions were still frequent but less violent, fading with the minutes then returning as the sweep continued, although not close enough to cause damage. Soon they were distant.

'Group down,' Sherman ordered and the whining eased.

They were safe for the time being. The enemy commander would never envisage a submerged boat travelling at normal surface speed.

Damage reports came. The boat was intact but Charlie Carroll was hurt. He had been thrown against the sharp corner of a panel and his face was ripped open.

'See what you can do with him, Oliver,' said Sherman. Traditionally the coxswain looked after wounds and ailments but since the boat was all but devoid of rank Woolcott was allotted the task.

Woolcott grimaced. He didn't like what he saw. 'I can't recall reading anything in the red book about this,' he said.

The red book was the navy's medical text book, explaining in detail what to do and when, but its scope was limited.

Sherman narrowed his eyes when he saw what Woolcott was getting at. Carroll's left cheek was torn open and they could see the teeth in his lower jaw through the hole. Parts of the flesh hung in shreds and blood poured from both the wound and his mouth.

'It needs surgery,' Woolcott looked up, 'stitching and God knows what else. I wouldn't know how to do that.'

'Christ!' Sherman swore, 'I knew this would turn into a disaster.'

From the hydrophone station Edward Rutledge looked on. He opened his mouth once or twice to speak then thought better of it.

'Stitch it then,' Carroll said through a froth of red bubbles, blood spattering Woolcott as he spoke.

'How?' Woolcott clenched his fists with despair. 'I don't know how. God! I could give you an infection and make it worse.'

'Do something, for Christ's sake! Use sticky-bloody-tape if you have to.'

Woolcott looked helplessly at Sherman.

'I'll do it, sir,' Rutledge said from his station. He was breathing heavily, having had to build up enough courage to speak.

'You can do it?'

'I've done something like it before, sir.'

'Do it, man!' Sherman said quickly.

'I need some equipment,' Rutledge came off his swivel stool. 'Needles and thread, pliers, boiling water, alcohol, cotton-wool and a sharp pair of scissors.'

'Do it!' Sherman snapped.

Most of the crew had come to see Carroll and were crowded around the control room, perched on pipes or pieces of equipment.

'Get him onto a bunk,' said Rutledge.

Wythe began boiling water and from the engine room came an assortment of pliers. Rutledge told Lynch, the Irishman, to kneel by the bunk and hold a tray at chest height.

'Now,' Rutledge said, 'when the water boils I want some of it poured over the tray. Then I want a piece of clean cloth placed on the tray and boiling water poured over that.'

Rutledge then went to the galley and supervised a second container of boiling water.

'Listen very closely,' he told Wythe, 'because it's

important. One lot of water will be poured over the tray and cloth and the second used to sterilise the equipment I shall use. When I begin all the equipment will be in boiling water, and as I need it I'll call out. I want you to clean your hands and douse them in alcohol, find yourself a soup ladle and sterilise that also then stand by. Use the ladle to take the stuff from the water and don't touch it with your hands. I shall take it from the ladle. You got that?'

Wythe nodded.

Everything Rutledge ordered was soon beside him. First he inspected the pliers. They were covered in oil. Using some of the medicinal alcohol he cleaned them as best he could then dropped them into the boiling water. Next the scissors were tested and dropped into the water, followed by three needles still on a piece of card, and finally a reel of cotton.

Again he washed his hands, doused them with alcohol and asked Lynch to take his place once more. Lynch knelt, holding the tray in front of him, and Rutledge called for Wythe to pour boiling water over it.

'Now the cloth.'

The cloth was a piece torn from a clean shirt belonging to Sherman.

'Pour off the residue,' said Rutledge when boiling water had been poured over it. 'And give me the cotton-wool and alcohol, someone.'

Using the alcohol-soaked cotton-wool swabs Rutledge began to clean Carroll's face. Carroll did not seem to feel anything for he made no sounds, and in fact tried to drop his eyes far enough to watch what was being done.

'Keep still,' Rutledge told him.

Very gently Rutledge lifted hanging flesh with the fingers of one hand and brushed the swab over it with the other. He took his time, ensuring every speck of dirt and oil was removed, then slowly opened Carroll's mouth to do the inside.

'Hell,' Rutledge looked up from his kneeling position.

I forgot a torch. Get me a torch for Christ's sake, someone!'

A torch came almost immediately. Rutledge told the holder to aim it into Carroll's mouth and went on working, leaning close to the injured man's face and tasting his foul breath. It took much longer this time. On the outside the blood was able to run away but inside it was congealing and more difficult to remove: and it had to be removed lest there be contaminants in it.

'Needles, thread and pliers!' Rutledge called out when he was satisfied the inside of Carroll's mouth was clean.

A path was made for Wythe who appeared gingerly toting his soup ladle. Using two fingers Rutledge quickly transferred them to the tray, then said. 'Pour boiling water over the tray again.'

The onlookers were filled with admiration for Rutledge. Without hurrying he threaded all three needles and laid them on the tray. He held out his hands and Sherman doused them with alcohol.

'Close your eyes, Charlie,' Rutledge said, 'and just let your head roll free. I shall want to move it to suit and I don't want you to be fighting against me.'

'Okay, doc,' Carroll attempted to joke.

'I'm going to do the inside of your mouth first. It will feel very uncomfortable but don't try to fight. It's not a very big area for me to work in and it must be done quickly. You got that?'

'Okay, doc,' Carroll mumbled.

Rutledge took hold of a set of pliers, held them up for dousing then used them to lift one of the threaded needles. The pliers were then inserted in Carroll's mouth where, working furiously, he proceeded to pull the shreds of flesh together. On the outside nothing appeared to be happening. The needle never came through. All the onlookers could see was Rutledge's fingers in Carroll's mouth and the tails of the pliers moving back and forth.

'Got to do it from both sides,' he said, giving a

commentary. 'If I don't it will reduce the stretch . . .' he completed another stitch, '. . . of that side of his face . . . and make him a bit lopsided. Scissors!'

He snipped the cotton off and wiped his brow. 'That's the inside done. The worst part's over. This side will be much easier.'

Again his fingers went to work, like a seamstress late in finishing a garment. 'Get me some sticking plaster, about a four-inch square of pink lint – double thick, Vaseline, and mix some hand soap and sugar into a paste.'

No one said a word. They just looked on with awe. Rutledge had never said much about himself and often the others had wondered if he was going to be the odd man out. But this: what he was doing now was commanding their respect.

'Okay,' he said, snipping the thread for the last time, 'that's it. I know it looks like a tailor's nightmare but under the circumstances it's the best we can do.'

The bleeding had stopped, which alone seemed to make the situation appear much less serious than it was. Someone applauded, it was picked up by others and in seconds the boat was resounding to claps and cheers.

'Good on yer, mate!'

'Well done, fella!'

Rutledge prepared a dressing. He coated the injured area with Vaseline and laid the lint on top, unfolding it so that one half hung loose. In the fold he applied a layer of the sugar-soap mixture then brought the second half over, smoothing it down and finally holding it in place with sticking plaster.

'What the hell's the soap for?' Bill Ellery asked.

'The Vaseline should keep infection out,' Rutledge told him, 'but in an environment like this where germs breed like rabbits, it might not be quite sufficient. So, if the Vaseline doesn't do the trick and an infection does get in, it will be drawn out by the poultice. That's an old-time remedy.'

'Okay, you guys,' Sherman broke them up, 'back to your stations.'

With the crisis over Rutledge's hands were shaking. Nothing he could do would stop them.

'You need a drink,' Sherman said.

'Give it to Charlie, sir,' Rutledge sat on the edge of a bunk with his head in his hands. 'He's going to be sore later on so a good sleep now will do him a world of good.'

'Okay, you're the doc.'

Sherman brought a bottle of scotch from his tiny cabin and handed it to Rutledge who, his hands still shaking, made Carroll drink nearly a third of the bottle.

'I know it's asking the impossible,' he told Carroll, 'but try as much as you can to lie on your back. Keep your mouth open but still breathe through your nose. This will help to dry the wound and make it heal quicker. And I should warn you that when you wake up you'll have a sore jaw, but I think the captain might have something for that.'

'Sure have,' Sherman smiled.

'Now, Charlie, get some sleep. If there is another alarm I'll come and look after you . . . Will that be all right, sir?'

'You got it, Ed.'

Rutledge waited until Carroll fell asleep, albeit a drunken sleep, then rose. He was still shaking and Sherman invited him to come to the officers' wardroom.

'Take a seat, Ed, and have a drink,' Sherman poured a stiff measure of scotch into a mug and pushed it over to him, nodding to Woolcott to join them. Rutledge gulped fiery liquid down in one swallow and gasped. Another was poured out which he also took in one go, after which he began to stop shaking.

'Okay, Ed,' said Sherman, 'you're here because you done something someone else didn't like, the same reason the rest of us are here. Now, you don't have to tell anyone what it was if you don't want to, but you're not just an ordinary medic, are you?'

Rutledge had his hands joined on the small table-top.

He stared at them to avoid Sherman's eyes. After some agonising seconds he said: 'No, I'm not a medic. For a while I was recognised as a doctor and surgeon.'

'You want to tell us what went wrong, doc?'

'I'm not a doctor, sir. You shouldn't call me that.'

'With all due respect, doc, I make the decisions on this boat. If I say you're a doctor then you're a doctor.'

Rutledge lifted his shoulders then dropped them, still without looking up.

'I'd be mighty interested, doc. It's not that I'm prying: it's just that I'd like to know about the guy who might one day be asked to save *my* life.'

There was silence for several moments before Rutledge replied.

'I was in France during the phoney war, a high-ranking regimental surgeon, and got caught up in the retreat to Dunkirk. A field hospital I was in charge of was overrun by SS troops. Jesus, they slaughtered our boys. They just came in and murdered them – badly injured boys who couldn't have hurt a fly never mind a Nazi soldier! Several of my staff were killed before they were driven off, but I remembered a lot of their faces. A few days later I took over another field hospital and there in bed were some of those same SS troops, being looked after by a nurse they'd injured a few days before. Christ, I saw red. I remembered one evil bastard in particular. He gave the order to murder my patients and took a perverse pleasure in cutting their throats with his dagger. Imagine yourself on a hospital bed, helpless, your arms and legs bandaged, and this bastard comes at you with his dagger, laughing when he cuts your throat. He was in bed, not laughing, but demanding the staff get him this and get him that. I wasn't having it. I carried a revolver. I took it out and shot the swine: shot him through the head. I went for some of the others but my staff thought I'd gone off my head and took the gun off me. The next thing I knew I was in a bed myself.

'The other prisoners made a terrible racket and word soon reached the general commanding the retreat. He arrived on the scene and questions were asked. The prisoner-patients described in vivid detail what had happened and, when they were questioned, my staff had to admit they had also witnessed me shoot one of my patients. Security people had me back in London double-quick where I was struck off the register, charged with murder and kept in solitary confinement. I was tried in camera, found guilty and promised the rope. Then I was kept in solitary confinement again while my appeal was heard. Not that I wanted to appeal: lawyers decided that. I was sickened. The trial didn't disbelieve me when I told them about the massacre of injured men in the field hospital, but said it was inadmissible as evidence without witnesses. I had witnesses but they were never called to speak in my defence, because when questioned they couldn't make a firm identification of the murderers. But everyone remembered me. So, I stayed locked up. That is, until your Mr Morton came along and offered me a job.'

'Bastards!' Sherman swore.

'How did Morton talk the army into letting you go?' Woolcott asked.

'I've no idea. He just came into my cell and started talking. I accepted his offer – I would have accepted any offer to get out. He just called the guard and that was that. We left the place and I was eventually taken to the hotel in Wimbledon.'

'Will you become our doctor, Ed?' Sherman asked him.

'I'm no longer qualified, sir.'

'For a guy who's no longer qualified you did one helluva good job back there.'

'That was an emergency, sir.'

'Everything that happens aboard this boat will be an emergency, Ed, and we need someone to do the doctoring. Will you do it?'

'I'm not allowed to practise, sir.'

'As I said already, Ed, I make the decisions here. You're the best damned doctor I've come across and the British Medical Council or whatever it's called can go to hell. These guys have seen you at work and they'll trust you with their lives – me included.'

'And me,' Woolcott added.

'It's against the rules, sir.'

'What rules?' Sherman said quickly in reply. 'We were told to make up our own rules. What do you say?'

Rutledge lifted his head for the first time and nodded. 'I'll do it, sir,' there were tears in his eyes.

'Good for you, doc,' Sherman held out his hand. 'Now I reckon you should get some sleep yourself. You deserve it.'

'What about Charlie?'

'Someone will wake you if Charlie needs help.'

'Thank you, sir,' Rutledge rose and trudged back to his bunk.

'He's had a raw deal,' Sherman said when Rutledge had gone.

'Hasn't he ever,' Woolcott agreed, his eye catching sight of Wilson creeping past the wardroom, 'and I've a feeling everyone will know about it before very long.'

'What's it matter?' Sherman had also noticed Wilson. 'They'd have got it out of him sooner or later.'

'I suppose so.'

Sherman ordered them to periscope depth and took a sighting. The ocean was clear and seemed to have calmed.

'Check all main vents!' he called through the tannoy.

'All main vents closed, sir,' the reply came back.

'Surface! Lookouts up-top.'

Chapter Twenty-One

The approaches to the Bay of Biscay were remarkably calm, a fact Woolcott relayed to Sherman.

'Generally it's rough 364 days out of 365.'

'Maybe our first good omen, Oliver.'

'Or the lull before the storm.'

'You sleepy?'

'Not yet.'

'What's your honest opinion, Oliver. Do you think we'll succeed?'

Woolcott drew a deep breath before replying. 'If I was to comment on any other crew I wouldn't give them a snowball's chance in hell but we've seen the determination of these blokes and it gives me the sneaky feeling that we might just make it.'

'God, I hope to hell we do. I want to do something right for a change.'

'Oh?' Woolcott leaned across the small table of the wardroom just as young Stone brought in fresh tea.

'Thanks, Tommy,' said Sherman affably. 'How are you getting on with it so far?'

'I'm shit scared, sir.'

'Then that's nothing to be ashamed of, kid. I was shit scared myself when we were depth-charged.'

'You, sir?'

'Why not, Tommy? I'm no hero. I'm only an ordinary guy like yourself. I'm just a bit older with a few more stripes, that's all.'

Stone grinned and went off, his confidence boosted no end.

'Were you going to tell me something?' Woolcott asked when they were alone.

'You want to hear?'

'Why not? We've all done something wrong, as you so rightly said.'

'Well,' Sherman sighed, 'I'd question that I did something wrong, although my opinion was not asked for.'

'What happened?'

'Something similar to yourself. I was out from Portsmouth on a training exercise, and at the same time there was a review of the Atlantic Fleet going on off Newport News in the Chesapeake. You could have made a fortune out of the brass that was there. I wasn't due to return for another day and I'd a bunch of recruits with me. They generally went out on the old *Burgot* before being given a permanent posting. One of them took ill and at first I thought it was only a stomach bug, but the kid became worse and I began to suspect appendicitis. So, I signalled my base and detailed the symptoms. Doctor there confirmed it was his appendix.'

Sherman paused while he sipped his tea. 'I had to make a decision whether to cut short the exercise and take him in or wait while a launch came out to fetch him. Okay, I signalled base and asked for a launch. None available, they said. Everyone's tied up with the review. Hell, Oliver, I'd a guy howling with pain and there was nothing I could do about it. I decided the hell with them and headed back, right into the middle of the review. Goddammit I never saw so many ships. There seemed to be hundreds of them. They were all sailing to a pre-arranged pattern and unfortunately I ballsed it up. I pushed this old tub as hard as she would go, as I had a feeling if I didn't get my guy to hospital quick he was going to die. Apparently all the brass were going crazy, wanting to know who the madman was who was ballsing up their arrangements. God knows how many Aldis signals were sent to me, and the radio was jammed with angry commanders telling me to get the hell out of the place. I signalled by lamp and radio to let everyone know my predicament but they didn't seem to care. They told me get out of the area and wait until the God-damned review was over.

'I got bloody angry and kept on. The lovely lines of ships got messed up and before long there was sheer chaos. Three ships collided, one ran aground and another tore off a double-bottom on a sand-bar. I got alongside and, shit, I had to plead for an ambulance to take my guy to hospital. It was as if they didn't believe me. Well, anyway, my appearance turned the whole thing into a joke. Admirals were fighting each other to get at my throat, and then my wife put in her two cents worth.'

'Your wife? What did she have to do with it?'

'My wife is the daughter of one of the top admirals. I was the prize boy up until then, you see. I'd gone through every training course, passed every exam and always came out top of the class. The world was my oyster, they told me. No one had ever scored so well. I was some kind of phenomenon and everybody who was anybody wanted me at cocktail parties and dinners. They liked to show me off, to be able to brag that they'd had this new whizz-kid as their guest. I met Kim at one of these parties and we seemed to hit it off first thing. What I didn't know was that her father and mine had arranged our meeting, and that Kim was in on it. It was to be the perfect marriage: the whizz-kid and the daughter of the man destined to become the most important figure in the US Navy. I was twenty-five then – thought my future was going to be a picture book: then came that. We'd been married three years and things weren't going too well. I wanted a family but Kim wouldn't hear of it. Nor would her father. They had an image to play up to and Kim being pregnant wasn't part of that image. Outwardly, though, we had to play lovey-dovey. That made me realise I had married into the wrong family. I wasn't a son-in-law or a husband: I was a tool, part of my in-laws' plan to get themselves to the peak of naval society. I suggested a divorce but again that was shoved under the table. I was never to mention the word again.

'I had made the navy a laughing stock. The newspapers had a field day and made the admirals look like fools. There was no mention of the guy with the bad appendix, only the stupid fool on the submarine and the bigger fools running the show. Before you could say John Paul Jones I was up before a court-martial to explain myself and do you know what? The bastards did me for disobeying orders and bringing the navy into disrepute. They still didn't want to know about the guy with the bad appendix. That didn't matter. What was important was that through me the review had turned into a disaster. At the time my rank was commodore 2nd class, and three grades were stripped off me as quick as you can blink an eye. I would never be given another command and was banished into obscurity, to an office dealing with enquiries on naval history.

'My in-laws treated me as if I had plague. Kim put the bubble in for me and people who had been my friends – more friends of hers really – cut me off. I was bad medicine. Even my own father disowned me. He'd retired a rear-admiral and was my father-in-law's drinking partner. So, my naval career was over. I was banished, completely forgotten about until a signal came one day ordering me to Boston. Then I ended up in England, discharged from the US Navy and unemployed, until the fat guy came along. I don't remember agreeing to work for him. From the first day I arrived in England I went on a continual drinking binge – or at least carried on with the one I started in the States.'

'When did this happen – the chaos, I mean?'

'Eleven months ago.'

'They were a bit rough on you.'

'According to them I was lucky I didn't get a term in the stockade.'

'What happened to the guy with appendicitis?'

'He died. Having that in mind was one reason I asked Rutledge to become our doctor. Seeing a man dying when you're helpless to do anything is something I don't want to experience again.'

'And you're officially discharged?'

'So Witherspoole tells me.'

'I wish I was. I'll be down as a deserter, the worst crime in war.'

'How'd you manage that?'

Woolcott recounted his meeting with Witherspoole and Morton at the Lyons Corner House.

'He asked you just to walk out there and then?'

'Just like that. I didn't even go back to the office to pick up my gas-mask or bits and bobs.'

Woolcott heard a movement behind the curtain screening off the wardroom and called out: 'Did you get that all right, Jimmy?'

'Yes, sir . . .' Wilson began, then swore at being caught out. 'Bleedin' twat!'

Sherman laughed. 'There's one like him in every crew.'

The ocean was still clear at daybreak. Wythe and Stone, self-appointed cooks, served up a breakfast of bacon and eggs. Carroll was still asleep although his face had become badly swollen, closing one eye and twisting his mouth into a death-like grin. Rutledge checked his pulse and temperature and cleaned the inside of his mouth with swabs.

'How is he?' Sherman came alongside.

'Good,' Rutledge nodded vigorously. 'He's a healthy lad. Being healthy helps to fight infection, you know. I could give him a jab now. Do you have any drugs?'

'Some,' Sherman took a key from his pocket. 'Open the cabinet and take what you need.'

Rutledge returned after a few minutes, preparing a syringe. 'This will help the swelling. It should bring it down in a few hours and let the wound heal properly.'

'Why didn't you give him that earlier, doc?'

'It would have made his pulse race. I wanted him to have a few hours on his own then feel his pulse. If it was racing then I'd know he had an infection. If it wasn't then I'd know he was recovering under his own steam. If the drug had made his pulse race, I wouldn't have known if he had an infection or not. I had to be sure.'

'You're the doc. How long before he can be on his feet?'

'Another twenty-four hours he should be up and about. He'll still ache a bit and it'll be a few days before he can eat properly. And if all goes well I'll have the stitches out in a week.'

'Keep up the good work, doc,' Sherman clapped Rutledge on the shoulder and did a tour of the boat.

'It's a lovely day,' Woolcott said on his return to the control room. 'A lot different to the weather we left behind.'

Sherman looked up. Sunlight was streaming down the conning tower hatch.

'Maybe we should give the guys a smoking break?'

'A breath of fresh air always works wonders for morale, sir.'

Sherman acknowledged Woolcott's comment and announced into the tannoy: 'Two each from fore and aft hatches. Five minutes, one all round.'

A cheer went along the boat and those who smoked looked for the tackle. Both Sherman and Woolcott went up-top to relieve the lookouts while they had their smoke.

'How far do you think, Oliver?' Sherman asked when the lookouts resumed their duties.

'Around four hundred miles, sir.'

'About twenty-four hours at our present speed. Make it thirty to be on the safe side.'

The ocean became calmer as the hours passed, like a mill pond. The crew rested to make the best of it, some lost in their thoughts and others recounting the experiences which eventually took them aboard the *Unwanted*.

Kean and Matthew Thornton, it turned out, had been shipmates, and both were deserters. Like many deserters they had envisaged sailing to exotic parts of the world, enjoying the delights and returning to tell others of the wonderful life. Thornton, only twenty-two, boyish, his face covered in pimples, was still disappointed. When offered a dangerous job he'd imagined being dropped by parachute onto some rocky crag to rescue someone important. The last thing he expected was to be cooped up in a submarine.

'What about you, Bill?' Braxton asked Whipple.

'Me?' Whipple feigned ignorance.

'Yeah, you. What have you done to deserve us? Have those scars got anything to do with it?'

Whipple's face and hands were a mass of scars. On his face particularly they looked sickly and gave him an evil appearance.

'Aw, I wasn't anything great,' he replied, averting his eyes. 'I just robbed post offices.'

'You *just* robbed post offices? Hell, man, robbing the mail is more serious than robbing a bank.'

'Yeah, come on, Bill,' Paca shouted, 'tell us about it.'

'I robbed post offices.'—

'But how did you get caught?'

'I left a trademark.'

'What kind of trademark, for Christ's sake?'

Whipple had turned robber the day he left school, training in small shops before graduating to post offices. His MO was to wait until one minute after a post office closed for the day then, wrapped in double layers of clothing, to throw himself through the window to put the fear of Christ up his victims.

'It worked,' he said. 'They didn't expect me and they didn't hang about when I demanded money.'

Each time he had thrown himself through a window he'd been badly cut, and the sight of his blood alone was enough for the hapless postmasters to hand over all their available cash, but at the same time his scarred face became his undoing. An observant resident of Hastings reported seeing him in town one morning and local police kept within reach of every post office when closing time arrived. Whipple, keeping to his schedule, ran from a car and crashed through a large window brandishing a shotgun, his favoured weapon, emerging minutes later with a bagful of cash to fall into the hands of the waiting constabulary.

At his trial the judge commented that he had seen too many Hollywood films, was as thick as two short planks and sentenced him to fifteen years on Dartmoor.

'So that's why you suggested you dive through the window back at Buckler's Hard?'

Whipple shrugged. 'It seemed a good idea.'

'George?' a head nodded to George Walton.

Walton was thirty years old, a thief and drunkard from Colchester in Essex. He was tall, slim and weak-looking, but his appearance was deceptive. The others had watched him in action in the New Forest and knew he possessed tremendous stamina, being able to walk or run for miles without having to catch a breath. He had begun his working life as a solicitor's clerk and in time had his first brush with authority for having his hand in the till. A thirty-day sentence was pronounced and on being freed he became a bus driver, holding on to the position long enough to convince a girl he would make a stable husband. His marriage foundered almost immediately. What his wife did not know was that he was a heavy drinker. He went through money like water, even going so far as to steal enough for a decent drink from his conductor's bag.

Walton soon lost both his job and his wife. He joined the army and seemed to settle in, then war came. He started drinking again and at least once a week awoke in the Catterick lock-up. Volunteers were wanted for special duties and he put his name forward. Catterick was glad to get rid of him, but the joy was short-lived when two weeks after he'd left, he returned, a reject. More drinking followed, with arrest after arrest, the crunch being when he flattened the guard and commanding officer. With two months of a six-month sentence served the offer of a job came along and Walton took it.

'And here I am,' he said.

'Watch change . . .' a voice called from the control room.

It was noon already, time for the watches to change over. Walton rose, glad to get out of the limelight and went to the control room. He was on wireless duty for the next two hours and looked forward to it. There was something about a wireless set that held him, although he couldn't explain why.

Except for the engineers everyone changed their station at each watch. There were to be no specialists. Each had to be able to do every job and to that end they were rotated.

'Aircraft approaching!' the call came seconds after the watch changed.

'Dive!' Sherman shouted.

The alarm was sounded and the engines seemed to stop dead. Men dropped into the boat, the officer of the watch slamming the lid behind him.

'Take her down, three hundred feet!'

They went down fast. The plane had been ten miles away but if it could do 250 mph it could be on them in around four minutes.

A bomb *crumped* not far away.

'His weaponry is limited,' Woolcott said. 'Two bombs, three at the most.'

Two more fell and Woolcott smiled. 'He's all out but he'll have heavy guns. We'd better stay below for a while, sir.'

Sherman nodded, not too proud to bow to Woolcott's experience.

They waited two hours before surfacing again, and both the ocean and sky were clear.

'Come dark,' said Sherman, 'we can start heading for the coast.'

'Very good, sir.'

The remainder of the day passed without incident, although Carroll woke and caused a stir. He demanded something to eat and when refused anything solid threatened to beat the living daylights out of young Stone. Rutledge calmed him, explaining what was necessary for a few days and advised him to get on deck for fresh air.

'Fresh air is the best thing for closing a wound,' said Rutledge, 'but for God's sake don't smoke.'

Willing hands passed Carroll to the after hatch and helped him through onto the deck. Razor Eddie and Rocard sat with him, ready to bundle him down should there be an alarm.

The weather was becoming even better.

'Just think of it,' Hancock remarked. 'Back home, or in England, they're freezing, and down here in Spain they're probably sitting out in the sun.'

'It ain't fair,' Morris put in.

'What's the name of that geezer what runs Spain now?' Wilson asked, looking around.

'Dick-Tater,' Lynch replied with a laugh.

'Franco,' Rooney said, 'a real nasty piece of work.'

'You was over there, wasn't you?'

'For a while. Me, Joe and Rick.'

'What was it like?'

'Pretty grim. And it wasn't much better afterwards.'

'Why's that?'

'They reckon Franco's soldiers and secret police killed a million people after the surrender, just to show the Spaniards who was boss.'

'He don't sound much like a music-hall turn, and that's a bleedin' fact.'

'He's none of that.'

'You ever kill anyone over there?' Bill Ellery asked.

'Some.'

'How many?' Ellery leaned close. He'd never met someone who'd killed face to face.

'A few.'

'How many, for Christ's sake?'

'A few hundred, I suppose.'

'Hundreds! Man, that's wild.'

Ellery kept silent for a few moments, trying to comprehend the remark. Rooney was so calm, as if he were talking about wild animals in the jungle. His thoughts were interrupted by Morris who came by carrying a Luger.

'What I could have done with this back home,' he said, stripping it down for a clean. 'I can just imagine walking into some classy joint and pointing it at the guy in charge. I could've been rich. Mind you,' he said with a dirty laugh, 'I'd sooner this was Betty Grable I was stripping.'

'Who?' Ellery asked, his face serious.

'You know,' Wilson replied for Morris, 'the bird with the lovely big top-bollocks, and the legs what go right up to her bum.'

Ellery shook his head. 'I wouldn't know Betty Grable from a bar of soap.'

'You're joking! Blimey, mate, you must be a right Gilbert if you doesn't know who Betty Grable is.'

The Americans within earshot narrowed their eyes. Another word had been added to their vocabulary but needed explaining. Hooper turned to Harewood and asked.

'A Gilbert?' Harewood's shoulders heaved with silent mirth. 'That's rather a long story, old chap. Perhaps in time one might explain it: or better still, illustrate.'

Nelson shook his head with bewilderment.

'Heh, Jimmy!' A deep Scots voice called out.

'What's up, Scotch-Jock?' Wilson answered.

'Not you, Jimmy, him . . .' Razor Eddie pointed to Nelson.

'My name's not Jimmy,' Nelson pointed out.

Harewood nudged his ribs and said with feigned panic: 'For God's sake, old chap, he comes from Glasgow where they eat their young and everyone is called Jimmy. Humour him!'

'What can I do for you, Ed?'

'You play chess, don't you?'

'Sure do.'

'I've made a set of pieces from nuts and bolts. Fancy a game?'

'Sure do,' Nelson rose and smiled at Harewood. His eyes said *animals don't play chess.*

Chapter Twenty-Two

'Surface craft bearing fifteen degrees starboard!'

'Dive!' Sherman leapt from the wardroom in a flash to superintend the dive but there was no need. As soon as the alarm had been given, fuel to the engines was cut off, the main vents opened and both lids shut simultaneously.

'Periscope depth.'

Conversations were forgotten. Razor Eddie's chess pieces were scattered about the floorplates and a sandwich lay on the edge of a bunk where it had been thrown at the sound of the alarm.

'Fishing boats,' Sherman announced, 'but fast buggers.'

He counted two dozen, Spanish by their flag.

'A long way from home,' Woolcott said with some suspicion. 'They might be German patrol boats disguised.'

'This far out?'

'Why not? Extra fuel tanks and they can have a range of a thousand miles. We're in the southern convoy lanes, don't forget, and they can cause as much damage as half a dozen U-boats.'

'They're turning north,' Sherman gave a commentary. 'Vee formation. Very, very disciplined.'

'Then they're German. So far as I know what is left of the Spanish Navy is nothing like that. Reports say they are very sloppy.'

'But from which base?'

'A Spanish base, maybe.'

'Could be,' Sherman agreed.

The boat remained submerged for an hour before resurfacing, by which time it was dark. Woolcott took over the watch on the tower and became lost in his thoughts.

He hadn't even said goodbye to his wife and little girl. Jean, his wife, would be in a state: not just because he hadn't come home, but because the naval police would have paid her a visit looking for him. There would be more than one visit and Jean would be watched twenty-four hours a day to see if they made contact. She would be a bag of nerves, poor dear. Little Allison would be wondering what was going on, perhaps asking her mummy why she was so sad. And a four-year-old knew when an adult was sad. They weren't fools.

And what would Jean think of him? By now she would have learned he was a deserter, and it wouldn't be long before neighbours found out, making her life worse. Would she get his pay? Bloody hell, that was something he hadn't thought of. Most of his pay was sent to Jean and it would more than likely be cut off until the navy determined his whereabouts.

'Bastards!' he swore aloud.

'Pardon, sir?' one of the lookouts said.

'Just thinking out loud.'

He hadn't thought of the navy being wicked either, but now, the more he thought of it the more it made sense. At the enquiry they hadn't given him the benefit of any doubt there might have been. He had exceeded his orders but not disobeyed them. Surely there was a difference? What's more, if he had had to pick up someone of prominence they would probably have told him to wait until that person made contact, regardless of how much time had passed.

The office job: that, he knew, was to humiliate him. Everyone in the office knew why he was there, and the Clerical Officer had treated him like some kind of serf, possibly putting the bubble in for him with the others. He recalled when he attempted to strike up a conversation he received short shrift from the majority of his colleagues. The exceptions had been two former commanders who had suffered a similar fate.

Which wasn't really very nice. Why humiliate and degrade a man for doing something he believed was the right thing to do at the time? All they had to do was give him a warning and put it on his record. And now Jean and Allison would be suffering, too.

'Rotten bastards,' he said again.

Woolcott reluctantly allowed himself to be relieved. The air, previously bitter cold, had become moderately bearable. They were moving into the warmer Southern European climate and it reminded him of the coming of an English summer.

'All quiet?' Sherman asked for the sake of starting a conversation.

'A beautiful night.'

Sherman nodded. The sea was a sheet of glass and moonlight reflected from it like a gigantic mirror.

'I've just increased speed to twenty-six knots,' said Sherman.

'I felt it,' replied Woolcott, 'in more ways than one.'

Sherman didn't reply. He didn't have to. The perpendicular bow threw up a spray that came back to shower those on lookout duty.

'If they give us another job,' Woolcott went on, 'we should insist on the bow shape being altered.'

'That's a fact,' Sherman eased himself onto the tiny steel seat projecting from the wall of the tower.

'Cup of tea, sir?' Wythe's head popped up.

'I'll have one below,' Woolcott took the mug and handed it to Sherman, 'then I'll get my head down.'

The night and the calm sea had the same effect on Sherman – made him remember the past. The fresh lookouts fastened their eyes on the horizon while he looked at the flat moonlit sea and thought back to three years before.

He had been deliriously happy then, madly in love with Kim and looking forward to having his own family. Their wedding day was something, without doubt the day of the year for the navy. Their respective parents went to the trouble of arranging the wedding to be held at Newport, Rhode Island, where the cream of American society spent their summers. That had opened doors for them.

And Kim had been a receptive lover – he had to give her that. But she'd insisted on him taking precautions. The idea of him not doing so appalled her and unless he did she kept her distance. In the beginning he'd imagined she was afraid of becoming pregnant for psychological reasons, but as time went on he realised she just didn't want to lose her figure or interrupt her hectic social life.

The arguments that followed after the first year! Hell, they were something. Kim behaved more like a broad from the Bronx than a respected member of society. And making-up was something else. Kim seemed to revel in it. Once, he remembered, they'd been to a function hosted by the country's Vice-President. He'd brought up the subject of having a family in front of the Second Lady and Kim could have strangled him. She didn't speak to him again that night until they were in the car going home, and only a dictionary of soft words in her ear got her round to being womanly again. It had got her going, so much so that once indoors she had her clothes off before they were half-way up the stairs of the over-large house his father-in-law gave them as a wedding present, and had him use his mouth on her as she lay sprawled on the third top step, reversing their positions several times until, when they were tired out, they were some way along the landing. But even then she wouldn't let him touch her in the conventional way unless he took the usual precautions.

Kim hadn't been a virgin when they married and recalling some of the things she could get up to his mind boggled as to what she had indulged in previously. To be as debauched as she was, she had to have had years of experience with different men.

But soon all the gloss and glamour fell away and there was nothing but fighting. Kim was her own person, and she wanted the marriage to be on her terms. He became a *thing*, something for Kim and her father to use. When her father called him he was expected to go running. Kim snapped at him when he spoke to her. He saw little of her, and when they were together he had to behave as though they were still madly in love with each other.

Divorce was absolutely outlawed. His own father would not hear of it, let alone Kim's. It would make them look bad in the eyes of the hierarchy. They had to keep pretending, he'd been told, even if it meant being married for forty years.

Well, all the doors were shut to him now. Kim was still the apple of society's eye, the darling girl whose husband turned out to be a wrong 'un. Immediately after the shambles of the Chesapeake they dumped him.

And the word *divorce* raised its ugly head again, but from the other side of the coin and as if it had never been mentioned before. Into the bargain, Kim's mother had snorted that she'd always known he was no good. What on earth Kim had seen in him was a mystery.

Who the hell cared? He came back to the present. Although the Chesapeake had ruined his naval career it was a blessing in disguise. It got him away from that God-awful family.

'Vessel bearing 155 degrees starboard, sir,' a lookout snapped him out of his reverie. At once he was on his feet, glasses hard against his eyes.

She was a big ship, fully lit and steaming north.

'Neutral,' he said. 'She won't see us.'

'Very good, sir.'

'You're from London, aren't you?' Sherman changed the subject.

'Bermondsey, sir.'

'I thought you were from London.'

'Bermondsey is a part of London, sir.'

'What happened to you? How did you end up with this job?'

Jim Adams shrugged, never taking his glasses from the sea. 'I suppose it started with wife trouble, sir.'

'You don't have to keep saying sir, Jim. At the moment we're just two guys having a private talk. You can tell me to mind my own business if you like, but I'm interested in my men.'

Adams said nothing for a few moments then began to speak. He was thirty-three, married with two daughters and had turned to crime to give them a decent life.

'We married young. I was eighteen and the missus seventeen. Bloody marvellous it was at first. Nookie at all hours of the day and night. She's a cracker, the missus, no mistake. Then the first nipper came along and Sandra had to stay at home a lot. I didn't earn much at that age and because she couldn't get out Sandra wanted more home luxuries. The only way I could get them was to become a tea-leaf. I started thieving, selling to a fence and buying Sandra the things she wanted. I got caught and got sent away for three months. Learned a lesson I thought when I came out, but not for the missus. She still demanded more and she was pregnant again. It went from bad to worse. I couldn't get a job because I'd been inside, so the only thing left was to get back to thieving. I done more time, and during this stretch I learned about diamonds. A bloke was doing twelve years for a big diamond robbery and anything there was to know about diamonds, he could tell you.

'He taught me all he could in the time I was with him and the next time I came out I went for diamonds. God-Almighty, I never had so much money. The missus loved it. I'd bank accounts all over the place. Of course, I was caught again, did three years and I still couldn't stop. The nippers were growing and the missus wanted this and that for them. She was giving me some stick by then about not looking after her. Then the war came along and we knew it was only a matter of time before I was called up. She tells me to do one big job, one that would keep her going until the war was over – whenever that might be. Off I goes, nicks the booty and makes twelve thousand quid. This time I didn't get caught but a mate of mine warned me that the Old Bill had my name. I told the missus we would have to move but, Christ, she didn't want to know, and before you know it the Old Bill's round my drum beating on the door.

'I just got away in time and a mate put me up for a couple of days, then when I thought things were quiet I sneaked round to the missus for some money. The bitch had gone, pissed off with everything, girls and all. Then it came out and, as it generally happens, I was the last to know. While I was in the nick she was living it up with a boyfriend, spending the loot. Anyway, I traced her and was on my way round to give her and the boyfriend a hiding when the Old Bill nicked me. Seven years, I got, and the missus living in luxury at my expense. Christ! I'd given her about £35,000 over the years, and wages during that time never rose above five pounds a week.

'I tried to escape twice. Nearly made it and all. I'd learned how to get in and out of just about every building there is and another couple of minutes would have seen me over the wall. I ended up in the security wing where I couldn't get near locks or windows. And it was just as well. Had I got out I would have been back in for murder. One of my mates came to see me and gave me the whisper that the missus had opened a brothel and that my eldest daughter, she was coming up for fourteen by then, worked in it. Not as a brass-nail, but as a receptionist and maid, and that the little one also acted as a kind of maid. My mate also told me that the boyfriend was trying to have it away with my eldest, and the missus had advised him to wait until she was sixteen. Christ . . .' Sherman could see Adams' hand grip the glasses tight. 'If it wasn't bad enough bringing the girls up in a brothel: but that! I saw red. I just wanted to get out of there and do her in. It wasn't to be, though: that is, until the Morton bloke came along and offered me the chance of getting out. I could have kissed him.'

'And I thought I had been hard done by,' Sherman looked at Adams' back. He suddenly felt humbled, and realised now why he'd never seen Adams smile.

Adams turned to face Sherman. Very slowly he said: 'If we get back, sir, I'm going to do both of them.'

Before Adams turned his face back to the sea Sherman could swear he caught sight of tears running down his cheeks.

'We'll get back, Jim, don't worry.'

Adams didn't reply. He maintained his watch, the glasses sweeping the sea in slow arcs. His shoulders seemed to be heaving in short, rapid movements.

Kean was on watch when faint lights were seen in the distance.

'Spain, I should think,' said Woolcott when he climbed onto the tower.

Those not on watch were invited to come up in pairs to see their first glimpse of Spain. And it could be nowhere else. More lights appeared, twinkling along the coastline from one side of the horizon to the other. To their left flashed the lighthouse on the Islas Cies, the three islands guarding the entrance to the Ria de Vigo.

'Dawn in an hour,' Sherman said, looking at the eastern sky. 'Get the men below and do a battery check.'

'Yes, sir,' Woolcott hurried below and put everyone on the shake. They would have to dive soon and spend a fair time submerged, and for that the batteries would have to be checked for leaks and be fully charged.

The lights on shore went out and the sky began turning colour but Sherman hung on, intent on waiting to the last minute, saving his batteries before diving.

When daylight was complete it was possible to see small coastal ships entering and leaving the Ria de Vigo. The lighthouse no longer flashed, and as they came closer to the shoreline they could make out trucks moving along the coast road. 'Large vessel leaving Vigo!' a lookout reported.

Sherman studied the ship. It *was* big, an ocean-going ship that seemed to be heading their way, possibly bound for South America.

'Dive,' he spoke into the tube, not shouting, but calm and purposeful. Staying on the surface any longer would put them at risk. The lookouts had vanished. He took one last look at the coast of Spain then dropped into the hatch, closing the top lid behind him. Woolcott was already standing by the periscope but Sherman shook his head.

'Let him go. We don't want him to see the 'scope. Are the charts ready?'

'On the chart table, sir.'

'Let's look them more closely, shall we?'

At 0930 hours they were 1200 yards off-shore, comparing the details on the charts against what they could see of the tall rocks from the periscope.

Sherman blew through pursed lips. 'I didn't realise how dangerous it would be. Look at that, would you.'

The rocks were close together, too close for a dinghy in most instances.

'Cruise up and down,' he told the helmsman. 'We can't give up. There must be some way in.'

For three hours they crawled up and down the short length of coastline examining it in minute detail, consulting the charts and making slide-rule calculations, then at 1300 hours a decision was made.

'There,' Sherman marked the chart with a pencil. The entire crew were crowded close to the control-room, perched wherever they could find a vantage point to listen in to the ultimate decision.

'It is barely forty yards wide but is at least straight and reaches within fifty yards of the base of the cliff face. It's very choppy in there and a small boat is liable to get thrown out of control, but if you all listen to my instructions and remember your training we might just make it . . .' Sherman explained at great length how they would approach the situation.

'Everyone clear?'

Heads nodded.

'It will be dangerous and risky, but this is the job we all agreed to do.'

Again heads nodded.

'Who goes ashore, sir?' Sherman recognised Braxton's voice call out.

'Lt Woolcott and I will discuss that now. Have a meal you guys, and sleep if you can. We'll go in as soon as it's dark and I reckon it'll be some time before some of us sleep again.'

The crew dispersed and Sherman and Woolcott went into a huddle.

'You make a list of the sixteen guys you think would be best suited to the job, Oliver,' Sherman said, 'and I'll do the same, then we can compare.'

They never got as far as making lists. Braxton put his head around the curtain and said: 'The men would appreciate a word, sir, if you wouldn't mind.'

'Oh? What's wrong?'

'If you wouldn't mind, sir.'

Most of the crew were squeezed into the crew's accommodation, their eyes fixed on Sherman when he stooped through the hatch.

'What's the trouble?' he asked.

'No trouble, sir,' said Braxton, bringing up the rear. 'We're just a little worried.'

'About what?'

'Well, sir . . .' Braxton lowered his head and

scratched the back of his neck. 'We look at it this way. If you send half the guys ashore and leave half behind, the guys on shore are in trouble if the boat is discovered. They will be stranded, at the mercy of the Spanish secret police, and we heard what can happen there. On the other hand, if the guys ashore are caught there won't be sufficient numbers left on the boat to get us the hell out of here. Whatever, we could be in deep trouble, and speaking personally, I don't want to be in either group.'

'We must all be in one or the other.'

'Yeah, I know, sir, but we've discussed the matter and we're all of the same mind. We don't want to be ashore not knowing if the boat is safe, maybe coming back to find it blown out of the water: and we don't want to be on the boat waiting for guys who might not come back. It's not knowing, sir, that makes the job unattractive.'

'Me, too,' Razor Eddie said. 'I wouldn't want to be sitting here if the lads ashore are in trouble, and not be able to do anything about it, sir.'

'You all feel that way?' Sherman looked about him, taken aback by the sudden militancy.

'Yes, sir!' the reply came back as a chorus.

For a moment Sherman didn't know what to say.

Every eye was on him: anxious eyes, each seeming to tell him something.

It couldn't be mutiny, he thought, since they weren't in the navy. Nor could it be their intention to take over the boat and sail to a neutral port. There were no real neutral ports worth speaking of and if they reached them anyway they would soon be tracked down and taken care of. They wouldn't be that stupid. They were also aware of the consequences of returning without carrying out the operation. Witherspoole had taken great pains to point out that the alternative, in many cases, was prison.

So what was eating them? Why had they suddenly chosen this moment to raise an objection? He looked at the eyes again. They *were* telling him something. They were bursting with a solution.

'Okay,' he drew in a breath, 'what do you suggest?'

Sighs greeted his words and Braxton became the spokesman again.

'Well, sir,' Braxton adopted the same stance as before – head slightly lowered while a hand scratched the back, 'we didn't approach you earlier as we didn't know how you would react. It ain't that we want to undermine your authority, you understand. It's just that we want to survive this job and we don't think we've got a cat in hell's chance if we split up. We suggest, and we'd like you to consider, all of us going ashore, sir. That way we stay together and if one guy is in trouble we all are.'

Sherman nodded to acknowledge the suggestion then put an obstacle in the way. 'Okay, so we all go ashore and do the job. What happens to the boat? We go in at night, and as soon as daylight comes the boat will be spotted. What then?'

'We've thought about that, sir . . .' Braxton went into a lengthy description of a plan Sherman saw as being too incredible for words, and said as much in reply. 'Have you tried it, sir?' Braxton asked.

'No, but I know from experience that there are certain things you can do with a boat, and some things you can't.'

'But have you ever tried it, sir?'

'No, I haven't,' Sherman admitted.

'And you, sir?' Braxton turned his attention to Woolcott. Woolcott shook his head.

'Could that be because navies follow recognised procedures, sir?' he asked, and did not wait for a reply. 'We aren't navy and don't have to follow recognised procedures, and since it hasn't been tried before we won't know if it will be successful if we don't give it a go, sir.'

Sherman let his eyes drop to the floorplates for some seconds to think. Braxton was right. It hadn't been tried before as far as he knew and, if they did try it and it went wrong, they wouldn't have a naval enquiry to answer to.

'What do you think?' he lifted his eyes and looked to Woolcott.

Woolcott shrugged, pushed his lips tightly together for a second then said: 'We can only try, sir.'

'Okay,' Sherman straightened, 'let's work out some details.'

The smiles that greeted his reply made Sherman realise how tense the crew had been, although it hadn't been noticeable before.

The remaining daylight hours were spent working out another approach, much more difficult this time since it involved taking the boat close to shore and between the rocks that could tear it to bits like a piece of driftwood.

But the crew seemed happy and Sherman noticed an odd incident occur over and over again as the time to go ashore came nearer. Before leaving England someone had printed *UNWANTED* in large letters above the fore and aft exits from the control room. The unofficial name had stayed there untouched until Braxton had raised the point about who would go ashore. He remembered looking at it at the time when trying to avoid the men's piercing eyes.

Afterwards, when the decision had been made for everyone to go ashore, he noticed the name was smudged and wondered what the significance was. So he watched, eventually working it out. As a man passed under the name, whether it was to go fore or aft, his hand went up and touched the blue chalk for luck.

Chapter Twenty-Three

Sherman took precautions before going into the shore. Once the details were established he took the boat out to sea and surfaced to recharge the batteries, then an hour before sunset turned at full speed and headed for the rocks, diving when five miles off-shore and reaching the take-off position at 1900 hours.

Everyone was prepared. Gone were the thick woollen pullovers and duffel coats supplied by Witherspoole and Morton. In their place were old shirts, jackets and pants that would hopefully give them the appearance of being Spanish. A silence fell over the boat when Sherman gave the order to make the approach. Both the search and attack periscopes were in use, Sherman on one and Woolcott on the other. The regular lighting had been turned off and a secondary circuit, two bulbs in each compartment, turned on. One bulb was blue-coloured and the second red, which produced an eerie atmosphere, but which was necessary to ensure that those on the periscope sights did not have their vision obscured by the brighter lights around them. Conditions inside the boat had to be as close as possible to the night conditions on the surface.

Every twenty seconds the distance from the rocks was called out by Matt Thorton on the range-finder, immediately followed by a sounding read from a chart by Kean. Theirs were the only voices heard, except for Sherman who every few minutes called for an alteration in course.

What Sherman was aiming for was an inlet one hundred yards wide and an approximate 350 yards long. Along the narrow path waves were slapping from one side to the other, crashing into the rocks to throw great volumes of spray into the air which, caught by a breeze, gave the impression of heavy rain falling.

Both Sherman and Woolcott were edgy, afraid in fact. Experienced as submarine commanders they knew the dangers of trying to get into narrow choppy channels. A boat could be caught in a sudden surge and dashed against the rocks, and for all its hull being made of thick steel it would be torn like paper. To make matters worse they were going in stern first at revs so reduced that were they to be caught they would stand no chance. To escape a surge required a boost from the engines or motors, but by the time the polarity in the motors was reversed to take it from astern to ahead, it could be too late.

This was what Braxton hadn't taken into consideration when the proposal for everyone to go ashore was put forward. Neither Sherman nor Woolcott had mentioned it at the time. They had concluded that Braxton couldn't have known and, had they raised the point, it would only have caused more tension.

Those not in the control room could tell when the boat entered the channel. The boat was still to begin with, gliding easily just below the surface, then began to rock when the slapping motion held them in its grasp.

'Group up,' Sherman ordered.

The revs increased but the slapping movement did not alter.

'Group up.'

Again the revs increased and again the boat had no control over its movement.

'We won't make it, sir!' Woolcott advised.

Sherman didn't have to be told twice. 'Reverse power!' he shouted quickly. 'All motors full ahead!'

The boat shuddered as it took command. The slapping stopped. Sherman and Woolcott swivelled their periscopes through 180 degrees and called for ranges and depths. The stillness returned and very shortly afterwards they were outside the danger area.

'We'll try again,' said Sherman, 'but this time on the surface.' He spoke into the tannoy. 'All hands prepare to surface.'

The order was given and the boat slid up into the quiet of the night. Lookouts were up-top within seconds, Sherman following, and reports given.

'All clear, sir.'

And it was. The sea was clear of shipping and the only movement was the twinkling of lights along the Spanish coast.

'Engines slow astern,' Sherman said down the voice-tube.

For some reason Sherman could not explain the throb of the diesels seemed to give him more confidence. The motors had done the same job, yet. . .

The water around the stern churned as the screws moved the boat's bulk back towards the channel.

'Stop port engine!'

The engine stopped immediately and the boat began to turn, lining itself up to take the channel head on.

'Both engines together!'

Instant reaction from the engine-room crew was crucial. A second either way could send them into the rocks at the mouth of the channel and oblivion.

'Half revs!'

The stern moved into the mouth of the channel and Sherman prayed to himself. One rev too many or too few and it wouldn't be just his command he would lose this time.

The slapping began again but less pronounced than before. For the time being at least, he thought, they were in command.

Then the bows were through. They were completely in the channel, and largely at the mercy of the elements.

'Five degrees starboard,' Sherman called down to correct their line.

A hundred yards had been covered and they were winning. The slapping was reducing and ahead, closer to shore, Sherman could see calmer waters.

'Reduce by twenty.'

The churning around the stern eased and Sherman could feel that he still had command.

'Minimum revs!'

The screws all but stopped although the boat continued to move through its own momentum.

'Sounding and range!'

The reply was instant. 'Fifty yards at eighty feet, sir.'

'I want fifty feet.'

'Fifty feet at ninety yards, sir.'

'Stop engines.'

For the next few minutes Sherman prayed some more. The boat was still moving under its own weight, lessening as they neared the shoreline but in calmer conditions now where they would not be thrown about.

'Both engines thirty revs ahead for ten seconds then stop!'

The roar of the diesels came up through the conning tower and Sherman counted mentally. After exactly ten seconds they were taken off, their short operation halting the gradual movement and completely stopping the boat, but allowing it to drift.

'Deck crew up-top!'

The deck hatches opened and men clambered through pulling equipment with them. Air hoses were passed up and dinghies inflated, the dinghies being pushed over the side and held while men clambered into them.

'All crew on deck except securing party!'

Within thirty seconds of the order being given four dinghies were ferrying men to the shore 150 yards away. This took time and before they returned Sherman had to order the engines started, to stop drifting too far from the middle of the channel. After thirty-five minutes the only people left on the boat were Sherman, Woolcott, Nelson and Braxton. The others, all ashore, looked out with expectancy.

'You guys know exactly what to do?' Sherman asked.

Nelson and Braxton nodded. They'd gone over the instructions a dozen times together.

'Okay. Count to thirty the moment you close the upper lid then open the main vents.'

'No worries, sir,' said Nelson.

'I am worried,' Sherman replied. 'Okay, go to it.'

Sherman and Woolcott climbed onto the tower and heard the upper lid being closed behind them, and for once he was glad the US Navy had chosen not to get rid of the ancient dog and cam arrangement on the hatch-covers.

A dinghy waited for them. They climbed in and Lynch, the Irishman, pulled away from the side.

'Ten seconds,' Woolcott said.

The boat sat alone, rolling on a gentle swell sweeping towards the narrow beach at the foot of the high cliffs.

'Five, four . . .' Lynch began a countdown, and on *one* the sea close to them boiled. Air rushed up in giant bubbles and the *Unwanted* very quickly dropped below the surface. Seconds later it was on the bottom, the tips of its periscopes just showing and the turbulence gone.

Inside the boat Nelson and Braxton, both naked, switched off the lighting system and using a torch to guide them stood at the bottom of the conning tower ladder.

'You first,' said Nelson and Braxton nodded.

Braxton pulled on a mask and air-bottle, tested that it worked properly then took the torch from Nelson and shone it on a second breathing set. Nelson pulled the second set on himself, tested it and nodded. They shook each other by the hand, shut off the boat's breathing air, then Nelson in the lead climbed to the lower lid.

The modern stirrup-style fastener had been left undone before the boat sank to the bottom and all reliance was now on the older dog and cam to stop the boat from flooding. Very carefully Nelson turned the handwheel securing the cover and when it reached the end of its travel, pushed upwards, his body stiffening, terrified that the Atlantic Ocean might come rushing in and sweep them to their death.

There was nothing other than the normal residual collection of water. He climbed through into the small compartment above and waited for Braxton to join him. It was a tight squeeze. Braxton dropped the torch into the boat then stood upright, pushing himself against the cold steel wall while Nelson closed the cover.

It was an even tighter squeeze trying to fit on flippers. They had to help each other, working in complete darkness and slapping each other on one shoulder or the other to signify a yes or no. Then, after what seemed an age, they gripped each other by both shoulders. They were ready to tackle the upper lid.

Mentally they went through the procedure first. They had to turn the handwheel its full travel then both had to push against the weight of water outside, allowing only a small gap for water to flow in rather than a large gap for water to rush in. A sudden rush of water could throw them back against the steel wall and perhaps knock them unconscious. When the compartment was full they would pull themselves through to the conning tower, secure the cover behind them in case the lower cover leaked, then kick to the surface.

On the surface Sherman and Woolcott waited with Lynch in the dinghy. Six minutes had passed since the boat went under. There wasn't so much as a ripple on the surface other than surf.

Another minute went by, then two more. Nine minutes.

'God help us,' Sherman whispered as the tenth passed.

Lynch was looking towards the shore where there seemed to be a considerable amount of movement, then a torch flashed once.

'The lads have found a way up the cliff, sir,' he said quietly.

'A lot of good that will do us if those two don't appear,' Woolcott said.

Suddenly, and to Sherman's great relief, bubbles broke the surface, then two heads.

'Quickly!'

Lynch rowed furiously towards the spot and the two naked men were hauled aboard. The breathing masks were pulled from their faces and a bottle of scotch pushed in front of them.

'One decent swallow,' said Sherman, then: 'Did it go okay?'

'Without a hitch, sir.'

'Thank God.'

Woolcott had joined Lynch in rowing. They knelt, backs bent forward, their arms pumping as they propelled the dinghy towards the shore.

Sherman looked back to the two periscopes still sticking out of the water. It was low tide now and when the tide changed the boat would stay on the bottom, the periscopes out of sight, but it only needed someone to come snooping along the cliff-tops at low tide . . .

Chapter Twenty-Four

Sherman was relieved to be on shore. Willing hands pulled the dinghy onto the narrow stretch of sand and helped him out. Braxton and Nelson were shivering from cold and although their clothing awaited them their job was not complete. They removed their flippers and breathing sets, tied them to the dinghy then began dragging it back into the sea until the surface was level with their chests. Nelson hung onto it while Braxton went back to the shore, took a large stone handed to him and went back out, gently dropping the stone into the dinghy then going back for another, continuing until the dinghy dropped to the bottom. The same procedure was applied to the other three dinghies and only when they, too, were out of sight did they put on their clothes.

As much as others volunteered to help the two Americans Sherman insisted that the fewer who got cold the better. Some wanted to carry stones out to the dinghies as they were, but entering the country wearing sodden clothing would have been a giveaway were they to be unexpectedly met and required to give an explanation of their appearance.

A way *had* been found up the cliff but to Sherman's horror it meant some measure of scaling. Wilson and Morris had done a quick recce and found an old path ending fifty feet from the top.

'Looks as though the top fell away at some time, guv'nor,' said Wilson, 'an' took the path with it.'

'But can we get up there, for Christ's sake?'

'Yeah, but it'll take us some time.'

'Then make a start. I'll follow with Tom and Carter when they're ready.'

Wilson and Morris scuttled off, the others following. They made no sound and were completely out of sight in seconds when the shadows of the cliffs swallowed them.

Nelson and Braxton were still shivering but nodded to Sherman they were ready to go on.

'Your hands and feet okay?'

'A bit numb, sir,' Braxton said, 'but we'll be okay.'

'That's no good. You won't be able to climb if your hands are numb. Look, I know this sounds a bit stupid at a time like this, but start beating the shit out of each other. It'll warm you up.'

The two Americans looked at each other in the dark and smiled. It did sound a bit stupid but at the same time it made sense. Simultaneously they went for each other and the cold was forgotten.

The cliff face was 150 feet high and the path, as Wilson and Morris had found, ended nearly fifty feet from the top. Several hundred tons of cliff had fallen away at some time and left a shelf twenty feet deep, towering above which was a near vertical climb.

Wilson, previously a trained commando, was already fifty feet up hammering in pitons to use as toe-holds. He worked fast and behind him Morris handed up pitons as they were required. The higher he climbed the more people came behind until, when he reached the top, seven others were in various stages of the climb.

Wilson uncoiled a rope wound round him then waited until the seven appeared over the rim.

'Okay?'

'No bother, Jimmy,' Razor Eddie laughed lightly.

Ropes were thrown over the edge, caught, equipment tied on and dragged up. Razor Eddie, Wilson and Morris armed themselves with the silent Stens and ran off some way to act as cover against any unwelcome visitors, while Harte, Carroll, Lee and Hewes used the ropes to pull up the remaining equipment, then their companions. They hauled quickly, relying on the man being pulled to help by 'running' up the cliff, bundling him over the top and immediately throwing the rope down to the next. The next four up relieved Harte and the others who joined the cover group, and so on until Sherman, bringing up the rear, was hauled over the top.

'Everyone and everything okay?' he asked as soon as he got to his feet.

'All ready to go, sir,' Woolcott replied.

'Then don't let's waste any time.'

Sherman gathered his men about him and gave last-minute advice. 'We run all the way, non-stop except for emergencies, so if any of you want to pee, do it now. It's about eight miles as the crow flies but with hills and dips we can double or triple that. We take turns in the lead, five minutes each, and whatever the lead man does you all do. Got that?'

Heads nodded.

'Okay, find somewhere to hide the ropes and then we'll get started.'

The countryside was hilly, undulating up to two hundred feet either way, demanding on the calf muscles and lungs and had it not been for the harsh training in the New Forest the group – possibly with the exception of Taylor, would have collapsed after a mile. Taylor took the lead initially, very quickly opening up a hundred yard gap and eventually having to slow in order that the others could catch up.

On shore the lights that had twinkled from the sea seemed to have disappeared. Small farm houses showed up every few minutes and where light did shine from their windows it came from oil lamps rather than electric bulbs.

Periodically they came across animals quietly grazing in the dark. The animals, unused to dark figures running across their normally undisturbed fields, bolted, whinnying and bellowing loudly with fright, the noise of their gallop cutting out the sound of thirty-five pairs of boots thundering across the land.

Bill Ellery wondered if he had done the right thing. As he vaulted over a low stone wall he thought of what could have been. The only son of one of America's most wealthy industrialists, he could have been sitting behind a desk in London or New York wielding as much power as the British prime minister.

In his own right he was an engineer, but only to oblige his father and not by any personal commitment. All through high school he'd wanted to be a dentist.

'A dentist!' his father had shouted in a tone of mixed indignation, horror and distaste. Anyone would have thought he'd suggested sweeping the streets of Harlem.

His place was with the corporation, taking over from his father when he had sufficient experience, part of which meant gaining an honours degree in engineering.

Reluctantly he'd gone to university, gaining his degree and immediately being given an executive position in the corporation. A marriage was the next item on his father's agenda. The daughter of another industrialist was waiting in the wings, a decent, pretty girl who undoubtedly would have made an excellent wife for someone, but who also did not like the idea of being traded as part of a business deal. His father had been furious when he'd said he had no intention of marrying just yet, and couldn't understand why he just wanted to be friends with the girl. He was being offered, he'd been told time and time again, an opportunity millions of guys about the world would have jumped at.

Angry, his father had him sent off to a plant in a remote part of Brazil hoping that the solitude and constant contact with Indian women would make him yearn for the bright lights and society in New York: a plan that failed miserably. Ellery rarely went to the plant and instead found himself a job as a dental assistant in a surgery that was no more than a shack in the jungle.

More furious than ever his father had him flown back to New York and questioned by psychiatrists. In Ellery senior's eyes there had to be something wrong with anyone who turned their back on power and money. The psychiatrists agreed; although they had determined the real reason they did not say so for fear of losing a lucrative client, and suggested instead that he be sent to Europe where he might learn from centuries of experience the necessity for power and money.

London had been the next stop and for once in his life Ellery enjoyed himself. He began to take an interest in the corporation's affairs, increasing the profits of the European operations, which seemed to convince his father that he had learned the error of his ways.

Invitations to meet England's nobility came his way and as the months went on he became a regular guest at receptions held by those whose pedigree went back to William the Conqueror. The unattached daughters of minor dukes and earls were skilfully presented for his inspection in the hope that a marriage might arise, and a subsequent injection of US dollars enhance the fading fortunes of one of the lesser families. Ellery had felt a little flattered by the attention but very quickly learned to reject it as skilfully as it was presented, causing his father back home to shake his head with amazement.

The war in Europe began and Britain's factories were nowhere near equipped to produce the amount of equipment required to fight Hitler. On the spot, Ellery approached the appropriate government department and put in a tender for the corporation to supply engines, gear-boxes and axles for a variety of vehicles ranging from staff cars to tanks. The tender was accepted and the corporation's plants in the United States began working flat out. After Dunkirk more plants were opened to increase production and as fast as components came off the production line they were shipped to ports in Britain where Ellery, now in even greater demand at receptions, learned something that caused him to take a step backwards.

The Battle of Britain had been in progress at the time, with Hitler building up an invasion force on the other side of the channel, yet certain members of the nobility behaved as if there was no war going on at all. While the general population had been told to pull their socks up and tighten their belts, the higher levels of society were still eating their gourmet foods, still employing

Savile Row tailors to make their clothes and spending the weekends at country retreats.

Ellery was attending a reception in West London and in conversation with an aging dowager duchess who was rather angry at Hitler's attempts to subdue the British.

'Someone should go over there and teach that nasty little man a lesson,' the duchess said. 'Go over in secret and get rid of him.'

A number of young men fawning around the old duchess nodded their heads in agreement and commented that such an event was overdue.

Ellery also agreed and asked why the men did not volunteer for the task instead of just talking about it. Were he British, he had said, he would have volunteered before now.

Conversation stopped dead for a second until the old duchess laid a sympathetic, condescending hand on his arm and said: 'My dear boy, you are from America, one of the emerging nations, and you could not possibly understand the complexities of our social structure. Out there . . .' she waved a limp arm, 'are millions of working people whose function in life is to serve. It is they who will volunteer for, or be allotted the more unpleasant tasks of this war. Not us. If we went to war the country would be without its educated classes, and we can't have that, can we? Who then would tell the millions what to do? and, anyway,' the old duchess suddenly smiled, 'why should you worry yourself with such trivialities? After all, the Ellery Corporation is doing rather well out of the war, isn't it . . ?' she went on to discuss the corporation's financial affairs.

Ellery had been appalled by this attitude towards the ordinary people; and taken aback by so much being known about the corporation's affairs. He asked how the old duchess had got hold of the information.

'Poor thing, you still do not understand. Most of the people in this room have money invested in your corporation. When it became evident that war would break out lots of lovely pounds went across the Atlantic and were invested in industries we knew would be asked to manufacture equipment. Why do you think you were invited here?'

The silence that followed told Ellery that he was there on sufferance. The old woman was telling him that he was not one of them and never would be, and that he was only there because he was making money for them.

They'd sickened and disgusted him and he'd said so, although none of them turned a hair during his attack. He'd gone on to say that, even though he was an American, not directly involved in the war, given the opportunity he would go into Europe and do what they should have been doing.

It was the last reception he'd attended. He'd stormed out at that point, although not without hearing the old duchess' parting words.

'But of course, my dear. That is your sole purpose in life. After all, you are actually serving *us* now . . .'

Back in his hotel suite that night Ellery had fumed. A hatred for his father grew, and a hatred for the British ruling classes. From what he'd heard it was plain that the upper crust would have invested in German industry had they been able to. Their only interest was in themselves, with a complete disregard for everyone else.

And boy, had they been making some money! The British government was in no position to haggle over costs and the corporation was making up to 500 per cent profit.

Three days later the approach was made. His conversation had been overheard and would he care to live up to his words? Whether his decision was made in anger or through a desire to be involved, Ellery wasn't quite sure, but a handshake soon confirmed his membership of a select group being recruited for possible work on the European continent.

The same day he'd decided to get his own back on society. He had full powers to negotiate deals and sign the relevant documents that made them legally binding, something he briefly thanked his father for, and before joining Witherspoole at the hotel in Wimbledon he paid a visit to the government minister whose signature was due to cost the British taxpayer $250 million.

The minister had been somewhat surprised when he quoted $5 million, but had not argued when Ellery told him it was the corporation's quiet contribution to the war effort. Instead of a 500 per cent profit on the deal – and the goods were already in the country – it was completely reversed. Had he done the right thing? He was only twenty-nine, he thought, a guy who could have become one of the richest men in the world. And now? Witherspoole had told him that the corporation's shareholders, both British and American, had put a price on his head, and from all accounts the British aristocracy were more adept at getting their pound of flesh than the Mafia could ever be. He was to be killed at the first opportunity and there was a million pounds waiting for whoever would do it.

What a turn round, he thought. Rich yesterday and a pauper today. Alive today and maybe dead tomorrow: drinking with the nobility one day and running across Spain like a fugitive the next.

'All I wanted was to be a dentist,' he said to Will Paca.

'Eh?' Paca turned his head.

'Nothing,' Ellery said and lengthened his stride.

No one got out of breath but they sweated heavily. The run was non-stop except when approaching roads or wide tracks, and then the pause was only momentary while they looked both ways before crossing, and they were all glad when Cousa came into sight.

They halted in a wood overlooking the village, found a convenient vantage point and kept still. One of the skills they had learned was fieldcraft, taught to them by none other than the Royal Gamekeeper from the Sandringham Estate, who impressed on them that a moving figure could be detected even in heavy darkness, and that the same figure keeping still would become part of the scenery and arouse no suspicions.

Church bells were ringing and a number of people

were walking through the village towards the church. There were no vehicles that anyone could see, but lighting in the village was minimal and it did not mean to say that there were none. Vehicles in a country recently ravaged by war would be in the hands of officials, and officials meant trouble.

Sherman waited ten minutes, then, without seeming to move a muscle, said: 'Will, Jesus and Joe . . .'

'Chief?'

'You guys know Spanish. I want you to go down and find this Ortega.'

'No sweat, chief,' Heroles whispered and slid off into the night with Paca and Hewes.

They returned after thirty minutes.

'Something going on down there, chief. As soon as we approached an old broad she ran off nearly screeching with fear. She seemed afraid to talk to strangers. Everyone we tried to stop ran away, but we did manage to get one old guy to point to his house. He's in there.'

'Which one?'

Paca pointed to a small house on the edge of the village.

'Okay, let's get down there.'

It took the group ten minutes to reach the back of the house where, keeping to shadows, Sherman crept to the door and gave it a light rap. No lights shone from the windows, nor was there any noise from behind the door.

Sherman rapped again and this time heard a movement. A bolt was drawn and the door opened a fraction. A woman's timid voice asked who was there.

'I wish to speak to Miguel Angel Ortega Gomez,' Sherman whispered.

'Why?'

'It has to do with Carlos Salinas de Gortari.'

'Who sent you here?'

Sherman hesitated then said: 'London.'

'Come in please, but hurry!'

Sherman signalled for Paca to join him and seconds

later they were inside. Outside, the remainder of the group kept watch.

The woman lit an oil lamp and introduced herself as Carmelita, Ortega's twenty-two-year-old daughter.

'He told me someone would come but we did not know when.'

'Where is he?'

'Through here,' Carmelita took them into a bedroom, using the lamp to show them a figure in bed.

'He is dying. A few days ago he tried to follow Valdes and was shot twice. They will not allow me to get a doctor.'

'Who are they?'

'The fascistas. They run our village now.'

'Will,' Sherman said quickly, 'go get doc.' He looked down at Ortega and pulled back the blanket covering him. Blood covered his chest.

'Who's Valdes?'

'It is he who killed Señor de Gortari.'

'Tell me.'

'People were brought to Señor de Gortari during the night when the fascistas were asleep, then left the next night. One night he was discovered and they arrested him. He was tortured for making a fool of the fascistas, and when they got the information they wanted they killed him. Soon after people still came but they were taken to Valdes' house. My father knew something was wrong and watched Valdes' house and saw the Britishers come and go. They did not know what was going on . . .'

At this point doc came in and began examining Ortega.

'He did not find out where they were taking the Britishers and for many weeks he stayed out all night trying to follow them, then two nights ago he was seen. They shot him then dumped him on the doorstep. I begged for a doctor but they would not allow it. Nor will they allow anyone to leave the village lest we tell of what happened.'

'Does this Valdes know where they are taken?'

Carmelita nodded. 'He knows. He is an evil man.'

'Where does he live?'

'The large house at the other end of the village.'

'Okay, Carmelita. Don't worry about Valdes any more. How's it going, doc?'

Rutledge spoke without looking up. 'He's lucky. Took one through the upper arm and another through the chest. Just missed his lung. Another day would have finished him though.'

'Can you do anything?'

'I can save his life.'

Carmelita held rosary beads and prayed while doc worked fast. His fingers and hands flashed with make-shift instruments. At times blood sprayed in his face but he never stopped.

'Tear a clean sheet into strips,' he said for Paca to translate.

Carmelita, weeping for her father, rushed away to do his bidding.

Rutledge completed his work in less than ten minutes, thankful that Ortega had been unconscious throughout otherwise he would have yelled with pain. He handed Carmelita a number of tablets and said: 'I have sprinkled powdered drugs over the wounds which should stop infection and help to heal him. If you cannot get a doctor to him, keep the dressings on for at least a week. He should recover consciousness in twelve or fourteen hours and when he does, give him one of these tablets every six hours. No food or drink for twenty-four hours after he wakes, and then it must be bread soaked in milk for three days. Do you understand?'

Paca quickly translated and Carmelita nodded her head vigorously. Rutledge looked to Sherman for his views on giving away precious drugs. They had been intended for the group were they to be injured during the operation and a fair proportion of them were now gone. Sherman nodded his assent. There was no way he could refuse help to someone who had risked his life to fight fascism.

'Is there some reason why the village is going to church at this time of night?' Sherman asked Carmelita.

'But of course . . .' she pointed out something Sherman had completely forgotten.

'Will Valdes be there?'

'No, the fascists will attend mass tomorrow.'

'Who else will be at Valdes' house?'

'His wife, children and servants. Maybe a guard. There are guards on the roads into the village. Did you not see them?'

'We didn't come by road. How do the British fliers come, and when?'

'They come in the early hours of the morning and enter Valdes' house by the back door, and usually leave the next night.'

'Okay, Carmelita, that's all we need to know. Will you stay with your father or attend mass?'

'I shall stay. Tomorrow the priest will say mass for him here.'

'He'll be okay. He's just been looked at by the best doc in the world. Now put out your lamp. We must leave and visit Señor Valdes.'

'Be careful.'

'Don't worry about us, Carmelita. In fact, forget about us.'

There were tears in Carmelita's eyes when Sherman and the others left, and when she bolted the door she returned to the darkened bedroom to kneel by her father's bed and pray.

The group used a long route to skirt the village and take up a new position behind Valdes' house. Sherman explained to the others what had happened and suggested a plan that shocked even himself.

Rodolfo Felix Valdes, Carmelita had told him, was the equivalent of the village mayor. Cousa wasn't really big enough to warrant a mayor but Valdes assumed the position and expected to be treated with the courtesy associated with the rank. He was also the local fascist leader with the power of life and death over everyone living in the village. Village thugs were his bodyguards, who made sure that his life was one of luxury, forcing former republicans to hand over most of the produce from their smallholdings for little or no payment.

'We shall have to hope for a measure of luck,' Sherman whispered. 'The girl only knows that they come in by the back, and whether there's a code of some kind we don't know. You guys ready, then?'

'No sweat, chief.'

'Right, Jesus, you go first.'

Heroles slipped into the darkness followed by Taylor, Razor Eddie, Hewes and Lee. The others waited a full minute then went after them, splitting up and taking positions that virtually circled the house on three sides.

A horse snuffled as Heroles crossed the backyard. At the door he stopped to listen, then satisfied there was no one lurking anywhere nearby, crept along to a window where a light shone, and carefully looked in. Inside, a man stood by a table wrapping a parcel and from the brief description Carmelita had given he had to be Valdes. Then a woman appeared. She came from a room at the front of the house, a wide smile across her face – not bad looking either, Heroles thought.

They kissed. The woman was no more than thirty but Valdes must have been ten years older. The kitchen they were in was modern, a hundred years ahead of the house they had been in a few minutes before. Not bad for a guy who five years before had looked after pigs.

Heroles crept back to the door and knocked lightly. Almost immediately Valdes opened it. He must have flown across the kitchen. Was he expecting someone, Heroles wondered, or did the unexpected visitor frighten him?

Valdes just looked at him without speaking and Heroles, playing the part of a peasant, appealed in an apologetic but agitated manner.

'Señor,' his shoulders were rounded and drooped, hands before him in supplication, and his Mexican face a picture of awe, 'an unexpected delivery, and we had trouble. Please, I beg you to help. It will mean trouble . . .'

Heroles played his part like an Oscar-winner. Valdes had no desire to leave his home at this particular time and rarely met his charges, but he didn't like mention of the word *trouble*.

'What kind of trouble?' he asked quickly. Not tonight, he thought.

'Señor, you must look for yourself,' Heroles said, backing away and pointing into the darkness.

Valdes, sucked in, closed the door and followed Heroles across the yard. As they turned the corner of the stable Valdes suddenly found himself being surrounded by dark figures. He sensed a trap although he could not imagine who in the village would have the nerve to harm him, and before he could call out a large hand was clamped over his mouth and a voice whispered in his ear.

'Don't fight it, Jimmy.'

Valdes recognised the voice as being English, a language he spoke slightly, and panicked. He kicked, then lost all sense of balance as strong hands lifted him into the air.

Taylor, Lee, Hewes and Razor Eddie carried Valdes on their shoulder like a casualty from a war zone. He bounced as the four ran fast, Paca guiding them, away from the village to a prearranged spot more than two miles away. Around them, coming from their cover, the remainder of the group formed a rear-guard, unnecessary as it turned out since their visit had been unobserved.

Valdes was lowered to the ground when they stopped and from the smell coming from him it was evident he had messed himself. Sherman went down on one knee before him and said: 'You are Rodolfo Felix Valdes. You are a Nazi agent. You murdered Carlos Salinas de Gortari and all but murdered Miguel Angel Ortega Gomez. You are also responsible for the disappearance of a number of English airmen. That much we know. Now, Señor Valdes, you are going to tell us where you send the Englishmen and the extent of your operations here.'

Valdes looked at the determined faces around him. Some faces, more cruel than determined, appeared to want to kill him there and then.

'I . . . I don't . . . know where they go . . . to,' he stammered. 'I . . . I just . . . w . . . w . . . wait for someone to come.'

Razor Eddie knelt beside him and took his arm. 'Yir a liar, Jimmy,' the big Scotsman said in a Glasgow dialect. 'Noo, if yae dinna tell the oul-man whit he wahnts tae know, ah'll blooter yae.'

Valdes looked to Sherman for an explanation. The words meant nothing to him – not that they meant much to most of the group either.

'I think he means,' said Sherman, 'that if you do not tell me what I want to know you will have problems.'

Razor Eddie began to talk quietly, his words meaningless to all but a handful, but the tone behind them clear. Then he suddenly stabbed Valdes through the forearm. Valdes opened his mouth to scream but a hand went over his mouth to stifle any noise. His arm was lifted so that he could see the blood spraying from the wound, and Razor Eddie continued to whisper in his ear.

Valdes fainted but was brought round after a few seconds and Paca put the fear of Christ in him by suggesting they bring his wife and family along. Razor Eddie enhanced the fear by stabbing him in the groin.

He told everything he knew, and when he seemed to hesitate the Scotsman quite calmly put another knife wound somewhere in his body.

'I don't think he's missed anything, sir,' Razor Eddie said in his normal voice.

Sherman agreed and gave a slight nod, whereupon Valdes was lifted to his feet and a knife drawn across his throat. He tried to cry out but all that came from his mouth was blood. His face, a mask of fear, began to contort, eyes bulging and mouth opening and closing like a turkey pecking seeds. Blood spurted several feet from the gash under his chin, forcing the group to move back. They just watched. Valdes resembled a puppet out of control. His hands went into the air as if to clutch something, jerking, fingers clenching and unclenching. His legs began running on the spot, then moved forward in bizarre, lengthy enlongated strides. He collided with trees, legs still pumping and arms waving, then, as the last ounces of blood left his body, he collapsed and lay still.

'Everybody should try everything once,' Morris commented to break the silence that followed, 'except kite-flying and the Highland Fling.'

Sherman said: 'Six months ago I would have shot anyone who'd done that to another man. Now I can't even feel sorry for him, and I wish his buddies could have been here to see it.'

No one felt sorry for Valdes. In their eyes he had deserved everything he'd got and more, although young Tommy Stone threw up at the sight of so much blood. Stones were gathered to cover the body and as it was in such a remote spot it would be some time before it was discovered.

They would have twenty-four hours' grace at least. From what Valdes had said his wife was used to him leaving the house during the night and returning the next day, although there should have been no deliveries on this particular day. She would be angry when morning came, and before nightfall next day would become worried.

Sherman reasoned that she would make telephone calls to try to trace her husband. Enquiries would be made, which could take hours, by which time the job should be complete and the group on its way back to the boat.

'Okay,' he said, 'we go south to Tomino and the Casa Solariega de las Flores. It's only five or six miles but hard going, so we get there quick and rest, then look the place over during the day, and as soon as it gets dark . . .'

Chapter Twenty-Five

The run south to Tomino *was* hard going and the group was glad of the rest, but before sleeping they viewed Tomino in the dark to gauge its layout. Tomino was much larger than Cousa and more spread out. Very few lights showed in the town itself, but the Casa stood out.

They were perched above Tomino looking down towards the town and the river beyond with Portugal on the other side.

'He doesn't trust anyone,' Taylor said, looking through glasses. 'I count four guards outside the walls and three inside. One large light illuminates the entire gardens behind the house and if I'm not mistaken there are lights along the top of the walls but not switched on.'

'We'll see tomorrow,' said Sherman. 'We might as well get some rest now.'

There was no need for guards. The training in the New Forest had primed their faculties to detect intruders even during the deepest slumber.

'Look across the river,' Wythe said fondly. 'Portugal, England's oldest ally. If only we could have taken the boat there.'

Many pairs of eyes looked across the river. Lights, too many to count, twinkled and the headlights of numerous cars threw their beams unashamedly into the night. Portugal, although a hot-bed of spies, was experiencing an economic boom. Goods were bought 'on spec' from South America and stored in warehouses along her coast and, when the warring factions in Europe wanted something in a hurry, it could be obtained at a price. The vehicles alone were indicative of the boom.

Carter Braxton also looked fondly at the other side of

the river. He'd been in Portugal some months before, after escaping from the Nazis. From Seattle, Braxton had been working in France for three years when the Nazis invaded, working as a demolition expert on a tunnel being pushed through the Alps. Following the invasion some of the French workers decided, long before there was any talk of Resistance, to destroy the tunnelling machinery lest it be of some use to the enemy. Collaborators informed on them and Braxton was among those rounded up. He had first-hand knowledge of the treatment handed out to saboteurs, having witnessed what happened to some of his former colleagues. The Nazis had knocked him about as well – a few beatings with a rubber truncheon, his head ducked into a bath of water – and were about to have him charged as a spy when he managed to escape.

He had a French gaoler to thank for that. At great risk to themselves some Frenchmen working under Nazi administration openly aided prisoners, and when it was known that Braxton was to be taken for 'intensive questioning' his escape was arranged. His cell door, and several other doors in the building, were left unlocked just before the early evening guard changed over, a time when their vigilance took second place to the thoughts of an evening out.

Braxton killed two Germans and a Frenchman during the escape and without help from anyone or any organisation, made his way across France, over the Pyrenees into Spain and then to Portugal. He'd enjoyed Portugal. There was even a girl there he'd like to have seen again.

How the British got on to him he never discovered but one day while he sat at a roadside café with his girlfriend a guy approached and began a conversation. The guy represented His Majesty's government, servants of whom were extremely interested in the tunnel. If he was agreeable he would be taken to London where he could explain in detail everything he knew about the tunnel to date.

Braxton remembered saying he didn't mind one bit, and the other guy saying that was splendid because they would have taken him to London anyway whether he'd agreed or not.

In London they asked questions until they came out of his ears. The guys asking never seemed satisfied no matter how detailed his answers were. They went further, even down to the size of nuts and bolts and to what proportion water was used when mixing cement and concrete. No one told him why they wanted so much. They just thanked him and sent him on his way, then the little fat guy came along with the offer of a job.

He looked over the river again and nodded. Yeah, it would be nice to slip into Lisbon and see Maria Elena. With memories stirring he lay down and closed his eyes.

Church bells tolled long before dawn, never seeming to stop, and immediately after the first peal, as if the faithful had been waiting for it, lights came on. Soon after, smoke rose from short chimneys. Women emerged from houses and attended to chicken coops, opening doors and collecting eggs from under a cackling hoard of frightened fowl. Life came to Tomino.

The bells were still tolling when the first people began heading for the church.

'Going to early mass,' said Lynch, 'where I should be. I just hope Our Blessed Lord will forgive me.'

'Why?' someone asked.

Lynch looked at the speaker as though he were an idiot. 'Tis a mortal sin to miss mass on a Sunday,' he replied in his lyrical Irish voice, making the sign of the cross at the same time.

'What's a mortal sin?'

'Tis an eejit you are, sir. If you were a Catlick you would know these things.'

'Ere, Paddy,' Wilson queried, 'how did you get mixed up with this mob? Shouldn't you be in the IRA or something?'

'The IRA?' Lynch snorted. 'Them's fools!'

'We know that, Paddy, but . . .'

'Listen here to me,' Lynch pushed out his jaw, 'now don't you go insulting my countrymen.'

'You just said . . .'

'I know what I just said, but 'tis not for you to say.'

'Okay, Paddy, keep your harp on. So how did you get mixed up with us lot?'

'Ach, sure now,' Lynch began, 'my ould father fought in the British Army during the last war and suggested I do the same this time. I came to London and joined up, then I decided I wanted t'join the commandos, but they wouldn't take me cos I'd had a little drink beforehand.'

'What'd you have to drink, for God's sake?'

'Sure, I only had eight pints of Guinness.'

'Bloody Norah!'

'What's Guinness?' someone asked.

'If you ain't heard of Guinness, mate, you must be a right Gilbert.'

'What the hell's a *Gilbert!*' Hooper growled.

'Go on, Paddy,' said Wilson, ignoring Hooper's question.

'I took offence at them suggesting I was drunk and knocked their heads together. I mean, had I been drunk I wouldn't have been able to stand. The rotten biddies locked me up then I got seven days' detention. When I got out I really did get drunk and I don't remember much after that until the little piggy-man pulled me out of the lock-up.'

The others were rolling about with laughter and in the background Sherman smiled. He'd read Lynch's brief military history. He was twenty-four, from Cork in Southern Ireland, brought up on a diet of potatoes and built, as Witherspoole had put it, 'like a brick shit-house'. He saw nothing wrong with getting blind drunk, and when angry became fighting mad. On top of that there was a childish naïvety about him that was very likeable.

'That's enough talk,' Sherman said. 'Keep your eyes on the place and memorise the layout.'

Conversations immediately stopped. The winter sun

was rising and the first rays of light beginning to streak into the village. Movement increaed. Men and women came into the streets and shook hands in greeting. The church bells stopped. Children appeared, running and squealing as they would anywhere else in the world.

'Look . . .'

Men and women, whole families, were descending on Tomino. Every road into the village was crowded. Some arrived in old beat-up cars, some in horse-drawn carriages, some on mules but the majority on foot. All were dressed in their best clothes, prayer books in one hand and the other guiding animals or children to the entrance of the church.

'It's time we moved,' Sherman said quietly.

In groups of three and four they moved out of their hiding place, taking detours to join the people on the roads and drawing only brief glances from locals who, normally suspicious of strangers, were prepared to welcome anyone on this happy and eventful day.

Bells tolled again and people of all ages streamed from the church. The first mass of the day was over and the new arrivals, lined-up outside, filed their way in for the next service. Lynch was among them.

'T'would be a sin were I not to attend mass,' he'd told Wilson and Morris on the road in. 'No matter where a Catlick is in the world, if there is a church there he is duty bound to attend. The Blessed Lord would never forgive me.'

'What about the bloke we knocked off last night?' Wilson asked. 'Worn't that a sin?'

'Not at all! The Blessed Lord knows that our work is to rid the world of an evil. And anyway, before I left home the priest absolved me from all sin and gave me Papal dispensation – except for missing mass.'

'Silly bleedin' sod,' Wilson muttered, shaking his head at the Irishman's ignorance of the danger he could be in, and went on with Morris to have a closer look at the Casa Solariega de las Flores.

In the Atlantic village at Oya, twelve-year-old Horacio

Aguilar Garcia rushed home from early mass, snatched a quick breakfast and hurried out again, mounted his brand-new cycle and made for his favourite observation post two miles further south.

Horacio had built the post himself. A semi-circular wall of rocks protected him from gunfire directed from the sea, the rocks themselves covered with twigs and branches for camouflage, a masterpiece of ingenuity even if he said so himself.

On reaching the post he hid his new bicycle lest it be seen by a keen-eyed enemy, first making sure that it would not fall over and mark the fresh paintwork. His day was already planned. There would be two or three hours at the post checking the sea, then an early lunch and an hour riding around Oya for the poorer children of the village to gasp in awe at his new bicycle. Then another hour at the post, home for a bath and evening dinner with his parents where he, an only child, would be the centre of attraction. He enjoyed being an only child. It was better than having brothers and sisters. They had to let each other play with their toys and presents.

And wouldn't the village children be jealous! They were already jealous of him but this would really make them hate him. He was the first person ever to have a brand-new French racer with drop-handlebars. He looked forward to that.

A small pile of stones acted as a seat from where he could watch the sea: cold in this weather but he'd brought along a cushion. After all, he'd told himself long before, wouldn't an admiral have a cushion?

Horacio caressed the new field-glasses hanging around his neck. They were big, much bigger than the other pair. Reaching to his tiny waist they were so big and so heavy he had to rest them on the parapet of the post. But the magnification. Phew! It was something out of this world. They were the best the Zeiss Company in Germany could make – and made specially for him, his father said.

He balanced the glasses on the top of the wall and

focused the sights on the horizon, sweeping them slowly in his daily search for shipping, and immediately felt a pang of disappointment. There was nothing out there. No one had bothered to come and let him try out his new glasses.

But then, he bucked up, an admiral would spend a lot of time at sea without spotting another ship. Admirals were patient. They waited, knowing that their patience would be rewarded.

This made him feel better and he took a writing-pad and pencil from his pocket, filling in the time and date. Admirals always filled in a log, and they didn't use shore-side time. They worked on the twenty-four hour clock.

He wrote down *0845 hours,* the date and his observations on the weather, then lifted the glasses again.

A ship passed at 0930: German: a fast cargo ship possibly just back from a trip to South America and now hugging the Spanish coast until it could get into German-controlled French waters.

The glasses were everything he wished for. They brought the ship so close he could make out the captain on the bridge. Anti-aircraft guns were dotted about the ship and men, continually on watch at their guns, had their eyes lifted to the sky watching for enemy bombers. Excitement rippled through him. He felt part of it, part of the new order that was sweeping across Europe and which one day would conquer the world.

Too soon the ship went out of sight and Horacio turned his glasses on the rocks. Sometimes it was possible to see parts of wrecks from years gone by, when unfortunate ships' captains were pushed into the rocks by strong currents and their ships destroyed.

But there was nothing to see. The sea was too calm: but that was probably fitting, remembering what day it was.

He turned his attention to the wildlife. Countless thousands of sea birds used the rocks as their home. They were secure there, except at a certain time of the year when eggs were collected and sent to Madrid where they were regarded as a delicacy. He watched the birds hover, then dive and pluck a fish from the sea, racing away when pursued by others too lazy to forage for themselves.

Then his eyes picked up something else. It looked like two poles sticking out of the water. Focusing the sights to home in on the poles he gasped with an excitement he hadn't experienced before. They weren't poles or part of a wreck. They were periscopes!

Horacio's hands shook so hard the glasses would not keep still. He laid them on top of the wall, lifted the pencil and entered the time in his log.

But here? What was a U-boat doing among the rocks? Had it lost power and been driven in by currents? Where was the crew? Were they still down there trapped, unable to get out?

He lifted the glasses again to make sure. Yes, he was certain, they *were* periscopes. Again he lifted his pencil, this time sketching what he could see: and he was good at drawing. Hadn't his tutor said so?

But if they were trapped something would have to be done. He would have to tell someone. That would make him a hero, and the thought of being a hero appealed to him. Grinning with delight he retreived his bicycle and rushed home.

'Papa! Papa!' his young voice reverberated through the house when he rushed through the kitchen.

Señor Aguilar imagined his son had fallen off his bicycle and hurt himself, and ran from his study to patch up any wounds.

'Papa! I have seen a U-boat,' he clung to his father's arm, breathless and extremely agitated.

'I told you those glasses were the best,' his father said, smiling fondly. 'You must be able to see for miles.'

'No, Papa, the U-boat is here, in the rocks. The crew will be trapped!'

Horacio Aguilar senior looked down at his son and wondered if he was getting carried away, yet at the same time he knew how meticulous the boy was in making reports on shipping.

'Are you sure, Horacio? You don't mean one passed far out?'

'No, Papa!' the boy became insistent. 'Look!' he held up his sketch.

Aguilar was proud of his son's ability to draw and at once realised this was not childish imagination. He recognised the rocks and, yes, sticking out of the water were what appeared to be periscopes.

'The tide, Papa! Soon the tide will cover them. We must tell someone!'

Aguilar stood still for a moment then said. 'Let's get into the car. I must see this for myself before bothering anyone.'

That was good enough for Horacio. He sped from the house and climbed into the passenger seat of the family Mercedes. His father joined him and seconds later they were driving along the bumpy track to the area of the rocks.

'My God, you're right!' Aguilar gasped with surprise when he looked through the glasses. There was no doubting the boy's word. They went back to Oya where Aguilar spread the word among his disciples, conveyed the news to his friend Doctor Acevedo who, committed to entertaining some important guests, suggested he contact the authorities in Vigo, which Aguilar did. Before noon, although the periscopes had since been covered by the rising tide, several hundred people had gathered to look down on the spot.

Mid-afternoon brought a rescue squad. Soldiers, experienced mountain fighters from the civil war, using ropes, lowered themselves down to the narrow beach. Divers and equipment followed then an attempt was made to row out, but the sea was coming up and the first dinghy was swept against sharp rocks, throwing its occupants into the cold water.

A diver swam from the shore and returned to confirm that there indeed was a U-boat there, although its conning tower did not carry a number and what was more, he reported, there was a dinghy at the bottom, close to the beach, which seemed to indicate that someone had come ashore.

More divers prepared themselves to go out but the weather worsened. Waves began smashing against the rocks, spraying into a shrouding mist, obscuring even the sea and preventing any further rescue attempts, and as the afternoon went on and light faded people began drifting home until only the soldiers remained, manning searchlights which were permanently trained on where they knew the boat to be.

In Oya, Horacio Aguilar Garcia was a celebrity. The whole town, those who admired the family and those who hated them, all came to pay their respects. Horacio, loving the limelight, stood at the front door of his home with his new glasses around his neck, his bicycle alongside him, pushed out his puny little chest and accepted the hands that wanted to shake his. It was the proudest day of his life.

Chapter Twenty-Six

The last mass in Tomino began at midday and ended shortly after one. Those who had attended the earlier masses were now indoors or making their way back to smaller villages and hamlets in the countryside beyond. Fewer people were on the streets. Children were seen less and less and the air was filled with the tantalising aroma of cooking.

The crew of the *Unwanted* had also left, mixing with those who lived elsewhere until out of sight of Tomino, then leaving the roads and making for their hiding place in a wood above the village.

'So far, so good,' Sherman said when the last of them arrived.

'The smell of food got to me,' said Woolcott. 'I'd

have given nearly anything to have gone into someone's house and asked for a lump of fresh bread.'

The others agreed. It had been some time since they'd eaten.

'And a drink,' said Hancock. 'I came very close to asking an old guy if he'd sell me a bottle of plonk.'

Alcoholism had been responsible for Hancock being given 112 days and a dishonourable discharge from the RAF. A twenty-four-year-old Canadian, Hancock had been with the RAF since day one as a radio operator, and had taken part in over fifty sorties before his nerve broke. The life expectancy of a bomber's crew had been estimated at six sorties. Every one after six was a bonus, although each could be the last and it preyed on Hancock's mind wondering which would be his. He had witnessed terrible scenes of carnage when colleagues were splattered around the inside of planes, so terrible that their remains were hosed out with high-pressure water.

Like many others who wanted to forget and who wanted not to think about which trip would be their last, Hancock took to alcohol. During bombing runs he was sober but immediately on returning took refuge in a bottle to escape the horrors of war.

On one occasion his binge went on too long. The others in the crew tried their best to sober him up before his condition was noted by the base commander, but to no avail. He was too drunk to take part in an important raid and, there being a drastic shortage of trained aircrew, the bomber never took off. The incident ended his career.

'Me, too,' said Lynch, 'but sure, they didn't have any Guinness signs up anywhere.'

Lynch's comment brought ripples of laughter.

'I got the impression they were afraid,' Taylor said. 'I've seen it before. They didn't give us much of a second glance, but they knew we weren't Spanish. I'd like to have known what they were thinking.'

'I'm Spanish,' Heroles said, 'and I even got a smile from a couple.'

'You ain't Spanish,' Paca snorted. 'You're a greasy Mex.'

Anger welled up in Heroles. He rose to his feet and very slowly drew a knife from inside his jacket. 'Yeah? And since when could a peon call himself Mex?'

Paca also rose, right up to his full five-foot-three inches, whipping a knife out and baring his teeth. Stung by the insult he was prepared to prove himself.

'Stop it, you guys!' Sherman snapped.

The two were pulled away from each other and Sherman shook his head. Of all places they had chosen this one to have a disagreement.

'What gives with you guys anyway?' he asked.

Casar Rooney answered the question. 'They apparently originate from the same area of Mexico, sir, and look down on each other. It isn't the first time they've had an argument.'

Sherman shook his head again and looked down on Tomino. Twelve o'clock mass had just finished and the congregation was tumbling into the street, hurrying this time, anxious to get home, and by half past one the village was deserted.

'Bit unusual for a village to shut down in the afternoon,' Morris said to no one in particular.

'You're an eejit, sir,' Lynch's voice called over quietly. 'Don't you know what day it is?'

'Nope.'

'It's Christmas Day, sure, the day our Blessed Lord was born.'

'Shit!' Morris swore. He'd lost track of days and dates.

As had many others. They turned to each other to shake hands, smiling, immediately thinking of happier Christmasses in the past.

'You hear that, Kazzie?' Wilson nudged Barcikowski. 'It's bleedin' Christmas.' The Pole looked up, not quite understanding.

'Christmas, you know . . .' Wilson made the movement of rocking a babe in arms. 'Yuletide: good will to all men an' all that swadlin'.'

In time Barcikowski understood. He nodded, made the sign of the cross and wept.

'Poor bleeder . . .'

Harewood had an amused smile on his face.

'What's so funny, Duke?' Hooper queried. 'You know what happened to his kids in Poland.'

'I'm not smiling at that, old thing, I'm smiling at our cockney friend. He has shortened the Pole's Christian name from Kazimerz to Kazzie.'

'And what's so funny about that?'

'The *Kazzie*, old thing, is London slang for shithouse.'

'Yeah?' Hooper had to chuckle himself, 'and what's a *Gilbert?*'

'This isn't the time, old thing. Perhaps later.'

Harewood turned his head at the sound of singing. Barcikowski, squatting on the ground, was singing quietly to himself in Polish. Although no one could understand the words they recognised the tune of *Silent Night*.

Lynch joined in, then Rocard and Henru, then others, until all of them, in voices no louder than that of a hum, celebrated the birth of Christ.

Afterwards no one spoke for some time. Some went off alone into the wood with their thoughts. Others dozed, the remainder just staring at Tomino rather than engage in conversation.

Around five o'clock Hooper broke the silence.

'Weather's turning,' he said.

The mood changed. The sun was partly obscured and rain-clouds were moving in from the Atlantic.

'That's all we need. Stuck up here when it's pissing down.'

'Hang about. There's a car coming.'

Every head turned. A car was speeding towards Tomino from the north.

'I wonder where that's going?'

The car did not slow down when reaching the village, but seemed to increase its speed and went through with a screech of tyres and stopped outside the Casa Solariega de las Flores.

It wasn't the only car outside the walls of the Casa. Three others had been there since early morning.

'A popular man, our Acevedo.'

Another car arrived, this time from a different direction, and a third and fourth.

'An' a merry bollocks to them as well.'

The sky became darker and the first drops of rain fell, light at first then the heavens seemed to open wide.

'At least it will keep them indoors.'

Lights came on around the Casa, showing guards patrolling the outside. Earlier they had counted four guards and although no weapons were seen no one doubted that they carried them.

'We'll give it another hour,' said Sherman.

The hour passed slowly, more so with rain teeming down and thunder crashing overhead, and when the time came to move every man was soaked to the skin.

'Okay, you guys,' Sherman gave the word to move. 'You know what to do. Good luck to you all.'

They broke up into four different groups, checked watches and with nods to each other moved out of the wood and down the hillside towards Tomino.

Guillermo Acevedo Soberon was a splendid host. The finest food and wines available on the Atlantic coast of Spain had been delivered to his home in the days prior to Christmas, ensuring that in his own corner of austere Europe his quests would want for nothing. Those guests who had joined him the previous evening had enjoyed twenty-four hours of luxurious over-indulgence and the new arrivals, marvelling at the feast laid out in the dining room, looked forward to several hours during which they could forget the war raging hundreds of miles to the north, and throw themselves into orgiastic scenes reminiscent of Berlin in the mid thirties. Acevedo greeted his recently arrived guests, made them comfortable with copious amounts of wine and excused himself for some minutes, retiring to a small room on the second floor of the house normally kept locked. Not even the maids were allowed into the room. Acevedo carried out any cleaning that was necessary, and the few pieces of paper that came from the room after periodic cleaning he took away and personally burnt to fine ash.

He unlocked the door, opened it just enough to slip through, then locked it behind him, only then switching on the light. On a table to one side was an extremely powerful transmitting and receiving wireless set. Acevedo sat before it and turned a switch, waited a few minutes for the equipment to warm up then began tuning the receiver.

Christmas Day or not, he had not been idle. The call from Aguilar in the morning had taken his breath away, although he had been able to keep any excitement out of his voice. Immediately afterwards he'd signalled Berlin that a U-boat was stranded and requested instructions. It was a tricky situation, for if British agents got wind of the incident they could have their Ambassador in Madrid insist on the boat being arrested and the crew interned.

At ten minutes past the hour as arranged a reply came through. The stranded boat was *not* German. This part of the signal was repeated so that there would be no misunderstanding. The whereabouts of all U-boats were known. Berlin, however, was extremely anxious to have a description of the boat and instructed Acevedo to utilise all his resources to that end.

If it wasn't German, Acevedo reasoned, it had to be British, and in that case how had it managed to get itself stranded in such an inhospitable place? Her commander would know from charts that the rocks were there. Unless, of course, they had been attempting a landing of some sort? He shook his head. That was impractical. There was nothing of any value in this area of Spain to interest the British.

Still, he had his instructions. Using the telephone extension in the room he called Aguilar at Oya.

Aguilar experienced a mixture of excitement and fearful awe when Acevedo informed him that the boat was not

German. He, too, although not as bright as his superior in Tomino, came to the same conclusion. Only once in his life had he met an Englishman, and he had been a seaman off a ship docked in Vigo. The thought of forty or fifty of them so close made him shudder.

Yes, he would endeavour to obtain a description of the boat, but what should he do about it in the meanwhile? Acevedo replied that this was a matter for the Spanish military authorities. Aguilar then sent for some of his subordinates and instructed them to keep watch through the night and to report to him should the weather abate.

In the background and keeping a low profile, young Horacio listened to his father's conversations and experienced an even greater thrill. A British submarine right here in Oya!

He recalled one of the divers saying that someone from the submarine had possibly come ashore. So, it maybe wasn't stranded after all. Whoever was still aboard was probably waiting for those ashore to return, unaware that he had discovered them.

Horacio sniggered as he thought how the men in the submarine would be imagining they were safe. But they hadn't reckoned on his vigilance as an observer. This would make him an even greater hero. Oh, that would make the poorer children of the village green with envy! They would wish they were him, every one of them.

But they weren't. They could never be, he reminded himself. He was a born leader and in time they would obey all his commands: just as their parents obeyed his father's commands now.

Chapter Twenty-Seven

Music drifted from the Casa Solariega de las Flores. Someone was playing gramophone records and voices, drunken, different from those on the records, joined in and virtually murdered the efforts of the professional singers.

Fifty yards from the west wall Sherman held up his arm for the men behind him to stop. The lights along the top of the wall had been switched off and underneath in the shadows an armed guard, wearing oilskins for protection against the wind and rain, patrolled back and forth along a well-trodden path.

A door was set in each wall, and on the south side, alongside a similar door, were the main gates, locked and chained to keep out both guards and unwelcome visitors. Woolcott, eight men with him, watched the guard patrol this wall. When the guard reached the west corner he nudged Paca. Paca nodded but did not speak and slithered snake-like to a position twenty yards from the wall and directly in front of the gates.

The third group, on the east wall and led by Taylor, were initiating the same move. When the guard reached the southern corner Heroles, a knife between his teeth, slid noiselessly across the wet earth.

On the rear wall Lee watched Morris disappear from sight as he wiggled his body through a clump of ornamental trees, then he began to count the seconds.

Sherman kept track of the dark figure moving between large cabbages in a well-kept vegetable patch and smiled in the darkness. It occurred to him that getting into the Casa would be easier than he'd first imagined.

The guard further ahead hummed in time to the music coming from the Casa and wished the guests would keep quiet. He would rather have listened to the singer on record than the broken voices of the drunken rich. And he would be glad when ten o'clock came round and the next watch arrived. It wasn't fair that he should be out in the wind and rain with his family at home waiting for him, and the doctor enjoying himself.

Why he needed an armed guard was a mystery. No one would have dared harm him, not with the power he had, but he seemed afraid of something. Still, the guard thought, he was being well paid for the job. His family's Christmas was the best they'd ever had since he'd gone to work for the doctor, and being in his employ gave him a high level of status in the village.

On the south wall the guard was having similar thoughts when something hard hit him on the side of the neck. For the briefest of moments he stopped, his brain instructing him to reach up and determine the cause of his flesh being punctured, then the world began to spin. He lost all orientation. In his mind he saw only a dark void, then he fell, dead before he hit the ground.

Paca raced the last five yards, pulled the knife from the guard's neck and waved. He knew there was no need to check if the man was dead. Woolcott and the others came running, ducked low, halted at the foot of the wall and began helping each other over.

Juan Gardogui still hummed. Not only would he be well paid for his work, but before he left for home he intended to take several winter cabbages from the doctor's garden. The doctor would never miss them and with the rain falling as heavily as it was, by morning the garden would appear as if nothing had been touched.

He never heard a sound until it was too late. A hand gripped his hair and pulled his head back, and just before his throat was slit from ear to ear a voice whispered: 'Heh, Jimmy: Merry Christmas.'

Twenty seconds later the doors in the rear and side walls opened. The group moved through, carrying the dead guards with them, searched the outbuildings then found cover. Woolcott's small unit was already behind shrubs with silent Stens aimed at the house, but there was no need for caution. The grounds inside the walls were empty and all the windows of the house were covered. Conveniently, Acevedo had the external lights still on, which gave Sherman the opportunity to decide on an entry.

The windows were thickly curtained on the inside and outside shutters had been swung together to give the house a more secure appearance.

He waved Harte over and whispered instructions.

Harte nodded and amid blazing light crossed an immaculate lawn to what appeared to be a kitchen door. Seconds later he raised an arm and pushed the door slightly inwards. There was no alarm and he went inside. Sherman rose, the signal for the others to follow, and ran across the lawn.

The sound of music was infinitely louder inside the house, broken at times by shrieks of female laughter and deeper, male guffaws.

Harte, experienced in entering buildings, led the way, picking his way along an unlit corridor and stopping when he came to a small dining room cum breakfast-bar. Ahead was a large opaque window separating them from the main room of the house, through which they could make out the silhouettes of men and women moving about.

The room was large enough for ten men to kneel in. The others knelt along each side of the corridor facing the window, tense now, rain dripping from their sodden clothing, wondering if they would meet with success or failure.

At a loss for something more original to make their entrance Sherman waved for Whipple to come forward, then pushing his mouth against the mail robber's ear whispered instructions. Whipple grinned and nodded. He enjoyed making a dramatic entrance.

Silently the group rearranged their positions. Nelson and Lee, the tallest and two of the strongest, crept to the window and stood facing each other, then joined hands, cupping them for Whipple to use as a catapult.

Whipple moved back several paces into the corridor, braced himself then ran forward. Nelson and Lee caught him, using their strength to help him along and threw him through the opaque window.

As the window shattered into a million pieces the men and women on the other side, all in various stages of undress, froze in a tableau of wickedness. A rain-soaked bundle came through the glass, landed on the floor with a bump, rolled once, then rose. They saw a scarred face grinning with malice, a frightening face that prompted one of the women to scream: just as a horde of other wet figures tumbled through both the window and the door alongside.

Whipple was already sinking his boot into a fat, bare stomach, its owner collapsing and exhaling air like a ballon being deflated.

The rough and tumble of the corridor in the New Forest came into its own. Six men and seven women were in the room, and although the men recovered their fright and attempted to protect their womenfolk they stood no chance. Fists and boots hit them with the power of hammers. Knives flashed. Women screamed with absolute terror. Someone took the opportunity to turn the volume on the gramophone up and Welrods popped.

A beautiful dark-haired woman, naked except for panties, suspender belt, stockings and high-heeled shoes slammed against a wall as bullets from a silenced Sten stitched her from groin to neck. A naked man appeared at the top of an ornate staircase holding an Austrian-made Steyr automatic pistol, not quite sure of the cause of the commotion. His eyes nearly popped out of his head when he saw the massacre below him. He raised the pistol but before he could take aim a Welrod popped and his lifeless body tumbled to the ground floor. At that moment the telephone rang.

Horacio Aguilar had received some disturbing news. Rodolfo Valdes, a close friend and business acquaintance, had disappeared. His wife had just telephone to say that she had been with him the night before when a visitor arrived. Rodolfo had gone outside and not returned. No one could find him and she feared for his life. Could the good Señor Aguilar help?

Aguilar replied that he would do all he could and when he replaced his receiver lines of worry crossed his forehead. He called his wife and told her, suggesting that Valdes' disappearance coincided with the submarine being among the rocks. The situation, if there was a connection, was getting beyond him, he said. His wife urged him to call Tomino, which he did, and became more concerned when Acevedo did not answer his call.

There was something wrong, he said. He knew Acevedo would be at home that evening. there was a party being held there and Acevedo was waiting for news of the submarine. He tried again, then a third time and, on the verge of panic, called the police chief in Tomino to investigate.

'Leave it,' Sherman said, when the telephone rang for the first time.

Two men were still alive. One, naked but for a woman's skirt, had been badly knocked about and the other, fully clothed, had been shot in the arm.

'I want information from them,' Sherman said without giving them another glance and instructed the others to search the house.

'This is the way a man should live,' Harewood commented, taking a bite from a roasted goose. 'Beautiful food and beautiful women. And, I think, the way a man should die.'

'You're welcome to any of them' Woolcott said while rummaging through a desk. 'I might just help myself at that, my good sir,' Harewood retorted and made for the stairs. The telephone rang again but was ignored.

A small arsenal of arms was discovered and enough ammunition to keep them going for some time, which delighted everyone. Someone found documents that were self-explanatory: a detailed description of how the escape line was broken and its history since.

'Find a briefcase or something,' Sherman ordered, 'and wrap them in something waterproof. They must get back undamaged.'

The radio was discovered and reduced to rubble. Lynch broke into song and had to be told to keep quiet since he sang in English. He was on his way to becoming drunk, Sherman noticed, having drunk the best part of a bottle of wine.

But Lynch wasn't alone. They were all hungry and

thirsty and the feast Acevedo had prepared was the best meal they would have for some time to come. Sherman shrugged and lifted a bottle of white wine to his lips.

The telephone rang a third time and someone commented: 'Whoever it is, is insistent.'

'He's wasting his time,' said another voice.

The two survivors had been uncooperative at first but a few telling stab wounds relieved them of any desire to be brave. They spoke rapidly, only too pleased to unburden their souls.

Wilson came rushing down the stairs laughing out loud. ''Ere!' he called. 'You know what? Old Duke's only up in a bedroom having it away with a bit of stuff!'

'You what?' heads turned in Wilson's direction.

'I ain't joking, guv'nor. He's givin' it one up there, and she's lappin' it up.'

There was a rush for the stairs as the group, deprived of women for some time, hurried to witness what was undoubtedly an unexpected turn of events.

'Bloody hell!'

They crowded into a large bedroom and as Wilson had reported Harewood was indeed making love. He had removed his filthy trousers and boots and was pumping hard into a Spanish woman of exquisite beauty, whose moans indicated she was enjoying herself.

No one spoke. They just stood, envious of Harewood, and watched the couple climax together. The woman entwined herself round Harewood and growled from deep in her throat, then her head went back, mouth wide open, and a long, thin baby-like whine emerged.

Harewood's body jerked several times before relaxing. He groaned and said: 'My God, did I need that!'

He rose from the bed and bowed to his audience who, rising to the spirit of the occasion, applauded.

'I think we can draw the line at rape,' said Woolcott.

'Rape?' Harewood appeared offended as he pulled on his trousers. 'The dear thing was lying here pissed as a pudding, sir, with her arms outstretched. She must have imagined me to be the chap on the stairs. The darling begged me to make love to her and I couldn't very well disappoint a lady of breeding. I mean, sir, one only has to look at her to realise she has aristocratic lines, and it was but fitting I should be the one.'

The woman was spreadeagled across the bed with a smile on her face, her sexual appetite satisfied and now in a drunken sleep.

Harewood fastened his boots and rose.

'Right, let's go,' Woolcott ordered. 'We've wasted enough time.'

'Aw, sir!' Wilson protested, his flies undone, 'I wanted to dip me wick as well.'

'Out!' Woolcott snapped, but could not help smiling at the same time.

'Jimmy,' Harewood smiled like a father to his son and waved an admonishing finger, 'she wasn't for the likes of you. The dear lady was nobility and one must keep one's nookie for one's own class.'

'Bollocks!'

'My goodness, yes, and those also. But, Jimmy, my friend, just for you I shall reveal what she said as she was wrapped in ecstasy . . .' Harewood piloted Wilson to the stairs, an arm around the cockney's shoulders and talking in low conspiratorial tones.

'She never . . . !' Wilson said, spellbound.

On the bed the sleeping woman still smiled.

A few moments later there was another unexpected turn of events. A cellar was found, with a tunnel leading to an outbuilding where three men were chained to a wall. They were barely conscious, badly beaten, and when keys were found to release them they had to be carried back to the house.

'Jesus!' Tommy Stone choked when he saw the state of the new arrivals. One of them had had the tip of his nose cut off.

Brandy was forced down their throats, a practice Rutledge was not keen on since he did not know the extent of any internal injuries, but some kind of tonic was need to revive the men so that they could identify themselves.

They coughed and opened their eyes. Fear immediately registered and Rutledge, his medical experience coming to the fore, calmed them.

'Who are you?' one of them asked in an Oxbridge accent.

'More to the point, old chap,' Harewood said, 'who are you?'

'Flying Officer Douglas Payne. They are,' he moved his head towards his companions, 'my navigator, Denis Lister and my flight engineer, Harvey Deane. Are you English?'

'It doesn't matter who we are, old chap. What matters is that we must get you out of here. You're in an absolutely shocking state. What do you think, sir?' Harewood looked to Sherman.

'Can you walk?' Sherman asked.

'I very much doubt it. Our host was rather sadistic and showed us in advance what he would do if we tired to escape. Not that we could.'

'Are you hungry?'

'Haven't eaten for days.'

'Okay, there's plenty here. Eat what you can and then we're leaving.'

'But, who are you all? What are you doing here?'

'No questions, friend. There isn't time, and I wouldn't tell you anyway.'

Bernardo Amor Sepulveda, Tomino's chief of police, respected by some and feared by most, was angered to get a call from Aguilar. Amor regarded himself as being superior to Aguilar and had the request been to investigate the safety of anyone other than Acevedo, he would have told Aguilar where to get off. It wasn't often he was off duty and Christmas Day was special. He'd enjoyed himself so far and was feeling the warmth of the day's wine inside him. His wife and family protested against him having to go out on a wild night,

Christmas night of all times. He had no desire to go out himself, but the good doctor had been responsible for his present good fortune and it would not do to be on his bad side.

Reluctantly he began to get ready.

'These guys are in no condition to walk seven yards, never mind run seven miles,' Hooper pointed out, 'and carrying them would slow us down.'

Sherman acknowledged the observation and gave the matter thought. He didn't want to leave the fliers behind yet they would become a burden he could do without.

'What about the cars outside?' Lyman Halls jerked his head.

Sherman brightened. 'How many are there?'

'Seven, and two in the garage.'

'Okay, forget about those in the garage. Everyone get outside and into the other cars. Take food if you need it, the arms, documents and passengers. Go!'

Although they seemed to have spent hours in the house in fact only twenty minutes had passed since the first man had climbed the wall. They began filing out, and before leaving Sherman supervised the rear-guard. The telephone was ripped from the wall, six records put on the automatic gramophone with one playing, then leaving no witnesses to tell of their visit he followed his men to the door in the east wall.

The cars' engines had already been started with keys taken from their dead owners, and apart from the noise they made the night was still quiet. Faintly, from the other side of the wall, came the voice of a Spanish opera singer.

Sherman locked the door, threw the keys over the wall and made for the leading car where the front passenger door was swung open waiting for him.

'Let's go,' he said, climbing in.

The cars, in line, revved hard then began moving in a motorcade through Tomino. Windows and doors in the village were tight shut, the streets deserted, except for a solitary figure huddled beneath a waterproof cape hurrying in the direction of the Casa. The figure stopped to allow the cars to pass, then with a last look at them continued on his short journey.

It was too murky for Amor to see the faces of the people in the cars and for a moment he wondered at them leaving so early. The doctor had said his guests would not be leaving until the next day.

What did he care? They were all depraved anyway.

No guards? Amor stopped when he reached the house. He looked about him but where there should have been men patrolling there were none.

He approached the main gate and looked through. The doctor's large collection of gramophone records was getting an airing, he could hear. But where were the guards? Amor called out, expecting them to come running. When they didn't he called again, louder, but still no one came.

Something *was* wrong, he reasoned. Aguilar had been right in his suspicions. His heart began to beat fast and wasting no more time he pushed his finger on the button that would sound the bell inside, holding it there and moving his feet as if starting a run, mentally willing the doctor to come out and harangue him.

When after two minutes no one appeared he threw caution entirely to the wind and climbed over the gate, tearing his uniform on barbed wire in the process, and approached the house. No one answered his knock or the bell. He went round to the side and rear, found no doors open and came back to the front, took a deep breath then smashed a window to gain entry.

Less than two minutes later Bernardo Amor Sepulveda was running through Tomino's streets yelling at the top of his voice. In the centre of the village he stopped, his face a mask of horror, and threw up, the vomit running down his cape to be washed away by the continually falling rain.

Doors opened a fraction and when keen ears heard the slightly incoherent tale they opened wide. Men, some barefooted and without coats, rushed into the open, oblivious of the rain, all heading in the direction of the finest house in Tomino. Amor had been yelling that the doctor had been murdered and they hoped that on this Christmas Day it was true. It would be the finest gift they could ever wish for.

Amor burst into his own home whimpering. He'd seen nothing like it since the civil war. With trembling hands he dialled Oya and between bouts of vomiting he told Aguilar of the terrible scenes at the Casa Solariego de las Flores.

'My God!' Aguilar nearly threw up himself when he put his telephone receiver back on its hook. 'It's horrible! Just horrible!'

Aguilar's wife had to sit down and be fed a measure of French brandy and beside her, holding her hand, Aguilar began to put two and two together.

An unidentified submarine, probably British, lying in the rocks making no effort to leave. A dinghy below the surface weighted down with rocks: Valdes' disappearance and now the horrible massacre in Tomino.

It couldn't have been done by one man, nor by a handful. To have gone into Tomino and got past the guards would have taken more than a handful: seven car loads – maybe the whole crew!

Aguilar jumped to his feet and grabbed the telephone, calling the local army chief and demanding he get more soldiers into the area at once.

'What!' he yelled into the mouthpiece, then slammed it down and turned to his distressed wife. 'The men along there are all he has! Thirty against how many? I've got to do something . . .'

There were few arms in the village. Following the civil war Franco's forces had searched just about every house in Spain – certainly in the areas where most of his opponents were – and confiscated any weapons they found. Franco was taking no chances on being deposed and made it a capital offence to carry or conceal a firearm of any kind.

Aguilar, loyal to Franco, was one of the few allowed to hold a firearm, as were some of his supporters in Oya, although between them they could only raise seven weapons. Aguilar's was a Hungarian-made Mannlicher rifle taken from a dead soldier of unknown origin fighting in one of the International Brigades against Franco. It was still in good working order and surrounded by his supporters he hurried south to the rocks.

Horacio Aguilar overheard every word his father said and when the door closed he rushed upstairs to a room his father normally kept locked. Horacio knew where the key was kept. Ever since he'd discovered the room three years before it had been his secret place. He'd rubbed the gold crucifixes packed in cases stacked in the room, played with the gold and silver coins and read the names on the lists of people his father had personally shot during and after the war. He had also played with the old Colt revolver at the bottom of one particular case.

Lovingly Horacio took the revolver from the case. He knew every inch of it. When left alone in the house he had always gone to the room and taken it out. He had taken it apart and reassembled it dozens of times. The Colt intrigued him. Made in 1915 for the British Army it had hardly been used. The barrel was extra-long, shiny where he had polished it, and now just began to fit into his small grip. The holster was just like the ones seen in American films about the Wild West. On a belt, it strapped to a man's waist and hung down his hip, and still had a fresh smell to it: practically new.

Horacio strapped the belt and holster to his waist, fastening the buckle through a hole he had made himself ready for a day such as this, then looked for the ammunition. There was plenty, he knew, carefully wrapped in protective paper to stop it deteriorating.

Like a cowboy he loaded the revolver then pushed it into the holster. On his small body it reached down to his knee. And it was heavy, but that did not matter.

Downstairs he could hear his mother weeping. She'd

been like that since his father had gone out. She wouldn't be weeping later when they returned. She'd cry, but with happiness, when she learned that her son had taken part in a battle with the British and killed them all single-handed. He wouldn't just be a local hero then. He would be given a medal.

Very carefully he closed and locked the door, crept downstairs and left the house by the kitchen door, collecting his new glasses and bicycle on the way and pedalled as fast as his young legs would carry him two miles along the coast.

Chapter Twenty-Eight

'Stop, for Christ's sake!' Sherman suddenly shouted.

So far the journey by car had been uneventful. The local population were too preoccupied with the festive season to worry about what was going on around them. No one, not even an animal, had been seen on the way. It had been bumpy but there had been no complaints. By car there was only twenty minutes of bad road to the boat.

Rocard braked so hard that the second car ran into him.

'Bloody stupid frog!' Adams, driving the second car, shouted from his window.

Then they saw the searchlights. Immediately the cars' headlights were switched off and Sherman signalled for everyone to get out.

'We've been tumbled,' Wilson said with a touch of fear in his voice.

'How many can you see?'

'Ten.'

'Twenty.'

'There could be more in the trucks.'

'Then we fight our way out, okay?' Sherman let his

voice carry to the circle of men around him. 'Wasn't that what we agreed on? Everyone or no one?'

'Right on, chief!' Morris replied.

'Are those guns loaded?' Sherman made reference to the captured weapons.

'All ready for the off, guv'nor.'

Acevedo's home had boasted five Beretta sub-machine guns, eleven Mausers, three Mosin-Nagant and two Lee-Enfield rifles: eighteen hand-guns of various manufacture and a box of British Mills bombs.

'Then here's what we do . . .'

'I tell you I saw lights down there!' Aguilar was close to hysteria.

'Where?' the young army major asked, with a shrug of his shoulders. 'I can see nothing.'

'They were there, I tell you! Several of them, like the headlights of cars, and remember what I told you about . . .'

'All right, Señor Aguilar,' the young major pacified him. 'I will send a squad down to investigate.'

Aguilar looked further south. He hadn't imagined it. He had seen the lights weaving along the twisting road then go out.

The bad weather hadn't abated. Waves still crashed into the rocks and the low tide once again showed the tops of the two periscopes. On the narrow beach under the cliffs tired and cold soldiers and divers waited in tents for the storm to blow itself out, cursing whoever had brought about the emergency that had taken them away from their Christmas feast.

Unseen, Horacio Aguilar leaned his bicycle against a tree several hundred yards from the cliff-top and crawled to his personal observation post. On reaching the post he wished he had brought his trenchcoat. He was soaked through already and would most certainly catch cold. Then he reminded himself that admirals did not always have the time to put on a coat, particularly in an emergency and that's what this was.

He heard his father shouting about lights to the south and focused his glasses in that direction.

'Magnificent!' he said in awe as the world of darkness came closer to him. Although the background appeared green he could see the cars clearly and dark figures running away from them, splitting up into groups and coming his way. He ducked his head and pulled the big revolver from its holster, resting it on the parapet of his observation post and pulling back the hammer. He'd pulled back the hammer on many occasions and squeezed the trigger, but there had been no bullets in the gun then.

Still no one had spotted him. He was pleased at that. It showed that the months of self-training hadn't been wasted after all. Not far away his father was moving into the glare of the searchlights to look down at the sea. A foolish thing to do, he thought. The glare would act like a screen and his father, and the soldiers, would not be able to see clearly into the darkness.

The cars moved again, two men to each, slowly, without lights, and drove closer to the top of the cliff where the ropes were hidden. In front of the cars three groups of men hurried forward, bent low, all afraid but determined to kill anyone who stood between them and their refuge. A fourth group hugged the cliff-top, carrying others in no state to walk by themselves, and gagged so that they would not call out in pain.

The main groups spread out in a long line, their goal to partially encircle the soldiers at the cliff-top and trap them: and once again they paid mental homage to the corridor in the New Forest. The incessant rain had turned the countryside into a bog and would have slowed down the strongest cross-country runners, but their muscles, toughened to a peak of perfection, pushed through the morass as if it were a mere puddle.

Figures came towards them. Everyone dropped. There were five men, soldiers judging by their caps, leaning into the rain and more intent on keeping dry than on what they had been sent out to do. They never stood a chance. One moment they imagined themselves alone in the bleak conditions and the next the lumbering hulk of the Pole rose from the ground. The soldiers stopped, frozen with fear. The apparition looked like a gorilla. They opened their mouths to call out but more figures rose from nowhere and seconds later they had spent their last Christmas on earth.

No one wasted time. The bodies were stripped of weapons, caps and waterproof capes and five impostors began to walk back to the cliff-top.

Horacio saw the cars coming. The German-made glasses really were incredible, he paused to muse. And he could see the soldiers returning. But, wait! One of them was very tall and he had made mental note that none of them who had gone out were taller than his father. He guessed what had happened and let the glasses fall onto his chest.

Now was the time, Horacio thought. He balanced the big Colt again, held it with two hands and squeezed the trigger.

The *boom* from the Colt took everyone by surprise. Aguilar, the major and his soldiers jumped round shielding their eyes from the searchlights and saw what appeared to be a convoy racing towards them.

'Shit!' Sherman swore when the gun went off. Immediately he switched on his lights and pressed his foot to the floor. The others copied him and Rocard overtook him seconds later, his hand slamming the horn to confuse the Spaniards. The cars spread out in an arc then turned to face the area where Aguilar waited, and as the length of the arc decreased the lights went out. Sherman rolled out onto the ground, waited a few seconds to see that the rest of his men were doing the same thing, then ran for the cover of some trees.

A grenade landed beside one of the trucks, one which contained a generator that operated a searchlight. The truck listed to one side for an instant and returned to an even keel, but it was on fire and almost immediately the searchlight on its roof went out.

Three soldiers dropped dead. As yet only the Colt had fired a shot. The major was stunned. He couldn't believe that three men could just drop dead. But when a fourth fell he realised that whoever was trying to get to the submarine possessed a weapon that was a military dream.

Then everything happened at once. Guns fired and grenades exploded. Men were running towards him, firing as they came. Those of his own men remaining took cover and returned the fire. The second searchlight went out and the night was suddenly plunged into darkness. Firing continued, heavier now, forcing him into cover with Aguilar who lay behind a rock gripped with terror.

Jefferson, Morris and Hancock ran from the trees carrying long ropes. Quickly and without making mistakes they tied the ropes to the base of the trunks then ran to the cliff-top and threw the coils over, running back to the trees and firing at the same time.

Hooper, Hewes, Lee and Stockton shuffled along the edge of the cliff towards the ropes. As they approached the firing intensified, holding the Spaniards down while they prepared to abseil down the cliff-face.

The passengers had been warned in no uncertain terms. Were they to do anything that would harm the retreat they would immediately be killed.

Hooper went over first with Flying Officer Douglas Payne hanging from his neck, legs around his waist. He kicked out, sailing into the night and dropped with a thump on the ledge not far below. Hewes landed a second later, then Lee and Stockton.

'Okay, the path,' Lee said, holding his charge up with one arm.

Then from the beach below came rifle fire.

'Jesus, they're down there as well!'

Hewes pulled the pin from a grenade and threw it over. The grenade exploded prematurely half way down and took a section of the cliff-face with it. Braxton and Nelson appeared and recognising the danger from the beach pushed ahead, loosing off shots at where they thought the enemy might be.

Above, Sherman concentrated his fire on the spot where the Spanish officer had taken cover and allowed his mind to stray for a moment. He couldn't explain it, but commanding a covert operation seemed to come naturally to him. He'd known exactly what to do when he realised their presence had been discovered, and so far it was going well.

Aguilar realised there was more to the submarine than met the eye and told some of his own men to get help. Using Aguilar's car they were quickly back in Oya, ringing the church bells to inform the countryside of an invasion and frantically telephoning Vigo for assistance. Aguilar himself, although horribly afraid, was holding his own. The initial panic had gone and in cover he was placing his shots carefully, fairly certain that he had made more than one hit, although he could not understand how so many men could have been aboard a submarine. There seemed to be hundreds of them.

Aguilar's confusion was the result of New Forest training. The crew of the *Unwanted* kept on the move, firing a shot from one position then running to another to fire again, giving the impression that their numbers were vast.

Conditions on the path leading to the narrow beach were far from ideal. Heavy rain, sea-spray and winds turned the path into a slippery and tortuous obstacle course. There was no time to feel one's way down. Gunfire from the beach forced Nelson and Braxton to roll, jump, and slide down the path, at times falling heavily from one level to the next, but always returning the fire from the beach.

Walton, Kean, Thornton, Carroll and Lynch were not far behind, and on hitting the beach Nelson and Braxton immediately ran into the sea. A grenade exploded above the tents which had housed the divers and soldiers on beach duty, for a second illuminating the beach with bright light and allowing the retreating force to assess their strength. The squad had retreated farther along the beach and were behind cover, beginning now to pin down the increasing numbers gathered on the ledge fifty feet below the cliff-top.

Above, the screams of wounded and dying men pierced the night. A searchlight came on, blinding Sherman on the cliff-top, a second later being knocked out, accompanied by a renewed barrage of battle-cries and fearful yells from the now dwindling numbers of invaders.

Eventually Sherman, Harewood, Stockton and Wythe were left. They lay flat by the edge of the cliff in a semi-circle, their rapidity of fire diminished, picking their targets with more care now that they were alone. Apart from the screaming of the wounded the yells and battle-cries had ceased, making the Spaniards realise that they were now in the majority on the cliff-top.

Sherman saw vehicles return from Oya, turned slightly for better aiming and shot out three headlights. The others were very quickly extinguished and the intensity of firing now went in reverse. Heavy machine-gun fire came from the general direction of Oya, forcing Sherman and the rear-guard to keep their heads down, allowing them only the odd shot in reply.

The quintet of Walton, Kean, Thornton, Carroll and Lynch were snaking along the rain-soaked beach towards the Spaniards who were pinning down the main force as they still tried to negotiate their way down the path. At times the defenders altered their aim, peppering the beach with bullets and grunting with satisfaction when they heard the unmistakable *thunk* of lead hitting human flesh: but the figures approaching them on their bellies kept coming.

Still wearing their clothes Nelson and Braxton swam out into the churning waters then dived to the bottom to remove the stones holding down the dinghies and breathing sets. To reverse what they had done the night before took six times as long. Struggling in icy-cold water they were forced up for air time and time again, eventually releasing the dinghies which shot to the surface out of their control and bobbed like corks on the tempestuous surface. Others, they could not tell who they were in the dark, plunged into the surf to retrieve the dinghies and pull them towards the shore.

Nearing exhaustion Nelson and Braxton removed their boots and fought the power of the sea while they pulled the flippers on their feet, then holding onto each other for support fastened the breathing sets on their backs. Each gave a thumbs-up sign and, still wearing their clothing, pushed out against the in-coming tide to where the boat lay.

One dive took them down to the conning tower and the top lid opened easily. Braxton went down first, pushed himself against the side and waited for Nelson, pulling hard on his companion's feet to save time. As he came, Nelson pulled the lid shut and used his remaining strength to lock it.

The bottom lid was the most dangerous part of the operation. The water trapped in the compartment between the lids was to be allowed to drop into the boat, and the pressure in the boat was less than atmospheric. Before leaving to carry out the mission the valves that delivered air for normal breathing in the boat had been shut. There had been more than enough air left in the hull for Nelson and Braxton to do what they had to do, but during the time they had been away the air was being gradually used up. It found its way into the cork lining. Hot machinery used it as a coolant, reducing its value to man, gradually turning it into a poisonous gas.

With the pressure in the compartment slightly greater, the interior of the boat was in a partial vacuum, which meant that when the bottom lid was opened the water trapped in the compartment would rush into the boat leaving a near-perfect vacuum behind it, fatal for the human body dependent on living in a pressurised atmosphere.

Braxton lowered himself and hauled on the large handwheel, growling beneath his face mask as it tried to fight against him. But it turned. The movement was slow but it turned, then he heard the cams coming off the dogs. He nudged Nelson's leg and began pulling on the wheel. A sucking sound penetrated their masks as the seal on the lid was broken. Water rushed through the small gap and Braxton had to brace himself to hold the lid as the lower pressure in the boat tried to pull it shut.

The water level dropped rapidly and when Nelson felt it reach his head he quickly tore off his mask and pushed it into the growing space above him, allowing the air to rush from his bottle and fill the space.

Below him Braxton was screaming with pain. His arms were stretched tight, trying to keep the lid from closing. The water level dropped agonisingly slowly and he knew that if the lid were to shut neither of them would have the strength to lift it again.

When the level dropped to half-way, Nelson removed his breathing set, jammed the valve open with the strap and let it drop. Precious air bubbled into the space and he lowered himself down into the remaining water to help Braxton. His lungs screamed in protest as he pulled on the handwheel but it gave Braxton a moment of respite. He, too, removed his breathing set, took several deep breaths and slid down to relieve Nelson, then taking it in turns they held on until the last drop of water was sucked into the boat.

The pressures equalised and the lid gave a sudden lurch, swinging upwards and crashing into Braxton's shin before dropping again. But the biggest danger was over. The lid lifted again, much more easily this time and nearly fainting from exhaustion they dropped into the warmth of the boat, trying to find their feet and falling against a bank of pipework. The boat listed acutely to one side and finding their bearings in the dark proved difficult. Time and again they fell over, standing on two feet only when Braxton found the switch to put on the emergency lights.

A penetrating scream arose from the beach when a knife thrown by Walton hit home. A Spanish soldier jumped from cover with the knife sticking from his chest, screaming, yet not quite believing that he was about to die. His screams unnerved his companions who also stood, prepared to surrender, then they, too, fell when soaking, determined men took their lives.

Although they were in the boat Nelson and Braxton had another danger to overcome. The pressure was still lower than atmospheric, which caused temporary deafness. Their lungs tasted the foul air and rebelled, hacking and swelling, demanding the right ratios of oxygen and nitrogen before they could function in the manner nature intended.

They felt their heads become light. Nelson laughed as if drunk then staggered to the valves that supplied breathing air, dragging on them and thanking God when he felt the zephyr of wind as the life-giving mixture swept through the boat.

Ears popping and lungs heaving, Nelson slid to the floorplates to recover. Nearby, Braxton was in a similar situation. They looked at each other, drawing heavy breaths, then smiled. Both had the same thought. It looked as though they were going to get away with it. Then they nodded, rose, Nelson making for the conning tower and Braxton for the levers that operated the blow-valves.

Nelson hung on to the conning tower ladder and took several more deep breaths. He still felt dizzy and lightheaded. Braxton watched and waited. Nothing would be gained by pushing Nelson. They could afford no mistakes at this stage and had to be certain that they were capable of carrying out the next part of the operation.

Nelson was bent over now, coughing and wheezing, then he came upright, turning, his face bright red.

'Now!' he tried to shout and climbed up to open the bottom lid.

Braxton pulled the levers, and air, compressed to 1,000lbs to the square inch, rushed into the ballast tanks. Immediately the boat began to rock, then regained an even keel as it lifted from the bottom and rose to the surface.

In the conning tower compartment Nelson dropped the breathing sets down into the boat and braced himself. He felt the unmistakable rise of the boat, counted to three and opened the top lid. Water rushed in but the boat was on the surface, bobbing in the storm and too close to the rocks for comfort.

A dinghy was already on its way out, filled with men. Another was being pushed from the shore and men were climbing into a third. Nelson clambered down to the deck and ran aft to wait for the first dinghy, aware now of heavy firing on the cliff-top.

Woolcott was in the first dinghy.

'Right!' he told Nelson breathlessly. 'Get down below and wait for my orders. The rest of you remain here and be ready to give the Old Man cover when he comes over.'

As the second dinghy arrived the first returned to shore, followed by the second and soon after the majority were aboard. The passengers were bundled unceremoniously through a hatchway on the after deck.

Under Woolcott's command the engines were started and the boat manoeuvred into the middle of the inlet. Fifteen men were on deck, kneeling with guns aimed at the cliff-top, waiting for a barrage they knew would come.

Eventually everyone was on board except for the four men on the cliff-top, and Adams and Whipple on the beach, each standing by a dinghy and with guns aimed upwards.

Woolcott switched a searchlight on and aimed the beam on the cliff-top, the signal for Sherman to make his retreat, and switched it off a second later.

'Okay!' Sherman paused in his firing and told Wythe to start moving. Wythe, still on his stomach, inched back towards the edge, felt for a rope and slid over.

'Now you, Duke!'

Harewood fired a last shot then disappeared.

'Rush!'

It was Stockton's turn. He raised himself slightly, pitched a grenade and as it exploded, rolled and vanished.

Sherman was alone. He fired two pistols at once to give the impression that he wasn't, then pushed them into his pockets and slithered towards the precipice until he touched the rope with his foot.

The instant the firing stopped the Spanish major realised he was now in the commanding position. He yelled to rally the remnants of his men and ran towards the spot where the invaders had been in cover. There he found the ropes taut and moving slightly from side to side.

'Bring lights!' he shouted, then began shooting at the ropes. One of them snapped and a yell from below told him that someone had fallen.

Torches arrived, and were beamed down to pick out men on the ledge below. Three were helping another to his feet, a sight that made the major grunt with satisfaction. Aguilar arrived and in moments the cliff-top was lined with armed men, each of them eager to be the first to kill one of the invaders.

Suddenly the night lit up. On the conning tower of the *Unwanted* Woolcott switched on a powerful search-light, instantly exposing the line of men high above, and in the same instant fifteen crew members, kneeling on the after deck of the boat, directed a barrage of fire in the same direction. Several of the enemy fell, some of them toppling over the edge and the remainder scattering to safety before the searchlight was switched off again.

On the conning tower Woolcott gripped the edge tight, praying that Sherman would be safe. He'd wanted to be part of the rear-guard but Sherman had ordered him to be one of the first aboard. Sherman was responsible for his crew's safety, he'd said, and there was no way he was going to leave any of them in a dangerous situation. He would be part of the rear-guard himself and, okay, he might be killed, but with Woolcott already aboard there would at least be one officer capable of commanding the boat.

Woolcott used the searchlight twice more before Sherman and the others reached the beach, each time sending the Spaniards scurrying for safety, then again while the dinghies were half-way to the boat. He gasped with relief when, after what seemed to be hours, they were dragged aboard and pulled down to safety.

The men on deck were hurrying down hatches when, quite unexpectedly, blazing lights came from the shore. All available vehicles had been driven to the edge of the cliff with their headlights on full-beam. Woolcott ducked as tracer bullets hummed over his head then, panic welling inside him, pushed his mouth to the voice-tube and gave the order to leave.

'Full ahead. All engines maximum revs!'

The sea immediately boiled when the screws fought to push the one thousand tons against the storm. The exhaust from the diesels roared even above weather noise and the boat shuddered. Then, finding momentum, it shot forward as if from a catapult and bulldozed into the first breaker.

Woolcott sat below the conning tower wall to avoid being hit, every few seconds lifting his head momentarily to monitor their progress and to call down the tube for changes in their course.

Their lives no longer in danger, the surviving Spaniards were standing upright on the cliff-top firing from every kind of weapon, screaming and swearing at the Englishmen who had caused so many deaths in their homeland. No one heard them. The wind and rain carried their words into the night, dismantling them, mixing them with other noises of the storm until they were just part of a giant cacophony of sound.

The local journalist, having hitherto reported on nothing more exciting than football matches and weddings, had reached what he imagined to be the peak of his career. His new German-made camera clicked repeatedly as he snapped the departing submarine, its lines fairly clear for a moment in the glare of the headlights, halting when it reached the limit of the beams and disappeared into the dirty night.

The women of Oya arrived, wailing and weeping as they searched through the dead for loved ones. More soldiers arrived, too late to take part, and began the grisly task of identifying their comrades and loading the corpses onto their trucks.

'Señor!' someone called to Aguilar.

Aguilar stood alongside the major. They were at the edge of the cliff looking out to sea, breathing hard and wishing they had been able to determine earlier how many men had come ashore. Although they had lost a lot of men Aguilar felt that he had acquitted himself with distinction. He hadn't run away. He'd taken cover and fired his gun as fast as he could reload. In a way he was proud of himself.

There was one thing which bothered him, though. He had presumed the boat and its crew to be English, but during the time they had been fighting, not once had he heard any of them speak. They had screamed and yelled, but hadn't spoken. Had they been English?

'Señor!' the voice called again. Aguilar turned to see a sad face trying to catch his attention.

'Yes?'

'Over here, señor . . .'

A grenade had exploded against the wall of Horacio's observation post, completely destroying it. Horacio lay among the ruins, his head crushed by some of the larger rocks he'd assembled with great care. His teeth were bared in a death grin and his small hand still gripped the big Colt.

'Mother of God!' Aguilar whispered and fell to his knees. He recognised the gun as his own. His face turned up to look at the sky. 'Why?' he implored. 'Why Horacio?'

Aguilar lifted the small limp arm and took the gun by the barrel, unaware that Horacio had pulled back the hammer before he'd been killed. As he pulled the barrel towards him Horacio's finger, still crooked as if to fire, was brought against the trigger, releasing the hammer. For the second time that night the big Colt boomed and Aguilar was thrown back, a large gaping hole appearing in his stomach. A look of surprise came onto his face, then fear. He cried out his son's name once, then died.

Horacio still grinned.

Chapter Twenty-Nine

Spain and the rocks were left behind. Woolcott looked back and saw the lights still aimed at the inlet, their intensity lessening now, and imagined he could make out one or two figures standing watching him.

'Prepare to dive,' he called down.

The lookouts went below. Woolcott took one last look at the horizon to satisfy himself that their departure had not been seen from the sea, then gave the order to dive.

It was an order he was glad to give. At maximum revs the boat was taking a terrible pounding. As Sherman had said, it was too old. Nor had it been built for speed. Every part of the boat shuddered and rattled, giving the impression of a truck running over a continual corrugated surface. As the vertical bow plunged into a high wave the boat momentarily stopped, the effect that of a car ramming a brick wall, then the wall giving way and the car going on in top gear. Sooner or later, Woolcott believed, the boat would shake itself to bits.

The diesels had stopped even before he went through the conning tower hatch, and as he closed the bottom lid they were submerged, at periscope depth, the violence of the sea gone and the boat enjoying a smooth ride.

Sherman had a broken arm, he discovered. Rutledge was working on him. The break had been reset and makeshift splints were being strapped on with electrical insulation tape.

'You okay, Oliver?' Sherman asked.

Woolcott nodded. He was cut and torn, as was everyone else, but he was in one piece. Abseiling down the cliff and running pell-mell down the path they had had no time to think about small things like cuts. They had all suffered, though. Somewhere about their body every man-jack had deep gashes, some so deep that surgery would be necessary to close the wounds.

The boat resembled a slaughterhouse. As well as cuts and gashes more than half the crew had been hit by gunfire and looked more dead than alive. Several sat wherever there was space, bent forward with their heads between their knees, blood dripping from wounds, shoulders heaving as their tired lungs drew deep and rapid breaths. Others were sprawled out, heads back, smiling, giving him the thumbs-up sign, too exhausted to speak.

Woolcott had to hold on to pipework himself. He felt that he just wanted to fall into a bunk and sleep for a week. In the engine compartment he found Nelson and Braxton, the heroes of the hour, and wanted to express his gratitude. But the moment was inopportune. The engineers were standing alongside their diesels, foreheads resting against a cooling water pipe, fast asleep. Woolcott didn't have the heart to disturb them.

Forward, the passengers, just as exhausted as the crew, looked up when Woolcott entered the compartment.

'Are you all right?' he asked them.

'Just a bit confused,' Flying Officer Payne replied. 'You chaps don't appear to be RN. What are you? Who are you?'

Woolcott just smiled and wiped blood from his mouth, then said: 'It would not be appropriate to ask questions, old boy, as you will get no answers. But be assured that barring any disasters you will be back in England within a few days.'

'We couldn't even have dreamed of something like

this happening,' said Payne. 'We had been told in no uncertain terms what our fate was to be, and they seemed to take great delight in telling us how they would shoot everyone involved in the escape line. That would have been terrible.'

'Oh, they'll be doing that all right.'

'God!' Payne lowered his head, shaking it from side to side, tears rolling unashamedly from his eyes.

'Horrible as it might be,' Woolcott went one, 'it is inevitable. The escape line is of no further use to Germany.'

Payne nodded but did not look up. His memory went back to a field in Belgium. He still had the picture in his mind of the bare feet and legs, the skirt: the witch-like figure that had slid into the ditch the night they crashed. He could still remember later, when the rain-soaked figure turned out to be a fourteen-year-old girl called Annette. He remembered Annette giggling at him, a child at that moment, while only minutes before she had risked her life on a mission many grown men would have balked at.

'What a waste . . .' he said, more to himself than to Woolcott.

Woolcott turned to walk away. Three months before he would have tried to say such things with some tact. Not now, he mused. He was part of a different war, a war in which there was no room for emotions.

'Just a minute,' Payne called him back.

'Yes?'

'Is there any way of getting word to the escape line so that they can go into hiding?'

Woolcott thought for a moment before replying. 'I'll ask,' he said.

'Thank you. It would be a shame if they were arrested by the Germans.'

'How do you know we aren't Germans?' Woolcott asked and returned to the control room.

'Why not?' Sherman nodded when Woolcott relayed Payne's request. 'Have a coded signal sent.'

Woolcott prepared the signal and gave it to Carroll who was doing his two hours on wireless watch.

'How are you, Charlie?'

'Knackered, sir,' Carroll took the signal and laid it before him.

'Periscope depth!' Sherman's voice reached them, then after a minute had gone by, 'Surface!'

Carroll's face, where Rutledge had done such a good job, was swollen. He also had a bullet wound in his thigh.

'Send the signal,' Sherman called over.

Carroll began tapping the key and a string of meaningless letters went into the night. That they would immediately be picked up by German listening stations caused Woolcott no concern. All SOE codes were based on poems, and unless the listener knew what the poem was the code was impossible to break.

Woolcott had chosen the poem himself. Literature had been one of his better subjects at college and the poem, Oscar Wilde's *Sonnet to Liberty*, seemed appropriate in title and text.

Several minutes passed before a reply came.

'Signal received and acknowledged, sir.'

How long it would take for the signal to reach Witherspoole was anyone's guess. As yet SOE did not have its own signals department and had to rely on MI6 for relaying wireless traffic both in and out of London, and since MI6 regarded SOE as a bunch of schoolboys playing cloak-and-dagger games, there could be a delay.

'Excuse me, sir,' Rutledge gently pushed Woolcott to one side and knelt to examine Carroll's bullet wound.

'It's clean anyway,' he said. 'A bit of torn muscle but that'll recover. How's your face, Charlie?'

'Bloody sore, doc.'

'Yes,' Rutledge rose, his eyes narrowing, 'no infection from what I can see. More than likely you've knocked it a number of times.'

'I've done that, doc.'

'No matter. I'll give you a jab and you'll be back to

normal in a day or two. In the meantime, let's get this wound dressed.'

Woolcott tried to imagine what was going through Carroll's mind as Rutledge probed into his leg. The son of an Irish boilermaker working at one of Birkenhead's shipyards, Carroll had been in the navy for seven years, and during the last two years of his service had repeatedly and unsuccessfully applied for a transfer to the army. None of the applications ever got past his commanding officer and, hoping that if he made a nuisance of himself the navy would only be too pleased to get rid of him, he deserted.

It was not to be. Like many others who imagined the same and were disappointed Carroll was arrested and locked up. On his release he deserted again, and on being recaptured was awarded a longer term behind bars. Doctors visited him. He was twenty-nine, mature and on the short list for officer training. Why, the navy wanted to know, did a man with so much naval experience jeopardise a fruitful future?

Carroll had had enough of the navy, he told them. Since completing his training he had been aboard an aircraft carrier and hated the cramped conditions below deck, food that wasn't fit to be fed to animals and the dictatorial, arrogant attitude of officers. For being disrespectful to the Sea Lords in this respect his commanding officer added another thirty days to his sentence which, from then on, gave him cause to hate everything about the navy.

Conditions aboard the *Unwanted* weren't much different, Woolcott thought. They were more cramped than any surface vessel and although the food wasn't bad it didn't always come at regular times. But Carroll seemed happy with his lot and had made no complaints.

Everyone was having a job keeping awake, a fact not lost on Sherman and Woolcott.

'We could be in trouble if we come under attack, sir,' Woolcott pointed out.

'I know, Oliver. What do you suggest?'

'Go back inshore and lie on the bottom for a while. We could all do with some sleep.'

Sherman nodded and asked for a sounding. He was too tired to argue.

'Seven hundred feet, sir.'

'Turn around and when we have 250 feet take us to the bottom.'

'Yes sir!' Halls replied with a smile.

Soon after, the boat sat on the bottom. Woolcott was told to sleep while Sherman kept himself awake by drinking mugs of coffee. Three others: Henru, Morris and Barcikowski also stayed awake, monitoring equipment; and Rutledge, refusing to close his eyes, continued to administer to the wounded.

Every few minutes Sherman did a tour of the boat, and on the first discovered that a mountain of food and drink had been taken from the house in Tomino. None of the food was worth eating. It was squashed, rain-soaked and plastered with mud and sand. Drink had fared no better. Jackets rattled when he brushed past them, the pockets half-filled with broken glass, although three empty bottles rolling on the floorplates showed that at least some had survived.

Blood seemed to be everywhere. Those whom Rutledge hadn't got to yet dripped blood from wounds, some caused by bullets and some by the sharp rocks on the cliff. Paca had stripped off and lay naked on his front. Part of his buttocks had been torn away when machine-gun fire raked him. Another bullet had gone through his shoulder and there was a deep gash on his lower leg where a rock had ripped it open during his cliff descent.

Paca was small, but he seemed to have no fear and made up for his size with guts and determination. He hailed from San Pedro in California, although he had originally been a migrant from south of the border. Sherman looked down at the small frame and smiled. There was a list of crimes against Paca outstanding in the United States, enough to have him put away for the rest of his life. They were mostly bank robberies and to escape justice he had done what many other crooks had cause to do when the law got close: he became a seaman, jumping ship in Belfast and living from the point of a knife until his inevitable arrest.

In the bunk below Paca lay Thomas Jefferson, twenty-two years old, an ex-US marine who'd jumped ship in Australia of all places. Jefferson reminded Sherman of himself: blond, hair in a crew-cut, and college-educated. Jefferson had planned to be a lawyer but got himself in with the wrong crowd, got drunk one night and the following morning learned to his horror that he'd joined the marines. That he had been drunk when signing held no sway with the recruiting officer and before he had sobered up he found himself in a training camp undergoing the most unspeakable torture in the form of drilling.

Immediately after base-training he'd been shipped out to the Pacific for advanced training, then on to Australia for leave. In Australia he simply did not return to his ship, but within hours of going ashore was aboard a British freighter bound for London. He learned that few questions were asked of a man when he asked for a berth aboard a British ship. The ships ran the gauntlet of German U-boats which deterred many from signing up and any able-bodied man was made welcome.

In the South Atlantic the freighter was torpedoed and Jefferson was one of the few survivors picked up by a British cruiser. Taken to England, his identity and reason for being aboard the freighter came to light. Interned, he waited with dread for the Marine Corps to take custody of him, but in the meantime SOE came along with the usual proposition.

Jefferson had not come out of this operation unscathed. He hadn't been hit with gunfire but his body was badly bruised and cut, having taken a tumble down the cliff. He would have tales to keep his grandchildren enthralled, Sherman mused.

Stockton seemed to be the only person relaxed in his

sleep. Although cut and bruised he had a contented look on his face.

Rutledge was working on Hancock. The Canadian still had two bullets in him and clenched his teeth as long-nosed pliers probed for them. In the chaos at the cliff-top, Hancock hadn't realised he'd been hit. He'd felt an ache which he put down to the battering his body had taken over the past couple of days and thought no more of it. Only when he was aboard the boat and noticed the colour of his clothing did he appreciate what had happened.

And he'd been lucky. One bullet was caught between two ribs, probably a ricochet, otherwise it would have gone straight through him; the other lodged in his forearm perilously close to an artery.

Sherman's heartfelt gratitude went out to Rutledge. Doc was as exhausted as the rest of them yet he hadn't stopped since coming back aboard, and how he could work so efficiently with his hands burned was nothing short of miraculous. All their hands were burned. Dropping on the rope, or abseiling down the top section of the cliff, they had just gone down as quickly as they could, the ropes burning their hands as they rushed through their fingers at an incredible speed. Sherman's own hands were badly burned, painful, and he had fallen part of the way. Large red blisters were forming on his palms, partly restricting movement. If that's what my own are like, he thought, God knows, what state the doc's are in.

In the control room Sherman found the Pole crying. He never seemed to miss an opportunity.

'You okay, Kazzie?' he enquired.

Barcikowski looked up from the Asdic. 'Yes, okay I am,' the Pole nodded vigorously.

'You're crying again.'

'I always cry. Much sadness cause crying.'

'We'll have our revenge, Kazzie, don't worry.'

'Revenge, yes. Revenge very good. Kill Germans.'

'Yeah,' Sherman walked on, 'we will kill Germans.'

The passengers were still awake and Payne sat up when Sherman approached.

'British and American,' Payne said. 'It becomes stranger all the time. What's an American doing here?'

'Am I an American?' Sherman raised his eyebrows.

'Your accent says so.'

'I can speak Spanish with the right accent, but it doesn't make me Spanish.'

'I'd love to know who you are,' Payne threw his arms wide, a smile forming on his lips. 'I haven't heard a single name so far, which points to you belonging to some secret government department. One hears about chaps like you but one never gets to meet you, and I am fascinated.'

'Fascinated you will have to stay, friend,' Sherman replied.

'You won't give me the slightest hint?'

'None whatsoever, and there will be no point in asking my men either. If anyone were to tell you anything I would have him shot . . . and you as well.'

The smile remained on Payne's face. He did not doubt that the boat's captain would have him shot, but he was still fascinated.

Sherman went on with his tour and eventually returned to the control room for more coffee. His head was beginning to throb and his legs were heavy. The break in his arm was beginning to cause swelling and the palms of his hands felt as if they were on fire. Not at all the condition the officer of the watch should be in. Stateside, he thought, he would have been whisked off the boat with anything worse than a bad cold and hospitalised, pampered by the best medical teams the navy could put together.

He chuckled through his pain. Rutledge could have put the finest doctors in the States to shame: and how many boats over there could be crewed by a bunch of misfits, all shot to buggery and half-battered to death? If details of the mission could be given out his old colleagues would never believe a word, it was so fantastic. An official log would have verified the facts, but there was no log. Nothing of the mission was ever to be recorded: which was a pity, for every member of the crew was a hero in his own right.

Sherman sat on the fold-away stool at the chart table and rested his arms, his mind going over the events of the past two days. He had been responsible for the deaths of God knows how many people, some presumably innocent of any warlike activity. Pictures of the men and women they had killed flitted before him, the blood and chunks of bodies, their screams when they realised they were about to die, yet he could not feel the slightest remorse for his actions. Months before he would have cringed at the thought of taking a life: indeed, he had always felt guilty when he'd had to warn a member of his crew for misconduct.

He shook his head, amazed at the transformation within himself. And the fat Englishman had warned him. He would lose all sense of propriety, Witherspoole had said. He would kill and experience a feeling of satisfaction. He would become an animal.

He hadn't believed Witherspoole at the time. He'd believed he would kill because it was necessary to rid the world of Hitler. But the fat man had been right. He *had* lost all sense of propriety. He *had* felt satisfaction and he *had* become an animal.

And he was tired: God-awful tired. In front of him the chart table began to spin, slowly at first, then increasing until the chart became a spoked wheel turning so fast the spokes became one. He let his head drop until it rested on his arms, then closed his eyes. A few moments was all he needed, he told himself. Just a few moments with his eyes closed would make all the difference in the world.

Chapter Thirty

Sherman woke with a start. Although his mind did not function for several seconds his subconscious told him he should be alert. He sat up, an instant later remembering everything that had occurred on their mission, but he couldn't remember having fallen asleep. A deep-throated roar told him that the diesels were running.

He was in his bunk and he shouldn't have been there. Frantically he pushed himself out of the bunk onto the plates, discovering now that he was naked and partly clean.

'Wha . . . how . . . I don't . . .' he stammered with bewilderment.

Woolcott pushed his head around the curtain. 'Morning, sir. How do you feel?'

'Fine. . . I think . . . How did I get here? I mean, I've no clothes . . .'

'The lads put you to bed, sir. Gave you a bit of a wash, too.'

'But . . .'

'A bomb wouldn't have roused you, sir. You were completely dead to the world.'

'How long have I been asleep?'

'About nine hours, sir.'

'Nine!' Sherman was horror-struck. 'I was on watch. My God!'

'No harm done, sir. The lads waited until you were out, undressed you, gave you a wipe over and put you to bed. When the watch changed they roused Mr Kean to stand the watch, after which I took over. Are you hungry?'

Sherman nodded. 'Thirsty and sore as well. God, I feel as if I've been run over by a tank.'

'I'll help you dress, sir,' Woolcott said, and carefully

took Sherman's clothing from a wire hanger hooked over a pipe.

'Your singlet, sir.'

Sherman's eyes opened wide. The clothing he'd come aboard with was spotless, and it had been ironed with a knife-edge crease in the pants.

'But . . ?'

'Wythie!' Woolcott suddenly shouted over his shoulder, 'do you have a meal ready for the captain?'

'Just about ready, sir!' Wythe's voice came back.

Sherman had no option but to accept Woolcott's aid. With his broken arm he was quite helpless and couldn't so much as fasten a button.

'Allow me to help you, sir,' Woolcott took Sherman's good arm and guided him beyond the curtain. Sherman felt a little light-headed and staggered as he took the first few steps, stopping suddenly when cheering broke out.

The crew was waiting for him, bloodied and bandaged, but cheering, smiling and applauding.

'What in the name of God . . . ?'

'Appreciation, sir,' Woolcott whispered in his ear. 'They appreciate what you have done for them, sir.'

'What the hell do you mean?'

'You stayed behind, sir. You were the last man aboard, and the lads went a lot on that, sir.'

Sherman became embarrassed when, to a man, the crew came to shake his hand. Then a meal was served.

'Bacon and eggs, sir,' Tommy Stone flourished a plate, 'with fried bread, onions and a bit of chicken we nicked ashore and managed to clean up. Guaranteed to contain nothing more poisonous than a spot or two of mud and oil.'

'And to wash it down, sir,' Wilson pushed his way through the throng holding a bottle like a well-trained waiter, 'a bottle of best Dago plonk what survived the journey back to the boat.'

Conscious of everyone watching him Sherman began to eat and discovered he was quite famished. He wiped the plate clean and to the delight of the crew asked for a second helping.

'Bacon and eggs coming up, sir!' Wythe called. 'Chicken's off, though. Couldn't get the cow-shit out of it completely.'

'Bacon and eggs will do fine, Wythie,' Sherman grinned.

Following the meal Sherman went to the control room to establish their position and unconsciously looked above the watertight doors. The name, *UNWANTED*, was still there, but obscured again by hundreds of fingerprints.

'Where are we?'

'Roughly, a hundred miles west of La Coruña, sir,' Braxton told him.

'You saved our lives, Carter,' Sherman said seriously, 'you and Nelson.'

'Nothing the others wouldn't have done, sir. We were all in the same boat, so to speak.'

Sherman doubted if they were all capable of the feat his fellow-Americans had carried out, but dropped the subject and with some difficulty climbed up to the conning tower.

It was a beautiful day. Kean, Henru and Paca were on watch and smiled when they saw him.

'You okay, sir?' Paca asked.

'I'm fine, Will, thank you.'

'We made it, sir,' Paca went on. 'I think we all gave ourselves little or no chance, but we made it,' a grin appeared on Paca's face.

'So far so good, Will.'

'I wonder where they'll send us next, sir.'

'Next? What makes you think there'll be another job?'

'You don't think the Limeys will let us run loose after what we've done, sir? We're the best thing that's happened to them since nookie was invented.'

Sherman allowed himself a smile. Everything Paca said was perfectly true. Witherspoole was one shrewd foresighted individual and would exploit them until they were of no further use to him. And why not? Sherman had to admit he had not found the mission so harrowing that he didn't want to take part in another. On the contrary, for the first time in his career he felt satisfied that he'd done something worthwhile.

Sherman spent two hours on the conning tower before going below and, as if compelled, looked above the watertight doors. Their name had been chalked in again: bright-blue lettering untouched as yet by a human hand, then Harewood passed through, sticking his hand up and touching the chalk for luck.

Where had the Goddamned chalk come from?

He went aft to suggest the crew might clean the weapons they'd acquired and found Wilson, Morris and Adams bent over a bunk talking ten to the dozen.

'Saying prayers, you guys?'

'You what?' Wilson turned, then: 'Sorry, guv, just sharing out a bit of tom.'

Two bunks along Hooper looked to Harewood for an explanation, his face saying all.

'Tomfoolery,' Harewood laughed, *'Jewellery.'*

The bunk was well sprinkled with jewels, watches, cash and gold and silver ornaments.

'Where in God's name did you get this little lot?'

'From the Casa de Whatsaname, guv. They aint got no more use for it.'

'Yeah, I suppose that's true. Anything valuable among it?'

'You what! Even flogging it to a fence we'd get fifty thousand nicker, not counting the old 'ot an' cold.'

'Eh?'

'The gold. That's worth a bob or two on its own, guv.'

'How much cash?'

'About ten thousand mostly in dollars.'

'And what will you do with it all?'

'Well, guv,' Wilson drew a breath, 'me'n Rob is going into business art'er the war, so we needs a bit of capital. Jim, here . . .' he jerked a thumb at Adams, 'knows something about jewels and will help out with advice, so he'll be taken on as a partner. We reckon we should be able to bank £30,000 each, comfortable like, and still have a stack to share with the lads. That's fair, innit, guv?'

Sherman could only laugh.

'But you can have the pick of the bunch, guv,' Wilson said quickly, thinking Sherman was offended.

'I'll take my share like everyone else, Jimmy,' Sherman went on laughing. It suddenly struck him as funny that any of them could have thought of stealing at the time, but then he conceded that it wasn't so strange, for hadn't Harewood taken the time to get his end away?

'Tis disgraceful!' a distinctly Irish voice cut in, 'thieving at a time of bereavement. The Blessed Lord will surely strike you down.'

'Bloody Norah! 'ark at the dirty beast. . . He was only slapping one bird about the tits telling her she was a dirty cow, an' every time he had a slap he had a feel.'

'I did no such ting!' Lynch retorted.

'Course you did! I could see the bulge in your pants. I wouldn't be surprised if you shot your duff just at the sight of them, cos, I mean to say . . .' Wilson played to his audience, 'ain't you Irish only allowed to 'ave it away once a year, roundabout Easter?'

'Rubbish!'

'Yeah, and you probably shot that and all.'

'Ach, you're an eejit, sir,' Lynch shook his head and turned his reddening face away.

'Know what?' Morris said, 'if Betty Grable is waiting at Buckler's Hard she can have all this just for one night with me.'

'Don't forget me,' Wilson gave a dirty laugh. 'We're partners, remember.'

'Yeah, well, if she thinks it's worth it after being with me.'

'Leave it out, mate. With me she'd think she had a return ticket on the Circle Line.'

'Who is this Betty Grable?' Ellery asked.

'You what?' Wilson and Morris went into great detail to describe the famous Hollywood actress, using grunts and moans to good effect, but Ellery kept his face straight.

'Never heard of her,' he said. 'Wouldn't know her from a bar of soap.'

'You bleedin' Gilbert! You probably don't know what a bar of bleedin' soap looks like either!'

Ellery shrugged and went forward to take his watch and as he turned his back he began to chuckle.

Hooper had jumped off his bunk and was appealing to everyone around him. He turned a complete circle twice, his arms wide, face tight with frustration, then yelled at the top of his voice: 'For Christ's sake, will somebody tell me what a *Gilbert* is!'

Someone blew a raspberry and a voice told him to keep taking the tablets.

By nightfall everyone was in an easy mood. The BBC came through loud and clear, and relayed over the tannoy it brought a feeling of homeliness to the boat. Comedians raised laughter and singers were joined by thirty-odd rough voices that would have been better employed in the London docks. All in all there was a happy atmosphere, until Thornton said: 'HE!'

'Dive!'

The BBC was cut off in mid-song as everyone scattered to their posts. Sherman threw himself against the periscope, forgetting he had a broken arm and yelled out in anger. He hooked his bad arm over the sight adjusting handles and slowly began a sweep.

'Nothing,' he said after a few minutes and nodded for Woolcott to man the after periscope. 'Any alarm, Oliver.'

Any alarm meant that both Sherman and Woolcott would man the periscopes, Sherman sweeping forward from the port beam through a 180–degree angle to the starboard beam, and Woolcott sweeping aft from the starboard beam through 180 degrees to the port beam where Sherman began. Sherman was still the commander but under circumstances of *any alarm* either of them could give the order to dive.

'Still nothing.'

'HE coming closer, sir. All around us.'

'Hell's teeth!'

For twenty minutes they maintained periscope depth before catching sight of the vessels causing the Asdic to sound off.

'Damned fishing boats,' said Sherman, 'the same ones we saw on the way down, and there seems to be more of them.'

'They might not have been fishing boats, sir, remember.'

'Coming closer, sir. Hey, they've circled us!'

'I don't like it,' Sherman pushed his head against the periscope. 'Shit! Look at this.'

Woolcott saw what Sherman meant. Fishing boats they weren't. They had obviously spotted the *Unwanted* and were closing in. High bow-waves said they were moving at a speed in excess of twenty knots.

'Dozens of the buggers!'

'Group up. Maximum power!'

The motors whined and pulled power from the banks of batteries, pushing the boat through the depths so fast that the outer tanks began to shake. Several depth-charges exploded at once, all perilously close. The lights went out and the boat rocked several times.

'As the man once said,' Harewood commented, 'for what we are about to receive let the Lord make us truly recover.'

'Enemy in three rows ten thousand yards dead ahead, sir.'

More explosions rocked the boat, closer this time.

'We need to surface,' Sherman said. 'They have our position and can keep up with us while we're submerged. But, Christ, we'll be a sitting duck!'

'Nine thousand yards, sir.'

'May I?' Woolcott raised his eyebrows.

'You can get us out?'

'Maybe, sir.'

'You guys take your time from Mr Woolcott,' Sherman announced.

'Lower periscopes,' Woolcott ordered, 'right into the wells.'

'Eight thousand five hundred yards, sir.'

'Speed?'

'Nineteen knots, sir.'

'Maintain . . . Range?'

'Eight thousand yards, sir.'

'Engine crew stand by. Stand by for blowing tanks and prepare for surfacing. Evacuate for'ard torpedo compartment and secure watertight doors.'

'Seven thousand five hundred yards, sir.'

Explosions ripped through the depths causing tremendous concussion on the boat's hull, at times giving the impression that it was a train being lifted from the rails.

'How could they get on to us so quickly?' Sherman asked no one in particular. 'They don't even know this boat exists.'

The Spanish had not been idle following the boat's departure. A description of it was sent on to Vigo then to Madrid, and passed on to the German Embassy from where it was radioed to Berlin. The description matched that supplied by Victor Brack in Boston and German Intelligence began to put two and two together. Since the boat had sailed from some unknown port in England it would have to return there, and during its journey it would have to run the gauntlet of German craft patrolling the Atlantic coasts of Spain and France. Signals went out to sink the rogue boat as soon as she was sighted.

'Five thousand yards, sir.'

'Maintain speed and depth.'

'Four thousand and closing fast, sir.'

'Man the hydroplanes.'

'Hydroplanes manned, sir.'

'Stand by to blow tanks.'

'Two thousand five hundred and closing, sir.'

'Maintain.'

'Two thousand yards, sir.'
'Stand by!'
'One thousand five hundred yards, sir.'
'Open the bottom lid!'
'Bottom lid open, sir.'
'Prepare!'
'One thousand yards, sir.'
'Maintain . . . maintain . . . maintain . . .'
'Five hundred yards, sir.'
'Blow all tanks!' Woolcott shouted. 'Hydroplanes in diving position!'

Gigantic volumes of air and water disturbed the surface, an indication to the converging patrol boats that they could go in for the kill. The *Unwanted* fought to surface. The tanks were filled with air trying to push her up, but the hydroplanes were in the diving position holding her, preventing her from going up or down.

'Three hundred yards, sir.'

The pressure hull was actually rippling as forces fought each other to take command of the boat.

'She'll break up!' a frightened voice screamed.

'Two hundred yards, sir.'

Above, the attackers were slowing, coming broadside to pitch their depth-charges into the sea where the enemy should be, waiting for the command from the lead boat so that dozens would explode at one time and put an end to the interloper.

'One hundred and fifty yards, sir.'
'This is it!'
'One hundred yards, sir.'
'Reverse hydroplanes! Surface!'

The hydroplanes were moved into the surfacing position and immediately the boat shot to the surface like a cork. The top lid opened and a second later the diesels took over the propulsion.

One patrol boat captain saw the giant dark hull suddenly leap clear of the surface and cried out with sheer terror, for an instant later it tore through his boat as if it were butter. Behind it a second patrol boat met the same fate with a third narrowly avoiding the sharp

'We're getting closer to England,' he said. 'It's damned cold up there now.'

The others said nothing. They just gazed at Ellery, thin smiles on their faces.

'What gives with you guys?' Ellery suddenly became conscious of the eyes on him: as if he was some kind of freak.

'Just talking, that's all,' someone muttered.

But the eyes were still on him. Ellery narrowed his eyes and looked around. They were still grinning. He looked down to see if his fly was undone, then, looking forward to a rest, shrugged and climbed into his bunk. Then he saw why he was the centre of attraction.

The grins on the faces of the others grew bigger. Ellery couldn't help but see the small newspaper picture of Betty Grable stuck to the hull curving over his bunk, and under the picture a bar of used soap.

Ellery had his back to them. They stopped talking and waited with baited breath. His hand reached out, hesitated a moment, then in one swift movement grabbed the bar of soap and kissed it, his body shuddering at the same time as if in the midst of a dirty dream.

A rousing cheer went up.

Chapter Thirty-One

The weather became progressively colder as the *Unwanted* neared the Channel approaches. Rain fell for hours, non-stop, making life for the lookouts most uncomfortable. Thick fog followed, and as they began the run into the Channel snow began to drop.

'At least it will give us a measure of cover,' Sherman commented.

'But also likely to make friendly forces trigger-happy, sir,' Woolcott pointed out.

During his training Woolcott had had it impressed on

him again and again that, if he was ever in doubt, to regard all unidentified shipping as hostile and take whatever steps he deemed necessary. The same advice was given to all naval commanders, and the navy did not know about the *Unwanted*, which put its crew in an unenviable position. They were unarmed and at the mercy of both British and German patrols.

'Then we increase our vigilance,' said Sherman.

At dawn they dived and kept a steady twelve knots to conserve power, keeping to the middle of the Channel as on the outward journey, and below periscope depth. Again no one could sleep. Tension reached even greater heights. With home so close the possibility of being caught unawares drove the very thought of sleep from their minds.

'A reference,' Sherman asked at 2000 hours.

'We should be off Portland Bill, sir.'

He nodded and gave the order to surface.

Bitter cold air swept into the boat which seemed to revive the crew to a great extent and relieve some of their tensions. Conversations began about what they would do when they were ashore. Tall stories came to the fore again and many a raucous roar of laughter reverberated along the boat as the explicit details of some forbidden love affair were revealed.

Sherman had a signal sent off informing Witherspoole that they were home and awaiting permission to approach the Solent. Thirty minutes went by before the signal was acknowledged, and another ninety minutes before instructions came. They were to sail closer to the coast and show two blue lights from the conning tower, shielded from the French side, and enter the Solent with extreme caution.

At 2345 the Isle of Wight appeared on their starboard bow and ahead was the reason they had been advised to proceed with caution. A flotilla of submarines was anchored: thirty boats in five rows of six in-line. Numerous small launches darted at speed from one to another, a few of them narrowly missing the *Unwanted* as she picked her way closer to the mouth of the Beaulieu River.

'Something big on by the looks of it,' Sherman observed.

The deck of the conning tower was crammed with bodies now that the danger was over. Sherman and Woolcott held the commanding position and viewed the boats with interest.

Woolcott nodded in the dark. 'Possibly to bolster the Mediterranean flotilla,' he said. 'From what I can recall we weren't doing so well down there.'

Two boats suddenly broke away from the flotilla and came towards them, taking up positions on either side and keeping pace.

'Now, I wonder what the hell they want?' Sherman muttered.

Word had been sent to all shipping in the Solent to stand-by while a submarine entered. Dozens of pairs of field glasses were trained on the *Unwanted* and, curious of her unusual lines and lack of identification, the fleet commander and the boat serving as his second-in-command decided to investigate.

'They're getting too bloody close,' said Woolcott.

The boats were close enough to make out the face of the flotilla commander who was leaning out as far as he dared to focus his glasses on Sherman.

They came closer until there was barely three yards between them.

'They're showing off, sir, and bloody stupid. All we need is someone's wash to lift us and we'll collide.'

'Goddamned fool!' Sherman growled and lowered his head to the voice-tube.

'Port ten at full speed, them immediately starboard twenty.'

The *Unwanted* swung to one side, thundering forward to bump one of the escorting boats. There followed a *clang* reminiscent of a bell ringing in an empty church, then a second as the *Unwanted* swung in the opposite direction. The boats immediately pulled away and blue Aldis lamps began flashing angrily.

'I'll give them collision,' Sherman growled again. 'Resume original course and speed,' he said.

Woolcott was laughing. 'My good God!' he threw his head back, 'that will really send the Sea Lords up the wall.'

The wash sent out by the *Unwanted*'s sudden burst of speed reached the boats and launches swarming around them. They began to bob as if in the midst of a violent storm. Men fell overboard and some of the smaller boats broke up when the thick steel of the submarines crashed into their flimsy wooden hulls.

The Beaulieu River appeared and as the boat slowed to turn, stern to the river, a rubberised dinghy raced alongside carrying a very irate naval officer.

'Just what the hell do you think you're doing?' he called up, his voice plummy and full of authority.

'Duke!' Sherman called down, 'get up here and bring . . .'

'Didn't you hear me, dammit?' the voice called up again.

'Deal with this goddamned fool,' Sherman pulled Harewood to the front as he climbed through the hatch, 'he speaks the same language as you.'

'My pleasure, sir,' Harewood leaned over and smiled. 'I say there, awfully decent of you to provide a welcoming committee. Much appreciated, but we'd rather do without the fanfare and just trot off home to bed. Jolly good of you, though . . .'

'I'm coming aboard,' the officer shouted, his anger now reaching a peak, 'and you are all under arrest!'

'Sorry, old chap,' Harewood waved an admonishing finger, 'not allowed don't you know? Now why don't you paddle off and play sailors, what? There's a good chap!'

They could see the fury in the officer's face. He was on his feet now, balancing against the rocking of the dinghy, his arms raised above his head in uncontrollable anger.

'I'll see that you get twenty years . . .'

'This guy just won't take a telling,' Sherman pushed

his way to the front again carrying the silenced Sten Harewood had brought up with him.

'Hey, shag-nasty!' he called down, using one of Wilson's greetings. 'You've got to the count of *one* to get the hell out of here.'

'You'd threaten m . . .'

The officer's words trailed off as Sherman squeezed the trigger of the Sten. It put those on the conning tower in mind of a record-player slowing down. The bullets cut a perfect line of holes across the dinghy, which immediately began filling with viciously cold water.

The for'ard deck-hatch aboard the *Unwanted* opened and men piled out, laughing and cheering at the officer who was still waving his arms but now standing knee-deep in water and gradually becoming smaller as he went under. Alongside him, his helmsman, a rating grabbed at the last minute for the occasion, sat stunned beside his outboard motor, not quite certain that what was happening was not a dream.

'Jolly nice to have met you!' Harewood called out as their boat began to move upriver. He waved with a royal salute. 'And we just *must* get together one day for drinky-poohs!'

Harewood's parting words were lost on the officer. The dinghy had vanished and all there was to see now were two small dark spheres sitting in the water.

'Dear God!' Woolcott said between sobs of laughter, 'the Sea Lords will comb the country for us now. They'll never live down the humiliation.'

'Goddamn them to hell!' Sherman was laughing now. 'Let 'em come. I'll back my guys against them any time!'

'I just hope,' Harewood said with feigned innocence, 'that poor chap isn't put on the carpet for misusing naval equipment.'

Shrieks of laughter greeted the remark and Wilson appeared, climbing onto the parapet of the tower with a megaphone, his cockney voiced echoing in rhyme across the water:

'May itching piles consume you
With syph and clap complete,
And lice as large as lobsters
Into your ballbag eat.

And when you're shagged and buggered
Like some old tossed off wreck
May you fall, inside out, through your arse
And break your bleedin' neck!'

More laughter and applause followed, as the *Unwanted* moved upriver.

The boat pulled into the covered shed at 0240. Witherspoole and Morton were on the quay in a state of excitement and jumped aboard before the gang-plank was moved into position.

'Welcome back!' they began shaking hands. 'Welcome back . . . welcome back,' they began to sound like a cracked record.

'Would you like to come below, sir?' Sherman asked.

'Yes . . . yes . . . of course!'

Sherman had never seen a grown man so excited.

'What happened to your bow?' Morton asked with some concern.

'A slight argument with the German Navy, sir,' Woolcott replied, enjoying himself. 'Had to make a few modifications to one or two enemy patrol boats. And talking of modifications, sir, there are several I should like to suggest . . .'

'Anyone hurt?' Witherspoole put in quickly.

Sherman and Woolcott burst out laughing. 'Not as you would notice,' said Sherman.

As they climbed into the boat Sherman put a finger to his lips and whispered: 'No names, sir.'

'My godfathers!' Witherspoole gasped when he saw the state the crew were in. Bruises, cuts and bloodstained bandages were very much in evidence, but through it all the men grinned.

'A present for you,' Rob Morris held out his hand.

Witherspoole held out his own, not knowing what to expect and was surprised to see so many bullets pile up in his palm.

'What's . . .'

'They're what doc pulled out of us,' said Morris.

'But . . . how . . . I mean . . .'

'All in good time, sir,' Sherman nodded to Woolcott who quietly slipped into one of the for'ard compartments.

'You did it!' Witherspoole suddenly began to giggle. 'You actually did it!'

'You didn't expect us to fail, did you, sir?'

'No, no, of course not.'

'We had a bit of a run-in with the navy guys down-river as we came in.'

'I heard,' Witherspoole's face became serious. 'You shouldn't have done that, you know. It could make things difficult for me.'

'You have any trouble, sir, you refer them to us. Ain't that right, you guys?'

'Yes sir!' a chorus came back.

'And another present,' Sherman said, waving for the others to make room. Woolcott returned leading the three airmen. They were blindfolded and holding each other's hands as a guide to the control room. Sherman introduced them but did not mention Witherspoole's name.

'They know nothing about us, sir, or any names. We found them at the end of the line.'

'Well done! Oh, I'm ever so pleased with you!' Witherspoole behaved like a small boy getting his first train set for Christmas.

'What about the escape line?' Flying Officer Payne asked, putting a sudden stop to the jollity.

Witherspoole coughed. 'I did managed to get signals out, but how many got away in time I couldn't say. I do know that the Gestapo went in to arrest everyone involved.'

'And what happens to us now?'

'You shall be taken to London and given into the

charge of RAF Intelligence who, no doubt, will ask you very many questions. Alas, though, you will be kept blindfolded until you reach London, and I should advise you not to attempt to remove the blindfolds. If you do I shall have no hesitation in having you shot. We value the security we have here.'

'I believe you would, sir, whoever you are. Your men made that very plain to us.'

'Then we shall not delay you further. I'm sure you have families who will be glad of the unexpected surprise.'

'We have that, sir.'

'Then . . .' Witherspoole nodded to Morton who escorted the airmen ashore.

With the airmen gone Witherspoole again gushed with gratitude.

'I'd settle for a plate of fish and chips an' a bottle of beer,' Wilson called from behind the main bunch.

'Tonight,' Witherspoole chuckled, 'as late as it is, you can have all the fish and chips you can eat, and all the beer you can drink.'

A cheer went up.

'I've arranged accommodation in the Forest for you. You won't be disturbed and I'll have the best doctors on call to tend to your wounds.'

'What do you say, doc?' Sherman asked Rutledge.

'Okay,' Rutledge nodded. 'I could do with a rest.'

'An' we need transport, guv.'

'I'll arrange some, don't worry.'

'And no corridors?' Woolcott said, raising one eyebrow.

'No corridors,' Witherspoole laughed, then: 'Well, you can go ashore now and leave the boat to the shore workers. There are some trucks alongside waiting to take you to your new quarters.'

'Not yet,' Sherman nodded to Woolcott once more. Everyone went quiet, including Witherspoole. Then his face took on a look of utter amazement. Woolcott was leading a fourth man, also blindfolded, by the hand.

'Another present, sir,' said Sherman.

The man was visibly afraid, Witherspoole could not help notice, but what held his attention more was that the man was barefooted, naked from the waist up and wearing a woman's skirt.

'Allow me to introduce Guillermo Acevedo Soberon, the gentleman responsible for the disappearance and probable murders of at least two dozen British airmen. Doctor Acevedo broke NIB and he has lots to tell you. We had to be a bit rough with him, you'll notice, but we persuaded him to fill some of the gaps there were in the documents.'

'You have documents?' Witherspoole nearly choked.

'Heaps of them, but I believe the good doctor will be more revealing than any documents. You see, in reality he is Heinz Riedenhuber, a member of Luftwaffe Intelligence who reports directly to the fat guy Goering himself.'

Witherspoole was shaking with excitement. 'Ooh!' he said, saliva running from the corners of his mouth, 'I have some friends who are going to enjoy Riedenhuber's company so much!'

'He's all yours, sir.'

'Yes, yes, I shall have to arrange transport.'

The German was taken away twenty minutes later and Witherspoole then led his men ashore, installing them in their new quarters where just about everything they asked for was provided. Afterwards he made a telephone call to London to give a brief account of the *Unwanted*'s eventful trip. The listener in London brayed jubilantly and offered Witherspoole his profound thanks.

Witherspoole replaced the receiver, smiled in triumph and danced a little jig. The mission had succeeded beyond his wildest dreams. He'd gained several bonuses, one of them being that the RAF might look on SOE a little more favourably now that he'd brought three valuable men back.

He punched one hand into the palm of the other. Dammit, he thought: keep a good thing going while you have it. They're still expendable. Ask around. There must be someone who needs a dirty job done.